WITHDRAWN

A12900 911966

ILLINOIS CENTRAL COLLEGE
PS648.S3I855 1983
STACKS
Isaac Asimov's space of her own /

A12900 911966

PS 648 .S3 I855 198

Isaac Asimov's space of her own
44766

WITH

D1247791

Illinois Central College
Learning Resources Center

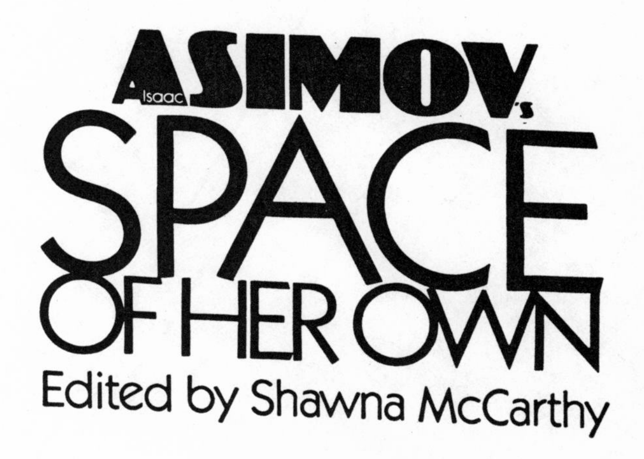
Isaac ASIMOV's
SPACE OF HER OWN
Edited by Shawna McCarthy

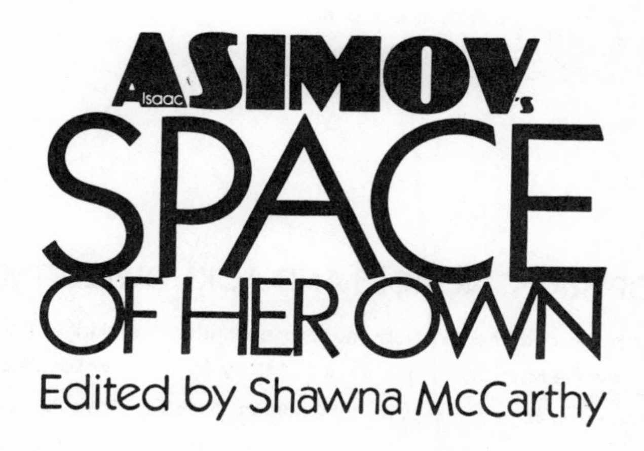

Edited by Shawna McCarthy

I.C.C. LIBRARY

The Dial Press
Davis Publications, Inc.
380 Lexington Avenue, New York, N.Y. 10017

44766

FIRST PRINTING

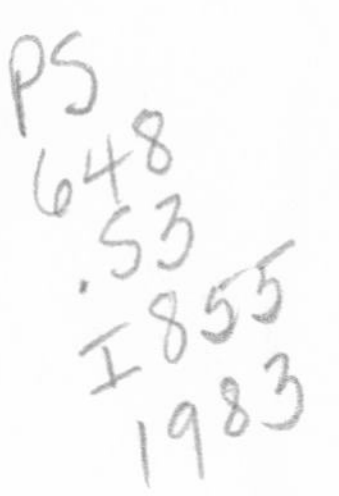
PS
648
.S3
I855
1983

Copyright © 1983 by Davis Publications, Inc.
All rights reserved.
Library of Congress Catalog Card Number: 78-60795
Printed in the U. S. A.

COPYRIGHT NOTICES AND ACKNOWLEDGMENTS

Grateful acknowledgment is hereby made for permission to reprint the following:

The Sidon in the Mirror by Connie Willis; © 1983 by Davis Publications, Inc.; reprinted by permission of the author.
The Sorceress in Spite of Herself by Pat Cadigan; © 1982 by Davis Publications, Inc.; reprinted by permission of the author.
Night of the Fifth Sun by Mildred Downey Broxon; © 1982 by Davis Publications, Inc.; reprinted by permission of Jarvis, Braff, Ltd.
The Jarabon by Lee Killough; © 1981 by Davis Publications, Inc.; reprinted by permission of the author.
The Horn of Elfland by J. O. Jeppson; © 1983 by Davis Publications, Inc.; reprinted by permission of the author.
Belling Martha by Leigh Kennedy; © 1983 by Davis Publications, Inc.; reprinted by permission of the author.
La Reine Blanche by Tanith Lee; © 1983 by Davis Publications, Inc.; reprinted by permission of Donald A. Wollheim.
Ancient Document by Hope Athearn; © 1982 by Davis Publications, Inc.; reprinted by permission of the author.
Miles to Go Before I Sleep by Julie Stevens; © 1982 by Davis Publications, Inc.;reprinted by permission of the author.
A Letter from the Clearys by Connie Willis; © 1982 by Davis Publications, Inc.; reprinted by permission of the author.
The Ascent of the North Face by Ursula K. Le Guin; © 1983 by Davis Publications, Inc.; reprinted by permission of Virginia Kidd, Agent.
$CALL LINK4(CATHY) by Cherie Wilkerson; © 1983 by Davis Publications, Inc.; reprinted by permission of the author.
Heavenly Flowers by Pamela Sargent; © 1983 by Davis Publications, Inc.; reprinted by permission of the author.
Exorcycle by Joan D. Vinge; © 1982 by Davis Publications, Inc.; reprinted by permission of the author.
Stargrazing by Beverly Grant; © 1982 by Davis Publications, Inc.; reprinted by permission of the author.
Shadows from a Small Template by Sharon Webb; © by Davis Pubications, Inc.; reprinted by permission of Adele Leone Agency, Inc.
Packing Up by P. J. MacQuarrie; © 1981 by Davis Publications, Inc.; reprinted by permission of the author.
Blue Heart by Stephanie A. Smith; © 1982 by Davis Publications, Inc.; reprinted by permission of the author.
The Examination of Ex-Emperor Ming by Cyn Mason; © 1982 by Davis Publications, Inc.; reprinted by permission of the author.
The Crystal Sunlight, the Bright Air by Mary Gentle; © 1983 by Davis Publications, Inc.; reprinted by permission of the author.
Missing by P. A. Kagan; © 1982 by Davis Publications, Inc.; reprinted by permission of the author.
Fire-Caller by Sydney J. Van Scyoc; © 1983 by Davis Publications, Inc.; reprinted by permission of the author.

CONTENTS

EDITOR'S NOTE

Back in the old, old days (gosh, fifteen or twenty years ago or so), there *were* no women in science fiction. They didn't read it, they didn't write it, and they certainly didn't star in it. (This is, admittedly, a bit of an overstatement. We cannot overlook the contributions of such women as Judith Merril, Leigh Brackett, C. L. Moore, and Kate Wilhelm [not to mention Mary Shelley].) However, the fact remains that perhaps one out of ten readers of SF were of the female persuasion, and the ratio of female to male writers was even lower. In order to write good SF, one must first read it and be familiar with its constructions, ideas, and assumptions.

For some reason (no one *really* knows why—and don't let anyone tell you it was the simmering sexuality of Mr. Spock in "Star Trek," either), in the mid-to-late 1960s, this situation began to change. Suddenly women were turning up at science fiction conventions; names like Joanna, Ursula, and Joan began appearing on the tables of contents of science fiction magazines; and real, honest-to-God female characters were showing themselves in stories. Sure, women had always had their place in science fiction; the problem was that that place was either dangling at the end of a long green tentacle, screaming, "Help me, Rock! Help me!" or swirling a mighty broadsword over her head (being careful not to dislodge her brass bra *too* far) while trying to rid peaceful Venus of the filthy male invaders.

To be certain, this sudden influx of women into the onetime hallowed halls of SF did not go unchallenged. One famous male editor maintained until the day he died that women just could *not* write science fiction. But despite all this *sturm und drang* (or maybe even because of it) female writers, readers, and fans hung on. Anthologies by and about women began to appear, and most everyone who read them agreed that, yes, this was good science fiction. And so it stands. Women have joined the club—at least with an associate membership, and the long-term members seem to have finally accepted them with grudging good grace. So why another anthology of women's science fiction? Well, we thought it might be nice to see what women have been turning out now that the storm has been weathered. Is it the literature of the radical feminist? Is it the literature of the cute, warm, and cuddly? Or is it, in a desperate attempt to gain full membership in the club, good, old-rousing macho-type sci fi?

Well, as you'll see, it's all of these and none of them. In many of these tales the gender of the author wold be unknowable were it not for the byline. In others, it's clear that a woman had a hand in their creation. Some of them are about women, some about men (as far as we can tell none of them are about the cute, warm, and cuddly), but all of them fit the most important criteria: they're damn good science ficiton. Enjoy.

THE SIDON IN THE MIRROR

art: Val Lindahn

by Connie Willis

Connie Willis, who recently won both the 1982 Nebula Awards for best short story and best novelette, would like us to make note in this space that she wrote this story while working under a National Endowment for the Arts government grant, and that their kindness made it possible for her to quit substitute-teaching and start writing full-time. If stories like the one that follows are the result of this kindness then perhaps we should all be grateful to the government.

We are near the spiraldown. I cannot see the mooring lights, and there are no landmarks on Paylay, but I remember how the lights of Jewell's abbey looked from here: a thin, disjointed string of Christmas tree lights, red and green and gold. Closer in you can see the red line under the buildings, and you think you are seeing the heat of Paylay, but it is only the reflection of the lights off the ground and the metalpaper undersides of Jewell's and the gaming house.

"You kin't see the heat," Jewell said on our way in from the down, "but you'll feel it. Your shoes all right?"

My shoes were fine, but they were clumsy to walk in. I would have fallen over in them at home, but here the heavier gravity almost clamped them to the ground. They had six-inch plastic soles cut into a latticework as fragile looking as the mooring tower, but they were sturdier than they looked, and they were not letting any heat get through. I wasn't feeling anything at all, and halfway to Jewell's I knelt and felt the sooty ground. It felt warm but not so hot as I had thought it would be, walking on a star.

"Leave your hand there a minute," Jewell said. I did, and then jerked my soot-covered hand up and put it in my mouth.

"Gits hot fast, din't it?" she said. "A tapper kidd fall down out here or kimm out with no shoes on and die inside of an hour of heatstroke. That's why I thought I bitter come out and wilcome you to Paylay. That's what they call this tapped-out star. You're sipposed to be able to pick up minny laying on the ground. You kin't. You have to drill a tap and build a comprissor around it and hope to Gid you don't blow yoursilf up while you're doing it."

What she did not say, in the high squeaky voice we both had from the helium in the air, was that she had waited over two hours for me by the down's plastic mooring tower and that the bottoms of her feet were frying in the towering shoes. The plastic is not a very good insulator. Open metal ribs would work far better to dissipate the heat that wells up through the thin crust of Paylay, but they can't allow any more metal here than is absolutely necessary, not with the hydrogen and oxygen ready to explode at the slightest spark.

The downpilot should have taken any potential fire-starters and metal I had away from me before he let me off the spiraldown, but Jewell had interrupted him before he could ask me what I had. "Doubletap it, will you?" she said. "I want to git back before the nixt shift. You were an hour late."

"Sorry, Jewell," the pilot said. "We hit thirty per cent almost a kilometer up and had to go into a Fermat." He looked down again at the piece of paper in his hand. "The following items are contraband. Unlawful possession can result in expulsion from Paylay. Do you have any: sonic fires, electromags, matches . . ."

Jewell took a step forward and put her foot down like she was afraid the ground would give way.

"Iv course he din't. He's a pianoboard player."

The pilot laughed and said, "Okay, Jewell, take him," and she grabbed up my tote and walked me back to St. Pierre. She asked about my uncle, and she told me about the abbey and the girls and how she'd given them all house names of jewels because of her name. She told me how Taber, who ran the gaming house next door to her abbey, had christened the little string of buildings we could see in the distance St. Pierre after the patron saint of tappers, and all the time the bottoms of her feet fried like cooking meat and she never said a word.

I couldn't see her very well. She was wearing a chemiloom lantern strapped to her forehead, and she had brought one for me, but they didn't give off much light, and her face was in shadow. My uncle had told me she had a big scar that ran down the side of her face and under her chin. He said she got the scar from a fight with a sidon.

"It nearly cut the jugular," my uncle had said. "It would have if they hadn't gotten it off of her. It cut up quite a few of the tappers, too."

"What was she doing with a sidon anyway?" I asked. I had never seen one, but I had heard about them: beautiful blood-red animals with thick, soft fur and sot-razor claws, animals that could seem tame for as long as a year and then explode without warning into violence. "You can't tame them."

"Jewell thought she could," my uncle said. "One of the tappers brought it back with him from Solfatara in a cage. Somebody let it out, and it got away. Jewell went after it. Its feet were burned, and it was suffering from heatstroke. Jewell sat down on the ground and held it on her lap till someone came to help. She insisted on bringing it back to the abbey, making it into a pet. She wouldn't believe she couldn't tame it."

"But a sidon can't help what it is," I said. "It's like us. It doesn't even know it's doing it."

My uncle did not say anything, and after a minute I said, "She thinks she can tame us, too. That's why she's willing to take me, isn't it? I knew there had to be a reason she'd take me when we're not allowed on Solfatara. She thinks she can keep me from copying."

My uncle still did not answer, and I took that for assent. He had not answered any of my questions. He had suddenly said I was going, though nobody had gone off-planet since the ban, and when I asked him questions, he answered with statements that did not answer them at all.

"Why do I have to go?" I said. I was afraid of going, afraid of what might happen.

"I want you to copy Jewell. She is a kind person, a good person. You can learn a great deal from her."

"Why can't she come here? Kovich did."

"She runs an abbey on Paylay. There are not more than two dozen tappers and girls on the whole star. It is perfectly safe."

"What if there's somebody evil there? What if I copy him instead and kill somebody, like happened on Solfatara? What if something bad happens?"

"Jewell runs a clean abbey. No sots, no pervs, and the girls are well-behaved. It's nothing like the happy houses. As for Paylay itself, you shouldn't worry about it being a star. It's in the last stages of burning out. It has a crust almost two thousand feet thick, which means there's hardly any radiation. People can walk on the surface without any protective clothing at all. There's some radiation from the hydrogen taps, of course, but you won't go anywhere near them."

He had reassured me about everything except what was important. Now, trudging along after Jewell through the sooty carbon of Paylay, I knew about all the dangers except the worst one—myself.

I could not see anything that looked like a tap. "Where are they?" I asked, and Jewell pointed back the way we had come.

"As far away as we kin git thim from St. Pierre and each ither so simm tripletapping fool kin't kill ivverybody when he blows himsilf up. The first sidon's off thit way, ten kilometers or so."

"Sidon?" I said, frightened. My uncle had told me the tappers had killed the sidon and made it into a rug after it nearly killed Jewell.

She laughed. "Thit's what they call the taps. Because they blow up on you and you don't even know what hit. They make thim as safe as they can, but the comprission equipmint's metal and metal means sparks. Ivvery once in awhile that whole sky over there lights up like Chrissmiss. We built St. Pierre as far away as we kidd, and there in't a scrap of metal in the whole place, but the hydrogen leaks are ivverywhere. And helium. Din't we sound like a pair iv fools squeaking at each other?"

She laughed again, and I noticed that as we had stood there looking at the black horizon, my feet had begun to feel uncomfortably hot.

It was a long walk through the darkness to the string of lights, and the whole way I watched Jewell and wondered if I had already begun to copy her. I would not know it, of course. I had not known I was copying my uncle either. One day he had asked me to play a song, and I had sat down at the pianoboard and played it. When I was finished, he said, "How long have you been able to do that?" and I did not know. Only after I had done the copying would I know it, and then only if someone told me. I trudged after Jewell in darkness and tried, tried to copy her.

It took us nearly an hour to get to the town, and when we got there, I could see it wasn't a town at all. What Jewell had called St. Pierre was only two tall metalpaper-covered buildings perched on plastic frameworks nearly two meters high and a huddle of stilt-tents. Neither building had a sign over the door, just strings of multicolored chemiloom lights strung along the eaves. They were fairly bright, and they reflected off the metalpaper into even more light, but Jewell took off the lantern she had strapped to her head and held it close to the wooden openwork steps, as if I couldn't see to climb up to the front door high above us without it.

"Why are you walking like thit?" she said when we got to the top of the steps, and for the first time I could see her scar. It looked almost black in the colored light of the lantern and the looms, and it was much wider than I had thought it would be, a fissure of dark puckered skin down one whole side of her face.

"Walking like what?" I said, and looked down at my feet.

"Like you kin't bear to hivv your feet touch the ground. I got my feet too hot out at the down. You didn't. So din't walk like thit."

"I'm sorry," I said. "I won't do it anymore."

She smiled at me, and the scar faded a little. "Now you just kimm on in and meet the girls. Din't mind it if they say simmthing about the way you look. They've nivver seen a Mirror before, but they're good girls." She opened the thick door. It was metalpaper backed with a thick pad of insulation. "We take our inside shoes off out here and wear shuffles inside the abbey."

It was much cooler inside. There was a plastic heat-trigger fan set in the ceiling and surrounded by rose-colored chemilooms. We were in an anteroom with a rack for the high shoes and the lanterns. They dangled by their straps.

Jewell sat down on a chair and began unbuckling her bulky shoes. "Din't ivver go out without shoes and a lantern," she said. She gestured toward the rack. "The little ones with the twillpaper hiddbands are for town. They only list about an hour. If you're going out to the taps or the spiraldown, take one iv the big ones with you."

She looked different in the rosy light. Her scar hardly showed at all. Her voice was different too, deeper. She sounded older than she had at the down. I looked up and around at the air.

"We blow nitrogen and oxygen in from a tap behind the house," she said. "The tappers din't like having squeaky little helium voices when they're with the girls. You can't git rid of the helium, or the hydrogen either. They leak in ivverywhere. The bist you can do is dilute it. You shid be glad you weren't here at the beginning, before they tapped an atmosphere. You had to wear vacuum suits thin." She pried off her shoe. The bottom of her foot was a mass of blisters. She started to stand up and then sat down again.

"Yill for Carnie," she said. "Till her to bring some bandages."

I hung my outside shoes on the rack and opened the inner door. It fit tightly, though it opened with just a touch. It was made of the same insulation as the outer door. It opened onto a fancy room, all curtains and fur rugs and hanging looms that cast little pools of colored light, green and rose and gold. The pianoboard stood over against one wall on a carved plastic table. I could not see anyone in the room, and I could not hear voices for the sound of the blowers. I started across a blood-red fur rug to another door, hung with curtains.

"Jewell?" a woman's voice said. The blowers kicked off, and she said, "Jewell?" again, and I saw that I had nearly walked past her. She was sitting in a white velvet chair in a little bay that would have been a window if this were not Paylay. She was wearing a white satinpaper dress with a long skirt. Her hair was piled on top of her head, and there was a string of pearls around her long neck. She was sitting so quietly, with her hands in her lap and her head turned slightly away from me, that I had not even seen her.

"Are you Carnie?" I said.

"No," she said, and she didn't look up at me. "What is it?"

"Jewell got her feet burned," I said. "She needs bandages. I'm the new pianoboard player."

"I know," the girl said. She lifted her head a little in the direction of the stairs and called, "Carnie. Get the remedy case."

A girl came running down the stairs in an orange-red robe and no shoes. "Is it Jewell?" she said to the girl in the white dress, and when she nodded, Carnie ran past us into the other room. I could hear the hollow sound of an insulated door opening. The girl had made no move to come and see Jewell. She sat perfectly still in the white chair, her hands lying quietly in her lap.

"Jewell's feet are pretty bad," I said. "Can't you at least come see them?"

"No," she said, and looked up at me. "My name is Pearl," she said. "I had a friend once who played the pianoboard."

Even then, I wouldn't have known she was blind except that my uncle had told me. "Most of the girls are newcomers Jewell hired for Paylay right off the ships, before the happy houses could ruin them," my uncle had said. "She only brought a couple of the girls with her from Solfatara, girls who worked with her in the happy house she she came out of. Carnie, and I think Sapphire, and Pearl, the blind one."

"Blind?" I had said. Solfatara is a long way out, but any place has doctors.

"He cut . . . the optic nerve was severed. They did orb implants and reattached all the muscles, but it was only cosmetic repair. She can't see anything."

Even after all the horrible stories I had heard about Solfatara, it had shocked me to think that someone could do something like that. I remember thinking that the man must have been incredibly cruel to have done such a thing, that it would have been kinder to kill her outright than to have left her helpless and injured like that in a place like Solfatara.

"Who did it to her?" I said.

"A tapper," he said, and for a minute he looked very much like Kovich, so much that I asked, "Was it the same man who broke Kovich's hands?"

"Yes," my uncle said.

"Did they kill him?" I said, but that was not the question I had intended to ask. I had meant did Kovich kill him, but I had said "they."

And my uncle, not looking like Kovich at all, had said, "Yes, they killed him," as if that were the right question after all.

The orb implants and the muscle reattachments had been very

good. Her eyes were a beautiful pale gray, and someone had taught her to follow voices with them. There was nothing at all in the angle of her head or her eyes or her quiet hands to tell me she was blind or make me pity her, and standing there looking down at her, I was glad, glad that they had killed him. I hoped that they had cut his eyes out first.

Carnie darted past us with the remedy case, and I said, still looking down at Pearl, "I'll go and see if I can help her." I went back out into the anteroom and watched while Carnie put some kind of oil on Jewell's feet and then a meshlike pad, and wrapped her feet in bandages.

"This is Carnelian," Jewell said. "Carnie, this is our new pianoboard player."

She smiled at me. She looked very young. She must have been only a child when she worked in the happy house on Solfatara with Jewell.

"I bit you can do real fancy stuff with those hands," she said, and giggled.

"Don't tease him," Jewell said. "He's here to play the pianoboard."

"I *meant* on the pianoboard. You din't look like a real mirror. You know, shiny and ivverything? Who are you going to copy?"

"He's not going to copy innybody," Jewell said sharply. "He's going to play the pianoboard, and that's all. Is supper riddy?"

"No. I was jist in the kitchen and Sapphire wasn't even there yit." She looked back up at me. "When you copy somebody, do you look like them?"

"No," I said. "You're thinking of a chameleon."

"You're not thinking it all," Jewell said to her and stood up. She winced a little as she put her weight on her feet. "Go borrow a pair of Garnet's shuffles. I'll nivver be able to git mine on. And go till Sapphire to doubletap hersilf into the kitchen."

She let me help her to the stairs but not up them. "When Carnie comes back, you hivv her show you your room. We work an eight and eight here, and it's nearly time for the shift. You kin practice till supper if you want."

She went up two steps and stopped. "If Carnie asks you inny more silly questions, tell her I told her to lit you alone. I don't want to hear any more nonsinse about copying and Mirrors. You're here to play the pianoboard."

She went on up the stairs, and I went back into the music room. Pearl was still there, sitting in the white chair, and I didn't know whether she was included in the instructions to leave me alone, so I sat down on the hard wooden stool and looked at the pianoboard.

It had a wooden soundboard and bridges, but the strings were plastic instead of metal. I tried a few chords, and it seemed to have a good sound in spite of the strings. I played a few scales and more chords and looked at the names on the hardcopies that stood against the music rack. I can't read music, of course, but I could see by the titles that I knew most of the songs.

"It isn't nonsense, is it?" Pearl said, "About the copying." She spoke slowly and without the clipped accent Jewell and Carnie had.

I turned around on the stool and faced her. "No," I said. "Mirrors have to copy. They can't help themselves. They don't even know who they're copying. Jewell doesn't believe me. Do you?"

"The worst thing about being blind is not that things are done to you," she said, and looked up at me again with her blind eyes. "It's that you don't know who's doing them."

Carnie came in through the curtained door. "I'm sipposed to show you around," she said. "Oh, Pearl, I wish you kidd see him. He has eight fingers on each hand, and he's really tall. Almost to the ceiling. And his skin is bright red."

"Like a sidon's," Pearl said, looking at me.

Carnie looked down at the blood-red rug she was standing on. "Jist like," she said, and dragged me upstairs to show me my room and the clothes I was to wear and to show me off to the other girls. They were already dressed for the shift in trailing satin-paper dresses that matched their names. Garnet wore rose-red chemilooms in her upswept hair, Emerald an elaborately lit collar.

Carnie got dressed in front of me, stepping out of her robe and into an orange-red dress as if I weren't watching. She asked me to fasten her armropes of winking orange, lifting up her red curls so I could tie the strings of the chemilooms behind her shoulders. I could not decide then if she were trying to seduce me or get me to copy her or simply to convince me that she was the naive child she pretended to be.

I thought then that whatever she was trying, she had failed. She had succeeded only in convincing me of what my uncle had already told me. In spite of her youth, her silliness, I could well believe she had been on Solfatara, had known all of it, the pervs, the sots, the worst the happy houses had to offer. I think now she didn't mean anything by it except that she wanted to be cruel, that she was simply poking at me as if I were an animal in a cage.

At supper, watching Sapphire set Pearl's plate for her between taped marks, I wondered whether Carnie was ever cruel to Pearl as she had been to me, shifting the plate slightly as she set it down or moving her chair so she could not find it.

Sapphire set the rest of the plates on the table, her eyes dark blue from some old bitterness, and I thought, Jewell shouldn't have brought any of them with her from Solfatara except Pearl. Pearl is the only one who hasn't been ruined by it. Her blindness has kept her safe, I thought. She has been protected from all the horrors because she couldn't see them. Perhaps her blindness protects her from Carnie, too, I thought. Perhaps that is the secret, that she is safe inside her blindness and no one can hurt her, and Jewell knows that. I did not think then about the man who had blinded her, and how she had not been safe from him at all.

Jewell called the meal to order. "I want you to make our new pianoboard player wilcome," she said. She reached across the table and patted Carnie's hand. "Thank you for doing the introductions, and for bandaging my foot," she said, and I thought, Pearl is safe after all. Jewell has tamed Carnie and all the rest of them. I did not think about the sidon she had tamed, and how it now lay on the floor in front of the card-room door.

That first shift Jewell decked me out in formals and a black-red dog collar and had me stand at the door with her as she greeted the tappers. They were in formals, too, under their soot-black work jackets. They hung the many-pocketed jackets, heavy with tools, on the rack in the anteroom along with their lanterns and sat down to take off their high shoes with hands almost as red as mine. They had washed their hands and faces, but their fingernails were black with soot, and there was soot in every line of their palms. Their faces looked hot and raw, and they all had a broad pale band across their foreheads from the lantern strap. One of them, whom Jewell called Scorch, had singed off his eyebrows and a long strip of hair on top of his head.

"You'll meet almost all the tappers this shift. The gaming house will close hiffway through and the rist of them will come over. Taber and I stagger the shifts so simmthing's always open."

She didn't introduce me, though some of the tappers looked at my eight-fingered hands curiously, and one of the men looked surprised and then angry. He looked as if he was going to say something to me, and then changed his mind, his face getting redder and darker until the lantern line stood out like a scar.

When they were all inside the music room, Jewell led me to the pianoboard and had me sit down and spread my hands out over the keyboard, ready to play. Then she said. "This is my new pianoboard player, boys. Say hillo to him."

"What's his name, Jewell?" one of the men said. "You ginna give him a fancy name like the girls?"

"I nivver thought about it," she said. "What do you think?"

The tapper who had turned so red said loudly, "I think you shid call him sidon and kick him out to burn on Paylay. He's a Mirror."

"I alriddy got a Carnelian and a Garnet. And I had a sidon once. I giss I'll call him Ruby." She looked calmly over at the man who had spoken. "That okay with you, Jick?"

His face was as dark a red as mine. "I didn't say it to be mean, Jewell," he said. "You're doing what you did with the sidon, taking in simmthing thit'll turn on you. They won't even lit Mirrors on Solfatara."

"I think that's probably a good ricommendation considering what they do lit on Solfatara," Jewell said quietly. "Sot-gamblers, tap-stealers, pervers . . . "

"You saw that Mirror kill the tapper. Stid there right in front iv ivverybody, and nobody kidd stop him. Nobody. The tapper bigging for mercy, his hands tied in front of him, and thit Mirror coming at him with a sot-razor, smiling while he did it."

"Yes," Jewell said. "I saw it. I saw a lot of things on Solfatara. But this is Paylay. And this is my pianoboard player Ruby. I din't think a man should be outlawed till he does simmthing, di you, Jick?" She put her hand on my shoulder. "Do you know 'Back Home?' " she said. Of course I knew it. I knew all the tapper songs. Kovich had played in every happy house on Solfatara before somebody broke his hands. He had called "Back Home" his rope-cutter.

"Play it, thin," she said. "Show thim what you can do, Ruby."

I played it with lots of trills and octave stretches, all the fancy things Kovich could do with five fingers instead of eight. Then I stopped and waited. The nitrogen blowers kicked off, and even the fans made no noise. During the song, Jewell had gone and stood next to Jack, putting her hand on his shoulder, trying to tame him. I wondered if she had succeeded. Jack looked at me, and then at Jewell and back at me again. His hand went into his formals shirt, and my heart almost stopped before he brought it out again.

"Jewell's right," he said. "You shiddn't judge a man till you see what he does. That was gid playing," he said, handing me a plastic-wrapped cigar. "Wilcome to Paylay."

Jewell nodded at me, and I extended my hand and took the

cigar. I fumbled to get the slippery plastic off and then had to look at the cigar a minute to make sure I was getting the right end in my mouth. I stuck it in my mouth and reached inside my shirt for my sparker. I didn't know what would happen when I lit the cigar. For all I understood what was going on, the cigar might be full of gunpowder. Jewell did not look worried, but then she had misjudged the sidon, too.

My hand closed on the sparker inside my shirt, the nitrogen blowers suddenly kicked on, and Jack said lazily, "Now whit you ginna light that with, Ruby? There in't a match on Paylay!"

Jewell laughed, and the men guffawed. I pulled my empty hand sheepishly out of my jacket and took the cigar out of my mouth to look at it. "I forgot you can't smoke on Paylay," I said.

"You and ivvery tapper that kimms in on the down," Jewell said. "I've seen Jick play that joke on how many newcomers?"

"Ivvery one," Jack said, looking pleased with himself. "It even worked on you, Jewell, and you weren't a newcomer."

"It did not, you tripletapping liar," she said. "Lit's hear simmthing else, Ruby," she said. "Whit do you want Ruby to play, boys?"

Scorch shouted out a song, and I played it, and then another, but I do not know what they were. It had been a joke, offer the newcomer a cigar and then watch him try to light it on a star where no open flames are allowed. A good joke, and Jack had done it in spite of what he had seen on Solfatara to show Jewell he didn't think I was a sidon, that he would wait to see what I would do before he judged me.

And that would have been too late. What would have happened when I lit the cigar? Would the house have gone up in a ball of flame, or all of St. Pierre? The hydrogen-oxygen ratio had been high enough in the upper atmosphere that we had had to shut off the engines above a kilometer and spiral in, and here the fans were pumping in even more oxygen. Half of Paylay might have gone up.

I knew how it had happened. Jewell had interrupted the down-pilot before he could ask about sparkers, and now, because her feet had hurt, there was a live sparker in her house. And she had just convinced Jack I was not dangerous.

I had stopped playing, sitting there staring blindly at the keyboard, the unlit cigar clamped so hard between my teeth I had nearly bitten it through. The men were still shouting out the names of songs, but Jewell stepped between them and me and put a hardcopy on the music rack. "No more riquists," she said. "Pearl is going to sing for you."

Pearl stood up and walked unassisted from her white chair to the pianoboard. She stopped no more than an inch from me and put her hand down certainly on the end of the keyboard. I looked at the music. It showed a line of notes before her part began, but I did not know that version, only the song that Kovich had known, and that began on the first note of the verse. I could not nod at her, and she could not see my hands on the keys.

"I don't know the introduction," I said. "Just the verse. What should I do?"

She bent down to me. "Put your hand on mine when you are ready to begin, and I will count three," she said, and straightened again, leaving her hand where it was.

I looked down at her hand. Carnie had told her about my hands, and if I touched her lightly, with only the middle fingers, she might not even be able to tell it from a human's touch. I wanted more than anything not to frighten her. I did not think I could bear it if she flinched away from me.

Now I think it would have been better if she had, that I could have stood it better than this, sitting here with her head on my lap, waiting. If she had flinched, Jack would have seen her. He would have seen her draw away from me, and that would have been enough for him to grab me by the dog collar and throw me out the door, kick me down the wooden steps so hard that the sparker bounced out, leave me to cook in the furnace of Paylay.

"Now whit did you do thit for?" Jewell would have said. "He din't do innything but tich her hand."

"And he'll nivver do innything ilse to her either," he would have said, and handed Jewell the sparker. And I would never have been able to do anything else to her.

But she did not flinch. She took a light breath that took no longer than it did for my hand to return to the keys and hit the first note on the count of three, and we began together. I did not do any trills, any octave stretches. Her voice was sweet and thready and true. She didn't need me.

The men applauded after Pearl's song and started calling out the names of other songs. Some I didn't know, and I wondered how I could explain that to them, but Jewell said, "Now, now, boys. Let's not use up our pianoboard player in one shift. Lit him go to bid. He'll be here next shift. Who wants a game of katmai?" She reached over and pulled the cover down over the keyboard.

"Use the front stairs," she said. "The tappers take the girls up the back way."

Pearl bent toward me and said, "Good night, Ruby," and then took Jack's arm as if she knew right where he was and went through the curtained door to the card room. The others followed, two by two, until all the girls were taken, and then in a straggling line. Jewell unfastened the heavy drapes so they fell across the door behind them.

I went upstairs and took off the paper shuffles and the uncomfortable collar and sat on the edge of the bed Jewell had fixed for me by putting a little table at the end for extra length. I thought about Pearl and Jack and how I was going to give Jewell the sparker at the beginning of the next shift, and wondered who I was copying. I looked at myself in the little plastic mirror over the bed, trying to see Jewell or Jack in my face.

I had left my cigar on the music rack. I didn't want Jack to find it there and think I had rejected it. I put my shuffles back on and went downstairs. There was nobody in the music room, and the drapes were still drawn across the door of the card room. I went over to the pianoboard and got the cigar. I had bitten it almost through, and now I bit the ragged end off. Then I chomped down on the new end and sat down on the piano stool, spreading out my hands as far as they would go across the keyboard.

"I understand you're a Mirror," a man's voice said from the recesses of Pearl's chair. "I knew a Mirror once. Or he knew me. Isn't that how it is?"

I almost said, "You're not supposed to sit in that chair," but I found I could not speak.

The man stood up and came toward me. He was dressed like the other men, with a broad black dog collar, but his hands and face were almost white, and there was no lighter band across his forehead. "My name is Taber," he said, in a slow, drawling voice unlike the fast, vowel-shortening accents of the others. I wondered if he had come from Solfatara. All the rest of them except Pearl shortened their vowels, bit them off like I had bit the cigar. Pearl alone seemed to have no accent, as if her blindness had protected her from the speech of Solfatara, too.

"Welcome to St. Pierre," he said, and I felt a shock of fear. He had lied to Jewell. I did not know who St. Pierre was, but I knew as he spoke that St. Pierre was not the patron saint of tappers, and that Taber's calling the town that was some unspeakably cruel joke that only he understood.

"I have to go upstairs," I said, and my hand shook as I held the cigar. "Jewell's in the card room."

"Oh," he said lazily, taking a cigar from his pocket and unwrapping it. "Is Pearl there, too?"

"Pearl?" I said, so frightened I could not breathe.

He patted his formals pockets and reached inside his shirt. "Yes. You know, the blind girl. The pretty one." He pulled a sparker from his inside pocket, cocked it back, and looked at me. "What a pity she's blind. I wish I knew what happened. She's never told a soul, you know," he said, and clicked the sparker.

It was not a real sparker. I could see, after a frozen moment, that there was no liquid in it at all. He clicked it twice more, held it to the end of his cigar in dreadful pantomime, and replaced it in his pocket.

"I do wish I could find out," he said. "I could put the knowledge to good use."

"I can't help you," I said, and moved toward the stairs.

He stepped in front of me. "Oh, I think you can. Isn't that what Mirrors are for?" he said, and drew on the unlit cigar and blew imaginary smoke into my face.

"I won't help you," I said, so loudly I fancied Jewell would come and tell Taber to let me alone, as she had told Carnie. "You can't make me help you."

"Of course not," he said. "That isn't how it works. But of course you know that," and let me pass.

I sat on my bed the rest of the shift, holding the real sparker between my hands, waiting until I could tell Jewell what Taber had said to me. But the next shift was sleeping-shift, and the shift after that I played tapper requests for eight hours straight. Most of that time Taber stood by the pianoboard, flicking imaginary ashes onto my hands.

After the shift Jewell came to ask me whether Jack or anyone else had bothered me, and I did not tell her about Taber after all. During the next sleeping-shift I hid the sparker between the mattress and the springs of my bed.

On the waking shifts I kept as close as I could to Jewell, trying to make myself useful to her, trying not to copy the way she walked on her bandaged feet. When I was not playing, I moved among the tappers with glasses of iced and watered-down liquor on a tray and filled out the account cards for the men who wanted to take girls upstairs. On the off-shifts I learned to work the boards that sent out accounts to Solfatara, and to do the laundry, and after a couple of weeks Jewell had me help with the body checks on the girls. She scanned for perv marks and sot scars as well as the standard GHS every abbey has to screen for. Pearl did not have a mark on her, and I was relieved. I had had an idea that Taber might be torturing her somehow.

Jewell left us alone while I helped her get dressed after the scan, and I said, "Taber is a very bad man. He wants to hurt you."

"I know," she said. She was standing very still while I clipped the row of pearl buttons on the back of her dress together.

"Why?"

"I don't know," she said. "It's like the sidon."

"You mean he can't help himself, that he doesn't know what he's doing?" I said, outraged. "He knows exactly what he's doing."

"The tappers used to poke at the sidon with sticks when it was in the cage," she said. "They couldn't reach it to really hurt it, though, and Taber couldn't stand that. He made the tappers give him the key to the cage just so he could get to it. Just so he could hurt it. Now why would he want to hurt the sidon?"

"Because it was helpless," I said, and I wondered if the man who'd blinded Pearl had been like that. "Because it couldn't protect itself."

"Jewell and I were in the same happy house on Solfatara," she said. "We had a friend there, a pianoboard player like you. He was very tall like you, too, and he was the kindest person I ever knew. Sometimes you remind me of him." She walked certainly to the door, as if she were not counting the memorized steps. "A cage is a safe place as long as nobody has the key. Don't worry, Ruby. He can't get in." She turned and looked at me. "Will you come and play for me?"

"Yes," I said, and followed her down to the music room. Before the shifts started, while the girls were upstairs dressing, she liked to sit in the white chair and listen to me play. She understood, more than any of the others, that I could play only the songs I had copied from Kovich. Jewell, to the end, thought I could read music, and Taber even brought me hardcopies from Solfatara. Pearl simply said the names of songs, and I played them if I knew them. She never asked for one I didn't know, and I thought that was because she listened carefully to the tappers' requests and my refusals, and I was grateful.

I sat down at the pianoboard and looked at Pearl in the mirror. I had asked Jewell for the mirror so I could see over my shoulder. I had told her I wanted it so she could signal me songs and breaks and sometimes the ropecutter if the men got rough or noisy, but it was really so I could keep Taber from standing there without my knowing it.

" 'Back Home,' " Pearl said. I could hardly hear her over the nitrogen blowers. I began playing it, and Taber came in. He walked swiftly over to her and then stood quite still, and between my playing and the noise of the blowers, she did not hear him. He stood about half a meter from her, close enough to touch her but just out of reach if she had put her hand out to try to find him.

He took the cigar out of his mouth and bent down as if he were going to speak to her, and instead he pursed his lips and blew gently at her. I could almost see the smoke. At first she didn't seem to notice, but then she shivered and drew her shinethread shawl closer about her.

He stopped and smiled at her a moment and then reached out and touched her with the tip of his cigar, lightly, on the shoulder, as if he intended to burn her, and then darted it back out of her reach. She swatted at the air, and he repeated the little pantomime again and again, until she stood and put her hands up helplessly against what she could not see. As she did so, he moved swiftly and silently to the door so that when she cried out, "Who is it? Who's there?" he said in his slow drawl, "It's me, Pearl. I've just come in. Did I frighten you?"

"No," she said, and sat back down again. But when he took her hand, she flinched away from him as I'd thought she would from me. And all the while I had not missed a beat of the song.

"I just came over to see you for a minute," Taber said, "and to hear your pianoboard player. He gets better every day, doesn't he?"

Pearl didn't answer. I saw in the mirror that her hands lay crossed in her lap again and didn't move.

"Yes," he said, and walked toward me, flicking imaginary ashes from his unlit cigar onto my hands. "Better and better," he said softly. "I can almost see my face in you, Mirror."

"What did you say?" Pearl said, frightened.

"I said I'd better go see Jewell a minute about some business and then get back next door. Jack found a new hydrogen tap today, a big one."

He went back through the card room to the kitchen, and I sat at the pianoboard, watching in the mirror until I saw the kitchen door shut behind him.

"Taber was in the room the whole time," I said. "He was . . . doing things to you."

"I know," she said.

"You shouldn't let him. You should stop him," I said violently, and as soon as I said it I knew that she knew that I had not stopped him either. "He's a very bad man," I said.

"He has never locked me in," she said after a minute. "He has never tied me up."

"He has never known how before," I said, and I knew it was true. "He wants me to find out for him."

She bent her head to her hands, which still lay crossed at the wrists, almost relaxed, showing nothing of what she was thinking. "And will you?" she said.

"I don't know."

"He's trying to get you to copy him, isn't he?" she said.

"Yes."

"And you think it's working?"

"I don't know," I said. "I can't tell when I'm copying. Do I sound like Taber?"

"No," she said, so definitely that I was relieved. I had listened to myself with an anxious ear, hoping for Jewell's shortened vowels and tapper slang, waiting in dread for the slow, lazy speech of Taber. I did not think I had heard either of them, but I had been afraid I wouldn't know if I did.

"Do you know who I'm copying?" I said.

"You walk like Jewell," she said, and smiled a little. "It makes her furious."

It was the end of the shift before I realized that, like my uncle, she had not really answered what I had asked.

Jack's new tap turned out to be so big that he needed a crew to help put up the compressors, and for several shifts hardly anyone was in the house, including Taber. Because business was so slack, Jewell even let some of the girls go over to the gaming house. Taber didn't go near the tap, but he didn't come over quite so often either, and when he did, he spent his time upstairs or with Carnie, talking to her in a low voice and clicking the sparker over and over again, as if he could not help himself. Then, once the compressors were set up and the sidon working, the men poured back into St. Pierre, and Taber was too busy to come over at all.

The one time he came, he found Pearl alone with me, he said, "It's Taber, Pearl," almost before I had banged a loud chord on the keys and said, "Taber's here." He did not have his cigar with him, or his sparker, and he did not even speak to me. Watching

Pearl talk to him, her head gracefully turned away from him, her hands in her lap, I could almost believe that he would not succeed, that nothing could hurt her, safe in her blindness.

We were so busy that Jewell hardly spoke to me, but when she did, she told me sharply that if I had nothing better to do than copy her, I should tend bar, and set me to passing out the watered liquor she had brought out in honor of the new sidon. She did the boards for the week herself while I ran the body checks.

Pearl, naked under the scan, looked serene and unhurt. Carnie had sot-scars under her arms. I did not report her. If Jewell found out, she would send Carnie back to Solfatara, and I wanted Taber to be working on Carnie, giving her sots and trying to get her to help him, because then I could believe he had given up on me. I did not dare believe that he had given up on Pearl, but I did not think that he and Carnie alone could hurt her, no matter what they did to her. Not without my help. Not so long as I was copying Jewell.

I told Pearl about Carnie. "I think she's on sots," I said. We were alone in the music room. Jewell was upstairs, trying to catch up the boards. Carnie was in the kitchen, taking her turn at supper. "I saw what looked like scars."

"I know," Pearl said, and I wondered if there was anything she did not see, in spite of her blindness.

"I think you should be careful. It's Taber that's giving them to her. He's using her to hurt you. Don't tell her anything."

She said nothing, and after a minute I turned back to the pianoboard and waited for her to name a song.

"I was born in the happy house. My mother worked there. Did you know that?" she said quietly.

"No," I said, keeping my hands spread across the keyboard, as though they could support me. I did not look at her.

"I have told myself all these years that as long as no one knew what happened, I was safe."

"Doesn't Jewell know?"

She shook her head. "Nobody knows. My mother told them he threatened her with the sot-razor, that there was nothing she could do."

The nitrogen blowers kicked on just then, and I jumped at the sound and looked into the mirror. I could see the sidon in the mirror, and standing on its red murdered skin, Taber. Carnie had let him in through the kitchen and turned the blowers up, and now he stood between the noisy blowers, smiling and flicking imaginary ash onto the carpet beside Pearl's chair. I took my

hands off the keyboard and laid them in my lap. "Carnie's in the kitchen," I said. "I don't know if the door's shut."

"There was a tapper who came to the house," Pearl said. "He was a very bad man, but my mother loved him. She said she couldn't help herself. I think that was true." For a moment she looked directly into the mirror with her blind eyes, and I willed Taber to click the sparker that I knew he was fingering so that Pearl would hear it and withdraw into her cage, safe and silent.

"It was Christmas time," she said, and the blowers kicked off. Into the silence she said, "I was ten years old, and Jewell gave me a little gold necklace with a pearl on it. She was only fourteen, but she was already working in the house. They had a tree in the music room and there were little lights on it, all different colors, strung on a string. Have you ever seen lights like that, red and green and gold all strung together?"

I thought of the strings of multicolored chemilooms I had seen from the spiraldown, the very first thing I had seen on Paylay. Nobody has told her, I thought, in all this time nobody has told her, and at the thought of the vast cage of kindness built all around her, my hand jerked up and hit the edge of the keyboard. She heard the sound and looked up.

"Is Taber here?" she said, and my hand hovered above the keyboard.

"No, of course not," I said, and my hand settled back in my lap like the spiraldown coming to rest on its moorings. "I'll tell you when he comes."

"The tapper sent my mother a dress with lights on it, too, red and green and gold like the tree," Pearl said. "When he came, he said, 'You look like a Chrissmiss tree,' and kissed her on the cheek. 'What do you want for Chrissmiss?' my mother said. 'I will give you anything.' I can remember her standing there in the lighted dress under the tree." She stopped a minute, and when I looked in the mirror, she had turned her head so that she seemed to be looking straight at Taber. "He asked for me."

"What did he do to you?" I said.

"I don't remember," she said. Her hands struggled and lay still, and I knew what he had done. He had locked her in, and she had never escaped. He had tied her hands together, and she had never gotten free. I looked down at my own hands, crossed at the wrists like hers and not even struggling.

"Didn't anyone come to help you?" I said.

"The pianoboard player," she said. "He beat the door down. He broke both his hands so he could not play anymore. He made my mother call the doctor. He told her he would kill her if she didn't. When he tried to help me, I ran away from him. I didn't want him to help me. I wanted to die. I ran and ran and ran, but I couldn't see to get away."

"Did he kill the tapper who blinded you?" I said.

"While he was trying to find me, my mother let the tapper out the back door. I ran and ran and then I fell down. The pianoboard player came and held me in his arms until the doctor came. I made him promise to kill the tapper. I made him promise to finish killing me," she said, so softly I could hardly hear her. "But he didn't."

The blowers kicked on again, and I looked into the mirror, but Taber wasn't there. Carnie had let him out the back way.

He did not come back for several shifts. When he did, it was to tell Jewell he was going to Solfatara. He told Pearl he would bring her a present and whispered to me, "What do you want for Christmas, Ruby? You've earned a present."

While he was gone Jack hit another tap, almost on top of the first one, and Jewell locked up the liquor. The men didn't want music. They wanted to talk about putting in a double, even a triple tap. I was grateful for that. I was not sure I could play with my hands tied.

Jewell told me to go meet Taber at the mooring, and then changed her mind. "I'm worried about those sotted fools out at Jick's sidon. Doubletapping. They kidd blow the whole star. You'd bitter stay here and hilp me."

Taber came before the shift. "I'll bring you your present tonight, Pearl," he said. "I know you'll like it. Ruby helped me pick it out." I watched the sudden twitching of Pearl's hands, but my own didn't even move.

Taber waited almost until the end of the shift, spending nearly half of it in the card room with Carnie leaning heavily over his shoulder. She had already gotten her present. Her eyes were bright from the sot-slice, and she stumbled once against him and nearly fell.

"Bring me a cigar, Ruby," he shouted to me. "And look in the inside jacket pocket. I brought a present back for everybody." Pearl was standing all alone in the middle of the music room, her hands in front of her. I didn't look at her. I went straight upstairs to my room, got what I needed, and then went back down into the anteroom to where Taber's tapper jacket was hanging, and got the cigar out of Taber's pocket. His sparker was there, too.

The present was a flat package wrapped in red and green paper, and I took it and the cigar to Taber. He had come into the music room and was sitting in Pearl's chair. Carnie was sitting on his lap with her arm around his neck.

"You didn't bring the sparker, Ruby," Taber said. I waited for him to tell me to go and get it. "Never mind," he said. "Do you know what day this is?"

"I do," Carnie said softly, and Taber slid his hand up to hold hers where it lay loosely on his shoulder.

"It's Chrissmiss Day," he said, pronouncing it with the Solfatara accent. He took his hand away from Carnie's so he could lean back and puff on his cigar, and Carnie took her red, bruised hand in her other one and held it up to her bosom, her sot-bright eyes full of pain. "I said to myself we should have some Chrissmiss songs. Do you know any Chrissmiss songs, Ruby?"

"No," I said.

"I didn't think you would," Taber said. "So I brought you a present." He waved the cigar at me. "Go ahead. Open it."

I pulled the red and green paper off and took out the hardcopies. There were a dozen Christmas songs. I knew them all.

"Pearl, you'll sing a Chrissmiss song for me, won't you?" Taber said.

"I don't know any," she said. She had not moved from where she stood.

"Of course you do," Taber said. "They played them every Chrissmiss time in the happy houses on Solfatara. Come on. Ruby'll play it for you."

I sat down at the pianoboard, and Pearl came and stood beside me with her hand on the end of the keyboard. I stood the hardcopies up against the music rack and put my hands on the keyboard.

"He knows," she said, so softly none of the men could have heard her. "You told him."

"No, it's a coincidence," I said. "Maybe it is really Christmas time on Solfatara. Nobody keeps track of the year on Paylay. Maybe it is Christmas."

"If you told him, if he knows how it happened, I am not safe anymore. He'll be able to get in. He'll be able to hurt me." She took a staggering step away from the pianoboard as if she were going to run. I took hold of her wrist.

"I didn't tell him," I said. "I would never let him hurt you. But if you don't sing the song, he'll know there's something wrong.

I'll play the first song through for you." I let go of her wrist, and her hand went limp and relaxed on the end of the keyboard.

I played the song through and stopped. The version I knew didn't have an introduction, so I spread the fingers of my right hand across the octave and a half of the opening chord and touched her hand with my left.

She flinched. She did not move her hand away or even make any movement the men, gathered around us now, could have seen. But a tremor went through her hand. I waited a moment, and then I touched her again, with all my fingers, hard, and started the song. She sang the song all the way through, and my hands, which had not been able to come down on a single chord of warning, were light and sure on the keyboard. When it was over, the men called for another, and I put it on the music rack and then sat, as she stood silent and still, unflinching, waiting for what was to come.

Taber looked up inquiringly, casually, and Jewell frowned and half-turned toward the door. Scorch banged through the thick inner door and stopped, trying to get his breath. He still had his lantern strapped to his forehead, and when he bent over trying to catch his breath in gasping hiccoughs, the strip where the hair had been burned off was as red as his face and starting to blister.

"One of the sidons blew, didn't it?" Jewell said, and her scar slashed black as a fissure across her cheek. "Which one?"

Scorch still couldn't speak. He nodded with his whole body, bent over double again, and tried to straighten. "It's Jick," he said. "He tried to tripletap, and the whole thing wint up."

"Oh, my God," Sapphire said, and ran into the kitchen.

"How bad is it?" Jewell said.

"Jick's dead, and there are two burned bad—Paulsen and the tapper that came in with Taber last shift. I don't know his name. They were right on top of it when it went, putting the comprissor on."

The tappers had been in motion the whole time he spoke, putting on their jackets and going for their shoes. Taber heaved Carnie off his lap and stood up. Sapphire came back from the kitchen dressed in pants and carrying the remedy case. Garnet put her shawl around Scorch's shoulders and helped him into Pearl's chair.

Taber said calmly, "Are there any other sidons close?" He looked unconcerned, almost amused, with Carnie leaning limply against him, but his left hand was clenched, the thumb moving up and down as if he were clicking the sparker.

"Mine," Scorch said. "It didn't kitch, but the comprissor caught fire and Jick's clothes, and they're still burning." He looked up apologetically at Jewell. "I didn't have nithing to put the fire out with. I dragged the ither two up onto my comprissor platform so they widdn't cook."

Pearl and I had not moved from the pianoboard. I looked at Taber in the mirror, waiting for him to say, "I'll stay here, Jewell. I'll take care of things here," but he didn't. He disengaged himself from Carnie. "I'll go get the stretchers at the gaming house and meet you back here," he said.

"Let me get your jacket for you," I said, but he was already gone.

The tappers banged out the doors, Sapphire with them. Garnet ran upstairs. Jewell went into the anteroom to put her outside shoes on.

I stood up and went out into the anteroom. "Let me go with you," I said.

"I want you ti stay here and take care of Pearl," she said. She could not squeeze her bandaged foot into the shoe. She bent down and began unwinding the bandage.

"Garnet can stay. You'll need help carrying the men back."

She dropped the bandage onto the floor and jammed her foot into the shoe, wincing. "You din't know the way. You kidd git lost and fall into a sidon. You're safer here." She tried the other shoe, stood up and jammed her bandaged foot into it, and sat back down to fix the straps.

"I'm not safe anywhere," I said. "Please don't leave me here. I'm afraid of what might happen."

"Even if the sidons all go up, the fire won't git this far."

"It isn't those sidons I'm afraid of," I said harshly. "You let a sidon loose in the house once before and look what happened."

She straightened up and looked at me, the scar as black and hot as lava against her red face. "A sidon is an animal," she said. "It kin't help itself." She stood up gingerly, testing her unbandaged feet. "Taber's going with me," she said.

She was not as blind as I had feared, but she still didn't see. "Don't you understand?" I said gently. "Even if he goes with you, he'll still be here."

"Are you ready, Jewell?" Taber said. He had a lantern strapped to his forehead, and he was carrying a large red and green wrapped bundle.

"I've gitta git another lantern from upstairs," Jewell said.

"There's nithing left but town lanterns," she said, and went upstairs.

Taber held the package out to me. "You'll have to give Pearl her Chrissmiss present from me, Ruby," he said.

"I won't do it."

"How do you know?" he said.

I didn't answer him.

"You were so anxious to get me my jacket when I went next door. Why don't you get it for me now? Or do you think you won't do that either?"

I took the coat off the hook, waiting for Jewell to come back downstairs.

"Lit's go," Jewell said, hardly limping at all as she came down the steps. I took the jacket over to him. He handed the package to me again, and I took it, watching him put the jacket on, waiting for him to pat the sparker inside the pocket to make sure it was there. Jewell handed him an extra lantern and a bundle of bandages. "Lit's go," she said again. She opened the outside door and went down the wooden steps into the heat.

"Take care of Pearl, Ruby," Taber said, and shut the door.

I went back into the music room. Pearl had not moved. Garnet and Carnie were trying to help Scorch out of the chair and up the stairs, though Carnie could hardly stand. I took his weight from Garnet and picked him up.

"Sit down, Carnie," I said, and she collapsed into the chair, her knees apart and her mouth open, instantly asleep.

I carried Scorch up the stairs to Garnet's room and stood there holding him, bracing his weight against the door while Garnet strung a burn-hammock across her bed for me to lay him in. He had passed out in the chair, but while I was lowering him into the hammock, he came to. His red face was starting to blister, so that he had trouble speaking. "I shidda put the fire out," he said. "It'll catch the ither sidons. I told Jick it was too close."

"They'll put the fire out," I said. Garnet tested the hammock and nodded to me. I laid him gently in it, and we began the terrible process of peeling his clothes off his skin.

"It was thit new tapper thit came down with Taber this morning. He was sotted. And he had a sparker with him. A sparker. The whole star kidda gone up."

"Don't worry," I said. "It'll be all right." I turned him onto his side and began pulling his shirt free. He smelled like frying meat. He passed out again before we got his shirt off, and that made getting the rest of his clothes off easier. Garnet tied his wrist to the saline hookup and started the antibiotics. She told me to go back downstairs.

Pearl was still standing by the pianoboard. "Scorch is going to be fine," I said loudly to cover the sound of picking up Taber's package, and I started past her with it to the kitchen. The blowers had kicked on full-blast from the doors opening so much, but I said anyway, "Garnet wants me to get some water for him."

I made it nearly to the door of the card room. Then Carnie heaved herself up in the white chair and said sleepily, "Thit's Pearl's present, isn't it, Ruby?"

I stopped under the blowers, standing on the sidon.

She sat up straighter, licking her tongue across her lips. "Open it, Ruby. I want to see what it is."

Pearl's hands tightened to fists in front of her. "Yes," she said, looking straight at me. "Open it, Ruby."

"No," I said. I walked over to the pianoboard and put the package down on the stool.

"I'll open it then," Carnie said, and lurched out of the chair after it. "You're so mean, Ruby. Poor Pearl kin't open her own Chrissmiss presents, ivver since she got blind." Her voice was starting to slur. I could barely understand what she was saying, and she had to grab at the package twice before she picked it up and staggered back to Pearl's chair with it clutched to her breast. The sots were starting to really take hold now. In a few moments she would be unconscious. "Please," I said without making a sound, praying as Pearl must have prayed in that locked room, ten years old, her hands tied and him coming at her with a razor. "Hurry, hurry."

Carnie couldn't get the package open. She tugged feebly at the green ribbon, plucked at the paper without even tearing it, and subsided, closing her eyes. She began to breathe deeply, with her mouth open, slumped far down in the white chair with her arms flung out over the arms of the chair.

"I'll take you upstairs, Pearl," I said. "Garnet may need help with Scorch."

"All right," she said, but she didn't move. She stood with her head averted, as if she were listening for something.

"Oh, how pretty!" Carnie said, her voice clear and strong. She was sitting up straight in the chair, her hands on the unopened package. "It's a dress, Pearl. Isn't it beautiful, Ruby?"

"Yes," I said, looking at Carnie, limp again in the chair and snoring softly. "It's covered with lights, Pearl, green and red and gold, like a Christmas tree."

The package slipped out of Carnie's limp hands and onto the floor. The blowers kicked on, and Carnie turned in the chair, pulling her feet up under her and cradling her head against the chair's arm. She began snoring again, more loudly.

I said, "Would you like to try it on, Pearl?" and looked over at her, but she was already gone.

It took me nearly an hour to find her, because the town lantern I had strapped to my forehead was so dim I could not see very well. She was lying face down near the mooring.

I unstrapped the lantern and laid it beside her on the ground so I could see her better. The train of her skirt was smoldering. I stamped on it until it crumbled underfoot and then knelt beside her and turned her over.

"Ruby?" she said. Her voice was squeaky from the helium in the air and very hoarse. I could hardly recognize it. She would not be able to recognize mine either. If I told her I was Jewell or Carnie, or Taber, come to murder her, she would not know the difference. "Ruby?" she said. "Is Taber here?"

"No," I said. "Only the sidon."

"You're not a sidon," she said. Her lips were dry and parched.

"Then what am I?" I moved the town lantern closer. Her face looked flushed, almost as red as Jewell's.

"You are my good friend the pianoboard player who has come to help me."

"I didn't come to help you," I said, and my eyes filled with tears. "I came to finish killing you. I can't help it. I'm copying Taber."

"No," she said, but it was not a "no" of protest or horror or surprise, but a statement of fact. "You have never copied Taber."

"He killed Jack," I said. "He had some poor sotted tapper blow up the sidon so he could have an alibi for your murder. He left me to kill you for him."

Her hands lay at her sides, palms down on the ground. When I lifted them and laid them across her skirt as she had always held them, crossed at the wrists, she did not flinch, and I thought perhaps she was unconscious.

"Jewell's feet are much better," she said, and licked her lips. "You hardly limp at all. And I knew Carnie was on sots before she ever came into the room, by the way you walked. I have listened to you copy all of them, even poor dead Jack. You never copied Taber. Not once."

I crawled around beside her and got her head up on my knees. Her hair came loose and fell around her face as I lifted her up, the ends of it curling up in dark frizzes of ash. The narrow fretted soles of my shoes dug into the backs of my legs like hot irons. She swallowed and said, "He broke the door down and he sent for the doctor and then he went to kill the man, but he was too late. My mother had let him out the back way."

"I know," I said. My tears were falling on her neck and throat. I tried to brush them away, but they had already dried, and her skin felt hot and parched. Her lips were cracked, and she could hardly move them at all when she spoke.

"Then he came back and held me in his arms while we waited for the doctor. Like this. And I said, 'Why didn't you kill him?' and he said, 'I will,' and then I asked him to finish killing me, but he wouldn't. He didn't kill the tapper either, because his hands were broken and all cut up."

"My uncle killed him," I said. "That's why we're quarantined. He and Kovich killed him," I said, though Kovich had already been dead by then. "They tied him up and cut out his eyes with a sot-razor," I said. That was why Jewell had let me come to Paylay. She had owed it to my uncle to let me come because he had killed the tapper. And my uncle had sent me to do what? To copy whom?

The lamp was growing much dimmer and the twillpaper forehead strap on the lantern was smoldering now, but I didn't try to put it out. I knelt with Pearl's head in my lap on the hot ground, not moving.

"I knew you were copying me almost from the first," she said, "but I didn't tell you, because I thought you would kill Taber for me. Whenever you played for me, I sat and thought about Taber with a sidon tearing out his throat, hoping you would copy the hate I felt. I never saw Taber or a sidon either, but I thought about my mother's lover, and I called him Taber. I'm sorry I did that to you, Ruby."

I brushed her hair back from her forehead and her cheeks. My hand left a sooty mark, like a scar, down the side of her face. "I did kill Taber," I said.

"You reminded me so much of Kovich when you played," she said. "You sounded just like him. I thought I was thinking about killing Taber, but I wasn't. I didn't even know what a sidon looks like. I was only thinking about Kovich and waiting for him to come and finish killing me." She was breathing shallowly now and very fast, taking a breath between almost every word. "What do sidons look like, Ruby?"

I tried to remember what Kovich had looked like when he came to find my uncle, his broken hands infected, his face red from the fever that would consume him. "I want you to copy me," he had said to my uncle. "I want you to learn to play the pianoboard from me before I die." I want you to kill a man for me. I want you to cut out his eyes. I want you to do what I can't do.

I could not remember what he looked like, except that he had been very tall, almost as tall as my uncle, as me. It seemed to me that he had looked like my uncle, but surely it was the other way around. "I want you to copy me," he had said to my uncle. I want you to do what I can't do. Pearl had asked him to kill the tapper, and he had promised to. Then Pearl had asked him to finish killing her, and he had promised to do that, too, though he could no more have murdered her than he could have played the pianoboard with his ruined hands, though he had not even known how well a Mirror copies, or how blindly. So my uncle had killed the tapper, and I have finished killing Pearl, but it was Kovich, Kovich who did the murders.

"Sidons are very tall," I said, "and they play the pianoboard."

She didn't answer. The twillpaper strap on the lantern burst into flame. I watched it burn.

"It's all right that you didn't kill Taber," she said. "But you mustn't let him put the blame for killing me on you."

"I did kill Taber," I said. "I gave him the real sparker. I put it in his jacket before he left to go out to the sidons."

She tried to sit up. "Tell them you were copying him, that you couldn't help yourself," she said, as if she hadn't heard me.

"I will," I said, looking into the darkness.

Over the horizon somewhere is Taber. He is looking this way, wondering if I have killed her yet. Soon he will take out his cigar and put his thumb against the trigger of the sparker, and the sidons will go up one after the other, a string of lights. I wonder if he will have time to know he has been murdered, to wonder who killed him.

I wonder, too, kneeling here with Pearl's head on my knees. Perhaps I did copy Pearl. Or Jewell, or Kovich, or even Taber. Or all of them. The worst thing is not that things are done to you. It is not knowing who is doing them. Maybe I did not copy anyone, and I am the one who murdered Taber. I hope so.

"You should go back before you get burned," Pearl says, so softly I can hardly hear her.

"I will," I say, but I cannot. They have tied me up, they have locked me in, and now I am only waiting for them to come and finish killing me.

THE SORCERESS IN SPITE OF HERSELF

by Pat Cadigan

art: Janet Aulisio

The author lives in Overland Park, Kansas, where she writes a line of humorous greeting cards for Hallmark. Her work has appeared in *Omni*, *IAsfm*, and many other science fiction magazines.

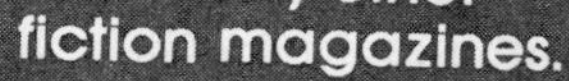

"Oh, damn it, *please* be here," she muttered for the millionth time, yanking open the top drawer of her bureau and pawing through the mess of lingerie inside. Her frantic fingers brushed a small green box and she flicked the lid open with her thumb. It was empty. She stared at it for several seconds, trying to remember what had been in it originally—the silver leaf brooch or the butterfly pin? She shook her head, putting the box on the cluttered dresser top. It was an old box, and she probably hadn't put any jewelry in it for ages. She continued searching the drawer.

"Lou?"

She jumped, making a small shriek and inadvertently tossing several pairs of panties into the air. In the mirror she saw Tony standing in the doorway of the bedroom, looking amused. She hoped he couldn't see the stricken expression in her own reflection at that distance. If she could get through the evening without his finding out, maybe she could get to a jeweler tomorrow and buy replacements. It would put her in hock up to her ears, which was as good a level as any, considering, but since they had separate bank accounts, it wouldn't be hard to conceal the expenditure from him. She'd done that often enough in the past.

"I realize turning thirty is traumatic," he said with gentle sarcasm, "but if you don't put a move on, we're going to be unforgivably late for your birthday dinner. They'll give our reservations away."

"Oh, yeah. Right." She looked down at the open drawer and then at the scatter of items on the bureau top. There was no use in continuing her search. This was the fourth time she'd ransacked the dresser, and if they weren't there the first three times, they weren't about to appear now. Besides, if she delayed any longer, Tony was going to be suspicious. She pushed the drawer closed, plucked her purse out of the mess on the bureau, and forced a bright smile as she turned around. "Well, then, let's go."

Tony shook his head. "Aren't you forgetting something?"

A cold knot gathered in Lou's stomach. "Ah, am I?"

Tony tapped his left earlobe. "I thought you wanted to show off tonight."

"Oh. Well." She shrugged, trying to look natural. "You know, I was reading the paper and there was this news story about a woman who was wearing some ruby earrings and a guy walked right up to her on the street and just ripped them right out of her ears. Tore her earlobes to shreds. She had to go to the hospital and everything." Lou shuddered. "It kind of scared me, you know? I mean, I'm thinking about not even taking a purse tonight."

She could tell he didn't buy the explanation by the stunned look on his face. "Oh, Lou, you didn't—"

"They're safe, honest, Tone, I put them away—"

"—didn't *really* lose them—"

"—in the box where I always—"

"—*please* tell me you didn't lose the diamond earrings that cost me half a year's savings—"

"—for Chrissakes, they're in the drawer now. Let's go! We're going to be *late!*"

They stared across the room at each other in the sudden silence.

"Oh, God, Lou," Tony said finally.

Lou burst into tears. That was a dead giveaway. She knew it as soon as she did it, but she couldn't control herself. She was a crier under pressure, and she could no more break herself of that than she could break herself of losing things. Sobbing as much over her lack of control as with sorrow for Tony's discovery of the loss, she groped her way to the bed and sat down.

Tony stood helplessly in the doorway for a few moments and then went to her. "Lou, Lou, Lou," he chanted, pulling her into his arms. The comforting sound he was trying to put into his voice was not quite there. She sobbed harder.

"Come on, now," he said after a minute. "Pull yourself together, and I'll help you look for them."

"It's no use, Tony," she wept, pushing him away. She went to the bureau and slid a tangle of necklaces off a box of tissues. Before taking one, she felt around the inside of the box, but it contained nothing but tissues. "They're gone for good. I looked everywhere and they're not in the house."

"Did you ever take them off at work?"

She wagged her head from side to side. "I never wore them to work. Diamonds in the office would be a little much." She blew her nose.

"Are you *sure?*"

"Yes, I'm *sure!*" she snapped. "I'm not a complete feeb, you know!"

Tony stood up and folded his arms. "Don't get mad at *me. I'm* not the one who lost your earrings."

"No? I'm not so sure about that." She lifted her head, her tears drying up almost instantly. "You're always cleaning things up and putting things away where I can't find them. Maybe you saw my earrings lying around and decided to put them in a safe place. Only it's so safe that it's even safe from me!"

Tony's face hardened. "Look you, you can't just leave diamond earrings *lying around.* And someone's got to pick up the clutter around here. If I didn't, we'd be ass-deep in junk and you know it!"

Lou's shoulder's slumped and she leaned on the bureau. "Oh, God, Tony. My *earrings.*"

He took a deep breath. "When did you see them last?"

"I don't know," she said sadly, staring at the floor.

"Try to remember. Did you wear them last weekend?"

"I don't know."

"Well, when was the last time you wore them that you *can* remember?"

She made a pained face. "I think I wore them to the company dinner. In fact, I *know* I did, because Jack Waverly said something about them."

"Okay. Then what? After we came home, what did you do?"

"How should I know? That was a week and a half ago."

"*Think.*"

"I must have put them where I always put them—on top of the bureau. In my jewelry box."

He got up and looked at the jumble of necklaces, pins, and other earrings in the shallow open box. "Are you sure they're not in there hiding under something?"

"I looked a million times, Tone."

"Goddamit, I don't see how you can find anything in that mess." He snatched the box off the bureau and upended it over the bed.

"Jesus, Tony, now you've made a bigger mess."

He spread the jewelry around, combing through it with his fingers. She stood and watched, waiting for him to give up. It was a scene they had replayed over and over through six months of marriage, with car keys, house keys, wallets, rings, eyeglasses, and a multitude of other things, usually hers, being the objects of the search. Long ago he had learned not to give her anything of his to hold, not even for a moment, because she would make it disappear. That was her special talent, making things disappear. Mostly they were small but important items, though she had, in the past, worked miracles with a ten-pound bag of charcoal briquets, a twenty-five pound frozen turkey and once, in an unparalleled feat of dematerialization, a full barrel of trash. She insisted even to herself that the barrel had been stolen on collection day. If that indeed had been the case, however, someone had stolen the trash in it as well, because Tony had discovered the loss before the collection truck arrived.

Now Tony picked up the jewelry box and shook it vigorously

over the bed again to dislodge anything that might have been jammed in there. Lou shook her head. He knew as well as she did that the box was empty. He dropped it on the bed and threw up his hands.

"How do you *do* it?"

She stared at his incredulous face, feeling like a monster.

"How do you make things disappear like that? Tell me. Tell me and I'll die a happy man!"

"Oh, Tony—"

"No, come on, now, Lou. How do you do it? Don't you have *any* idea?"

She brushed past him and began to gather up the scattered jewelry on the bed, dumping it back into the box by the handful. "Magic."

Tony slapped the bureau with his hand. "Well, goddamit, why didn't you just say so? Magic. That's great. Better than I thought. If you were just careless or disorganized, I'm not sure what I'd do. I mean, here you are, a woman with a Master's degree in Business Administration who spends her days keeping the largest manufacturing firm in the state rolling along turning out widgets, gidgets, and gadgets but who can't keep track of her possessions from one moment to the next—that would be too absurd to believe. But *magic*. Now *there's* an explanation that's not only rational, but full of potential for profit! We could both quit our jobs and tour the country with our own magic act. Louise Belmont performing prestidigitation and sleights-of-hand before your very eyes, aided by her faithful husband Tony. We'll play everywhere—Vegas, the Borscht circuit, who knows? Maybe even a command performance for the Queen in London! Your Majesty, where did you say you remember seeing the Crown Jewels last?"

Lou straightened up slowly, holding the box tight against her stomach so she wouldn't fling it in her husband's face. "That's no way to talk to a woman with a curse on her."

Tony exploded with laughter. She ignored him and set the box on the bureau. Then she sat down on the edge of the bed and watched him coldly until he wound down.

"Oh, God," he said, grabbing for a tissue. "If this weren't so serious, it really would be funny." He dabbed at his eyes and laughed a little more.

Lou's mouth was an angry line. "Funny to *you*. I'm the one with the curse."

Tony's smile faded away. "You don't actually believe that—"

"I don't know what else it could be." She looked away from him.

"I've tried everything to keep from losing stuff—making lists, memory courses—I even went to a fancy, high-priced psychiatrist for some industrial strength analysis. You know what he told me? I tend to lose things. What an analysis. I knew that already." She wiped her light brown hair away from her forehead. "The only explanation left is magic. Sorcery. I'm an inadvertent sorceress. Somehow I put spells on things and make them go away."

Tony bent and squinted into her face. "Lou."

"What."

"Look at me."

She raised her eyes to meet his.

"Now I want you to look me square in the face and say all that again without laughing."

She turned away. "Lay off, Tone."

"I mean it, Lou. If you actually believe all that garbage you just said, you've got a bigger problem than just losing things. Not only am I going to have to lock up everything of value, but I'll have to have you deprogrammed as well."

"I'm not crazy."

"Oh, no?"

Lou sat up sharply, bouncing a little on the mattress. "I'll prove it. Give me something."

Tony rolled his eyes. "Sweetheart—"

"I'm not kidding. Give me something."

"For God's sake—"

"*Give me something.*"

He picked up one of her necklaces from the bureau.

"Not that. Something of yours. Something important to you. Something you don't want to do without."

After a moment of thought, he began pulling off his wedding ring.

"Oh, thanks a lot, *pal.*"

He held the ring up. "Something important to me."

Lou's eyes narrowed. "You're putting me in a bad spot, Tone. If it disappears, it's gone forever. You'll never see it again. But if it doesn't, that'll say more about you than it does about me. All of it bad."

"It's important to me," he insisted. "And you can't make things disappear by magic. You're just careless."

"I am not." She took the ring from him. It was a simple white-gold band, just like her own, with their initials and the date of their wedding engraved on the inside. "Now. Observe." He groaned as she reached down and pulled her blazer pocket inside out. "An ordinary pocket, perfectly intact, no holes in it—"

"Lou, you're getting silly—"

"*Perfectly intact, no holes in it.*" She pushed the lining back down again. "Now. I'm going to drop the ring into this pocket." She did so and held the pocket open. "Look. Look down inside and make sure the ring is still there."

Tony sighed.

"Do it or you'll never believe me."

He looked and nodded. "I see it."

"Fine." She folded her hands on her knees. "Now we wait."

"For what?"

"For the ring to disappear. I think it takes me a little longer with precious metals than with ordinary objects." She tilted her head thoughtfully. "I must have a lot of trouble vanishing precious gems. You gave me those earrings three months ago at least."

"Lou, this is insane."

She arched her eyebrows at him. "Is it?"

"Yes, it is. There's no such thing as real magic. And if there were, you wouldn't be able to perform it by accident. Magic requires a lot of ritual."

"If there's no such thing, how would you know that?"

"I've read about magic, just like anyone else has. Including you, it would seem. Except I never heard you mention any of this stuff before." He frowned at her suspiciously. "Did you ever fool around with witchcraft?"

"I don't know anything about witchcraft. That's probably part of my problem. If I did study up on it, maybe I could find out what I was doing or saying and stop it." Lou wet her lips. "I never said anything before because it sounds as crazy to me as it does to you. For a long time I never considered such a thing. But all my life I've been a loser. Literally. I don't know how I got through school. I had to pull all-nighters constantly to do papers. If I didn't, I'd have too much time in which to lose them. I wrote my Master's thesis in a week and even then I lost it three times. If I hadn't kept copies with all my friends, I'd probably still be trying to write it." She gave a small laugh. "When I went to work, I really had to learn how to think fast. I used the multiple copy device from college, but even so, an awful lot of important contracts were, ah, lost in the mail. The day I got a secretary was the best day of my life. I just dumped everything with her and called for things as I needed them. Now I've got a whole battalion of assistants, and I do just fine. Except with the office supplies. I've taken to buying my own at a stationery store. It's expensive, but it's easier than trying to explain how I can go through all those paper clips, rubber bands, manila envelopes, and pens so quickly."

Tony stared at her, his mouth partially open.

"If that doesn't sound like magic to you, then what in hell would you call it?" she asked plaintively. He didn't answer. "You can look in my pocket now. I'm sure your ring is gone."

He looked. She kept her face averted as he stood bent over her pocket, transfixed. He made her stand up and patted her down the way cops frisked suspects on television. He felt around on the bed and on the floor underneath, crawling back and forth, digging his fingers into the nap. He took off her shoes and shook them out, peered into her mouth, ran his fingers through her hair.

"Satisfied?" she asked when he finally plumped down on the bed, holding his ringless left hand up in front of his face.

"I don't believe it," he murmured, "but I believe it."

"Wonderful. Now let's go celebrate my thirtieth birthday. Thirty years of losses probably totaling in the hundreds of thousands, including a hundred dollar wedding ring and a pair of earrings worth over two grand." She laughed bitterly. "Happy birthday to me."

It was a quiet ride to the restaurant.

"Maybe it's swearing," Tony said to her suddenly over their third cocktail.

She nearly spat her daiquiri out onto the table. "Maybe *what's* swearing?"

"Your vanishing act. Your making things disappear."

At the next table, a man glanced up from his menu at them and then looked down again. Lou speared a fried mushroom from the appetizer dish and chewed it sullenly. "What are you talking about?"

Tony leaned over the table, blinking at her. He'd been drinking Black Russians, and she couldn't really blame him. "You said it was magic, a curse on you, right? Maybe it is. Literally. Maybe every time you curse, you lose something." He tried to stab a mushroom for himself, missed, and tried again.

"That's the dumbest thing I ever heard."

Tony switched his attention from mushrooms to black olives with success. "Listen to that," he said to the olive on the end of the plastic pick he was holding. "She tells me there's a magic curse on her, and when I make a suggestion as to what's causing it, she says it's dumb." He popped the olive into his mouth and gave her a dirty look.

"Before you put all that alcohol in your system, you thought it was all pretty dumb."

"Of course it's dumb." Tony took a sip of his Black Russian. "I'm drunk. And well I should be. Today my wife disposed of a pair of diamond earrings and my wedding ring. Right now everything else sounds reasonable."

Lou sighed, rested her elbow on the table, and plunked her chin in her hand. "All right. But just what made you come up with the idea that my swearing would make things disappear?"

"I made the association. Curse—cursing—swearing. Simple as that."

"There's only one thing wrong with that theory, bright guy. I didn't curse when your ring disappeared."

Tony's chin lifted abruptly. "Yes, you did. You said 'hell.' "

"I didn't." Lou frowned. "Did I?"

"Yep. You said something about how if your losing things wasn't magic, what the hell was it? Or something like that." He looked around for the waitress and signalled for two more drinks.

"I guess I did." Lou rubbed the side of her face. "I don't really remember. I'm a little toasted myself. Wish the food would come."

"We're lucky you didn't say, 'Wish the *goddam* food would come.' God knows what you'd lose now."

"It still doesn't work, Tone."

"And why not?"

"Because I must have cursed hundreds of times during the three months I had the earrings."

"Regular little potty-mouth, aren't you? So?"

"Well, I didn't lose them till tonight, *dear*," she said with exaggerated patience. "Do you see what I mean?"

"Ah." He nodded, grimacing at the appetizer plate. "*Ah.*" He pointed a finger at her. "But maybe conditions weren't right."

"Conditions?"

The waitress came and set down two more glasses, picking up the empty ones. "It shouldn't be much longer," she told them. "Chicken Cordon Bleu takes a little time to do right." Neither of them paid any attention to her.

"Remember what you said when you did the magic act in the bedroom?" Tony asked. "How I had to give you something I really cared about?"

The waitress gave Lou a strange look before she walked away.

"I cared about my earrings," Lou said huffily. "They weren't just trinkets, for Chr—"

Tony put up his hand. "Restrain yourself. I may not have this right, but let's not take any chances, okay?"

Lou looked up at the ceiling. When she looked down, she found the man at the next table was staring at her again. She wrinkled her nose at him. "Okay, okay. But I still cared about my earrings."

"Sure. In a distracted way. Tonight, though, you really wanted to wear them. So you went looking for them and as soon as you did, you started worrying because you know you always lose things. The pressure was building up, you probably said something like 'hell,' and—" He popped his cheek with his finger. "Gone without a trace. Just like my ring, which was as important to you as it was to me."

Lou sat perfectly still. "I said, 'damn it.' "

Tony's eyes widened. "Oh. You did?"

She nodded.

"Uh-huh." He tapped his fingers on the table. "You know, I still didn't quite believe it. I mean, I was just talking. One absurdity's as good as another absurdity. Now I'm getting nervous." He took a large drink from his glass. "And sober. But not for long, I hope."

Lou sipped at her own drink without tasting it. "That isn't going to help me figure out how to beat this thing."

Tony shrugged. "Try watching your mouth?"

"It would be better if I could find a way to get un-cursed. I don't want to be a sorceress. I've been making things disappear all my life, ever since I was a little girl—"

"Sneaking little curses under your breath, no doubt."

"No. *No.*" Lou rapped her knuckles on the table. "Now that I do know. I was a very clean little kid. The worst thing I ever said was 'Oh, my God.' "

"Which is technically swearing."

"It *is?*"

"Taking You-Know-Who's name in vain. That's swearing. Cursing."

"Oh, G—great."

Tony brightened. "Hey. Maybe we can figure a way to bring things back."

"What?"

"Yeah. Now that we've figured out how you're losing things, maybe we can dope out some way you can reverse the spell and find them again."

The waitress came with their meals, setting the plates down

in front of them slowly, in case there was any more interesting talk about magic acts in the bedroom. When there wasn't, she left. Lou picked up her knife and fork and began sawing at her chicken.

"I don't think so," she said. "Tonight was the first time I'd done anything like I did with your ring. I was always too terrified that it would work. Which it did. It took me thirty years to get to that point. I'll probably be sixty before I stumble over a reversing spell. And I don't think there is one."

"There has to be," Tony said around a mouthful of red snapper. "Magic is symmetrical. Yin and yang, all that."

"You're talking about the magic you've come across in books. Popular culture stuff and covens in California. What we're dealing with is magic that works. That stuff doesn't."

Tony dragged his head from side to side. "If it works one way, it's got to work the other. Even magic—real magic—must have laws, just like nature. Hell, you're even governed by one of them. Action: swear. Reaction: disappearance."

The light buzz Lou had been feeling was beginning to wear off as her stomach filled. "All right. That sounds reasonable, about as reasonable as it can sound, considering. H—heck."

Tony winced. "That was close."

"I thought there had to be *conditions*."

"Don't tempt fate."

"This is peachy," she said sourly. "I can spend my life either losing things or sounding like Little Mary Sunshine. What the— What is this, anyway? I didn't ask to be a sorceress."

"Relax." Tony patted her hand clumsily. "Cheer up. I helped you find out why you always lost things. I bet I can help you find them again." Much to her dismay, he signalled for another drink.

By the time they were ready to leave, Tony was nearly in a stupor. She managed to get him to walk from the restaurant to where the car was parked but there was no question of his driving. "Thanks a lot, Tone," she muttered as she buckled him into the passenger seat. "*My* birthday and *you* get bombed. Thanks a *bundle*."

His eyes opened to slits and he smiled at her sleepily. "You're welcome. Happy birthday." Then he was out again, really out. She slammed the car door and stalked around to the driver's side, not very steady herself. She hated driving when she'd had even just one drink, but she'd always been able to hold her alcohol better than Tony. Still, she couldn't remember the last time she'd seen him so drunk.

Not that she wouldn't have liked to be smashed herself, she thought, keeping to an even twenty-five miles per hour all the way home. She had more reason for it than Tony did certainly. She glanced at his limp form, drooping like a rag in the shoulder harness, and felt a little surge of anger. Here she was, an unwilling sorceress in the middle of a modern American city with a power that could do her absolutely no good at all, and when she needed his help, what did he do? Got drunk and passed out.

She clamped her lips together. Don't say it, she told herself. Don't say it or you're sure to vanish the house keys, because in a few more blocks they're what you're going to want most.

She maintained control, not even allowing a sigh to escape her until she drove the car into the garage attached to their house. If Tony had been not indisposed, he would have insisted on backing the car in so he could just drive out the next day, but she wasn't about to attempt such a thing. Tony could just back out of the driveway for a change. It wouldn't kill him.

She got out of the car and went to unlock the door to the kitchen, fumbling with the keys in the dark. She flipped the garage light switch and found to her great annoyance the bulb was burned out. Now she'd have to practically carry Tony inside in the dark. Sighing, she unlocked the door and began feeling her way around to Tony's side of the car.

"Tony? Tony, we're home." She heard a faint answering moan. He was going to be righteously sick in the morning. "Tony, wake up so I can get you in—" Her foot hit something hard with an alarming clatter and she lost her balance, falling sideways onto the hood of the car. "Oh, god*damm*it!" she yelled, struggling to push herself upright.

Then she froze, leaning on the car, realizing what she had said.

"Tony! *Tony!*" She pushed herself around the front of the car, banging her knee on the bumper. "Tony, I said it! I slipped and said 'goddam', Tony, quick, wake up, we've got to find out what I lost this time. The house keys—"

She yanked the car door open. The flash of the dome light hurt her eyes, and for several seconds she could only stand blinking at the empty front seat.

"Oh, darn," she said miserably. "Oh, goshdarn it all to blazes."

The front seat stayed empty.

by Mildred Downey Broxon

NIGHT OF THE FIFTH SUN

art: Ron Logan

Mildred Downey Broxon, who has lived all over the North and South American continents, now lives in Seattle, Washington with her two cats. Her novel, *Too Long a Sacrifice*, will soon be re-released as an illustrated trade paperback from Blue Jay Books.

Four suns have died before us, say the Aztecs. The first was destroyed by jaguars, the second by wind, the third by fiery rain, and the fourth by flood.

Then was born ours, the fifth sun. The god Huitzilopochtli must be fed or the sun will die. At the end of every fifty-two-year cycle, the sun grows weak.

The proper food for the sun is human hearts and blood.

Winter breathed dead cold toward the city centre. The metropolis sprawled out from what was once an island in a shallow lake. Yellow through the smog, the Pleiades wheeled up the sky. The wind ghosted through centuries of history, tossed trash down streets once trod by feathered warriors, and slithered toward the ancient place of sacrifice. No temple stood there now; the wind crept in through hospital windows.

In the basement, Jesus-Maria Lopez shivered and drew near the furnace. He opened the fire door: light glinted off shards of broken glass. Piles of it stood in cartons. He'd helped straighten the laboratories this week, and should really have carried out the trash, but time enough for that tomorrow. This was a night of death. A cold god danced in the wind.

His mother had taught him to keep careful count: tonight ended a cycle. Fifty-two years since the last New Fire: he'd been a boy of four. His aunt went into labor that night. In the morning the sun rose as usual, but his mother said Carmelita was dead. Jesus-Maria remembered weeping.

He shivered again. It was nowhere near as cold as the winter nights in Europe, during the Second War, but then he'd been twenty-one, an eager warrior. Even if death struck all around, there was honor to dying in battle. Never mind the wife and child at home.

But he'd come back; and now he would end his days as a janitor in the old hospital, in the heart of Mexico City.

Tonight the shadows lived. Beneath the silence he could hear feathers rustle and water lap on wooden hulls. The archaeologists said a canal once lay here, a waterway to serve the temple. It had been filled in long ago, the pyramid leveled; and the conquerors had raised one of their churches on the sacred spot. A larger church, a convent, and finally a hospital followed, in an attempt to claim the site. Still, tonight he heard lapping water. And tonight tied up a bundle of years: the sun was weak and hungry.

The feather-rustle grew, became a scratching, as if bony fingers clawed the windowpane. He did not want to see what stood outside, but he rose to his feet and squared his shoulders like a man. After all, he had custody of this place.

The basement was sunk half a story into the ground, so the window stood at eye-height. First, through the darkness and grime, he saw nothing; then, by the wall, he made out a figure. Bare legs beneath a calf-length skirt, a woolen shawl over the head—what woman would seek him here? He pulled the window open.

"Grandfather?" It was a croak.

He stepped back. Of his five granddaughters, only one would roam the streets at night. At least she was alive. It was so long since he'd heard—his heart hammered. He caught his breath. "Luisa?"

The figure doubled over. He heard a stifled moan. Then, "Let me in. I'm cold, and—"

"Come around to the side." So it was down to this, for Luisa: a slut on the street, with nowhere to sleep. He latched the window and fumbled for his keys.

The cold wind, the death-wind blew her through the door. Lopez looked at the sky, but saw only yellow haze throwing back the city lights. "Come close to the fire, child." Whatever she wanted, she'd tell him in time.

The young woman fell to her knees and bit back a cry. She crouched motionless a minute, then straightened. She crept toward the furnace and held out her hands. Her fingers were thick as sausages, and the scarlet nail enamel was chipped. When she threw back her woolen shawl he saw that her features—once as fine as her mother's—had grown puffy. She dropped her shawl to the floor and faced him. He stared at her swollen belly.

"You see," she defied him, "how it is with me." Then she grew pale. Again she doubled over, but made no sound.

"Mother of God!" The old man was aghast. As an afterthought he added silently, "Saint Mary Magdalene, pray for her." Should not that saint have pity on a sister whore? "Tell me, child, have you no one?"

She waited until the pain stopped, then shook her head. "No one." She laughed. The sound cut like the wind. "I've been unable to—ply my trade—of late."

"Come, then, let's get you upstairs quickly." At home in the village women thought little of giving birth, but those were women of the old, pure stock. City people, even his own granddaughter, were not as strong.

He put his hand under her elbow and helped her to her feet. Behind him a cold wind made the furnace flicker. He turned back and closed the door against the draft.

* * *

In the small Coronary Care unit a man slept hooked to wires. Machines traced the ragged beating of his heart. It was weary, and parts of it had already died.

Amid the green-lighted dusk, blackness bulked in a corner. Eagle claws scrabbled across tile. Invisible wings beat the air.

The man stirred. His heart tracing leapt and twisted; the shadow flowed forward, then stopped. This was no warrior. This heart was not fit to feed the sun.

When the nurse ran into the room the man was asleep. His cardiogram seemed unchanged. She looked at the print-out and shook her head: it had been a near thing. Only then did she notice the scratches on the tiles. Someone had been moving heavy equipment, no doubt. But she'd not seen those marks when she made her rounds . . . She sniffed: a smell like surgery. She pulled back the covers to check. The wizened body lay in a white gown on spotless sheets. Why, then, was the air heavy with fresh blood?

The emergency clinic was bright and noisy. Lopez stood, a drab quiet figure, in the treatment room.

The young white-coated doctor was a Yankee, new to the staff. "Ah, Hay-soos," he said, in halting Spanish, "would you please step outside while I examine her?" Jesus nodded and left. The Yankees always had trouble with his name—as if to speak it were blasphemy. Name of God, why should that be so?

He found a bench along the wall and waited, staring straight ahead. Time passed.

The young doctor tapped him on the shoulder. Jesus looked up. "She's been in labor for a long time, and she's sick, also. Tox-e-mi-a." Jesus nodded at the unfamiliar word. Yes, Luisa was sick. He could see that. "I'll admit her, even though she's not our patient," the doctor went on. "She says she's had no care." He looked disapprovingly at Lopez. "She's malnourished, as well. Your granddaughter, you say?"

"Yes." Jesus-Maria did not explain. This was a private shame.

"You'll have to sign the papers, then." The doctor gestured; an orderly wheeled Luisa away.

At the admitting desk he had trouble: his eyes were poor. The receptionist helped him, a bit impatiently. There was a space on the form for the husband's name. Shamefacedly, he printed "none."

The ward windows were barred. The mirrors on the wall were steel. Sleepless, an old and hollow-eyed woman paced the night.

Darkness paused at the locked doorway, then oozed inside. The old woman cowered, and a mad smile flicked across her face. She held out her hands to the cold: "I will go with you. I will be proud to feed the sun. I shall dance up the steps, singing: take me and see!"

Years had scored her face, and madness nibbled at her brain. She was no proper sacrifice. The darkness shrank from her touch.

She stared after it, sobbing, then ran to the window. She clutched the bars and looked up at the sky. Through a rift in the smog the Pleiades gleamed, a scatter of diamonds. "The end of the cycle," she whispered, "the death of the Fifth Sun. I would have gone, but I was not chosen."

She strode to the end of the room and stared at the clouded steel. "It has come," she whispered. "The God of the Smoking Mirror rules the night." The tears on her cheeks glittered like stars.

Jesus-Maria Lopez followed his granddaughter to the labor room, but they'd put a needle in her arm to make her sleep. He could do nothing, so he went back to the basement. He was worried about the furnace.

He fretted over Luisa: she looked very ill, and the doctor seemed concerned. Women sometimes died in childbirth. Rosalia, his wife, had been lucky. She bore six; and it was cancer, at the last, that sent her to the Little Dead Ones. But remember Carmelita, his mother's youngest sister. . . .

> Sunset. Sleepy chickens pecked in the dust one last time. Charcoal smoke dimmed the autumn air. The women bustling inside the hut, Carmelita's cries like a bleating goat, the men huddled in groups against the creeping dark.
>
> His older sister hurried him off to bed; in the morning he heard Carmelita had died. His mother had tried to comfort him: "Carmelita is a *cihuateto,* she is in the Heaven of the Sun, now. She died in childbed; that is the same, for a woman, as being a warrior. And besides," as an afterthought, "her soul is surely with the Blessed Virgin. She was a good Catholic."

Not until later in life had he wondered at that. Such thoughts were common in his village, where his family could trace its line to before the Conquest. They were Aztec—and never, his mother added proudly, was there any Spanish blood. Those of the women who were raped or captured hanged themselves for shame.

Time passed, and in Europe the war began. Jesus-Maria wanted glory, so he crossed the ocean to fight. He came home to find the village dried up like a gourd. His mother was dead. He stayed on for a year, but finally followed the rest of the young people to the city. He, Rosalia, and the children had never been back, even on the Feast of the Dead.

Years later, at the Anthropology Museum, he saw the stone statues of *cihuatetos,* their hands clenched, their teeth bared in skull-like grins. With a shudder he remembered Carmelita.

In the city his children learned city ways and wed whom they wished, without asking advice or permission. So Spanish blood at last came to their line. Pedro, his eldest, married a bank teller, a handsome woman who bore him three children before running away to Los Angeles. Of those three, the first was Luisa.

Such was life. Now he tended the furnace and swept floors in the hospital, and Luisa sold her body on the street.

He shrugged and checked the furnace. The fire was almost dead.

The young woman lay alone in a two-bed room. Her face was shiny with sweat, her black hair spread tangled on the pillow, and her fingers clutched the sheet. Every few moments she was wracked by contractions. She made no sound.

In the corner, darkness grew solid. A woman in childbirth—yes, here was a tasty sacrifice. The bravery, the fear, the pain all added spice. It was proper, it was as things should be. This woman came mostly of the old stock, from those who had known proper reverence, and fed their gods with human hearts and blood.

The darkness hefted an obsidian knife and savored the future.

The burner showed only one low flame. Jesus-Maria muttered under his breath, a combination curse and prayer. According to the old ways all fires should be extinguished tonight, until the new one was kindled on the breast of a sacrifice. But there were no sacrifices any more. Surely the ancient gods no longer expected to be fed with lives.

Water slapped against a wood-hulled boat, and feathers rustled. A whisper: "The star-cluster is high. A bundle of years has been gathered and tied. Tonight the fifth sun will gutter out."

In the darkness Jesus-Maria saw a glint as of black volcanic glass, held by a dim shape. No, that was only his old coat swaying in the draft, and the light shone off broken lab ware. The shards were long and dangerous. He should have carried the boxes out, but he had no wish to brave the death-cold wind.

It was blowing away the overcast, he saw. The Pleiades gleamed like a shattered wineglass.

He turned back to the furnace. Nothing worked, no matter how he adjusted the oil flow. It must be some trick of air currents. He'd have to figure a way to screen it. Tomorrow. Tonight he was so tired, so cold. . . .

The knock woke him from a doze. He opened the door. Julio the orderly stood, impressive in his white smock. "They—they sent me to find you, Jesus. Your granddaughter—" he swallowed. "They have summoned the priest. You should go to her."

Wordless, Jesus followed.

Yes, it was good. The world might be spared for another cycle. This woman would suffice. By the time she claimed her reward as a cihuateto, *she would have earned it well.*

It seemed she was a willing sacrifice. Yes, the sun would be fed. The world need not end tonight.

The darkness waited to take the offering. It was patient. Old as it was, it could afford to be.

The priest closed the door and wiped spittle from his cheek. His hand shook. "She would not see me," he muttered. Then, to Lopez, "Are you her grandfather?"

Lopez nodded.

"Reason with the child. Tell her to confess, no matter what she has done. Her life is in danger. She may well die in her sins! I will wait." He turned, went to a chair, and opened a prayer book. His movements were angry.

The doctor looked up as Lopez entered. "As I thought, she's been in labor for days. The water broke a long time ago. There may be infection."

Lopez heard all this but paid little heed. The face of the girl on the pillow could have been that of Rosalia, his wife, now that Luisa's sharp Spanish features were blurred by swelling. Mixed-blood or no, she resembled their side of the family, too.

"Luisa—"

"Go away! I do not want your Sacrament!"

"Luisa, it is your grandfather, not the priest. There is no priest here, Luisa."

She opened her eyes and searched the room. Her gaze lingered in the darkest corner. She licked her lips. "Grandfather?" She did not look away from the shadows.

"I am here, Luisa. Why did you send the priest away? You know you are very ill."

"I do not wish to make confession. I am not sorry. I regret nothing.

Not even—this." She looked into the distance and half-smiled.

Lopez saw nothing in the dimness. But as he turned back, out of the corner of his eye—*the plumed headdress, a flash of bright color, a black knife*—no, when he looked again there was only a curtain swaying in the breeze.

Luisa began to cry out; to stop herself she sank her teeth into her wrist. "You'd better leave now," the doctor said. "She must stay quiet. We will keep you informed." He pulled back the sheet: Lopez caught a glimpse of bright blood.

The priest looked up as he passed. Lopez shook his head. "Pray for her. Perhaps she is mad."

The priest's face smoothed. "Perhaps so, indeed, poor child."

They knew where to find him. The furnace needed tending. Best a man have something to do on a night when death danced in the wind.

"I go gladly," Luisa murmured in Nahuatl. "Take me."

"What did she say?" the Yankee doctor asked the nurse. "I didn't understand."

"Nor did I," the nurse replied. "She is probably delirious." Neither of them spoke the ancient Aztec tongue.

The old man opened the furnace door and peered inside. All seemed as it should be, but the flame was dying. —In preparation for the offering: a high-born victim, a worthy sacrifice. This is the fifty-second year, the end of the cycle. Tonight the sun will be destroyed and the world will end, as it has four times already—

"Of course no one now believes that." *He must raise his voice over the sound of lapping water, paddles dipping into the canal: more of them, now. The canoes were gathering on the ancient waterways. The square of the window had been grey with street lights and starshine, but of a sudden it grew black. He stepped over and saw, near the hospital, dwarfing it and the old church, the pyramid dark against the sky. On its top torches flared and were snuffed; in the distance he saw the sheen of a long-buried lake.*

On nearby rooftops people gathered. They wore feathers, blankets, bright woven garments; and, like the buildings that held them, they were somehow insubstantial. Children cried and were hushed.

The furnace spat one yellow-blue flame against the dark. He hurried back, turned the dial for more oil, and struck a match. The flame shrank to nothing in his hand.

Julio knocked on the door. "Hurry, Jesus, hurry!" His voice was urgent. "She's had a convulsion—the doctor says she is dying. If you wish to be with her—"

"I will come immediately." *So.* At the end of the cycle, in the fifty-second year, Luisa, my little Luisa, goes to feed the sun. Was it all for this? The withered village, our move to the city, Luisa's birth, her taking to the streets—was it all that she might be sacrificed in childbirth and serve the sun as a *cihuateto?* There are no more offerings, in this last hungry age. My little Luisa will die in her sins, unconfessed and unabsolved. Will it be Hell or the Western Paradise of the Sun for her?

If the sun is not fed it will die, and the world will perish. No matter that no one believes this now. It is nonetheless true.

Julio knocked again. "Jesus! Hurry, I beg you!"

"Go ahead. I follow in a moment." —Even if no one knows, it is still true. Luisa, child, you should not die in your sins. I am an old man. The sun must be fed.—"Go ahead, Julio," he called, and waited until he heard footsteps fade away.

He dragged the carton of broken glass into the last glow of firelight and selected a long, thick shard. He held it before him. "Dear God, receive my spirit." He did not know which god he meant. "We do not believe. We fear." The glass point gleamed. He raised it high and bore downward to his heart.

He breathed pain. Through a veil he saw the furnace flicker out.

The darkness tasted a warrior's death. It left the room where the young woman lay. Tonight the sun would feast.

The city woke. Traffic hooted over ancient causeways. Few who hurried to work knew that today began another cycle of fifty-two years. None cared that they lived because Huitzilopochtli, and the sun, had fed.

The nurse handed Luisa her newborn son. The mother took him and smiled. "I'll name him Jesus-Maria." Through the window, a shaft of sunlight touched the child; she shuddered and clasped him to her breast.

DEC JAN
G. Barr - 1981

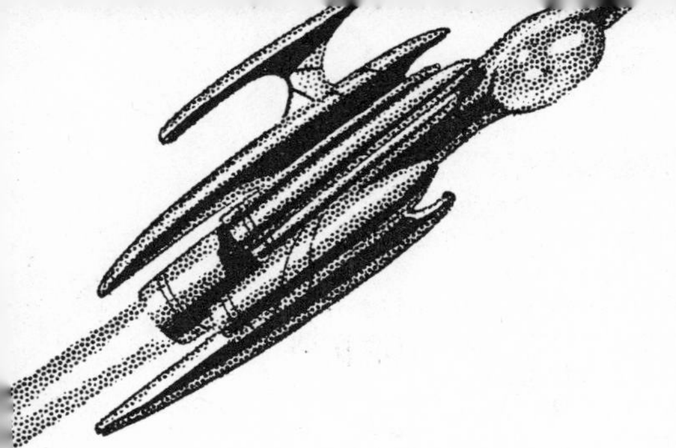

THE JARABON

by Lee Killough

art: George Barr

Mrs. Killough was born in Syracuse (in 1942), grew up in Atchison, and now lives in Manhattan—all in the state of Kansas. She gave up on horses after two broken legs and a concussion; between her work as a Radiologic Technologist at the Kansas State University's College of Veterinary Medicine and her writing *(Deadly Silents* and *Aventine,* both from Del Rey), she's more than busy.

The things I do for Sperrow, Kele thought with a sigh. She had considered wearing stars for the occasion, something appropriate for interstellar travel, but in the end, could not resist a web instead. Spangled with tiny syngems, the painted pattern radiated outward across her face from the sooty, lurking spiders of her eyes. *Come into my parlor, little fly,* she thought toward the man walking before her down the concourse of Chelsea Station to the berth of the Cunard galley *Marchlight.*

He blended well with the other passengers . . . boots just as high on his thighs, sleeves as sweeping, the fabric of his clothing as tasseled, fringed, and glittered, topped by an elaborate embroidered and jeweled yoke. Riffers—thieves—looking for a tag, though, would instantly recognize the cheap ostentation for what it was—from all of seven meters away Kele had no trouble appraising the "jewels" on the yoke as inexpensive synthetics—and pass him over in favor of the woman ahead of him, say, whose face gems and clothing reflected genuine wealth. The man walked to avoid attention, too . . . not boldly, yet not timidly enough to mark him as an easy victim. No one without Kele's special knowledge of him would suspect him of carrying anything of real value. Which made him an ideal courier for Sidakar Vermilion.

But not a perfect one, Kele hoped.

"He's carrying a package. I want you to secure it for me before he can turn it over to Vermilion on Northfire," Belas Sperrow had said when his call jerked Kele out of a sound sleep just a few hours before.

"Thanks for giving me so much time to plan," she had grumbled.

"I didn't know about the delivery until a short time ago." Sperrow was not a large or imposing man—small, in fact—but a lean whip of a man, a knife blade of a man, with eyes brilliant and hard as blue diamonds. From the screen of the phone, the eyes shot icy glints at her above a persuasive smile. "Kele, my little sparrow, you can do it. I keep telling you, you're the best thief in the Hundred Worlds."

As she followed Vermilion's courier, Kele reflected wryly that Sperrow seemed to enjoy finding increasingly more difficult assignments to make her prove it, though. She wondered why she accepted some of them, then answered herself. For the fun, partially. What other job offered the same challenge and excitement in performance, the same exultation in success? And she owed Sperrow. She owed him gratitude and loyalty and service. She owed Sperrow everything.

Eighteen years ago she had been one of the hundreds of nameless, homeless children living in the streets of Windward's ironically named Newhope City, stealing for a living and sleeping wherever she could. The sailcar had looked so enticing with its expensive gleam and the bar in the passenger compartment open so she could see its glass and silver accessories. Only, as she worked at matching the tone of her whistle to the lock frequencies of the door, a hand closed on her neck.

She had turned biting and clawing on her captor, but even her speed and desperation were no match for his strength, and he threw her, bruised, at the feet of his smaller companion . . . Sperrow.

"What were you doing?" Sperrow demanded.

She had looked up, her sooty eyes meeting the hard glitter of his. "Nothing," she replied sullenly.

The taller man jerked her to her feet. Her teeth cracked together as he shook her like a snakehound killing an angelmaker, then dropped her again.

"What were you doing?" Sperrow repeated.

This time she whispered in terror, "Whistling open the car."

The taller man laughed in derision. "What? Ridiculous! Bel, I'll call a badge."

But Sperrow had shaken his head and with eyes narrowed, squatted down in front of Kele. "You can really do that?"

She eyed him, uncertain what to make of his suddenly friendly tone.

"That's the best quadtone on the market, supposedly untamperable. If you can whistle it open," he said, "I'll *give* you everything you were going to steal."

Licking her lips at the thought of the car's contents, she had whistled open the lock.

"How old are you?" Sperrow asked.

"Ten."

He raised a brow. "I'd have thought six or seven. Do you have a home?"

She eyed him. What was this? "No. Are you going to give me what you promised?"

Sperrow had smiled thinly. "That and more, if you'll work for me."

He had made her his ward, had housed, fed, clothed, and educated her, sparing no expense. She moved in the most elite of circles, living and looking like the rich bitch playgirl Sperrow wanted people believing her to be. When all Sperrow asked in return was a little theft and espionage, how could she reasonably refuse him?

Kele never had and did not this time, either. Staring back at his image on the screen, she shrugged. "Well, there's nothing like the challenge of a riff on the fly. What's the package?"

"Do you know what a jarabon is?"

Kele knew. The Copians—the extinct, original inhabitants of Cornucopia—had carved gems into replicas of flowers so realistic they looked like petrified blossoms. Each diffracted light in such a way as to glow internally. Achingly beautiful, they were very old; very rare; and very, very valuable. Few existed outside of museums.

"So having learned that Vermilion is about to put his greedy paws on one, you've developed an uncontrollable desire to possess it instead?"

"Oh, no." Sperrow had smiled, a thin gesture with little amusement. "I want it in order to give it back."

She stared at him. "To give it *back?"* Industrial espionage she understood, but these other games Sperrow and his competitor peers played grew complex beyond all comprehension. She sighed. The things she did for him. "As you wish."

Easy enough to say, Kele reflected, watching her quarry approach the boarding hatch, but that had been before she realized she would not locate the courier until he reached Chelsea Station. Observing him up in the lounge area, she had not been able to guess where he might be carrying the jarabon. That meant she would have to search him and his luggage, and she knew only one place offering time enough for that . . . the flight to Northfire.

The time, but . . . was she physically capable of making use of the opportunity? Would the timewind let her? She hoped Sperrow appreciated what she was about to put herself through on his behalf. Taking a deep breath, she held out her embarkation pass to the boarding steward.

He examined and returned it with the smile of deference ship stewards gave someone of her apparent wealth. "Nidra Saar. Welcome aboard. You'll be in bunk 43-C."

This close to the courier, Kele needed cover. She found it by putting herself on the other side of a matron with painstakingly pampered skin and jeweled butterflies around her eyes. "I think it's unfair that we have to spend the entire voyage in dreamtime," she told the butterfly woman in a petulant tone. "Why should only pilots be able to see the stars in hyperlight?"

The butterflies around the matron's eyes fluttered. "But, my dear, it's the only way one *can* travel in hyperlight. Everyone knows that."

Dreaming was the only way most people could, anyway, an unfortunate fact which had been thrust upon humanity in the testing of Emile Gallipeau's new FTL drive. Two of the three crewmen on the Gallipeau-ship's first field trial came back with severe psychological disturbances that affected them the remainder of their lives, and subsequent tests had shown complete sedation to be the only effective preventative measure. It established the pattern for all future interstellar travel.

"I have a friend who once tried to ride the timewind," the butterfly woman said, "and though she took her dream dust just minutes after the ship went hyperlight, she nearly lost her mind. She had nightmares about it for years."

Kele bit her lip. This was just what she needed to hear.

She glanced around the hatch, corridors, and passenger cabin as she followed her companion in, searching for security devices. She did not like what she saw: no spy eyes anywhere but at the hatch, none in the corridors or cabin.

"How does the pilot monitor us?" she asked a steward in feigned anxiety.

"With telltales built into the bunks, miss," the steward replied. He gave her a reassuring smile. "Don't worry; he'll know immediately if you slip too deep or start to wake prematurely, and he'll correct you with the proper drugs. He's trained and licensed to administer dream dust and its antagonists."

Kele smiled back. Inside, she frowned uneasily. No viewscreen monitoring. Bad news. The absence of such security devices in a galley whose owning company had been shipping passengers and cargo between stars for five hundred years could only mean they felt no need for them. The first thief successfully riffing passengers inflight would have caused the installation of enough safeguards to prevent a re-occurrence. Was the so-called timewind, the effect produced in hyperlight by forward motion in space and treading in place in time, *that* debilitating to the normal human body and mind? Kele wished there were another way to take the jarabon.

She had no choice but to try for it here, though; there would be no other chance before the courier delivered his package to Vermilion. If it had been anyone but Sperrow asking her to do this, or if it had not offered such a challenge—stealing where no one had dared to before—she would have refused to do it.

Another steward greeted the butterfly woman and handed her a blue capsule and a small glass of wine. The butterfly woman promptly swallowed one with the aid of the other, then let herself be assisted up into her bunk.

The steward fastened the safety net over her and turned to Kele. "Some wine with your dreamdust, miss?"

Kele accepted the wine but waved the capsule away. "I don't intend to sleep this time."

The butterfly woman turned her head drowsily. "But you *must,* my dear. I told you what happened to my friend."

The steward, however, smiled. With the air of one who had dealt with the situation many times before, he said, "You won't enjoy being wide-eyed. Believe me, hyperlight is intolerable."

"Pilots don't find it so," she said stubbornly . . . and smiled to herself, enjoying her own performance.

"A pilot is a unique individual. Only one person in five hundred thousand is hyperlight Tolerant."

Around her, other passengers frowned, waiting with impatience for the steward's help. Kele tried not to look at Vermilion's courier. Most agents in her and the courier's position tried to avoid attracting attention. However, her web design hid the features of her face, even if he had been told about her by Vermilion, and an elaborate dark wig covered her natural moon-pale hair . . . and she hoped that the very act of calling attention to herself, in fact, would disarm him about her.

She tossed her head, hamming hauteur. "I'm a unique person, too . . . one in a *million,* I'm told." With satisfaction, she heard the impatient sighs around her and bit back a grin. She folded her arms. "You can't *make* me take the dream dust."

The steward's patient smile fixed in place. "Of course not, and I wouldn't dream of forcing you, miss, but . . . the ship isn't really designed for conscious passengers. Those four chairs at the front are all we have for a lounge and the only food provided is for the pilot."

"I'll fast. It's good for the spirit, anyway."

Behind her, a man whose face had been painted with seams and rivet heads to mimic metal plates snapped, "Take your capsule and stop delaying take-off."

"I have a suggestion," the steward said mildly. "Keep your capsule. Then if you change your mind, you can still sleep. The pilot can assist you into your bunk."

She heard *when* beneath *if*.

Kele conceded. "Very well." Her character should not be *too* unreasonable. Besides, if she could not tolerate the timewind, Kele very much wanted the option of dreamtime. She held out a hand for the capsule, then tucking it into a sleeve pocket, sat down in one of the deep chairs at the front.

She hoped no one else felt the urge to ride the timewind this trip.

Near her chair, a screen gave the illusion of looking out into space, past the station and down toward the misty blue-and-brown of Chelsea below. Staring at the image, Kele tried to remember everything she had heard about hyperlight and the timewind, particularly accounts by people who rode it successfully; but all she recalled were the nightmare stories of failure. No pilots ever seemed to publish articles about themselves; but then, pilots had little in common with ordinary people. They did not even communicate. Two she had seen in Chelsea Station shot unseeing by her, hyperkinetic, quicksilver, babbling to each other in rapid sentences that dominoed against each other and jumped subjects in midthought.

The stewards fastened the last of the safety nets—everyone else obediently took their dream dust—then with a glance at Kele and a shake of their heads, left the passenger cabin. Minutes later she felt a vibration through the ship as the outer hatch closed after them. The image of the station on the screen fell away in wheeling stars.

Kele gripped the arms of her chair nervously. Any minute now the galley would begin its dive into the gravity well of Chelsea's sun. Swinging around the sun with the momentum the dive gave them, they would shoot away slingshot style toward Northfire, and Gallipeau's drive would activate, boosting the galley into hyperlight. Then—then Kele would learn personally if the timewind had earned its killer reputation.

The bronze sun filled the screen, hurtling at her. She swallowed. She had been told that galleys came very close to the sun, but . . . *this* close? Sweat beaded her forehead and upper lip and trickled down from her underarms. She saw nothing but blinding light and boiling flame. Sunspots like immense dark cauldrons looked close enough to reach out and touch.

The play of bright and brighter light blurred by ever faster. Suddenly it disappeared, replaced by fire-spangled blackness. That changed, too, even as she watched, the stars stretching from points to ovals to a rainbow of streamers, blue ahead and red at the edge of the screen. Then the red streamers vanished, leaving the blue streaks dissolving into black nothingness . . . and, howling, the timewind struck.

Her mind called it by the scientific term, contra-chronic pressure, but she experienced it as a wind. It sounded like wind, a low roar in her ears, a symphony of the slowed sounds of her heart and lungs and the ship around her; and it felt like wind, pushing, buffeting her, pressing her hard into the chair so that movement came as though through cold-thickened syrup. Worse, it battered at her mind, too, pushing back her very thoughts. Thinking became like pulling against heavy gravity, or pushing a great burden uphill on a frictionless surface. Her mind strained, fighting, but formed a thought only with agonizing slowness. On some deep, subconscious level, where she did not have to think, Kele counted time—seconds, minutes, hours—and sensed with horrified astonishment the span needed to frame an idea in the face of the timewind.

Two days of this? she thought with dismay.

Perceived by the ship and the rest of the galaxy, it would be just two days—two days longer than she cared to spend like this—and in that time, she might manage to drag herself through two days of motion and possibly think a day's worth of thoughts, but somewhere deep in her, a clock would count the actual time spent treading in place against the timewind, every endless moment of the months and years.

She fought to keep from reaching for the blue capsule. How could she withstand this even long enough to search the courier? Her mind felt as though it were being shredded. Could she manage to work at all? How did pilots tolerate this hell? There must be some trick to it. Granted that some people thought and reacted faster than others, but she had always considered herself to be among those faster individuals, and here she sat virtually helpless.

Kele locked her hands on the arms of her chair and, with her deep clock counting the hours, forced herself into a standing position. However the pilots did it, she could not. She would have to do the best she could this way. She did not try to think that thought; she simply understood it.

She had noted the location of the bunk where the courier slept. Fighting the pressure against body and mind, she dragged herself down the row of bunks toward him. The timewind howled and boomed in her ears, reverberating through teeth and bones in maddening bass frequencies. The wine in her stomach churned threateningly.

Fumbling at the catches of the safety net, Kele discovered with dismay that opening them required three steps which must be thought through before executing them in the proper sequence. Even struggling to think and act when the mental phrases felt as though they were unraveling faster than she formulated them, her spirits rose. A catch of this complexity must mean that at least one successful or near-successful riffer had preceded her.

The catches yielded after intense concentration, and with time ticking off—*hurry, Kele, hurry; you're taking weeks*—she drove her sluggish body into an exhaustive search of the sleeping man. Normally, her blood would have been racing with heady excitement, lifting her to a peak of mental performance, tuning her body into an instrument of lightning-fast precision. This time, however, her blood eddied turgidly. She could hardly move, let alone think.

Painfully, she joined one thought to another. It was like building a feather mosaic in a gale. If she were the courier, she would have hidden the jarabon with care, not taking chances with losing it even during the supposed security of the flight. But trying to guess what he might consider a good hiding place exhausted her. She worked through his clothing, rolling him onto his side to check the material down his back. His pockets held a variety of objects, but none of them the jarabon or any container which might conceivably hide the jewel.

Faster, Kele.

Why had she let Sperrow talk her into this? She ought to give it up, quit. Right now she wanted to quit the whole business and find another job. But even as the thought fought to form, she let it dissolve. She had grown accustomed to her lifestyle. She feared losing it, or perhaps it was that she feared that giving it up would return her to the desperate street life which still haunted her dreams. And she owed what she had to Sperrow.

She tried to think: was the jarabon small enough to be swallowed? She hoped he had not chosen that most secure cache of all; slitting him open to check was not her style.

The cabin door hissed, sliding open.

Kele could not have moved faster if she had teleported. She slammed the safety net closed and leaped away from the bunk. By the time the door finished opening, she stood with heart galloping, clinging to the rail of a bunk two sections beyond the stack where the courier slept.

Astonished, she began asking herself how in the Hundred Worlds she had managed—

But the thought dissolved unfinished as she blinked at the galactic display sweeping into the cabin. A naked man wore it—the pilot, surely—a brilliant display of gold, silver, and syngems, glittering in nebulas and constellations and clusters . . . the universe painted and glued to skin the color of burnished copper. He moved on feet shod in whisper-soft deck slippers.

"Raven Windust, pilot." He spoke abruptly, but smiled. "Tuck you in?"

Suns, she wished she could let him. Kele felt exhausted enough to sleep for two days without any help at all from drugs. But she lifted her chin as the spoiled, stubborn Nidra Saar *persona,* unwilling to admit a poor choice, would do. "No. I'm enjoying myself watching the stars and listening to the timewind."

She caught her breath in a self-conscious laugh. The drag of the timewind had lowered her voice to a deep, husky drawl that drew the words out interminably.

If he found the voice a ludicrous contrast to her petite stature, Windust did not show it. The pilot came across the cabin to take her arm. "Come."

She hung back. "Come where?"

"Control room. A better view of the stars there."

"Oh, I'm fine here." *Go away, pilot. I've no time to socialize!*

"More comfortable, too, and food; I'll share mine."

"I'm not hungry."

His eyes widened. "You don't want to come? I don't usually ask wide-eyes forward."

A woman like Nidra would be flattered at the invitation. Kele went with him, wondering how to leave. Perhaps if she annoyed him, he would banish her back to the passenger cabin.

She launched into a hopefully boring monologue, gushing on the "romance" of riding the timewind, on the display presented by the stars turned to blue streamers— ". . . like the fireworks at the Winterfest on Frost, don't you think?" —and on the growl of the timewind— "With imagination, you can turn the undertones into music. It's so exotic. I can hardly wait to reach Northfire and tell my friends all about it."

Curiously, she felt that she could be speaking at almost normal speed if she wanted, but she let her voice continue dragging. She read impatience in the angles of Windust's head and shoulders, but

instead of asking her to return to the cabin, he merely stopped listening to her. Once in the control room with its screens and instruments, and doorway connecting it to the pilot's quarters, he busied himself checking the controls.

Kele fell silent. She lowered herself into the enveloping softness of a chair in his quarters and through the open door watched the glittering stars on his buttocks. Presently, she called to him, "Do you *really* like this?"

He looked around. "I love it; it's life; docking's dying and port's just waiting."

"But how can you—"

But he had turned away again. She continued the thought silently while her inner clock measured the real-time hours necessary to think it: how could he love the ceaseless pressure and sound? Of course, he managed to move and apparently think with normality despite it. If only she could, too. Then maybe she could finish what she needed to do before the *Marchlight* docked at Northfire Station.

She had moved normally, too, but only for a moment, when he nearly caught her in the cabin. She could have talked at normal speed, as well. What made the difference?

Mind, she decided after reflection. She had not thought while talking, just run on, and her actions in the cabin had come as reflex reaction. Thinking appeared to be the bottleneck. Disengage the mind, and the animal body proceeded at due speed. Now, she thought sardonically, if she could only avoid thinking.

A moment later she pressed her fingers to her temples, swearing silently at Sidakar Vermilion, Emile Gallipeau, the courier, and even Belas Sperrow. She had to find a way back to the cabin . . . had to find the jarabon before she went mad. Lord, how she wanted that capsule in her sleeve pocket. Soon, she promised her aching body and mind; she would take it as soon as she had the jarabon.

Windust came into his quarters and rummaged through a cabinet and refrigerator. He eyed her with what Kele read as a puzzled expression. "Something to eat?"

She swallowed. "No, thank you." Her stomach was rebelling enough at the wine she had drunk. The thought of spending subconsciously perceived hours or days throwing up food only added to her nausea. "I couldn't."

He smiled in sympathy. "I understand. Sleep, then?"

She straightened. "I told you, this is the most exciting experience of my life. I don't want to miss a minute of it."

"Seeing the stars in hyperlight?"

"Yes."

"Listening to the timewind?"

Some note in his voice sent a ripple of wariness through her. What was he doing? "That, too."

His eyes fixed steadily on her. "Disturbing the passenger in 38-D?"

Every cell of her went still, watching him . . . waiting. She felt like the small wild creature she had once seen at night on the lawns of Sperrow's country estate, frozen in the light of her hand lamp. Had its heart slammed against its ribs as hers did now?

His constellations shot off icy glints of light. "Telltales told me he was moving without vital signs going up to indicate consciousness, meaning someone moving him . . . you: why?"

In over ten years of industrial espionage for Sperrow she had never been caught before. She *would* have to be caught now . . . now when any attempt to plan what to say blew away in the hellish hurricane of the timewind.

Then, looking up at Windust, she saw his expression . . . not grim, not accusatory. Rather, he regarded her with that previous puzzlement. He did not suspect her of theft, she realized in a flash of understanding; he expected, or perhaps even hoped, for some reasonable explanation. Her outward appearance still protected her!

She gave up trying to think and let her reflexes take over. "I was trying to recover something he stole from my father."

He raised a brow but said nothing.

Did he believe her? "We've had a Cornucopian jarabon in our family for generations. Last night my father gave me permission to wear it out. I met a man and went home with him. When I woke up, he and the jarabon had vanished. I found out, though, that he works for a man named Sidakar Vermilion, who is one of my father's business rivals. I think he stole the jarabon at Vermilion's request and is taking it to him. I have to get it back before my father finds out what happened."

As she talked, she watched Windust. The expression on his face told her he believed her; but instead of feeling satisfaction, she regretted the necessity of the lie . . . and wondered at her reaction.

"Why not report it?" Windust asked.

"Report it? You mean to law enforcement people?" She did not have to pretend surprise; it colored her voice naturally. "We don't report such incidents. It isn't really a theft; men like Vermilion and my father play games with each other. Vermilion probably intends to give the jarabon back."

Windust stared at her. "Then why worry about it?"

"Because—" She sighed. What was it about him that made her want to be truthful and make him understand? "In the game, if Vermilion takes possession of the jarabon, even if he returns it my father loses face." He seemed familiar somehow, she decided, struggling with the thought, as though they had known each other for years. How strange. "I can't let him lose face, can I? Not my father."

Windust's constellations shimmered as he shook his head in bewilderment. "He doesn't have to; Security on Northfire Station can search and recover the jarabon before it reaches this Vermilion."

"But that's an *official* agency," Kele protested. "That's cheating." Very true, but even if not, she dared not put herself in official hands. Any inquiries into her background would almost certainly prove embarrassing, if not dangerous to her liberty. "If I recover the jarabon myself, *Vermilion* loses face. Please, come with me to the cabin and watch me search the man. You can make certain I take only the jarabon."

But now Windust eyed her doubtfully. "I've only your word it's yours; Security'll investigate."

Cold trailed down her spine. "Is this a kind of arrest, then?"

He shrugged in a splintering play of light off painted stars. "You can be a guest here the rest of the run or I can shoot you with dream dust."

She bit her lip in chagrin. After all the successful operations she had run for Sperrow, avoiding traps laid by professionals, here she fell prey to a naked pilot. Compounding her humiliation was his willingness to leave her conscious and loose despite his suspicions of her, reflecting his judgment of how helpless the timewind had rendered her. That bastard timewind!

Rubbing her temples, she touched the syngems on her face and remembered the design painted there. Her hands came down again, hope rising. *Patience, Kele. Play the spider. Surrender and wait for a chance at the courier.*

She looked up at Windust. "Consider me your guest."

Windust returned to the control room. To distract herself from the relentless march of the chronometer and the thought of being given to Security, she pushed up out of the chair and leaned against the doorway watching the pilot work. After a bit, that became a pleasant entertainment worthy of being enjoyed for its own sake. He had the sturdy muscular development of a gymnast, a result of constantly riding the timewind? and moved with the gliding grace of a dancer that set his painted and glued starfields glittering. The familiarity of him struck her more strongly than ever.

"Why are you a pilot?" she asked. "Isn't it lonely?"

"Solitary," he replied. A black nebula glinted across one rippling shoulder. "A significant difference. I like solitude."

That was why he seemed familiar; he reminded her of Sperrow, and of herself. All of them liked solitude, and Windust carried the same aura of self-containment Sperrow did and which she felt around herself, as though they lived in closed systems needing virtually nothing from the outside.

"That's what you enjoy about hyperlight?"

He turned in spattering rainbows of light. "The timewind sings all songs for those who listen . . . supports . . . insulates. Without it there's just void and endless falling."

She pictured the two pilots she had seen in Chelsea Station, moving and talking like quicksilver. Another image followed, her in their place, feeling the absence of the accustomed pressure, not a relief but a vacuum through which body and thoughts hurtled headlong, uncontrolled. She shivered. "Is that why you call docking a death?"

Stars twinkled. He stared at her in surprise. "You understand?"

She felt surprise in herself, too, but not at her understanding. Belatedly, she realized that the last thoughts had come quickly, as thoughts should, without effort. She reached back for them, trying to determine how they had been different from previous thoughts. Images . . . that was it; they had been pictures and not words. Was that Windust's trick?

Excitedly, she asked, "Do you think in pictures instead of words?"

A glow flared in his eyes. He nodded. "Yes. Images and concepts. Faster than words. You *do* understand." He paused. "Do *you* think images or words?"

She heard excitement in his voice and wondered at it. Why him? "Both, but words, mostly."

The glow in his eyes flared to incandescent brilliance. "Forget words; concentrate on only pictures."

She blinked at him. "What?"

Light shattered from him as he whirled across the control room to take both her hands. "Images," he said in an intense voice. "Make your mind a vid screen and see the action but just *feel* the sound. Train yourself."

The timewind tore at her mind, shredding the thoughts as she tried to comprehend what he wanted from her. "Why—"

He interrupted. "One in half a million is Tolerant; fewer can withstand the solitude. There's never enough pilots. We need."

Her breath caught as she understood his emotion. He saw her as someone like himself, as new kin. He wanted to recruit her. Excitement rose in her. In a dazzling vision, she saw herself at the helm of a galley, stars streaming from blue to nothingness around her, the timewind singing. "Do you really think I could be a pilot?"

"Let's see; think pictures."

Between instrument checks he worked with her. The trick of thinking images and concepts came hard at first, but once she began, it grew easier. Like a stream cutting a bed, her mind flowed into the path of least resistance, into the fastest, least painful method of thinking.

Windust grinned in approval. "A Tolerant, and functional. Congratulations."

Grabbing her hands, he pulled her into his arms and danced her around the control room. Kele followed in triumph. With the function time of her mind reduced, she could move as quickly as she desired. The buffeting weight of the timewind vanished. Moving to the rhythm of the timewind, they danced across it as lightly as thistledown on a summer breeze. Images played in Kele's mind, shivering a little in the gale tearing at them, but each holding undissolved until replaced by the next. She soared on a delirious wave of exultation.

"This isn't hard at all," she said in delight. "Why can't everyone do it?"

Windust shrugged. "Don't know; maybe a combination of reasons, beginning with not being willing to stay wide-eyed long enough to learn. But you've learned." And he kissed her.

Kele became suddenly aware of the warmth of his bare skin beneath her hands and through the fabric of her dress. She hesitated only a moment before kissing him back. After all, she reflected, neither of them were *completely* self-contained. They needed to reach out of their preferred solitude once in a while.

She discovered an interesting aspect to making love in hyperlight. Counting time on a subconscious level, the peaks of emotion and sensation lasted for days at a time.

Afterward, Windust dozed but Kele could not. Her mind raced, building images: Kele Sperrow at the helm of a galley feeling as much excitement and satisfaction as a riff had ever brought her . . . Kele, once nameless, once homeless, a gutter brat from Windward but now joining the company of a rare, priceless few . . . human jarabons.

But there the images froze and dissolved. Jarabon. She sighed and rolled away from Windust's warmth. How foolish she was, letting herself be carried away by the pilot's vision of what she was. Maybe she had the ability to be a pilot, but she was not free to do as she wanted; she owed too much to Sperrow. And Sperrow wanted her to bring him the jarabon.

She dressed quietly and with guilt gnawing at her—Windust slept so trustingly, apparently having forgotten his suspicions of her in his delight at discovering a new Tolerant—slipped out of the control room, back to the passenger cabin. The safety net unfastened without difficulty now. The timewind interfered no more than a gentle breeze. Her body still did not operate as smoothly and quickly as it had on other riffs, however. She felt no excitement as she returned to searching the courier. The fun had gone, she realized. Only a sense of obligation remained.

With a picture of the telltale section of the control panels warning-clear in her mind, she moved him just minutely, not enough to register as suspicious on the pressure telltales.

She kept an ear tuned for the opening hiss of the door, too, praying Windust remained asleep. Not only did she not want him catching her, she did not want to be caught by *him*. She felt too much akin to him. She saw in him what, under other circumstances, she might have become. He might even have been a friend.

Anger stirred in her, resentment of her debt. She had felt it occasionally before, but never so strongly. It plagued her while she flipped pictures through her mind, trying to imagine where she would hide the jarabon. Then her gaze fell on the yoke. What if he were hiding the jewel in plain sight? What if one of those syngems were a shell with the jarabon tucked inside it?

She reached for the yoke.

The courier's eyes opened.

Kele froze with a hand on the yoke. The two of them stared into each other's eyes for hours of eternity, then abruptly, like snakes, the courier's hands shot toward her throat.

Kele leaped backward. How could he move so fast? Was he Tolerant, too? Then she realized that he was doing as she had when Windust walked in on her, reacting purely on instinct. He saw a threat to the jarabon and reacted in defense.

She jumped, but not far enough, not soon enough. His reach was long and he rolled, coming after her. His fingers closed around her throat. He fell out of the bunk, taking her to the deck with him.

As her lungs struggled for air and her vision blurred, Kele cursed herself as a fool. She had broken an important rule; she had relaxed and become overconfident. She knew people woke in mid-flight; the steward told her so on boarding. It stood to reason that the courier, anxious about what he carried, might be one of the few, but she had overlooked that possibility. Now not only would Sperrow lose the jarabon but the services of the best thief in the Hundred Worlds.

She fought panic. She could not allow herself that; it would kill her before strangulation did. Pinned under the courier with his fingers biting ever deeper into her neck, crushing her windpipe, and with her consciousness dimming, she twisted, clawing, struggling for defense room.

To combat the panic, she created anger, fury aimed at the courier. She would not let him kill her! Damn him! Damn Sperrow, too, for getting her into this! Reason told her he could not have known this would happen, but she did not feel like being reasonable; she dared not; she needed her anger. Kele grabbed at the emotion and built on it. Sperrow had sent her into this game with a glib smile. Did he care what happened to her? Would he mind if he lost her? Probably not; he could always hire another thief.

Suddenly, with consciousness slipping away from her, she saw that that was true. Playing pieces did not matter, only the game. And with that realization came *real* anger, berserker fury. She owed him; she owed him a great deal, but maybe not *everything* . . . not, by God, her *life!*

She freed one arm. Her finger plunged like a dagger into the courier's eye. As he reared back, screaming, his hold loosened. She scrabbled out from under him. Air rushed into her lungs. Gasping and coughing, Kele staggered to her feet and kicked him hard under the chin.

The door hissed open. Fields of stars in a copper sky swarmed into the cabin. Windust held a pressure capsule tipped with a needle. "Telltale alarm went off warning me a passenger was coming up."

Kele coughed. She rubbed her throat. In a hoarse voice she said, "I put him down again." She drew a deep breath. The air burned all the way down her throat but reached her lungs unobstructed. She took another breath, just to reaccustom herself to the pleasure of it, then leaned against the rail of a bunk, her knees trembling.

Windust stared narrow-eyed from her throat to the courier stretched out on the deck. Icy glints reflected from his starfields. "A game, you say?"

The timewind roared in her ears. "Yes, a game." She swallowed tentatively. It hurt. "But you can still die of it."

"You wrote that into the rules?"

The disgust in his voice stung. Looking up, she said quickly, defensively, "It was never *my* game. I'd like to quit."

He raised a brow. "Why don't you?"

She sighed. "Because—" Because why? She remembered her thought that she did not owe Sperrow her life. Now, massaging her neck, it occurred to her that these bruises ought to entitle her to some compensation. Could they write off part of her debt, maybe even all of it, as close as she had come to death? What if she told Sperrow that? What would happen to her then? She bit her lip, thinking of Windward's despairing streets. "Do you still think I can be accepted as a pilot candidate?" she asked.

He eyed her. "We need pilots. Training'll tell what you're made of. Besides, if anything disappears in-flight there's only one suspect." He paused. "You'd have to tell them your real name, though."

The heat and cold of guilt washed through her. So he had suspected far more than she realized. And he had still not shot her with dream dust after realizing she was a Tolerant? "Pilots are *that* important?"

"That rare," he replied.

She took a deep breath and through the pain of it, tasted freedom.

"The name is Kele Sperrow. Would you help me apply when we reach Northfire?"

He nodded, smiling as one kinsman to another. "Tolerants stick together because we've no one else. We'll all help you."

She hugged him. So she would gain a kind of family as well as a new job. That was not bad for a former gutter brat and thief, even one who had been the best in the Hundred Worlds.

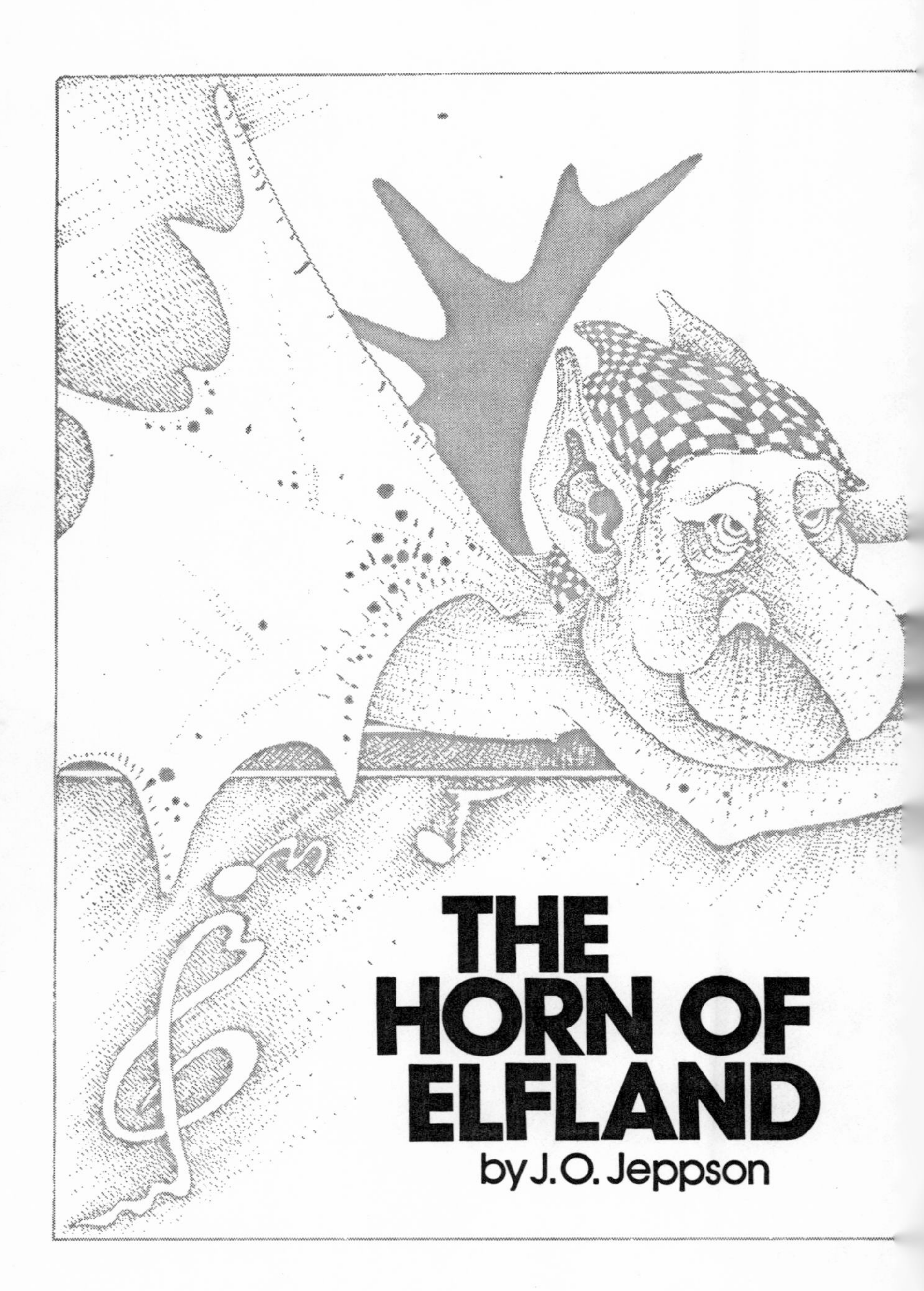

THE HORN OF ELFLAND

by J. O. Jeppson

art: Roland Wolff

Dr. Jeppson, a psychiatrist and psychoanalyst, says she has a "zen yen for the New York Philharmonic." Here she presents us with one of her tales from the casebooks of Pshrinks Anonymous.

One of the Interpersonal members of the Psychoanalytic Alliance put a plastic container on the lunch table and said, "I have brought blueberries for dessert, to celebrate the Horn of Elfland faintly blowing."

Startled, the other members of Pshrinks Anonymous stopped trying to dissect Stressed Squab without spilling Primal Peas off their plates. "How did you get blueberries in mid-winter?" asked a Pshrink.

"Don't you mean *horns* of elfland?" asked a literary Pshrink.

"No, she doesn't," said the Oldest Member, "and wherever you got those berries, m'dear, they will go well with these cookies I brought to thank you for giving me your Philharmonic ticket in the emergency."

"Chocolate-chocolate chip!" said the Interpersonal. "Food being the music of love . . ."

"I disapprove of all these misquotations," said the literary Pshrink, "as well as the references to food."

"Silence!" said the Oldest Member. "I intend to tell a story about music."

"Perhaps it will be a story with Zen implications," said the Interpersonal.

"Don't be ridiculous," said the Oldest Member, staring at her with heavy suspicion.

She seemed to be meditating on a cookie. "When I'm eating, I eat. When I'm listening to music . . ."

"That will do," said the Oldest Member.

Last week [he said] I received a call from my internist, who is not only one of my oldest colleagues but someone upon whom I depend heavily since—you will be astonished to learn this—I find it incredibly difficult to acquire a reliable authority figure at my age, much less another M.D. who isn't a complete ass. My internist doesn't quite measure up, but he's the best I know, so I'm always willing to help him out when I can. His problem was his ne'er-do-well grandson, now about thirty, who seemed to be in urgent need of psychiatric attention.

I reminded my internist that his grandson was obviously not suitable for classical Freudian analysis, my specialty, but that I would consent to doing a few emergency consultations.

When I saw the patient, last Thursday morning, he proved to be a short, energetic chap with a sparse brown beard and a wild look in his eyes.

"Hullo," he said, sitting down on my couch. "I suppose grandpops has told you his diagnosis—that I'm crazy and that I've wasted my life trying to find myself. I suppose I have. I've tried finding myself in graduate schools, business, hard labor, and what grandpops calls idleness, but mostly I live on money left in trust for me by my other grandfather, and I pursue my three main interests—music, gourmet food, and Tolkien, not necessarily in that order."

Since I wasn't doing analysis, I questioned him, to speed things up. El, as I will call him, could play guitar and piano well enough to earn money with them, but had never tried. He was such a good cook that his one experiment with marriage had ended when his wife (a busy lawyer) complained that he was more interested in heating up the oven than her.

His obsession with Tolkien took the form of a preoccupation with *The Lord of the Rings* that was getting so out of hand it hadcertainly passed beyond the bounds of respectable neurosis.

El believed—believes—that Elves exist.

"Grandpops thinks it's insane," said El, waving his naked toes back and forth from his perch on my couch. Although it is winter, he was in sandals. Perhaps he expected fur to sprout from his feet.

"It's true," continued El, "that I may have been a trifle overenthusiastic when I changed my name to Elrond—say, do you know what I'm talking about? Do you realize that I'm referring not to little pixie-like creatures in silly stories, but to *Elves*, those tall, majestic, more-than-human creatures of Tolkien's masterpiece?"

"And you believe you are one of them?"

"Hell, no. I just believe there's a real place, inhabited by Elves, which can be entered by transcending the boundaries of this dimension. Tolkien unconsciously divined the truth, that there's another universe, in another dimension, where Elves live, making potent music and eating beautiful food. I'll go there with the ring."

He paused and chuckled as if he knew he'd titillated me.

"Ring?"

"Tolkien was wrong, you know. It's not the sort of ring he described. It's a ring of music. True power comes from completing the sequence of proper vibrations, closing that ring and pushing us into the other dimension. I'm a little worried, however, about what it will do to Avery Fisher Hall."

I raised my eyebrows inquiringly. They always have notable effect.

"An earthquake will swallow up the building," he said, "but I'm going to the concerts anyhow. All of them—Thursday, Saturday, Tuesday nights and Friday afternoon. Something is bound to happen, because they're playing Pinkton's Seminal Seriatum."

"Whose what?"

"Serial music!"

"Cereal as in breakfast?" I asked. For some odd reason, food was on my mind.

"Serial music as in mathematical series, the major themes fitting a chosen form using a carefully constructed pattern of the twelve pitch classes of the equal tempered scale, intervals arranged in rows creating harmonic succession or hinting at harmonic possibilities that may or may not be fulfilled. The seriality of the piece may include timbre, rhythm, pitch—and Pinkton's will overdo the resonance properties of Fisher Hall."

"Oh?"

"The arrangements of lights over the stage, in particular, will no doubt respond when the serial music builds up resonance, in the metal lamps, shaped like more rounded oriental brass bells. Each row of lights has a different arrangement of balanced numbers—five-seven-seven-five in the first row at the edge of the stage ceiling, four-twelve-four in the next row, three-six-three in the next, and twenty-four straight across in the last row. Similarly balanced but totally different grouped numbers of lights are in rows over the audience, but it's the hot ones over the stage that will react."

I was skeptical, to say the least. Perhaps my expression—although ordinarily I am the most poker-faced of Freudians—revealed my opinion, because El scowled and suddenly slapped his hands on his thighs.

"You might *try* to believe me! I know what I'm talking about! When I first saw Avery Fisher Hall after it was rebuilt inside a few years ago, I was fascinated by the possibilities. That's when I started attending as many concerts as I could. I decided at first that the repetitive *dah-dah-dah-DAH* in Beethoven's Fifth would produce interesting effects, or perhaps something Baroque and contrapuntal would, but no. I turned to more modern stuff, but only when the most serial of serial music was performed did I begin to be certain that eventually there would be the ideal composition to make Fisher Hall enter another dimension."

"And you expect to find superhuman beings? Perhaps your problems with your father—an unresolved Oedipus complex—and with subsequent male authorities . . ."

"Bosh," said El. Actually, that was not exactly what he said, but at lunchtime I will bowdlerize his speech a trifle.

"Have you met this Pinkton?" I asked, feeling that El was still in search of a father figure more suitable than his own father or, heaven forfend, his grandfather.

"Pinkton's a young punk of twenty-five who lives in Boston and has nothing to do with this except that he wrote it. He may be a modern musical genius, but I'm sure he has no idea what his mathematical build-up of sound will do to the world."

"What do you mean, build-up?"

"That's the whole point. The particular composition to be played tonight builds up tonality and amplitude, with increasing dissonance, until the sound becomes unbearable for most people—and just at that moment it softens, and a door at the side of the stage opens. In the darkness beyond there is an extra French horn player hired for the purpose. We won't be able to see him, but suddenly we'll hear what seems to be an incredibly sweet note, like the faraway sound of an Elven horn."

I don't know what made me do it. Most unanalytic. I found myself muttering, out loud, "Blow, bugle, blow . . ."

"That's right," said El, obviously pleased. "Tennyson described it perfectly. Wild echoes flying out into the auditorium, sweet and clear, as if from afar. Not a real bugle, not even a trumpet, because only the French horn of all the brasses can sound that sweet, that sad, that mellow—the whole irony of Pinkton's masterpiece."

"I don't understand."

"You wouldn't, unless you go to the concert. Remember, now, the audience has been barraged with the build-up of unpleasant serial music, then reprieved, and then seduced by the off-stage horn into thinking they'll be soothed and relaxed. What happens then is sheer genius. The horn immediately peaks upward into incredible dissonance."

"I don't understand how one horn can create . . ."

"Remember that the rest of the orchestra, onstage, is still playing dissonantly but softly enough so that the audience believes that everything's going to be harmonic and beautiful eventually. The horn offstage adds its sound as if to sweeten while joining the orchestra, but all at once it interrupts the mathematically precise configuration with another kind of dissonant note that sets teeth on edge, forcing the seriality of the music into fever. The orchestra goes wild and the whole thing ends in a blast."

"Sounds awful."

"I love it. I've heard it in Boston and Philadelphia, but none of those places has the right kind of hall. Fisher has a mysterious seriality built into the metal light fixtures."

"I still don't understand. What does that one French horn do that could possibly cause an earthquake?"

"Before it, there's an incredible build-up of tension, in people as well as in metal, and I believe the tension increases precisely because people are then deluded into expecting relief. When the horn's unexpectedly cruel dissonance occurs, that will complete the ring of powerful sound waves and electromagnetic waves and possibly psi waves, and that dissonance will push us into Middle Earth or whatever the place is called in the other dimension. Possibly only with a minor earthquake."

"That will happen tonight?"

"Anytime the Seminal Seriatum is played in Fisher Hall. I'm convinced that the first sign will be some electrical phenomenon, possibly a light exploding, just before the earthquake."

I was having trouble controlling my sarcasm. "I suppose you've calculated whether or not it matters if the lights in the ceiling are on or off?"

"Of course. During the concert, only certain dimmed lights are left on over the audience, but those over the musicians are bright and hot. All the lights are lit in a balanced pattern, so that if one light goes, the pattern will be upset, starting to unravel our ties to this dimension. . . ."

He went on like this for some time, discoursing as well on Tolkien's brilliance in tuning himself to the universe of Middle Earth, although—said El—Tolkien had been led astray by his preoccupation with language when he should have been concentrating on the music of the Elves, a music that may be drawing us to the other dimension just as we are pushed by the dissonance in this.

I could get nowhere with any sort of regular psychiatric interview, but El did promise to return the next morning, Friday.

When he showed up, late, his depression and anxiety would have been obvious even to a non-Freudian.

"I've been too upset to eat," he said. "Perhaps I should have counted the studs."

"The *what?*"

"The studs in the stage walls and ceiling—eight in the side panels, I think six in each ceiling one. Yet perhaps they don't matter. If I start trying to include the vibration tendencies of that metal, I suppose I should include the steel beams in the building proper and the metal in the chair seats, too."

"Are you trying to tell me that nothing happened?"

"And I forgot about metal in eyeglasses, jewelry, dental fillings, watches—my God, watches, ticking away, disrupting the seriality of the piece subliminally! And what about battery watches like my Accutron, adding a ghost of a hum. And piano wires! Oh hell, I forgot about the metal in the stage machinery to raise and lower the piano! And kettledrums are the worst . . . What am I saying? This is crazy!"

I was glad he thought something was. I had begun to worry about an out-of-control manic excitement, an obvious diagnosis even if he had not begun to neglect his food intake, which makes it worse. I remembered that my wife had put a bag of cookies in my briefcase when I left home that morning, but to give a patient food! It is almost unthinkable for a Pshrink of my persuasion. Perhaps it would be unnecessary now that he was beginning to show a slight degree of insight into his own pathology.

"That's right!" he shouted. "I'm crazy to consider all the other kinds of metal, even the kettledrums. After all, tympani are tuned to different pitches, while those lights are in mathematical sequence like the music, each light identical to the others, the lighted ones warm and the unlighted ones cold."

"Since nothing happened last night, why do you persist in believing that something will?" I asked, rummaging in my briefcase.

"I wasn't quite accurate. What I wanted—I mean, what I expected to happen didn't. There was no earthquake. We didn't get to the other dimension, but at the height of the serial music, when the offstage horn came in with that incredibly dissonant addition to the rest of the blast, I'd swear that the wires for those three suspended microphones began to vibrate. All we need is for that inexperienced guest conductor to play the thing *right* next time. You'll see. The world will see!" El laughed maniacally.

"Have a cookie," I said.

He grabbed it. "Thanks. I seem to be hungry after all. It's so depressing. Last night I didn't sleep, because I kept thinking that I was wrong."

"About the whole idea of Elfland?"

"Oh, no. That exists—somewhere. What I may be wrong about is the Pinkton. Maybe it won't send us to where I can hear Elvish music and eat Elvish food."

He finished the cookie. "The right kind of food is important to adjust our physiology to higher planes of existence, and music will keep it there. Maybe by mistake Pinkton's music, if played *right,* is exactly the wrong music. I'm afraid—all those people sitting in Avery Fisher Hall with non-Elvish food in them and listening to music that perhaps isn't Elvish—I'm afraid! So afraid!"

"Afraid of what?"

"Being sent to Mordor, of course! All in Avery Fisher Hall . . ."

"Have another cookie," I said.

"They're good cookies, but I can make them better," he said. "Did you know that I'm a good gourmet cook? I've been trying new combinations of spices and other ingredients, creating food fit for Elves, but my conservative family disapproves."

"What about Mordor?"

His face creased as if he were going to cry. "During the music last night, watching the microphone wires sway, I thought all at once about what New York is like, about what the world is like, and now I fear we won't transcend the limitations of this universe and enter another, better one. Perhaps Tolkien combined the two possible other dimensions, better known in primitive thought as heaven and hell, and Mordor is hell. Perhaps we'll go there when the music succeeds."

"But . . ."

"Gee, grandpops says you're a Freudian. I thought you guys aren't supposed to keep making interrupting noises."

I said nothing. I did not tell him that I may have caught the disease from certain colleagues in the other camp. [The O.M. cocked one eyebrow at the Interpersonal.]

"Maybe," El continued, in a sadder tone, "that's why so many people walked out during the Pinkton, the last thing played. I know that Philharmonic audiences have a tendency to dribble out early to catch trains to whatever posh suburbs they came from, but this was almost a stampede. It's possible that's why the Pinkton didn't work."

"Couldn't it be that serial music is not to everyone's taste?"

"Most of it is harmonious and dull," said El, "but this Pinkton is an exception. Yet, if it does work, and . . . and . . . then Mordor! I don't think I could stand that. Yet it's so logical. Perhaps the opening to Mordor is created here in this dimension by the intricacies of carefully structured dissonance."

"That's the way it sounds," I said drily.

"You've heard Pinkton!"

"Ah, no, but . . ."

"Then you've got to go to one of the concerts. Go tomorrow. Get a ticket from somebody or try at the box office. Usually subscription holders who can't use their tickets call up so the box office can resell their seats. Please go. My grandfather is so angry with me. I've always been such a failure. I'd like one of his friends to be there when I prove myself." With that, he ran out of my office.

I decided that I had better go to the concert as a favor to my internist. You [he nodded politely to the Interpersonal] were kind enough to give me your subscription ticket to the Friday matinee concert, and I went.

Unfortunately I was sitting in the third tier, as far up as you can get, controlling my slight tendency to agoraphobia, when the concert finally ended with markedly subdued clapping for the horrendous Pinkton thing. Perhaps the audience, what was left of it after the predictable exodus, was too shell-shocked to hiss.

Suddenly I saw El weaving his way through the exiting crowd, and before I realized what was happening, he was up on the stage just as the conductor was taking his first bow after the Pinkton.

"Play it again!" shouted El. Then he turned crimson and ran over to the conductor to whisper in his ear. Some in the audience tittered, but they did not stop their determined march out to the lobby. Talking earnestly, El wouldn't let go of the conductor's arm.

The concertmaster stepped up to the conductor's box and helped the conductor march El out to the wings. After a minute, while the applause died away completely, they came back without him. Another smattering of applause, clearly for politeness, was all the audience would give, and that was the end of the concert.

By the time I got down to the stage level—the elevators work slowly in Avery Fisher Hall, and I am too old to run down all those flights of stairs—the backstage guards had taken El to Bellevue Psycho for observation.

Yes, I see by your faces that you read about it in one of the daily papers—not the *Times*, of course. El gave a phony name to everyone, so no one realized for a while that he was my patient. It wasn't until Sunday morning that he was released in my custody.

In the meantime, the Saturday night concert went off without a hitch and without El's presence. He was chastened and depressed, and he promised all of us, including his angry grandfather, that he would behave himself.

"I suppose that means I can't buy an air pistol and shoot out one of the lights when the offstage horn plays." he said.

He was clearly in need of long-term treatment.

After being sheltered in the bosom of his family the rest of Sunday and Monday, on Tuesday morning he came for another office visit with me. He seemed agitated again.

"I've just realized that someone must warn people with pacemakers not to listen to the Seminal Seriatum," said El, still obsessed. "When the damn music is played properly—and I don't believe it has been so far—then not only will we go to Mordor, but the electronic vibrations will louse up pacemakers. At least I think so. Did you know that grandpops has one?"

"No," I said, unaccountably troubled. My own internist—a man my age—with a pacemaker! I have always felt in my prime. Now I began to have doubts. Mordor indeed!

"And I've been wrong about the lights," said El, pulling at his beard. "I thought the hot ones over the stage were the ones that counted, but maybe the others over the audience are important, especially the first row nearest the stage—six and twenty-six and six. Do you think the rows with even numbers in the sets are more likely to be affected than the rows with odd numbers?"

It was hopeless. I could not get him to concentrate on anything but Avery Fisher Hall and Pinkton. I regretted not bringing more cookies, and I was afraid that if he went through with his plan to go to the last concert, that night, he would have such a psychotic episode that he would not recover for a long time. I was completely unsuccessful in persuading him to stay home, but he did promise to sit still and leave quietly no matter what happened. He persuaded me *not* to go, and to trust him.

It's a good thing that our Psychoanalytic Alliance luncheon was on Wednesday this week, because I felt like describing this case, which has, after all, turned out well. My patient came to an early morning session today and seemed considerably improved. He even brought me a present.

"After the concert last night I stayed up late and made these cookies," he said as he walked into the room. He seemed different—somehow taller, even handsome, certainly poised and calm. His grandfather must have revealed to him my penchant for chocolate-chocolate chip cookies.

"What happened at the concert?" I couldn't help asking. I had spent a restless night worrying about him, when I should have been reviewing the psychodynamics of the case and deciding on the appropriate psychoanalytic formulation.

"I guess I was wrong about the Pinkton," said El. "I should have known that in spite of the theoretical plausibility, in actuality it's impossible for any orchestra to play the music so perfectly that the proper resonance affects the light fixtures and sets up the conditions for entering another dimension. On top of that, the horn player was completely off last night."

There was a pause, and El shrugged. "It's funny, but the other dimension doesn't matter much any more. Maybe I've accepted that we're all stuck in this one and I intend to make the best of it. It's odd, but while listening to the Seriatum I had a brilliant idea. I'm going to open a restaurant. Grandpops says he'll give me the money."

"Then . . ."

"I thought of calling it Elrond's Way, but there might be copyright difficulties, so I'll think of something else. I'll serve the gourmet recipes I invented while trying to discover Elvish food, and I'll have a music and light show every night—modern music and maybe computer graphics in color, projected on a large screen. I think I've finally found"—he winked at me—"my s—elf."

So you see, my fellow Pshrinks, that while El is still quite crazy, he has transformed some of it into a possibly worthwhile endeavor. I, for one, intend to go to his restaurant, although I doubt if I'll stay for the music. Have one of his cookies, and I think you'll understand.

The Oldest Member stopped talking and passed around the bag of cookies.

"Best I ever ate," said several Pshrinks.

"Terrific," said the Interpersonal. "They go well with my blueberries."

"For someone who never gets fat," said the O.M. enviously, "You have always been notably interested in food."

"And in the endings of stories."

"I've told you how it ended."

"You don't know the rest of the story. I went to the concert last night."

"But your ticket was for Friday afternoon, and you gave it to me."

"I got one at the last minute at the box office. I was curious. Your patient was wrong. Something did happen."

"All right, all right. I didn't suppose I could tell a case history without your being involved in some way," said the Oldest Member. "Tell us."

"Well," said the Interpersonal through a cookie, "I was sitting not in my regular seat in the third tier but in the lower middle section of the orchestra seats. I could see the stage lights quite well. When the Pinkton horror was played, the offstage horn does at first sound as if it were out in Elfland, promising a ring of happiness."

"Happiness?" said the O.M. "I heard it, and as El said, the horn only tempts you to think that, just before it triggers off that God-awful cacophony in the orchestra."

The Interpersonal shook her head. "Last night when the horn player was supposed to switch to dissonance, the note cracked—French horns can do that even with the best players—and instead of a horrible clashing sound, we heard . . ."

"What?" asked the Oldest Member as the Interpersonal stopped speaking and stared into nothingness.

"Um. It was just as one of the lights in the stage ceiling winked out. I forgot to count exactly where it was, not being very mathematical, and of course the orchestra did eventually go on to finish the damn piece but it was ruined as far as the expected effect . . ."

"What happened?" shouted the Oldest Member.

"And afterward, I noticed that everyone around me looked a little paler and rather tense . . ."

"At this rate," said the Oldest Member, "I will need a pacemaker myself. If you don't tell us what happened . . ."

"Oh, yes. You see, the cracked note, instead of being the one that produced the worst dissonance, did just the opposite. After what we'd been subjected to, that note sounded as if the promise of happiness had been kept. We didn't move into Elfland. It came in to us. Perhaps the horn player, fed up with Mordor, did it on purpose."

"I suppose you had an extraordinary experience, as usual."

The Interpersonal grinned. "I was sitting on the slope of a mountain eating sun-warmed blueberries that grew wild all around me. The little boy in front of me turned to his mother and said, loudly, as soon as the music ended, 'I was on the space shuttle, having a great time and eating watermelon. I could taste it. I was *really there*. Where were you, Mommy?"

"Now you can't expect us to believe . . ."

"Fortunately his mother had slept through most of the last part of the concert, so she was able to say confidently, 'You're always imagining things too much, dear.' Everyone around me sighed, obviously with relief, and we all left Avery Fisher Hall, which was still completely intact."

"I suppose," said the Oldest Member with resignation, "that you're going to say food comes into it because it's a more primitive experience, and what happened was some sort of right brain activity induced by the amplification of vibrations in the electromagnetic fields of the neurons?"

"Well . . ."

"And I know what you're like. You'll insist that El's partial cure was in surrendering to his better self in response to my concern, and that I handled the case well because I was more interpersonally active."

"Um," said the Interpersonal, taking another cookie and pouring milk on her blueberries.

"And now you're probably going to pontificate about how we Pshrinks overdo the seeking out of internal pathology, as if the human mind contained only Mordor, when we should be helping the patient find in himself what's true and noble and . . ."

"Elvish?" said the Interpersonal.

"I knew it!" said the Oldest Member triumphantly.

"Well, I . . ."

"Furthermore," said the Oldest Member, scowling, "you will now undoubtedly insist on ending with some impenetrably obscure Zen remark that you think illuminates the mystery of life."
"Enjoy your blueberries," said the Interpersonal.

BELLING MARTHA

by Leigh Kennedy

The author,
who was raised in Colorado,
now lives in
Austin, Texas, but says
that it is much
warmer there now than
it is in this story. She's sold several
stories to various
science-fiction markets and,
when she isn't writing,
she enjoys fishing and photography.

art: Janet Aulisio

Martha was looking for her daddy.

By the time she saw the lights of the cabins on the stark hillsides outside the gates of Austin, she'd nearly forgotten her goal. Especially as she knew not to travel the road, it had been enough to survive one hill, the next, and then another . . .

She sniffed the frigid wind blowing toward her from the notorious stove vents of those who lived just outside the city.

Someone was roasting human flesh in their fires.

The thin leather boots issued by the Central Texan Christian Reform Camp were scant protection for slogging through two feet of snow. Breaking the icy crust had made her shins sore, even through her jeans. Wind flapped her sleeves and collar and battered her ears until a dull ache throbbed through her skull. She'd stopped three times on the way from Smithville to build a fire and revive her feet, and sleep a bit.

The aroma quickened her progress. It had been a long time since Martha had smelled that particular odor. The biscuits and apples she'd carried with her—stolen from the camp kitchen—had long ago been eaten.

The closer she struggled toward home and warmth, the more stinging the dry snow felt. Gradually, she could discern details of the cabin she'd spent most of her life in—the heavy drapes at the window, the flat boulder that she used to perch on while she watched her father chop wood, the daub patches on the east wall.

Wise enough not to approach the house from the road, where stray travelers, legal or not, were watched with interest, she came upon the rear door. She pushed the door open and stepped inside.

"Daddy?"

The house had changed only a little—different colors and smells; she noticed that her small bed was gone from beside the fireplace. On the stone of the hearth, a cracked head and shoulder lay with its hair stiff and awry. Strips of flesh hung from hooks above the fireplace, and a kettle bubbled on the high grate above the fire. The meat smelled old. It was apparently not a kill, but probably a body tossed out the gates because there was no one to pay for a burial inside the city.

She heard a sound behind her.

"Dad . . ." she said, turning.

A woman poised toward Martha, holding a garroting wire in her hands. Martha stepped back and knew as she spoke that she was imitating the cool of her father's manner. "Hey, neighbor," she said.

The woman's eyes narrowed. She was still ready to strike. Martha would have to work fast to get out of the situation if the woman was a Crazy.

"Neighbor?" the woman repeated.

"What are you doing in my house?" Martha said.

The woman smiled wryly. "Like hell *yours,* kid. I live here."

Now Martha speculated. It had been over a year since her father's last letter had reached her at the camp. Could it be that he'd found himself a companion? "With my daddy?" she asked.

"Don't think so," the woman said. Her hands lowered a bit. "Not unless the old fella hasn't told me all."

"My daddy's Harry Jim Skill."

"Well, then, your daddy ain't here," the woman said irritably. "What are you doing out here anyway?"

"Looking for my—"

"Yeah, okay," the woman said. She unwound the wire from her hands and stuffed it into her pocket. "He didn't teach you a bit of sense, did he? If you're really neighbors with folks like us, I'll let you go. Go on now!"

Martha wasn't ready to have the decision made for her. She couldn't believe her father was not nearby. She shouted, "Harry Jim!"

"You little fish, I'll stew you. . . ." the woman said, walking toward her again.

The back door swung open. Martha swiveled to look. The face could have been handsome or beetle-like, she didn't notice, but it was wrong, all wrong, and that made it horrible.

"Git!" the woman shouted, and Martha hesitated only long enough to shake the uncertainty of terror out of her bones, then pushed through the front door.

As soon as she'd come in sight of the city gates, she knew she'd lost her caution. She stopped. Before her was the battered sign on a brick wall just outside the gates:

WELCOME TO AUSTIN, TEXAS STATE CAPITAL

Above her, the sentry leaned out of his watchbooth, sighting her down his gun barrel. "Don't move," he said through a loudspeaker.

Martha stood completely still. For the first thirteen years of her life—until she'd been taken to the camp—she had seen the walls of Austin, but she'd never been so close as now.

"Drop that bag."

Martha let her bag of possessions slip from her hand onto the frosty mud.

Still, the guard kept his weapon on her. "Do you have a pass?"

She started to say no, but thought better of it. "I got jumped in the back of a government truck. They stole my pass, then shoved me out. Been walking for three days."

The sentry paused. After a moment, the box that he stood in eased down the wall on a track. When it was about a meter from the ground, it stopped with a mechanical bounce. One of the spotlights atop the wall swiveled until it shone directly on her. She raised her hand to shield her eyes.

"Throw your bag over here."

Martha picked up her bag and flung it toward the box. The sentry moved cautiously, watching her, and stepped sideways to pick the bag up with a hook. He examined it inside his box. "Take your clothes off."

"It's too cold!"

"Do you want inside the city?"

She peeled everything, including her boots, shivering so hard that she could barely throw the heap toward him. After a few moments, the voice in the loudspeaker said, "Come in." The gate opened just a bit; Martha squeezed through the opening. Someone grabbed her arm as she entered. Peripherally, she saw the sentry box rising up the wall again.

She stood naked inside the gates of the city—for the first time. Trampled pathways glittered coldly under the bowed heads of streetlamps. Small houses shouldered one another as if for comfort, their windows dark. The wind whined eerily through broken panes of glass. The sound of loose metal clanged in the wind.

She'd imagined cities to be clean havens for good folk, but it looked more miserable than outside to her. Still, she thought, surveying all the possible places for residence, there must be a lot of food here. . . .

The soldier who had her arm stared hard at her face. "What's your name?"

Martha blinked. "Uh . . . Martha . . ."

"Hey, Carrie," called the sentry above. "Take my post awhile."

"Shit," the soldier with Martha muttered. "Come on down," she said impatiently. As the other hurried down a metal stair, she took on a warning tone. "You're going to get caught one of these days, you horny dog. Someday the governor's daughter will come through WP."

"This isn't the governor's daughter," he said, taking Martha's hand. "Come on, now, I got to check you in. You want in the city, right? You got relatives?"

As he pushed her toward a metal shed, Martha said, "Don't

know if they're still in the city." She was getting hazy from the cold and from being shoved around.

"We'll just find out in a little while." He opened the door. In the shed was a table with tools, greasy notices pinned on a board, and the kind of radio she'd seen in Brother Guy's office at the camp. Against one wall, a cot listed in a mended way.

"Lay down, spread your thighs. Ever done this before?" he asked, unbuckling his coat.

Martha tested the cot and figured it would hold her. "Do I have to?"

"Sure would make things easier for you, sweetie."

She shrugged.

The jeep shot through the city, sometimes leaping off crevasses in the streets, sometimes jerking to avoid potholes, sometimes dipping one wheel in a hole with a thump. Martha sat beside the policeman driving, hunched over the bag in her lap.

They'd found her Aunt Jenny Skill in the directory. Martha couldn't remember much about what her father's sister had become, except she'd married in the city and either left or lost her husband. The check-in police told her that if her Aunt Jenny couldn't (or wouldn't) take her in, she would have to go to the WP camp.

Martha knew vaguely about WP camps. Sometimes they kept people doing construction or working in government janitorial jobs for years. One could get out by playing political or buying a bureaucrat's attention. Martha figured her aunt might know where her father was; even if he'd gotten stuck in a camp himself, she could find him. He would help her.

Wouldn't he?

She thought about the last time she'd seen him. . . .

"Renounce your ways!"

She'd run outside to see the battered truck with a chicken wire cage on the back. Standing inside the cage was an old woman with two apples in one hand and a potato in the other. Though she was grey and fragile, when she spoke to Martha straight through the cage, she had a strong voice.

"Renounce your ways!" she shouted, then pointed to Martha's father standing just behind her. "Come with us to the Lord's commune. We have food, we have warmth. Don't let your child be damned by your sinning ways!"

"Martha," her father said, but then was silent.

"Look at all the food," Martha said, noticing the lumpy bags of potatoes, apples, beans, and cheeses with heavy rinds in boxes, loaves of bread wrapped in paper.

"Forty miles to happiness," the woman shouted. "Forty miles to regular meals, a warm bed, and God-given peace of mind." She beckoned to Martha with an apple, unlatching the door of the cage. "You won't have to eat the flesh of your brothers and sisters. Brothers and sisters in God's eyes! Renounce your ways! We understand! We forgive! We will save you!"

"Martha," her father said again with a voice as soft as snowfall, "do you want to go?"

Martha looked at more food than she'd ever seen at once in her life. She thought of the nights that her father wept and sighed after an especially trying capture and kill. She was still young enough to believe that a different life meant a better life, and if her father was willing . . .

"Yes!"

"Come, child," the woman said, "come with us to pray with thanks for salvation."

Martha caught hold of the tailgate of the truck and boosted herself up to the cage door. Then she looked over her shoulder and saw that her father was standing still, just watching.

"Daddy!"

The woman grabbed her shoulders and pulled her headlong into the truck, shouting, "Take off, Brother Guy!"

The truck lurched. Martha skinned her knees falling forward. She crawled up to look out at the figure standing down the road and screamed, "Let me out, let me out, you old bitch!"

And far away, her father yelled her name through cupped hands. "Martha, I love you!" he said.

From the jeep she could see broken-down houses. To her left, she saw the tall outline of buildings she'd seen distantly for years. They seemed close and large, and yet still a coherent shape.

A wish came to Martha—perhaps if she couldn't find her father, maybe her aunt could take his place.

After she'd first been taken to the Christian camp, she'd been bitter and angry, feeling deserted by the only person that had ever meant anything to her. His few letters to her there had eventually made her realize that he had thought it was the best thing for her. During the numb years at the camp, Martha mouthed the phrases and sang the verses, but they hadn't touched her. She'd made adequate, tentative friendships, but none so profound that she would grieve at separation.

She leaned back and slid down the seat, face turned outward to passively watch the scenery. She'd seen pictures in old books of cities, but all this seemed a ruined imitation. Dried weeds poked out of the thin crust of snow. Parts of houses had been hacked away, probably for firewood or to patch other houses. Fleetingly, she saw someone prying a windowframe from an abandoned garage. She saw one tree enclosed within a fence.

Slowing down, the driver for the first time spoke to Martha. "Is this it?"

Martha looked at the house beyond the posts of what had once been a chain-link fence. The house was a square two-story with symmetrical windows. "I don't know," she said.

She followed the policeman up the path to the house. The roof overhung the door a bit, but looked chopped away. A layer of gritty snow covered the boxes and other odd shapes on the porch. The policeman pounded on the door and turned toward the street uneasily.

When the door opened, four people stood behind a heavy mesh. Others looked through the parted drapes. The policeman unfolded a piece of paper and held it out. "Is there a Jennifer Skill here?"

It reminded Martha of the time she'd first arrived at the camp. Faces, faces, looking back at her.

A woman came forward out of the other room and stood behind the mesh. "What do you want?"

Martha couldn't superimpose her father's stories of his childhood companion on this tight-lipped, thin woman.

"This girl claims you'll take her in."

Jenny Skill looked at Martha speculatively. "Who is she?"

"Martha Gail Skill, she says," said the policeman.

"Where's my daddy?" Martha asked her.

No answers came for a moment. The policeman and Martha stared inward and the others stared outward and no one said anything. Jenny reached above her head and there were sounds of metal locks slipping as her hands crept down the side of the mesh.

The door opened. Martha stepped inside and stood behind her aunt. The policeman thrust his notebook in the door. "Sign this," he said. "She has no papers. You'll have to get them for her in ten days or pay the fines."

Jenny only nodded as she signed the paper.

After the policeman left, Jenny took Martha's coat collar between her thumb and forefinger and guided her into the living-room. Furniture crowded the room, as if several households' worth of things had to be arranged in a single place.

Fifteen or so people came into the room, some sitting on the sofas or chairs, but most stood around them. Jenny lifted her chin. "She's kin to me and I'll take responsibility for her. You know that she's my brother Harry's kid, but she won't pull anything here." Then Jenny took Martha's jaw in her hand and jerked her face around so that Martha stared straight into Jenny's eyes. "Will you?" she said.

"Where's my daddy?" Martha whispered. She felt a cramping in her lower gut. The bright electric bulb overhead, the strangers all intent on her presence, and Jenny's roughness confused her.

"Poor thing," one of the grannies whispered.

"You just forget about your daddy," Jenny said. "He's not here."

"But where is he?"

"No use worrying about it."

"Now, wait a minute," a man said.

Jenny let go of Martha and for the first time she was able to focus on the people around her. There were two old grannies sitting together. There were several men about her father's age, and even more women. Younger people nearer her own age numbered only about five. Later, she discovered that six children had been put to bed.

The large man who'd spoken shouldered closer. He had an aggressive, troubled kind of look that Martha had seen on some of the Crazies at the camp. "I don't feel safe about having your brother's kid here. Nothing against you, Jenny, but we all know what your brother was, and what's to say—"

"Tell 'em where you've been," Jenny said, nudging Martha.

Martha stood dumbly. She'd heard the word *was* referring to her father. Was? What did it mean?

"She's been in the Christian Reform Camp," Jenny said. "Okay, look, Darren, we'll move Terry out of the closet under the stairs and hang that big brass bell over the door. Anyone will hear her coming out at night. Send her out with the kids to scavenge. If she gets fed like the rest of us, she won't be looking to carve anyone up."

"You'll have to feed her better than that," one of the grannies said.

"Well, where am *I* going to sleep?" one of the young ones asked. She was kind of pretty, but she kept narrowing her eyes at Martha.

Martha listened vaguely as sleeping places were rearranged. Someone was sent to lock up the knives in the kitchen. Jenny searched Martha's pockets. Sweat formed on Martha's upper lip; she clenched her teeth as her bowels churned nervously.

"Jenny," she said, "what happened to Daddy?"

Jenny turned quickly. "He's dead! Now I don't want to hear another word about it."

Martha nodded slowly. She had expected her to say exactly that, but somehow she couldn't believe that she really had. Her ears buzzed and she felt weak. "I need to go to the john."

"Kaye, take her out back," Jenny said.

A young dark-haired woman shuddered melodramatically. "*Me?*"

"All right, all right," Jenny said impatiently. "Switzer."

A blond, rosy-cheeked young man motioned to Martha. She followed him through the kitchen, which was clean, but dishes, boxes, cans, and bottles crammed together on narrow shelves and utensils and pots hung everywhere there was room. Switzer unbolted the back door. She saw the john and ran for it.

She stayed longer than she needed to, in spite of the cold, rocking back and forth, sobbing. She thought of the last time she'd seen her father, the words he'd written to her about how they would go south together someday when he had money to pass the boundary. She revived old memories of him telling her stories, the little jokes they had with each other, songs he would sing while cooking or sewing, the way he looked when he was "just thinking."

She didn't want to go back inside with those people. At the camp, everyone had done their best to act nice, though the feelings were usually at odds with their behavior.

She stopped crying. She felt dry and cold and used up.

On the way back into the house, Switzer said, "I'm sorry about your father." There was a sort of anger in his voice.

Jenny met her in the kitchen and led her to a dim room lined with several mats. Two small forms lay under blankets, but the rest were flat. "Here. We're giving you a warm place. Keep that in mind." Jenny opened a closet door. A bell jangled. One of the sleeping children sat up. Martha saw that the dark closet was the inverse shape of a stairway, lined with boxes and various shapes, all of which seemed to lean dangerously inward. Jenny urged Martha forward.

The door shut behind her with another jangle, then a bolt slipped into place.

She sank down, only then realizing her weariness. As her eyes adjusted to the darkness, she saw the ghost of her hand against a rough blanket. Voices and footsteps scattered randomly around her. Someone went up the stairs above her.

She was hungry—awfully hungry—now. Beyond her door were so many people.

She knew her own ribs and hipbones and spine as hard places on her body. But there were those in the house who were not so lean. She could crawl from mat to mat and search for their hipbones and find none so sharp as her own.

"People are not food," Brother Guy had said to her on her second day in the camp. "When God gave Moses the laws, he said, 'Thou shalt not kill.' It's better to die of hunger than to kill your fellow man. It is wrong, Martha, *wrong*. You will pay for doing wrong by torment of eternal fire, eternal pain, eternal sorrow in the depths of lonely Hell if you don't get on your knees right this moment and swear—swear!—to God that you were wrong. That you will no longer eat the flesh of humans. That you were an innocent child of circumstances. That you beg His forgiveness. That you repent with a soul full of anguish and remorse. That you will face hunger with a heartful of love for Him! On your knees and pray, Martha! Pray for your soul!"

And Martha had gotten to her knees and prayed, hoping that would relieve all the grief. But over the years, she'd come to recognize that Brother Guy didn't see the world the way she did. In fact, he saw things differently than almost everyone else. Her hope of salvation and fear of an infinite Hell broke little by little, until she behaved the way they expected her to merely out of custom—and respect for the supper table.

Now she was free of that.

When Aunt Jenny fetched her from the closet in the morning, she dragged Martha to a tiny room with a disconnected bathtub. Tepid water still stood from probably two or three others' baths. Martha didn't relish wallowing in scummy water, or that dampness after washing. They hadn't made her wash but every week at the camp.

"Wash your hair, too," Jenny said, closing the door.

She obeyed out of habit. Half way through her bath, someone tossed in a shirt and pair of pants for her, which were slightly large when she dressed. Outside the room, Switzer sat on the floor, apparently waiting for her. "Hungry?" he asked.

Martha knew that her face changed with the suggestion of food.

Switzer led the way back to the kitchen. Six or seven people crowded the kitchen, fixing their breakfasts, washing up, or passing through and chatting.

Switzer motioned for her to sit. Taking the edge of the bench at the table, she noticed the lull in the conversation. A boy stared at her, but the weak-chinned man resumed eating, and the woman stared out the window. Switzer returned with two bowls of white mealy soup and a chunk of bread. He tore the bread, gave her half, and began to eat rapidly.

As she began to spoon in the cereal, the man glanced toward her with a studied casualness, as if curious about the table manners of her kind.

She didn't waste time on manners.

As she stuffed the last of the bread in her mouth, Switzer said, "Let's go."

"Go?"

"C'mon." He strode across the room. In the entry hall, he put on a coat and knitted cap; his fair hair stuck out around his collar. He wrapped his throat with a cloth sack. Martha found her own coat on a peg.

"Where are we going?" she asked as they walked away from the house. The day was clear but for a few grey clouds in the south, but the sunlight was dulled by a persistent chill breeze.

"Scavenging," he said. He looked at her sidelong. "You've gone scavenging, haven't you?

"Yesterday I brought home a whole door," he said. He sensed Martha's skepticism and touched the bag around his neck. "I chopped it up first, of course." And then he opened his coat and showed her a small axe hanging in the lining of his coat.

They walked without conversation for a long while. All the uninhabited houses she saw had been plundered. Inedible and non-fuel trash hugged chain-link fences. Ahead was the tall yellow tower she'd seen often in the distance.

"This used to be the University," Switzer said.

They passed into an open area which was crowded with hand-built shacks.

"There used to be trees everywhere," he said. "I've seen pictures of this place where all this was green grass except for walkways, and there were trees . . ."

Martha had seen an area covered with trees outside of Smithville once.

"Maybe it will warm up before we have to ruin everything," Switzer said.

"Warm up?" Martha said. "Hah."

"It might." Switzer slowed down. "I've read that this a temporary thing, not an actual climactic change. An abberation because of those three volcanos and a fluctuation in the sun. If it goes on for another twenty years or so, then it might really be a permanent change, but it *could* warm up." He was straightforward, not fanatical like the Christians; Martha could see that it meant a lot to him.

But she didn't understand what he was saying. "Oh," she said, and squinted.

He smiled vaguely, as if knowing that she didn't follow.

"I don't know any different from now or the good times, anyway," she said. "My daddy told me about how it used to be a little, though. It just sounded like stuff he made up. You know how they talk."

"We'd be happier."

They were walking through the shacks. Martha saw faces listlessly watching from windows that had once been in automobiles. Even inside the scrap metal and cardboard huts with makeshift stovepipes, the occupants' breath condensed in little puffs. Only a few moved around outside their shanties, hands and feet and heads wrapped in rags, nostrils frosted. Martha thought they looked dulled somehow. She'd seen more people inside the city who looked like they belonged in the Other Yard at the camp than she imagined possible.

Even Switzer was subdued as they quietly walked the edge of the village-within-a-city. He glanced uneasily over his shoulder as two, then three men, trailed them as they moved toward the street. Martha flinched when Switzer took her arm, but he held.

"It's slippery here," he said, indicating the steps ahead. Martha figured that was an excuse.

When they had descended, Switzer walked at a faster pace. Martha saw that those who'd been following stood like sentries at the edge of what used to be the campus.

"I thought you should know about this place," he said. "And now you know where *not* to go."

Martha shrugged. "What would they do to *me?*"

He didn't answer.

They walked for a long time. Martha's feet began to grow numb and she had chills between her shoulder blades from the wind. The buildings around them were taller and closer to the street as they moved forward. Fractured glass, abandoned brick and concrete—she realized that was the insides of the city she'd only viewed from afar—not the spun-sugar she used to imagine.

"Pigeons," Switzer said, pointing to the roof of a three-story building. "Right in my favorite place, too." He took a slingshot out of his pocket. Martha wondered how many weapons and tools he carried. They scrounged the ground for chunks of concrete and rocks, or chips of metal.

He let loose with a rock. A burst of pigeons came outward in a wave. He loaded and reloaded with dexterity but out of the ten or so birds, only one dropped. They both ran to retrieve it from the middle of the street.

Martha saw that the bird still fluttered and twisted its neck. "Let me," she said, holding her hand out for the slingshot.

Switzer handed it over. She looked up at the ridge just below the roof where the pigeons were settling again. The sky was a flat grey now, the clouds having moved in part way over the city, but it was still bright enough to make her squint. Switzer flushed them again, then she shot with the same speed he had, only this time three pigeons dropped.

"Damn lot of birds here," she said simply, as they walked toward the kill.

"You do all right," he said with admiration.

"I've had to." She remembered her father's coaching—"Right here," he had said, tapping his temple, "hard as you can."

"At the camp?"

"Yeah." She handed him one of her birds so that they each carried two. "They took care of us so that we could hunt, farm, and chop wood for 'em. They've got one of those greenhouses the government gives out to folks they like."

"Why did you leave the camp?"

Martha shrugged. "Just seemed like the right time."

"Were they mean to you?"

Martha looked at the sky. A bleak day altogether. The only vivid color was the pink weather-pinch in Switzer's cheeks. "I don't know. . . . Naw. They just didn't pay much attention unless you got out of line."

"Did you?" he asked, smiling conspiratorially.

"Sometimes."

Martha had been standing in the short-season garden with three others when old Randall fell. He'd had attacks before, but they'd been mild and a few days of resting had usually put him back on his feet.

This time he pitched face forward into the mud, scattering the basket of asparagus he'd gathered at the fence's edge. The four of them watched, and each of them knew the thoughts of the others without so much as an exchange of words or glances.

They waited.

Summer, Martha remembered, and the sky was cloudy without thunderheads, threatening only to blow over without rain. A mockingbird made a sound like a dry wooden wheel squeaking. Martha stood, not even waving away the gnats.

Old Randall made no move.

At first they walked calmly, then more rapidly toward the fallen man. The dry grass shushed under their bare feet as they ran.

No one ever found the bones of old Randall. God moved Brother Guy to leave twenty children without food (only two of whom had the memory of fat sizzling on the fire and a full stomach) just in case they'd forgotten that they lived in His mercy.

They swung their pigeons in tandem as they wandered the city. Switzer talked about things that she couldn't really understand. Like trying to imagine the shape of the city if she'd only seen the ruins they'd passed through, she couldn't follow his words.

"We're driven to excesses," he said. "If we have food, we eat it until it's gone. If there's more than we can eat at once, we eat until we're sick, and go back for the rest before we're hungry. If we have enough fuel, we burn it until we're hot, even if the next day we have to be cold again. People are stupid and greedy when they're hungry and cold. If the government hadn't deserted us, they would try to fix things. But everyone with money and power moved to the equator. We've been deserted. After the Tropical War, all the people who could help moved away from the situation, and now they've forgotten."

"What about the governor?" Martha asked, trying to take part.

"Oh, he's greedy, too," Switzer said with disgust.

As they crawled through empty structures, overturned heaps of trash, opened cans and boxes and wrecked cars, he talked about scientific farming in cold weather, building places to live in space, and the lack of research in fission, solar power, and other energy sources.

"They were working on all those things before the weather changed. But it was all so half-hearted because they never really believed we would need it. By the time we did, everything was too ruined to make any constructive moves. My parents owned a company that designed solar homes."

Martha wondered if his parents lived at the house, and what "solar homes" were, but didn't ask.

He was quiet as they headed back. The kind of quiet that sounded like he was trying to think of something to say. Finally, he asked, "Can I sleep with you tonight?"

"I guess so," Martha said. "But . . ."

"I'll fix the bell. Don't like it anyway."

The longer she was with him, the more peculiar he seemed, but she thought it would be nice to have someone to play with anyway.

Jenny greeted them at the door when they arrived just after dark. She stared at Switzer a long time, then rifled through their bag and nodded at the pigeons with approval.

"Martha got most of them," he said.

"Maybe she'll earn her keep then," Jenny said.

It hadn't been such a good day for the others. For dinner they each ate a few spoonsful of pigeon and potato in a paste of water, flour, and lard. Martha ate the sparse amount, hoping there would be seconds. There were none. She scarcely spoke a word, but conversation was limited to general comments about the events of the day or the assignment of chores. Martha noticed for the first time that even though her Aunt Jenny said little, most of the conversation was addressed to her, or in her direction, or with an eye for her approval or amusement. It had been exactly the same with Brother Guy at the camp.

Jenny was the head of the house, no doubt.

Martha didn't like her. Simply, without wondering why, she didn't like Jenny's silent appraisal of all that occurred around her. She didn't like the way she held her fork, or tilted her head and half-closed her eyes when someone asked her a direct question. Even the clothes she wore were crisp and characterless. Jenny was neither relaxed nor tense, neither cheerful nor irritable. She was obscure and remote. Martha didn't think of people in intimate enough ways to actually realize it was this obscurity that bothered her, she only felt that Jenny didn't care for her. In return she didn't like Jenny, and that was that.

Switzer was as quiet as herself through the meal. Guessing his anticipation for the night, she smiled a few times.

Jenny gave her choices for evening entertainment; she could read in one of the upstairs bedrooms until it was time for the children to go to sleep, or play cards in the living room, or just chat in the kitchen and dining room. Martha heard mention of a fiddle, but heard no music that evening.

She wanted to play cards when she heard there would be a game. Not since she'd lived with her father had she played. Switzer mumbled something about reading and left the room with a disappointed look on his face.

"Here you go, little Martha," said one of the granddads, indicating a chair for her. Martha would've felt friendly to him, but she saw his quick glance at her aunt and felt the politics of the situation. She sat down. One of the other players was Darren, the man who'd spoken against her the night before.

They played rummy for a few rounds without much talk. Martha did all right, but it was obvious that the others played just about every night. She got bored with losing and stood.

"Where are you going?" one woman asked, alarmed. She'd been sitting in a nearby chair the whole time, chatting with the players while she sewed rags together.

Martha just stared at her.

"Where are you going?" the woman repeated in a higher voice.

"I don't know."

"You just sit back down then," Darren said.

"Honey, go get Jenny," the woman said.

They all stared at Martha. Martha stared back. At first, she meant to hold Darren's gaze without a flinch, knowing that a straight look was the best way to deal with anger. But something wavered within her and she began to study his throat, his meaty forearm and measured the breadth of his shoulders.

"Jenny!" he shouted. "Why are you looking at me like that?" he asked Martha, eyes narrowed.

Martha turned away from him. When Jenny came into the room, each oriented toward her. "What's going on here?"

"Are you going to let her wander around loose?"

Jenny sighed. "Come with me." She took Martha into the dining room and guided her to a straight-backed chair. "Sit here and just keep away from Patricia and Darren." And then she was gone again.

Martha watched children play with jacks and miniature houses built from welded tin cans. They begged attention from adults and older children. The elderly women sat together, as if they could only find interest in each other, occasionally patting a child. The room smelled of damp diapers and old, flaking skin. The women chattered about the people they used to know.

Martha sighed and wiggled in her chair.

"So you're Harry's?" one of the grannies said, noticing Martha's presence.

Martha nodded.

"You look a lot like him, yes," she said. "But last time I saw him, he was so changed, you know. It was the first time in . . ." She calculated, ". . . eighteen years."

Martha had not dared speak about her daddy. But she found her restlessness disappearing as she leaned toward the granny. "When did you see him?"

"Oh, it was just last summer. I remember because I was thinking the weather wouldn't be too bad for him at first."

"Weather?"

"At that prison. In Dakota." She lowered her voice and peered around the room as if she were about to tell Martha every confidence she'd stored up for several years. "I think myself that people eatin' people ain't so bad—maybe killin' 'em is. We tried to tell 'em years ago that there were too many people, and that things were going to go bad one way or another. They thought we were just anti-Establishment, you know? Well, we didn't know that the weather—"

"Then he's not dead?"

"Last I heard he was alive. I used to know him a long time ago. I was a friend of Jenny and Harry's father a long time ago." The granny smiled.

"Jenny told me he was dead," Martha said slowly. It was easy for her to believe it had been a lie.

"Oh, I don't think so," the granny said helpfully. "She probably didn't want you running off after him. He talked about you a lot."

"Sharon," said the other old woman.

The granny continued in a cheerful way. "Jenny just knows that you can't go see him. These days family doesn't count for much. It never used to, I thought, but it's even worse now. Why half the folks that live here don't know if their relatives are dead or alive, and most of 'em probably don't care. Just another mouth, another bed. They'd take a stranger sooner, if he was useful. When I was young, we all believed in love and peace and helping each other. . . ."

"Sharon," said the other again, placing her bony hands on the sagging flesh of her companion's arm. "These people here, they're like rats. You can't turn your back on any of 'em, and they're still better than some. Remember that."

"Watch me, Sharon and Candy!" shouted one of the children. "Watch me!"

Just as the conversation had involved her, it left her again. Martha began to shiver. She turned her head slowly, gazing intently, as if to see through the walls of the house the bell that imprisoned her.

She stirred, hearing a muffled tap at her door. It was an inadvertent sound, followed by more movement brushing against her door. Then the bolt-lock slid.

"It's me." Switzer's voice.

Martha sat up and drew her knees to her chest. He crawled onto the mattress and pulled the door closed quietly. "Waring may have heard me. I couldn't tell if he woke up." He spoke softly and put his fingers on her thigh. "I brought something."

She couldn't see him in the darkness, but sensed that he reached within his shirt. She felt something smooth and hard on her arm. "What is it?"

"An apple. We can share it. I could only get one this time."

She took a couple of eager bites and realized that she had eaten her half already. Reluctantly, she passed it over. Her mouth felt rough and dry from its tartness.

"What did you do to the bell?" she asked.

"I tied the clapper with cloth." He searched for her hand with his. Finding it, he put the apple core in her palm. Martha ate it. He rubbed small circles on her thigh.

She pulled her shirt off over her head, elbows knocking against the boxes around her. "Hey, Switzer."

"What?" It sounded as though he were undressing, too.

"Did you know that my daddy was sent to Dakota?"

"Yes."

"Why didn't you tell me?"

He was silent.

"Is he dead or not?"

"I don't know," he said. "The first I heard of it was what Jenny said to you last night. I was going to find out for you. We can't ask Jenny, of course. She knows that you'll try to leave."

"Why didn't you tell me?" she asked. Her voice raised.

"Shh." He was quiet for a moment. "I wanted to wait until I knew for sure, so you wouldn't get your hopes up. And then I thought we could save up some supplies and . . . Well, I want to go with you."

"With me! To Dakota? Why?"

"Because I want to."

"Yeah, sure," she said, "*everybody* wants to go to Dakota."

"You'll see. You remember that I got you an apple? I can do even better than that. We can have everything we need in just a few days, or a week." He paused. "I knew you would want to go. I really was going to tell you."

She believed him. He had an eager sound in his voice. He'd told her before that he'd done a bit of traveling; that would make him a good companion for the road. He gradually moved closer to her and she adjusted with his moves until they were parallel shapes on the shallow mattress.

She could figure the route to Dakota; she'd heard talk about it all her life. It was wretched, even though spring was coming on. Glassy snow covered even the most traveled areas. Open stretches of land made it difficult to travel without goods to exchange for safe passage from those who made their living off highway traffic.

I will need food, she thought, feeling Switzer's skin touch hers. He was warm.

She saw him by her side as they trudged through the snow, talking of times when technology would take care of misery, and everyone would have food and shelter. He was serene and calm, looking forward to things she couldn't see. And vulnerable because she had him in the white light of snow and sun at a casual moment. She drew out of her coat the axe he had lent to her.

She dug her fingertips into his shoulders. He was not lean. Everywhere he touched her, she blazed. Never before had she been so warm that sweat was like a mist hovering over her pores. Their breathing, kisses, and suppressed voices became a secret between them.

She sliced his carotid easily with the axe and hardened herself against the look of betrayal that became his death mask. Her fingers clamped the wound as he fell, so that the blood flowed into the tissues rather than spilling wastefully on the ground.

Never before had her body been so confusing to her. A feeling overcame her that would have been soothing had it not been so urgent, had it not been pushing her to something further. . . .

When the pulsing stopped completely, she dragged him by his coat collar off the road under a clump of shrubs where she quickly gathered stones and built a fire. She heated the axe in the flames until it sizzled when tested in the snow. With one stroke, it would cauterize the flesh it hacked through. First—the arms, cut through until she could disengage the ball and socket. Then, the kneejoints, then the thigh from the hip. . . .

Her breathing spurted from her uncontrolled. Switzer made a sound that was like weeping, but she felt his face against hers and it was dry.

"Martha," he said softly. He didn't speak to reproach her, to call her attention, or to order her. She hadn't heard her name said that way for a long time, and only by one other person.

As she dozed, she thought of her father.

She woke, but with the feeling that she'd been coming awake for a long time.

The night was not hers; it belonged to the people whose sleeping presences oppressed her. Something obliged her to remain in the position dreams had shaped for her until the sound of someone muttering in their sleep freed her from the silence.

With stealth natural to her, she disentangled Switzer's fingers from her hair, dressed, and carefully opened the door.

The bell made a muffled clunk.

She stood for a moment, listening. No one moved. She made her way to the entry way and found Switzer's coat. In the pocket, the sling; in the lining, the axe.

She was hungry. She held the axe and stood in the darkness.

"People are stupid and greedy when they're hungry," Switzer had said earlier. She thought of the way he'd said her name, and she knew what hunger would drive her to. He was something warm in her life, but she would not consume it to extinction.

Quietly, she unlatched the door and left, wearing his coat.

LA REINE BLANCHE

art: D. Della Ratta

by Tanith Lee

This prolific English author has been writing since the age of nine in a wide variety of fields. In addition to her work in science fiction and fantasy, she's written for the BBC, composed songs and poetry, and written books for children. *Anackire,* the sequel to her epic fantasy, *Storm Lords,* is just out from DAW Books.

The white queen lived in a pale tower, high in a shadowy garden. She had been shut in there three days after the death of her husband, the king. Such a fate was traditional for certain of the royal widows. All about, between the dark verdures of the dark garden, there stared up similar pale towers in which similar white queens had, for centuries, been immured. Most of the prisoners were by now deceased. Occasionally, travelers on the road beneath claimed to have glimpsed—or to have thought that they glimpsed—a dim skeletal shape or two, in senile disarray, peering blindly from the tall narrow windows, which were all the windows these towers possessed, over the heads of the trees, towards the distant spires of the city.

The latest white queen, however, was young. She was just twenty on the day she wed the king, who was one hundred and two years of age. He had been expected to thrive at least for a further decade, and he had left off marrying until absolutely necessary. But he had gone livid merely on seeing her. Then, on the night of the nuptual, stumbling on his wife's pearl-sewn slippers lying discarded in the boudoir—symbol of joys to come—the king was overwhelmed. He expired an hour later, not even at the nude feet of his wife, only at the foot of the bridal bed. Virgin, wife, and widow, the young queen was adorned in a gown whiter than milk, and on her head, milk-white-coiffed like that of a nun, was placed the Alabaster Crown of mourning. With a long-stemmed white rose in her hand, she was permitted to follow her husband's bier to the mausoleum. Afterwards, she was taken by torchlight to the shadowy garden beyond the city, and conducted into a vacant tower. It contained a suite of rooms, unmistakably regal, but nevertheless bare. She was to commune with no one, and would be served invisibly. Such things as she might need—food and wine, fuel, clean linen—were to be brought by hidden ways and left for her in caskets and baskets that a pully device would

raise and lower at a touch of her fingers.

Here then, and in this way, she would now live until she died.

A year passed. It might have been fifty. Spring and summer and autumn eschewed the garden, scarcely dusting it with their colors. The shadow trees did not change. The only cold stone blossoms the garden had ever put forth were the towers themselves. When winter began, not even then did the trees alter. But eventually the snow came. Finding the unaltered garden, the snow at last covered it and made it as white as the gown of the young queen.

She stood in her window, watching the snow. Nothing else was to be seen, save the low, mauvened sky. Then a black snow-flake fell out of the sky. It came down in the embrasure of the window. A raven looked at the young queen through the glass of her casement. He was blacker than midnight, so vividly different that he startled her and she took half a step away.

"Gentle Blanche," said the raven, "have pity, and let me come in."

The white queen closed her eyes.

"How is it you can speak?" she cried.

"How is it," said the raven, "you can understand what I say?"

The white queen opened her eyes. She went back to the narrow window pane.

"The winter is my enemy," said the raven. "He pursues me like death or old age, a murderer with a sword. Fair Blanche, shelter me."

Half afraid, half unable to help herself, the white queen undid the window catch and the terrible cold thrust through and breathed on the room. Then the raven flew in, and the window was shut.

The raven seated himself before the hearth like a fire-dog of jet.

"My thanks," he said.

The white queen brought him a dish of wine and some cold meat left on the bone.

"My thanks again," said the raven. He ate and drank tidily.

The white queen, seated in her chair, watched him in awe and in silence.

When the raven had finished his meal, he arranged his feathers. His eyes were black, and his beak like a black dagger. He was altogether so black, the white queen imagined he must be as black inside as out, even his bones and blood of ebony and ink.

"And now," said the raven, "tell me, if you will, about yourself."

So the white queen—she had no one else to talk to—told the raven how she came to be there, of her wedding, and her husband one hundred and two years old, and of following his cadaver with her white rose, and the torchlit journey here by night, and how it was since the torches went away. It had been so long. Fifty years, or one interminable year, unending.

"As I supposed," said the raven, "your story is sad, sinister, and interesting. Shall I tell you, in turn, what I know of the city?"

The white queen nodded slowly, trembling.

The raven said, "There is still a king in the palace. He has had the walls dyed and the turrets carved with dragons and gryphons and swans. He loves music, dancing, and all beautiful things. He himself is young and handsome. He has been many months looking for a wife. Portraits and descriptions were brought from neighboring kingdoms. None will do. The girls are too plump or too thin, too tall, too short, not serious enough, too serious. He sends back slighting messages and breaks hearts. There have been suicides among the rejects. He himself painted an image of the girl he wants. Slender and pale, with a mouth made to smile and eyes that have held sorrow in them like rain in the cups of two cool flowers. I have seen this portrait," said the raven. "It is yourself."

The queen laughed. She tossed a pinch of incense on the fire to make the room sweet, and so console herself.

"How cruel you are," she said, "when I have tried to be kind."

"Not at all. In seven hours it will be midnight. Do you not guess I am the cousin of midnight? It can therefore sometimes be made to do things for me. And you, as you say, have been kind. I am warmed and fed. May I sleep now by your hearth, fair Blanche?"

The white queen sighed her assent.

Beyond the casement the snow-dusk deepened, and on the hearth the fire turned dense and gave off great heat. The raven seemed to melt into a shadow there. Soon his hostess thought she had dreamed it all, though the empty dishes still stood, dull-

shining in the twilight.

At midnight she woke, perhaps from sleep, and she was no longer in the tower. For a year of years it had contained her, all the world she knew. Now she was free—but how?

She walked over the snow but did not feel the cold through her slim thin shoes. A moon, the condemned white widow-queen of heaven, blazed in the west, and lit the way beyond the walls of the garden, on to the straight road that led to the city. Although the gates were obscured, Blanche passed directly through the mortared stones of the wall. So she knew. "This is only a dream." And bitterly, wistfully, she laughed again. "All things are possible to a dreamer. If this is the raven's gift, let me be glad of it."

Even at these words, she made out a vehicle on the road, which seemed waiting—and for whom but herself? As she stepped closer, she saw it was a beautiful charrette, draped with white satin, and with silver crests on the doors that were like lilies or maybe curved plumes or feathers. White horses in gilded caparison with bells and tassels drew the carriage, but there was no man to drive or escort it.

Nevertheless, the white queen entered and sat down. At once the carriage started off.

Presently, shyly, she glanced at herself. Her mourning garments were gone. The white silk of her gown was figured and fringed by palest rose and sapphire. Her slippers were sewn with pearls. Her hair flowed about her, maiden's hair, heavy, curled and perfumed with musk and oleander. A chaplet of pastel orchids replaced the Alabaster Crown of widowhood and living death.

"And there are moonstones at my throat, silver bands on my fingers. And how the bells ring and sing in the cold night air."

They came into the city, through the gates, unchallenged, through dark slight streets, and broad boulevards where torches flashed and lamps hung like golden fruit from wide windows and bird-cage balconies.

Along this same route Blanche had been driven to her marriage. They had warned her from the beginning the king was old, and not easy, but even that had not put out her pride or pleasure. Until she met him on the mountainous stair and gave up her hand to his of gnarled wood and dry paper. He had glared at her

in terrified lust, fumbling at his throat to breathe. But now she wished to forget and she forgot. Everything was novel, and fresh.

In the courtyard, the charrette stopped still. Blanche left the carriage. She looked and saw the wonderful gryphons and swans and dragons new-made on the turrets where the banners of the king floated out like soft ribbons. Every window was bright, an orchard of windows, peach and cherry and mulberry.

The guards on the stair blinked but did not check or salute her as she went up between them. Some gasped, some gazed, some did not see her. And some crossed themselves.

The doors glanced open without a sound. Or else she thought that they did. She came across several lamplit rooms into a moon-tinctured walk where only glow-worms and fountains flickered, and nightingales made music like the notes of the stars. At the end of the walk, Blanche the white queen saw a golden salon where candleflames burned low. She had known the way.

As she entered, she found the young king of whom the raven had told her. He was dark as she was pale, his own hair black as the branch of a tree against the snow. He was handsome, too. And she felt a pang of love, and another of dismay, though not surprise.

He caught sight of her at once, and started to his feet.

"Are you real?" he said. His voice was musical and tensed between delight and anger.

"No," said Blanche. "I am a dream. Mine, or yours."

"You are a painting come to life."

Blanche smiled. The raven, who surely was to be her tormentor, had spoken the truth to her. Or else, for now, it was the truth.

"I would," he said, "have waited all my life for you. And since you may not be real, I may have to wait, still. Having seen you, I can hardly do otherwise. Unless you consent to stay."

"I think I may be permitted to stay until sunrise. It seems to me I am in league with darkness. Until dawn, then."

"Because you are a ghost."

Blanche went to him across the golden gloom and put her hand in his outstretched hand.

"You are living flesh," said the king. He leaned forward and kissed her lips, quietly. "Warm and douce and live. Even though a dream."

For an hour, they talked together. Musicians were summoned,

and if they saw or feared her, or whatever they thought, they played, and the young queen and the young king danced over the chequered floor. And they drank wine, and walked among roses and sculptures and clocks and mysteries, and so came eventually to a private place, a beautiful bedroom. And here they lay down and were lovers together, splendidly and fiercely and in rapture, and in regret, for it was a dream, however sweet, however true.

"Will you return to me?" he said.

"My heart would wish it. I do not think I shall return, to you."

"I will nevertheless wait for you. In case it chances you put on mortal shape. For this is too lovely to believe in."

"Do not," said Blanche, "wait long. Waiting is a prison." But she knew these words were futile.

Just then a bird sang far away across the palace gardens. It was not a nightingale.

"Let me go now, my beloved," said Blanche. "I must leave instantly. I am partly afraid of what the sun may do to me before your eyes."

"Alas," he said.

He did not hinder her.

Blanche quickly drew on her garments, even the chaplet of orchids which showed no sign of withering. She clasped her jewels about her throat. A frosty sheen lay on the window-panes that the stars and the sinking moon had not put there. "Adieu," she said. "Live well. Do not, do not remember me."

Blanche fled from the chamber and away through the palace, the rooms all darkling now, the silent fountain walk, the outer salons, the stair. In the courtyard the charrette and its horses remained, but it was half transparent. This time, none of the guards had seen her pass. As she hastened on she realized that she had after all forgotten her pearl-sewn slippers. She felt only smooth cobblestones under her feet—there was no snow, and now it came to her that there had been none, in any corner of the city or the palace that she had visited.

The carriage started off. It flew like the wind, or a bell-hung bird, into the face of the dawn. And when the dawn smote through, the carriage fell apart like silver ashes. The sun's lilting blade pierced her heart. And she woke alone, seated in her chair before

the cold hearth, in the pale tower, in the shadowy garden. As she had known she would.

"Cruel raven," said the white queen, as she sprinkled crumbs of meat and bread along the embrasure of her window. She was full of pain and stiffness, and even to do so much made her anxious. Nor did she think he would come back. The winter day had passed, or had it been the whole of the winter which was gone? The snow faded between the shadow trees. The white queen looked from her narrow window and pulled her breath into her body without ease. "Spring will come," she said. "But not any spring for me."

She turned and went back to her chair. Within the white coif, under the Alabaster Crown, her face was like a carved bone, the eyes sunk deep, the cheeks and lips. Her hands were like slender bundles of pale twisted twigs. As she sat, her limbs creaked and crackled, hurting her. Tears welled in the sunken pools of her eyes. They were no longer two flowers holding rain.

"I am old," said the white queen. "In one night, I grew to be so. Or were they fifty nights, or a hundred nights, that seemed only one?" She recalled the young king, and his hair black as a raven. She wept a little, where once she would have laughed at the bitter joke. "He would despise me. No magic now and no demoiselle of dream. I should revolt him now. He would wish me dead, to be free of me." She closed her eyes. "As I wished my own aged husband dead, for I thought even this pale tower could be no worse than marriage to such a creature."

When the white queen opened her eyes, the raven stood in the opened window like a blot of ink.

"Gentle Blanche," said the raven, "Let me come in."

"You are in," she said. "My heart is full of you, you evil magician. I gave you food and drink and shelter and you did harm to me, and perhaps to another. Of course you did."

"Also you, my lady, told me a story. Now I," said the raven, "will tell one to you."

"Long ago," said the raven, "there was a maiden of high birth. Her name was Blanche. She might have made a good marriage among several of the great houses, to young men who were her peers. But it was told to her that she might also make a marriage with the king and rule the whole kingdom. He was old, decaying

and foolish, she was warned of this. But Blanche did not care. Let me agree; he will die soon, thought Blanche. Then I will be regent to any who come after, and still I will rule the land."

"Oh," said the white queen, "I remember."

"However," said the raven, sitting on the hearth like a gargoyle of black coal, "when Blanche was given to the king and saw and touched him, her courage failed her. By then it was too late. They were lighted to their bed and priests blessed it. As he had come from his disrobing, the king had stumbled on Blanche's discarded slippers, and called out, and fallen. As he was revived by his servitors, the aged monarch muttered. He had dreamed of a girl like Blanche eighty years before. Or else it was a spirit who visited him. The girl of his dreams had been his wife for one night, and he had worshipped her ever since, refusing to marry, looking only for his lover to return to him. In his youth he had been mad, ten whole years, following the uncanny visitation, wandering the earth in search of his ghost bride. He had even unearthed tombs and dug up embalmed corpses, to see if any of them might be she. All his life, even when the madness left him, he waited. And it seemed that Blanche, whom he had now wedded, was the image of the ghost-bride and, like her, had left her pearl-sewn slippers lying behind her."

"Yes," said the white queen, "I recall." She leaned her head on her hand, on her sore wrist thin as a stick.

"However," said the raven again, "Blanche barely listened to these ramblings of her senile husband. She lay in the silk covers shrinking and in horror. She thought, he is decrepit and weak and easily distressed, and so easily destroyed. When the servants and the priests were gone, she kneeled up on the bridal couch and taunted her old husband and railed at him. Her tongue was sharp with ambition and loathing. She broke his heart. He died at the foot of the bed."

"I called at once for help," said Blanche. "I thought they would judge me blameless. But it seems someone had stayed to listen and had overheard. For a certain kind of murder, the murder of a king by his queen without the brewing of a draught, the striking of a blow, this is the punishment. Confined alive until death in a tower in a cemetery garden. A white queen, a murderess. I am punished. Why," said the old white queen, "is fate so malicious, and are you fate? If I had met him as he was that night, young

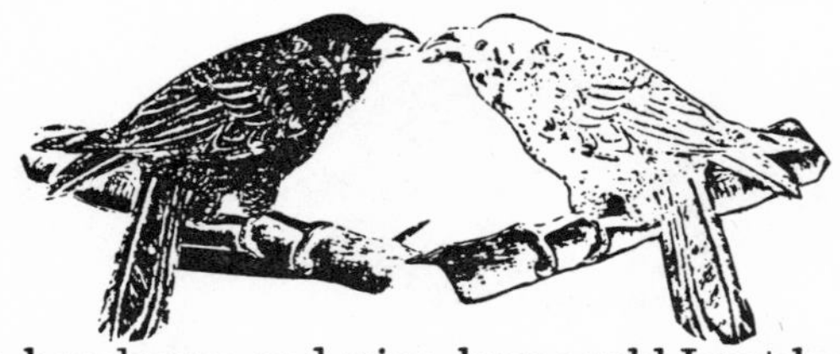

and strong, handsome and wise, how could I not have loved him? Yet I was sent back eighty years to harm him, as I would harm him eighty years in the future. And as he has harmed me."

"You were his punishment," said the raven. "His pride and his own malign tongue had broken hearts, as his would break. He would brook only perfection, a single sort of perfection, and was intolerant of all others. So this perfection came to him and was lost to him. He might have relinquished the dream still, and would not. He waited until he was a hundred and two years of age to claim a girl of twenty, such, even then, was his overbearing blind pride. It cost him dear."

"While I was punished for my wickedness, willing and casting his life away when I might have been happy elsewhere, and he left in peace."

"Each the other's sentence and downfall," said the raven. "As perhaps each knew it must be."

"And you," she said, "are an angel of chastising God. Or the Devil."

"Neither," said the raven. "Should we not chastise ourselves, that we learn?" He flew to the embrasure of the window. Beyond the tower, the trees were dark as always, the tops of the other dreary towers pushed up. But the sky was blushed with blue. Over the wall it would be spring.

"Despite all sins and stupidities," said the raven, "I love you yet and yet have waited for you, gentle, fair Blanche. And you, whether you wished it or no, waited for me in your bone tower, and at the last as at the first, you were kind."

The white queen wept. Her tears were like pearls.

"Let us," said the raven, "be together a little while, in freedom and innocence.

"Oh, how can you speak?" she cried.

"Oh, how can you understand what I say?"

Then the white queen left her chair. She left her body and bones and old pale blood, for she was white now inside and out. She flew up into the window embrasure. From the prison towers only the souls of dreamers or the wings of birds could get out. Up like arrows flew two ravens, one black as pitch, one white as snow, and away together over the trees, the wall, the road, the city, the world, into the sky of spring.

ANCIENT DOCUMENT

(excavated on an overpopulated planet while preparing a bomb shelter)

When this new empty land, our chosen home,
Leapt up to meet Mayflower III, we knew
Despair. Grey sand, cracked rocks, a single dome
Heavy and squat. Nothing familiar grew.
Far off, a pewter ocean under rain
Was fed by sullen rivers dull as dung.
Our ship roared in to meet an empty plain.
Then silence fell, where birds had never sung.

Comfort my blistered hands, the steady ache
Of lifting blasted stone. Hold me tonight,
In this sweet interlude before we wake
I'll dream of unborn children laughing, white
Linen, cream. Too soon the morning horn
Will call us out to plant tomorrow's corn.

—Hope Athearn

MILES TO GO BEFORE I SLEEP

by Julie Stevens

The author is 34, a lawyer,
and the mother (by single-parent adoption)
of 15 year-old Michelle.
This was the last of
twelve stories she wrote during
the 1980 Clarion SF Workshop
and the first to be published.

art: Robert Walters

Man's greatest achievements were conceived and realized not in the bracing atmosphere of plains, deserts, forests and mountains but in the crowded, noisy, and smelly cities

—Eric Hoffer.

Cheyenne read the sentence several times, wondering if the words chiseled into the granite cliff overlooking Thomas Creek Gorge were a specific quote or the ramblings of a passer-by named Eric Hoffer. Parts of the carved letters were defaced by a white, spray-painted scrawl that promised salvation if the author would repent.

Cheyenne sighed with frustration partly engendered by the sentiments of the second writer, and partly brought on by the unalterable fact that the Thomas Creek bridge was impassable to automobiles. After crossing back over the two remaining concrete standards, she turned her Mustang around, left a note on the steering wheel to tell the next traveler how to use the methane cannisters in the trunk, and put the keys in the glove compartment. Then, in the cursive script used only by city dwellers, she carefully scratched her name and destination under the hood. CHEYENNE WYO, DES MOINES CITY.

She hefted the backpack onto her shoulders and started across the girders. At least there were walkable remnants. A hundred miles back, Silver Canyon bridge had been completely destroyed. It had taken two extra days to rappel down the canyon walls and climb the other side. Then, the only transportation on the eastern bank had been a small Italian Vespa which had proved to be unwieldy and uncomfortable. She had ditched the Vespa as soon as she discovered the '92 Mustang. Blessing her good fortune, she had tried not to think of why the Mustang was abandoned. The last entry on the hood read: TOM MENDELSON, HELL. In the back seat, she had found a box full of sketchbooks, each drawing dated and signed. They were not particularly good, the work of a talented but untrained hand. The Mustang had been left in the Rockies; and Tom Mendelson, whoever he was, had had a thousand opportunities for a suicide leap.

On the eastern side of Thomas Creek Gorge, Cheyenne found a choice of vehicles. She picked a Jeep. It was low on meth, and she lost time siphoning fuel from the nearby cars. Since it was so close to dusk she decided not to drive further. It took her a while to find a promising side road, but the one she selected led to a quiet stream running through a rockstrewn meadow. She spread out the sleeping bag in the back seat of the Jeep and was asleep within minutes.

Sometime during the night she heard the sound of motorcycles; and, remembering past encounters with other roving gangs, she drew her revolver and waited until the roars swept past her and grew faint in the distance. No longer sure how safe her campsite was, she dozed off and on for the rest of the night, afraid to risk sleep. At the first tenuous rays of dawn, she set out once again on Highway 80. There was a little traffic along the route, mostly farm families using the paved road as a short cut from one small community to the next. She was careful to slow down and wave at the robust, solemn-eyed children, and to ask their parents if they wanted a ride, grateful when none did.

Just outside of Sutherland, Nebraska, she was stopped by two village rangers. The men were polite but effective as they searched through the Jeep and the contents of her pack. They found the wrapped jams and jellies with the tags that read *to Gramma Jean from Ann,* and they accepted her pre-crafted explanation that she was to join her grandmother's commune in Illinois. She even evoked a sincere air of sadness when she fabricated a story of how her two brothers who had accompanied her had been killed in a stonefall two days back and how the revolver was the only part of their effects she had been able to recover. There was no sense raising their suspicions by admitting that she was traveling alone.

"Honey, you hang on to that gun. You just might need it, what with the city-types on the road right now," the taller of the two rangers said, helping her to repack her belongings. His partner handed her a crumpled Sutherland methcard. "You stop at the pump in Sutherland and give this to Ed Crenshaw. He'll see you get the meth you need. Eighty's clear all the way to Grand Island but don't make any stops. And be sure you go 'round Des Moines City. There's evil brewin' in the city, and it's bound to spell trouble for us regular folk."

She nodded, thanked them for the methcard and the advice, and scarcely dared to breathe until the two men were back on their motorcycles, leaving trails of dust westward on the highway.

The encounter left her shaking. The rangers had been nice, not in the least terrifying; and once they decided she was respectable, they had been helpful. But she could not help wondering what would have happened if they had known she was Cheyenne Wyo. The last Cheyenne had been a middle-aged black man with one blind eye. He had spared her no detail as he told her how the citizens of a village much like Sutherland had put the eye out when they realized the stranger in their midst was a city mayor. The thought of her predecessor was depressing. It reminded her too well of how she was likely to wind up—old before her time, forever fighting the myth that the cities had caused the Great Conflagration and were responsible for the germ warfare that had followed. Blaming the victim was nothing new in psychology, but when it was applied to what remained of the American States—

Deliberately pushing such thoughts out of her mind, she pulled into the only meth station in Sutherland. She took out the ranger's card and flashed a smile at the old man who hobbled out to greet her.

" 'Fraid I can't help you today, Miss," he said after taking the card. "Our stills don't make more'n we use for ourselves. We run out yesterday afternoon and Hank won't have a new load ready till morning." He looked her over, as if evaluating her worth. "You could ask, six houses down, if the Reeds'll put you up for the night. Bethie Reed's my daughter and a good cook."

Cheyenne silently cursed the Jeep's nearly empty meth tank. She could not refuse the invitation to stay in Sutherland. To do so would needlessly invite suspicion. She was already showing too much independence for a properly raised village woman.

"Thanks. I need a place to stay."

Later, installed in a second-floor bedroom, listening to Bethie Reed hum to herself in the kitchen below, Cheyenne was not sorry she had been coerced into staying.

"The stove's got the water hot. You best take your bath before dinner," a voice said from the doorway.

Cheyenne whirled around to find herself face to face with a frail, porcelain-complexioned girl whom she judged to be around fifteen. The girl entered the room uninvited and wandered about, picking up those possessions Cheyenne had left scattered on the bed. Cheyenne saw then what she had not noticed while the child stood still. The girl was crippled, the misalignment of her right hip painfully obvious as she used the furniture to propel herself from one place to another, dragging her twisted foot behind her.

"It's pretty," the girl said, fingering the fabric of the dress Cheyenne had laid out on the bed. "I always wear these." She indicated the printed cotton wrapper that tied at the waist but did not conceal her thin, blue-veined legs.

Before Cheyenne could respond, Bethie was in the room, half-carrying, half-dragging the girl out. "Don't let my Cora bother you none, Miss. She's been sick but she'll be fine any day now." Bethie's brown eyes begged her to accept that explanation.

"I hope you feel better soon, Cora," Cheyenne called as the mother took the girl down the hall. She heard the slam of a door at the far end of the corridor and the sound of a slap followed by the girl's stifled cry.

At dinner, no place had been set for Cora. Cheyenne was not surprised by that, only that the Reeds had managed to hide a deformed child for so long. Cheyenne City was full of people like Cora, driven out of their villages as children because if they could not work in the fields or the stores, they had no useful function. A fraction of these outcasts made their way to the nearest cities and disappeared into the streets. Some died, a few became criminals, and one or two rewarded the city with their art, their music, their creativity.

Eight people sat at the dining table. Bethie was at one end; and her husband, Cal, sat at the other. In between were their four sons, whose names came so fast that Cheyenne could not remember which name belonged to which freckled redhead. Then came Ed from the service station, and next to Ed, a dark-eyed, sandy-haired man who pulled out a chair for her when she entered the room.

"I'm Allen Curtis. I was passing through Sutherland on my way to Minnesota and ran into the same lack-of-meth problem."

His smile was open and amiable. There was no reason for the tenseness she felt when she looked at him, but she could not deny to herself that it was there. Something about his tall, muscular body brought to mind the two rangers.

Cal, Ed, and Allen kept up an enthusiastic conversation that ebbed and flowed with scarcely any help from the others at the table. Cheyenne concentrated on her meal, Bethie's home-grown meats and vegetables a welcome change from the monotony of city synthetics. The voices swirled around her, requiring nothing more than an occasional nod or noncommittal answer when a question was directed to her. However, she glanced up at least twice to see Allen's gaze resting upon her. When she returned his stare, he shrugged and looked away.

At some point she noticed the tone of the conversation around the table had become more intense. Ed had her complete attention when his voice boomed out, "They're going to open up the cities, that's what. And come after our kids with sweet promises of soft living. We know that the cities got nothing to offer but sin and corruption, but our children don't. The freaks and do-nothings'll be using our women to make more of their kind. They'll take us over if we let them, and then it's back to war and plague. That's what they're doing in Des Moines City right now, organizing against us, plotting our destruction."

"I never heard the cities were closed to anyone," Allen interjected softly. "From what I gather, the meeting in Des Moines is simply to discuss a greater freedom of movement between the villages and the cities."

"Freedom to do what? Trade our good life for three rooms in a filthy city? Turn us into a bunch of freaks? Maybe we're too small to take on a whole city full of people, but we got to stop 'em any way we can. Sutherland's doing its part and you can bet towns like us all over the country are doing the same." Crenshaw's voice grew louder and shriller until Cal put his hand on his father-in-law's shoulder and commanded him to be silent.

"You keep yelling like that, Dad, and I won't let you go with us tonight. As for you, Mr. Curtis, I'd warn you to keep statements like that to yourself. You'll have people wondering if you are who you say you are."

"Anybody can check me out. I've got kin from Texas to Minnesota," Allen said, his easy manner taking the edge from the tension in the room. "Where I grew up, there weren't any cities, so I guess I just don't take the threat as seriously as you do. Maybe if I lived this close, I'd worry more."

Bethie began to clear the table. "You don't have children, Mr. Curtis, or you wouldn't talk like that. They're the ones that go to the city. And they never come back."

One of the redhaired boys nodded vigorously. "Sometimes when kids are ugly enough or can't do a day's work, we send 'em to the city. We don't want 'em back." He grinned at his mother. Cheyenne saw the look that passed between mother and son, and was afraid for the lovely, deformed girl upstairs.

Bethie wiped her hands on her apron and feigned a smile. "Dad, you best be getting your good clothes on for tonight's meeting."

Ed Crenshaw pulled his arthritic body to a standing position and shuffled out of the room. Cheyenne watched him go, with conflicting emotions. It never failed to puzzle her how villagers all over the country revered their old, and willingly cared for aged relatives regardless of the disabilities, yet condemned their children to death without a second thought.

Later that evening, long after Bethie had knocked at her door to say the family was going to the town meeting, Cheyenne changed into her jeans and sat in the rocking chair planning the speech she would deliver to the Mayors' Conclave in Des Moines City. At thirty-three, she was still younger than most of the mayors; and if the meeting in Des Moines City was anything like the council sessions she had attended over the past six years in Cheyenne, she would be more radical, more inclined to rebellion, more insistent upon linking together the network of cities around the country, than any other mayor.

A high, lilting voice sang through Cheyenne's thoughts, and she suddenly realized the sound was coming from Cora's room. Cheyenne peered down the dimly lighted hallway, wishing she had thought to ask Bethie where Allen Curtis was. She paused in front of his door but could hear nothing. She decided against knocking and went instead to Cora's room. The door was partly open. Cora was seated on her bed with a stringed instrument on her lap. Her voice rose high and clear over the chords she picked from the instrument. Cheyenne knocked softly and pushed the door open.

Cora never looked up, but Allen Curtis was on his feet in an instant. Cheyenne did not know who was more surprised, she or the blond stranger. The fear that crossed his face for a brief moment startled her. They stared at each other and she had the feeling she was being appraised. Finally, Allen broke the awkward silence and extended his hand to her.

"Albuquerque N-M."

Cora continued to sing as though there had been no interruption. A chill started in Cheyenne's stomach and spread its icy fingers upward. She refused the proffered hand, saying only, "I don't know what you're talking about, Mr. Curtis. I came because I heard the music."

He held her gaze a moment before smiling. "Whatever you say." He gestured toward the girl on the bed. "She's rather good for being untaught, isn't she?"

Cora's song came to an end, and she looked up expectantly at Cheyenne. "Mom says I sing pretty."

"Your mother is quite right," Cheyenne replied. She was going to say more when a distant noise caught her attention.

"The meeting will go by the window," Cora said serenely, as she plucked a few random notes. "Cal Junior says there's a burning tonight."

Allen and Cheyenne exchanged shocked looks. Cheyenne grabbed the girl's shoulders. "What kind of burning? Who do they have?"

Cora's eyes filled with tears and she tried to pull away. "You're hurting me. It's just somebody going to Des Moines City. A ranger brought him in yesterday and there was a meeting about it tonight. There's always a burning when they catch someone."

The sound of the crowd was drawing closer. When she looked out the window, Cheyenne could see the flickering torches. Her stomach tightened into a hard knot. Glancing at Allen, she saw the thin sheen of perspiration that covered his forehead.

"Provo Utah," he said, his tone bleak. "I was supposed to meet him yesterday outside of Sutherland but he never showed up."

She had heard of Provo, a giant bear of a man who was to chair the General Assembly. She swallowed her doubts and turned to Allen. "I've got a gun in my room."

He nodded. "Cora, you stay in here. Ann and I are going downstairs. I don't think you had better sing any more."

The girl smiled. "I'll turn off the lights too. Mom says I shouldn't let anyone see me."

Cheyenne and Allen stopped in the room to pick up the revolver. Cheyenne tucked it into the waistband of her pants, and they hurried down the stairs. A windbreak of trees lined the northern end of the Reed's property. Allen pulled Cheyenne against the rough bark, and together they watched the mob moving down the main street. Cheyenne had no doubt now that it was Provo the crowd was dragging by a rope that bound his hands in front. The man's face was a mass of cuts and bruises, and he staggered uncertainly as several of the Sutherland men yanked on the rope. She could see two of the Reed boys running behind Provo, taking turns poking at him with a long stick. Cal carried a torch and stood several feet away with Ed, who was one of several people swinging fuel cans. Cheyenne looked for Bethie and finally spotted the woman trailing along behind. For a moment Bethie turned toward the windbreak, and Cheyenne shrank back, almost certain she had been seen. But Bethie continued to move with the crowd.

The horde passed by the Reed house, pushing toward the town square less than six blocks away. Allen and Cheyenne ran from yard to yard, hugging the sides of the buildings and keeping to the shadows.

Cheyenne pulled the revolver from her belt, but it was obvious to them both that the weapon had too short a range and was hardly enough to disperse a crowd this size. Allen had nothing but his knife. He grabbed her arm and pointed down a dark side street to two propane tanks along the side of the general store. Cheyenne caught his meaning immediately. The town square was not visible from the store. A fire here might provide a sufficient distraction. She waited until the crowd was just past the store; then, using the corner of the building for cover, she fired twice in quick succession. The force of the explosion sent shock waves through the building. Within seconds, the first blue and yellow flames began licking their way through the wood-frame store. Allen jerked Cheyenne's arm and directed her to the shelter of a nearby porch.

The townspeople were in disarray, surging toward the burning store, leaving their bound prisoner kneeling on the brick pavement of the town square with only four men standing guard.

"My God, no!" Cheyenne whispered desperately as she saw one of the men empty the contents of a fuel can over the helpless victim.

Allen gave a strangled cry and, before Cheyenne could stop him, ran into the square with his knife drawn. One of the guards saw him coming and grappled him to the ground. Their two figures tumbled over and over in the flickering torchlight until one lay still and the other, whom she saw to be Allen, staggered to his feet.

The men raced to their companion's aid but not before one threw his torch at Provo. The prisoner's clothing caught fire immediately. Provo pulled himself to his feet, his body ablaze, and lurched in Cheyenne's direction. Then he fell heavily to the ground and rolled about, trying to quash the flames.

Cheyenne ran into the square and fired her revolver at the man who had thrown the torch. Her first shot missed but not her second. Allen left the last two guards lying on the pavement, whether dead or unconscious she could not tell. He rushed past her and flung himself upon Provo, using his hands and body to beat off the remaining flames.

When the fire was completely out, Allen pulled himself away and gently touched Provo's face. The man's skin came off in Allen's fingers. He stared in horror. Provo's eyes were glazed with pain as he reached out toward Cheyenne.

"Please."

The word was clear and distinct though she could see the effort it took him to say it. She understood before Allen did that the man was reaching not for her but for her gun.

Slowly, carefully, without letting Allen's anguished "No! You can't!" stop her, Cheyenne squeezed the trigger.

Provo's body jerked back, then fell against Allen.

"We have to get out of here," Cheyenne said, trying to loosen Allen's grip on the body. She saw that his hands were badly charred.

"How could you kill him?" The words were flat, as though the emotion that lay behind them had to be restrained or it would engulf him.

"It was his right," Cheyenne answered.

Allen looked at her oddly for a moment before laying Provo's body on the brick pavement.

There was nothing she could say to comfort him. She put her arms around his waist and helped him out of the square, back to the safety of the shadows.

They made their way to the outskirts of Sutherland. It was slow going as the pain of his burned hands began to take hold. In the distance, Cheyenne could see the red glow of the burning building. There was a new frenzied pitch to the sounds as the mob apparently discovered its prisoner dead. She knew it would not be long before search parties were organized. She slid down the bank of the creek that bordered Sutherland to the south, pulling Allen after her.

They both staggered as he fell against her. His words came irregularly and in spasms. Now that she had time to look him over, she realized his neck and chest were burned as well.

"Leave me here. When the Reeds find me missing, they will know I tried to free Provo. There must be no connection between you and me."

Cheyenne was torn between the truth of what he was saying and her unwillingness to leave him. He must have sensed her reluctance.

"I'll walk due east and try to stay near Highway 80. You can pick me up there tomorrow. If you don't find me within the first three miles, you will know I couldn't come."

They both knew he had little chance of making it to the highway alive, but she nodded anyway and agreed. She started to hand him the revolver, realized the futility of it, and tucked the weapon back into her belt.

She felt his eyes upon her as she scrambled up the bank and straight into the plump, quiet figure of Bethie Reed. Cheyenne gasped and reached for her revolver.

"You won't need a gun," Bethie said. Her voice was curiously level. "Is Mr. Curtis still alive?"

Cheyenne took a breath, then decided there was nothing to be gained by lying.

"He's burned but alive. He's down there." She pointed to the creek, knowing that Allen was there somewhere, listening to every word.

"I'll help you both, but there's a price."

"Yes?"

"You take care of Cora. You take her with you to the city." Bethie's hand clenched into a fist, then spread wide, then repeated both actions. "Dad and Cal can't understand how it is when a woman has a child, even a girl like Cora. They've put up with my fancies for a while now; but the time's coming when Cora will be put out of the village, if they don't burn her instead. You've seen her legs. She don't stand a prayer of getting to a city. I've got some money. . . ." Bethie's voice broke, and Cheyenne felt a sudden urge to put her arms around the older woman. But she stayed where she was and let Bethie recover her composure.

"Mrs. Reed, the cities are not at all what you think. Cora can learn there. She has musical talent; you must know that already. I won't let anybody hurt her."

After a long silence, Bethie nodded and started walking toward the creek bank. "You best be getting to bed. You got a long journey tomorrow."

The next morning, having eaten one of Bethie's mammoth breakfasts, endured Cal's account of the events of the previous night, and received a full tank of meth personally pumped by Ed Crenshaw, Cheyenne prepared to leave Sutherland. While Cal Junior wedged her backpack under the seat of the Jeep, she hugged Bethie very tight.

She pulled the vehicle out of the driveway and drove slowly through town. An elderly woman was scrubbing the blackened bricks of the town square. The woman smiled and waved.

It was not until she was two miles down Highway 80 and saw the pale-haired crippled girl clinging to the waist of a tall man with bandaged hands, that the mayor of Cheyenne City allowed herself the luxury of tears.

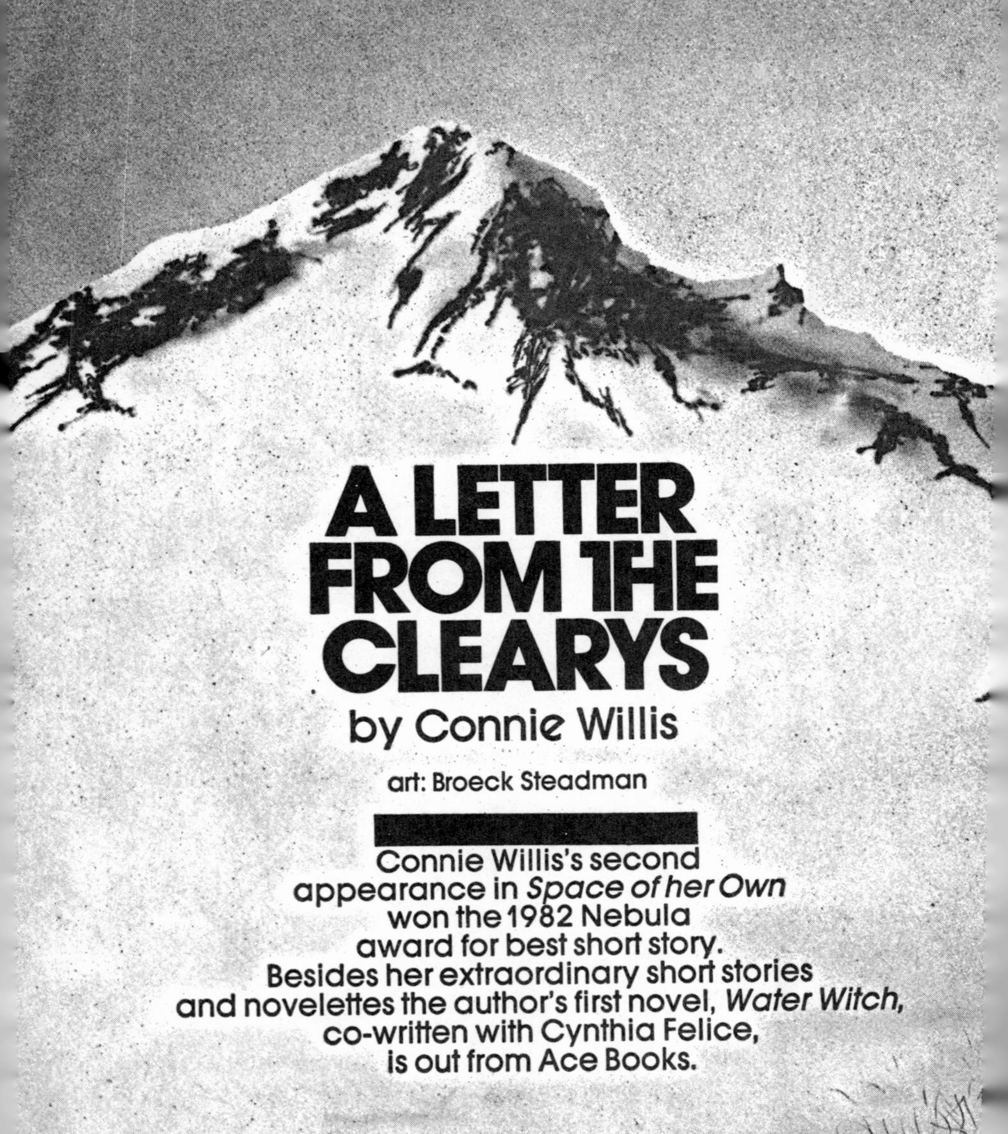

A LETTER FROM THE CLEARYS

by Connie Willis

art: Broeck Steadman

Connie Willis's second appearance in *Space of her Own* won the 1982 Nebula award for best short story. Besides her extraordinary short stories and novelettes the author's first novel, *Water Witch*, co-written with Cynthia Felice, is out from Ace Books.

E.T. Steadman '82

There was a letter from the Clearys at the post office. I put it in my backpack along with Mrs. Talbot's magazine and went outside to untie Stitch.

He had pulled his leash out as far as it would go and was sitting around the corner, half-strangled, watching a robin. Stitch never barks, not even at birds. He didn't even yip when Dad stitched up his paw. He just sat there the way we found him on the front porch, shivering a little and holding his paw up for Dad to look at. Mrs. Talbot says he's a terrible watchdog, but I'm glad he doesn't bark. Rusty barked all the time and look where it got him.

I had to pull Stitch back around the corner to where I could get enough slack to untie him. That took some doing, because he really liked that robin. "It's a sign of spring, isn't it, fella?" I said, trying to get at the knot with my fingernails. I didn't loosen the knot, but I managed to break one of my fingernails off to the quick. Great. Mom will demand to know if I've noticed any other fingernails breaking.

My hands are a real mess. This winter I've gotten about a hundred burns on the back of my hands from that stupid wood stove of ours. One spot, just above my wrist, I keep burning over and over so it never has a chance to heal. The stove isn't big enough, and when I try to jam a log in that's too long, that same spot hits the inside of the stove every time. My stupid brother David won't saw them off to the right length. I've asked him and asked him to please cut them shorter, but he doesn't pay any attention to me.

I asked Mom if she would please tell him not to saw the logs so long, but she didn't. She never criticizes David. As far as she's concerned he can't do anything wrong just because he's twenty-three and was married.

"He does it on purpose," I told her. "He's hoping I'll burn to death."

"Paranoia is the number-one killer of fourteen-year-old girls," Mom said. She always says that. It makes me so mad I feel like killing her. "He doesn't do it on purpose. You need to be more careful with the stove, that's all." But all the time she was holding my hand and looking at the big burn that won't heal like it was a time bomb set to go off.

"We need a bigger stove," I said, and yanked my hand away. We do need a bigger one. Dad closed up the fireplace and put the woodstove in when the gas bill was getting out of sight, but it's just a little one, because Mom didn't want one that would stick way out in the living room. Anyway, we were only going to use it in the evenings.

We won't get a new one. They are all too busy working on the stupid greenhouse. Maybe spring will come early, and my hand will have half a chance to heal. I know better. Last winter the snow kept up till the middle of June, and this is only March. Stitch's robin is going to freeze his little tail if he doesn't head back south. Dad says that last year was unusual, that the weather will be back to normal this year, but he doesn't believe it either or he wouldn't be building the greenhouse.

As soon as I let go of Stitch's leash, he backed around the corner like a good boy and sat there waiting for me to stop sucking my finger and untie him. "We'd better get a move on," I told him. "Mom'll have a fit." I was supposed to go by the general store to try and get some tomato seeds, but the sun was already pretty far west, and I had at least a half-hour's walk home. If I got home after dark, I'd get sent to bed without supper, and then I wouldn't get to read the letter. Besides, if I didn't go to the general store today they'd have to let me go tomorrow, and I wouldn't have to work on the stupid greenhouse.

Sometimes I feel like blowing it up. There's sawdust and mud on everything, and David dropped one of the pieces of plastic on the stove while they were cutting it and it melted onto the stove and stank to high heaven. But nobody else even notices the mess; they're too busy talking about how wonderful it's going to be to have home-grown watermelon and corn and tomatoes next summer.

I don't see how it's going to be any different from last summer. The only things that came up at all were the lettuce and the potatoes. The lettuce was about as tall as my broken fingernail and the potatoes were as hard as rocks. Mrs. Talbot said it was the altitude, but Dad said it was the funny weather and this crummy Pike's Peak granite that passes for soil around here. He went up to the little library in the back of the general store and got a do-it-yourself book on greenhouses and started tearing everything up, and now even Mrs. Talbot is crazy about the idea.

The other day I told them, "Paranoia is the number-one killer of people at this *altitude,*" but they were too busy cutting slats and stapling plastic to pay any attention to me.

Stitch walked along ahead of me, straining at his leash, and as soon as we were across the highway, I took it off. He never runs away like Rusty used to. Anyway, it's impossible to keep him out of the road, and the times I've tried keeping him on his leash, he dragged me out into the middle and I got in trouble with Dad over leaving footprints. So I keep to the frozen edges of the road, and he moseys along, stopping to sniff at potholes; when he gets behind, I whistle at him and he comes running right up.

I walked pretty fast. It was getting chilly out, and I'd only worn my sweater. I stopped at the top of the hill and whistled at Stitch. We still had a mile to go. I could see the Peak from where I was standing. Maybe Dad is right about spring coming. There was hardly any snow on the Peak, and the burned part didn't look quite as dark as it did last fall, like maybe the trees are coming back.

Last year at this time the whole peak was solid white. I remember because that was when Dad and David and Mr. Talbot went hunting and it snowed every day and they didn't get back for almost a month. Mom just about went crazy before they got back. She kept going up to the road to watch for them even though the snow was five feet deep and she was leaving footprints as big as the Abominable Snowman's. She took Rusty with her even though he hated the snow about as much as Stitch hates the dark. And she took a gun. One time she tripped over a branch and fell down in the snow. She sprained her ankle and was almost frozen stiff by the time she made it back to the house. I felt like saying, "Paranoia is the number-one killer of mothers," but Mrs. Talbot butted in and said the next time I had to go with her and how this was what happened when people were allowed to go places by themselves, which meant me going to the post office. I said I could take care of myself, and Mom told me not to be rude to Mrs. Talbot and Mrs. Talbot was right, I should go with her the next time.

She wouldn't wait till her ankle was better. She bandaged it up and we went the very next day. She didn't say a word the whole trip, just limped through the snow. She never even looked up till we got to the road. The snow had stopped for a little while, and the clouds had lifted enough so you could see the Peak. It was like a black-and-white photograph, the gray sky and the black trees and the white mountain. The Peak was completely covered with snow. You couldn't make out the toll road at all.

We were supposed to hike up the Peak with the Clearys.

When we got back to the house, I said, "The summer before last the Clearys never came."

Mom took off her mittens and stood by the stove, pulling off chunks of frozen snow. "Of course they didn't come, Lynn," she said.

Snow from my coat was dripping onto the stove and sizzling. "I didn't mean *that*," I said. "They were supposed to come the first week in June. Right after Rick graduated. So what happened? Did they just decide not to come or what?"

"I don't know," she said, pulling off her hat and shaking her hair out. Her bangs were all wet.

"Maybe they wrote to tell you they'd changed their plans," Mrs. Talbot said. "Maybe the post office lost the letter."

"It doesn't matter," Mom said.

"You'd think they'd have written or something," I said.

"Maybe the post office put the letter in somebody else's box," Mrs. Talbot said.

"It doesn't matter," Mom said, and went to hang her coat over the line in the kitchen. She wouldn't say another word about them. When Dad got home I asked him too about the Clearys, but he was too busy telling about the trip to pay any attention to me.

Stitch didn't come. I whistled again and then started back after him. He was all the way at the bottom of the hill, his nose buried in something. "Come *on*," I said, and he turned around and then I could see why he hadn't come. He'd gotten himself tangled up in one of the electric wires that was down. He'd managed to get the cable wound around his legs like he does his leash sometimes, and the harder he tried to get out, the more he got tangled up.

He was right in the middle of the road. I stood on the edge of the road, trying to figure out a way to get to him without leaving footprints. The road was pretty much frozen at the top of the hill, but down here snow was still melting and running across the road in big rivers. I put my toe out into the mud, and my sneaker sank in a good half-inch, so I backed up, rubbed out the toe print with my hand, and wiped my hand on my jeans. I tried to think what to do. Dad is as paranoic about footprints as Mom is about my hands, but he is even worse about my being out after dark. If I didn't make it back in time, he might even tell me I couldn't go to the post office anymore.

Stitch was coming as close as he ever would to barking. He'd gotten the wire around his neck and was choking himself. "All right," I said. "I'm coming." I jumped out as far as I could into one of the rivers and then waded the rest of the way to Stitch, looking back a couple of times to make sure the water was washing away the footprints.

I unwound Stitch and threw the loose end of the wire over to the side of the road where it dangled from the pole, all ready to hang Stitch next time he comes along.

"You stupid dog," I said. "Now hurry!" and I sprinted back to the side of the road and up the hill in my sopping wet sneakers. He ran about five steps and stopped to sniff at a tree. "Come on!" I said.

"It's getting dark. Dark!"

He was past me like a shot and halfway down the hill. Stitch is afraid of the dark. I know, there's no such thing in dogs. But Stitch really is. Usually I tell him, "Paranoia is the number-one killer of dogs," but right now I wanted him to hurry before my feet started to freeze. I started running, and we got to the bottom of the hill about the same time.

Stitch stopped at the driveway of the Talbot's house. Our house wasn't more than a few hundred feet from where I was standing, on the other side of the hill. Our house is down in kind of a well formed by hills on all sides. It's so deep and hidden you'd never even know it's there. You can't even see the smoke from our wood stove over the top of the Talbot's hill. There's a shortcut through the Talbot's property and down through the woods to our back door, but I don't take it anymore. "Dark, Stitch," I said sharply, and started running again. Stitch kept right at my heels.

The Peak was turning pink by the time I got to our driveway. Stitch peed on the spruce tree about a hundred times before I got it dragged back across the dirt driveway. It's a real big tree. Last summer Dad and David chopped it down and then made it look like it had fallen across the road. It completely covers up where the driveway meets the road, but the trunk is full of splinters, and I scraped my hand right in the same place as always. Great.

I made sure Stitch and I hadn't left any marks on the road (except for the marks he always leaves—another dog could find us in a minute, that's probably how Stitch showed up on our front porch, he smelled Rusty) and then got under cover of the hill as fast as I could. Stitch isn't the only one who gets nervous after dark. And besides, my feet were starting to hurt. Stitch was really paranoic tonight. He didn't even quit running after we were in sight of the house.

David was outside, bringing in a load of wood. I could tell just by looking at it that they were all the wrong length. "Cutting it kind of close, aren't you?" he said. "Did you get the tomato seeds?"

"No," I said. "I brought you something else, though. I brought everybody something."

I went on in. Dad was rolling out plastic on the living-room floor. Mrs. Talbot was holding one end for him. Mom was holding the card table, still folded up, waiting for them to finish so she could set it up in front of the stove for supper. Nobody even looked up. I unslung my backpack and took out Mrs. Talbot's magazine and the letter.

"There was a letter at the post office," I said. "From the Clearys."

They all looked up.

"Where did you find it?" Dad said.

"On the floor, mixed in with all the third-class stuff. I was looking for a magazine for Mrs. Talbot."

Mom leaned the card table against the couch and sat down. Mrs. Talbot looked blank.

"The Clearys were our best friends," I explained to her. "From Illinois. They were supposed to come see us the summer before last. We were going to hike up Pike's Peak and everything."

David banged in the door. He looked at Mom sitting on the couch and Dad and Mrs. Talbot still standing there holding the plastic like a couple of statues. "What's wrong?" he said,

"Lynn says she found a letter from the Clearys today," Dad said.

David dumped the logs on the hearth. One of them rolled onto the carpet and stopped at Mom's feet. Neither of them bent over to pick it up.

"Shall I read it out loud?" I said, looking at Mrs. Talbot. I was still holding her magazine. I opened up the envelope and took out the letter.

" 'Dear Janice and Todd and everybody,' " I read. " 'How are things in the glorious West? We're raring to come out and see you, though we may not make it quite as soon as we hoped. How are Carla and David and the baby? I can't wait to see little David. Is he walking yet? I bet Grandma Janice is so proud she's busting her britches. Is that right? Do you westerners wear britches, or have you all gone to designer jeans?' "

David was standing by the fireplace. He put his head down across his arms on the mantelpiece.

" 'I'm sorry I haven't written, but we were very busy with Rick's graduation, and anyway I thought we would beat the letter out to Colorado. But now it looks like there's going to be a slight change in plans. Rick has definitely decided to join the Army. Richard and I have talked ourselves blue in the face, but I guess we've just made matters worse. We can't even get him to wait to join until after the trip to Colorado. He says we'd spend the whole trip trying to talk him out of it, which is true, I guess. I'm just so worried about him. The Army! Rick says I worry too much, which is true too, I guess, but what if there was a war?' "

Mom bent over and picked up the log that David had dropped and laid it on the couch beside her.

" 'If it's okay with you out there in the Golden West, we'll wait until Rick is done with basic the first week in July and then all come out. Please write and let us know if this is okay. I'm sorry to switch plans on you like this at the last minute, but look at it this way: you have a whole extra month to get into shape for hiking up Pike's Peak. I don't know about you, but I sure can use it.' "

Mrs. Talbot had dropped her end of the plastic. It didn't land on the stove this time, but it was so close to it, it was curling from the heat. Dad just stood there watching it. He didn't even try to pick it up.

" 'How are the girls? Sonja is growing like a weed. She's out for track this year and bringing home lots of medals and dirty sweat socks. And you should see her knees! They're so banged up I almost took her to the doctor. She says she scrapes them on the hurdles, and her coach says there's nothing to worry about, but it does worry me a little. They just don't seem to heal. Do you ever have problems like that with Lynn and Melissa?

" 'I know, I know. I worry too much. Sonja's fine. Rick's fine. Nothing awful's going to happen between now and the first week in July, and we'll see you then. Love, the Clearys. P.S. Has anybody ever fallen off Pike's Peak?' "

Nobody said anything. I folded up the letter and put it back in the envelope.

"I should have written them," Mom said. "I should have told them, 'Come now.' Then they would have been here."

"And we would probably have climbed up Pike's Peak that day and gotten to see it all go blooey and us with it," David said, lifting his head up. He laughed and his voice caught on the laugh and cracked. "I guess we should be glad they didn't come."

"Glad?" Mom said. She was rubbing her hands on the legs of her jeans. "I suppose we should be glad Carla took Melissa and the baby to Colorado Springs that day so we didn't have so many mouths to feed." She was rubbing her jeans so hard she was going to rub a hole right through them. "I suppose we should be glad those looters shot Mr. Talbot."

"No," Dad said. "But we should be glad the looters didn't shoot the rest of us. We should be glad they only took the canned goods and not the seeds. We should be glad the fires didn't get this far. We should be glad . . ."

"That we still have mail delivery?" David said. "Should we be glad about that too?" He went outside and shut the door behind him.

"When I didn't hear from them, I should have called or something," Mom said.

Dad was still looking at the ruined plastic. I took the letter over to him. "Do you want to keep it or what?" I said.

"I think it's served its purpose," he said. He wadded it up, tossed it in the stove, and slammed the door shut. He didn't even get burned. "Come help me on the greenhouse, Lynn," he said.

It was pitch dark outside and really getting cold. My sneakers were starting to get stiff. Dad held the flashlight and pulled the plastic tight over the wooden slats. I stapled the plastic every two inches all the way around the frame and my finger about every other time. After we finished one frame, I asked Dad if I could go back in and put on my boots.

"Did you get the seeds for the tomatoes?" he said, as if he hadn't even heard me. "Or were you too busy looking for the letter?"

"I didn't look for it," I said. "I found it. I thought you'd be glad to get the letter and know what happened to the Clearys."

Dad was pulling the plastic across the next frame, so hard it was getting little puckers in it. "We already knew," he said.

He handed me the flashlight and took the staple gun out of my hand. "You want me to say it?" he said. "You want me to tell you exactly what happened to them? All right. I would imagine they were close enough to Chicago to have been vaporized when the bombs hit. If they were, they were lucky. Because there aren't any mountains like ours around Chicago. So they got caught in the fire storm or they died of flashburns or radiation sickness or else some looter shot them."

"Or their own family," I said.

"Or their own family." He put the staple gun against the wood and pulled the trigger. "I have a theory about what happened the summer before last," he said. He moved the gun down and shot another staple into the wood. "I don't think the Russians started it or the United States either. I think it was some little terrorist group somewhere or maybe just one person. I don't think they had any idea what would happen when they dropped their bomb. I think they were just so hurt and angry and frightened by the way things were that they just lashed out. With a bomb." He stapled the frame clear to the bottom and straightened up to start on the other side. "What do you think of that theory, Lynn?"

"I told you," I said. "I found the letter while I was looking for Mrs. Talbot's magazine."

He turned and pointed the staple gun at me. "But whatever reason they did it for, they brought the whole world crashing down on their heads. Whether they meant it or not, they had to live with the consequences."

"If they lived," I said. "If somebody didn't shoot them."

"I can't let you go to the post office anymore," he said. "It's too dangerous."

"What about Mrs. Talbot's magazines?"

"Go check on the fire," he said.

I went back inside. David had come back and was standing by the fireplace again, looking at the wall. Mom had set up the card table and the folding chairs in front of the fireplace. Mrs. Talbot was in the kitchen cutting up potatoes, only it looked like it was onions from the way she was crying.

The fire had practically gone out. I stuck a couple of wadded-up magazine pages in to get it going again. The fire flared up with a brilliant blue and green. I tossed a couple of pine cones and some sticks onto the burning paper. One of the pine cones rolled off to the side and lay there in the ashes. I grabbed for it and hit my hand on the door of the stove.

Right in the same place. Great. The blister would pull the old scab off and we could start all over again. And of course Mom was standing right there, holding the pan of potato soup. She put it on top of the stove and grabbed up my hand like it was evidence in a crime or something. She didn't say anything. She just stood there holding it and blinking.

"I burned it," I said. "I just burned it."

She touched the edges of the old scab, as if she was afraid of catching something.

"It's a burn!" I shouted, snatching my hand back and cramming David's stupid logs into the stove. "It isn't radiation sickness. It's a *burn!*"

"Do you know where your father is, Lynn?" she asked.

"He's out on the back porch," I said, "building his stupid greenhouse."

"He's gone," she said. "He took Stitch with him."

"He can't have taken Stitch," I said. "Stitch is afraid of the dark." She didn't say anything. "Do you *know* how dark it is out there?"

"Yes," she said, and looked out the window. "I know how dark it is."

I got my parka off the hook by the fireplace and started out the door.

David grabbed my arm. "Where the hell do you think you're going?"

I wrenched away from him. "To find Stitch. He's afraid of the dark."

"It's too dark," he said. "You'll get lost."

"So what? It's safer than hanging around this place," I said and slammed the door shut on his hand.

I made it halfway to the woodpile before he grabbed me.

"Let me go," I said. "I'm leaving. I'm going to go find some other people to live with."

"There aren't any other people! For Christ's sake, we went all the way to South Park last winter. There wasn't anybody. We didn't even see those looters. And what if you run into them, the looters who shot Mr. Talbot?"

"What if I do? The worst they could do is shoot me. I've been shot at before."

"You're acting crazy. You know that, don't you?" he said. "Coming in here out of the clear blue, taking potshots at everybody with that crazy letter!"

"Potshots!" I said, so mad I was afraid I was going to start crying. "Potshots! What about last summer? Who was taking potshots then?"

"You didn't have any business taking the shortcut," David said. "Dad told you never to come that way."

"Was that any reason to try and *shoot* me? Was that any reason to *kill* Rusty?"

David was squeezing my arm so hard I thought he was going to snap it right in two. "The looters had a dog with them. We found its tracks all around Mr. Talbot. When you took the shortcut and we heard Rusty barking, we thought you were the looters." He looked at me. "Mom's right. Paranoia's the number-one killer. We were all a little crazy last summer. We're all a little crazy all the time, I guess. And then you pull a stunt like bringing that letter home, reminding everybody of everything that's happened, of everybody we've lost. . . . " He let go of my arm and looked down at his hand.

"I told you," I said. "I found it while I was looking for a magazine. I thought you'd all be glad I found it."

"Yeah," he said. "I'll bet."

He went inside and I stayed out a long time, waiting for Dad and Stitch. When I came in, nobody even looked up. Mom was still standing at the window. I could see a star over her head. Mrs. Talbot had stopped crying and was setting the table. Mom dished up the soup and we all sat down. While we were eating, Dad came in.

He had Stitch with him. And all the magazines. "I'm sorry, Mrs. Talbot," he said. "If you'd like, I'll put them under the house and you can send Lynn for them one at a time."

"It doesn't matter," she said. "I don't feel like reading them any more."

Dad put the magazines on the couch and sat down at the card table. Mom dished him up a bowl of soup. "I got the seeds," he said. "The tomato seeds had gotten water-soaked, but the corn and squash were okay." He looked at me. "I had to board up the post office, Lynn," he said. "You understand that, don't you? You understand that I can't let you go there anymore? It's just too dangerous."

"I told you," I said. "I found it. While I was looking for a magazine."

"The fire's going out," he said.

After they shot Rusty, I wasn't allowed to go anywhere for a month for fear they'd shoot me when I came home, not even when I promised to take the long way around. But then Stitch showed up and nothing happened and they let me start going again. I went every day till the end of summer and after that whenever they'd let me. I must have looked through every pile of mail a hundred times before I found the letter from the Clearys. Mrs. Talbot was right about the post office. The letter was in somebody else's box.

by Ursula K. Le Guin

THE ASCENT OF THE NORTH FACE

art: John Pierard

If we were to attempt to list all of the author's works, prizes, and places of publication here, this introduction would probably be longer than the charming, atypical little piece which follows. However, for those few of you who do not devour her latest book as it appears, her most recent is *Compass Rose* (1982, Harper & Row).

2/21. Robert has reached Base Camp, with five Sherbets. He brought several copies of the *Times* from last month, which we devoured eagerly. Our team is now complete. Tomorrow the Advance Party goes up. Weather holds.
2/22. Accompanied Advance Party as far as the col below The Verandah before turning back. Winds up to 40 mph in gusts, but weather holds. Tonight Peter radioed all well at Verandah Camp.
The Sherbets are singing at their campfire.
2/23. Making ready. Tightened gossels. Weather holds.
2/24. Reached Verandah Camp easily in one day's climb. Tricky bit where the lattice and tongue-in-groove join, but Advance Party had left rope in place and we negotiated the overhang without real difficulty. Omu Ba used running jump and arrived earlier than rest of party. Inventive but undisciplined. Bad example to other Sherbets. Verandah Camp is level, dry, sheltered, far more comfortable than Base. Glad to be out of the endless rhododendrons. Snowing tonight.
2/25. Immobilised by snow.
2/26. Same.
2/27. Same. Finished last sheets of *Times* (adverts).
2/28. Derek, Nigel, Colin, and I went up in blinding snow and wind to plot course and drive pigils. Visibility very poor. Nigel whined.
Turned back at noon, reached Verandah Camp at 3 pip emma.
2/29. Driving rain and wind. Omu Ba drunk since 2/27. What on? Stove alcohol found to be low. Inventive but undisciplined. Chastisement difficult in circumstances.
2/30. Robert roped right up to the NE Overhang. Forced to turn back by Sherbets' dread of occupants. Insuperable superstition. We must eliminate plans for that route and go straight for the Drain Pipe. We cannot endure much longer here crowded up in this camp without newspapers. There is not room for six men in our tent and we hear the sixteen Sherbets fighting continually in theirs. I see now that the group is unnecessarily numerous even if some are under 5 foot 2 inches in height. Ten men, hand picked, would be enough. Visibility zero all day. Snow, rain, wind.
2/31. Hail, sleet, fog. Three Sherbets have gone missing.
3/1. Out of Bovril. Derek very low.
3/4. Missed entries during blizzard. Today bright sun, no wind. Snow dazzling on lower elevations; from here we cannot see the heights. Sherbets returned from unexplained absence with Ovaltine. Spirits high. Digging out and making ready all day for ascent (two groups) tomorrow.

3/5. Success! We are on the Verandah Roof! View overwhelming. Unattained summit of 2618 clearly visible in the SE. Second Party (Peter, Robert, eight Sherbets) not here yet. Windy and exposed camp site on steep slope. Shingles slippery with rain and sleet.
3/6. Nigel and two Sherbets went back down to the North Edge to meet Second Party. Returned 4 pip emma without having sighted them. They must have been delayed at Verandah Camp. Anxiety. Radio silent. Wind rising.
3/7. Colin strained shoulder on rope climbing up to the Window. Stupid, childish prank. Whether or not there are occupants, the Sherbets are very strong on not disturbing them. No sign of Second Party. Radio messages enigmatic, constant interference from KWJJ Country Music Station. Windy, but clear weather holds.
3/8. Resolved to go up tomorrow if weather holds. Mended doggles, replaced worn pigil-holders. Sherbets non-committal.
3/9. I am alone on the High Roof.

No one else willing to continue ascent. Colin and Nigel will wait for me three days at Verandah Roof Camp, Derek and four Sherbets began descent to Base. I set off with two Sherbets at 5 ack emma. Fine sunrise, in East, at 7:04 ack emma. Climbed steadily all day. Tricky bit at last overhang. Sherbets very plucky. Omu Ba while swinging on rope said, "Observe fine view, sah!" Exhausted at arrival at High Roof Camp, but the three advance Sherbets had tents set up and Ovaltine ready. Slope so steep here I feel I may roll off in my sleep!

Sherbets singing in their tent.

Above me the sharp Summit, and the Chimney rising sheer against the stars:

That is the last entry in Simon Interthwaite's journal.

Four of the five Sherbets with him at the High Roof Camp returned after three days to the Base Camp. They brought the journal, two clean vests, and a tube of anchovy paste back with them. Their report of his fate was incoherent. The Interthwaite Party abandoned the attempt to scale the North Face of 2647 Vine Street and returned to Calcutta.

In 1980 a Japanese party of Izutsu employees with four Sherbet guides attained the summit by a North Face route, rappelling across the study windows and driving pitons clear up to the eaves.Occupant protest was ineffective.

No one has yet climbed the Chimney.

by Cherie Wilkerson

$CALL

art: John W. Pierard

LINK4(CATHY)

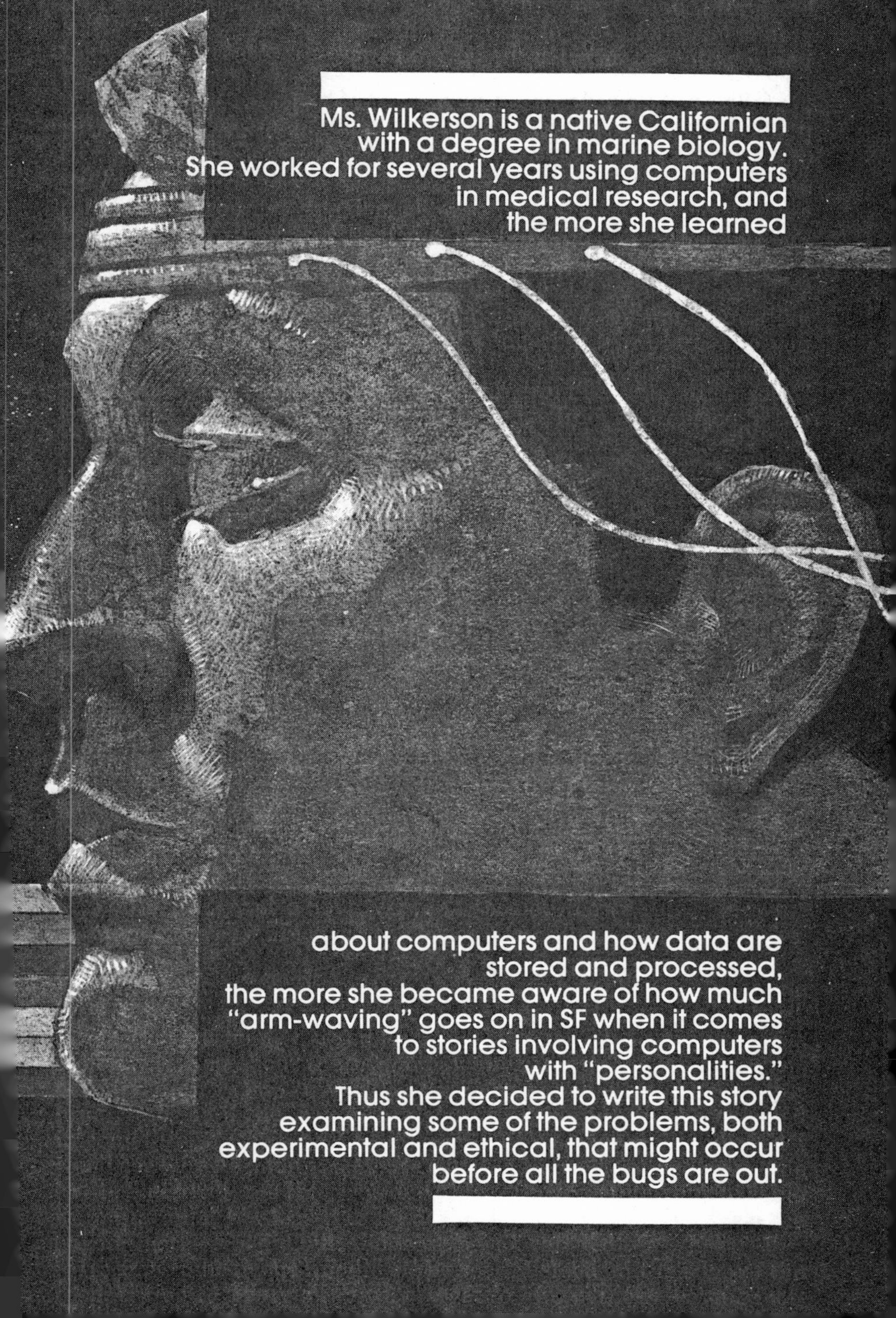

Ms. Wilkerson is a native Californian with a degree in marine biology. She worked for several years using computers in medical research, and the more she learned about computers and how data are stored and processed, the more she became aware of how much "arm-waving" goes on in SF when it comes to stories involving computers with "personalities." Thus she decided to write this story examining some of the problems, both experimental and ethical, that might occur before all the bugs are out.

The red-haired woman slipped out of her blouse and arched her back seductively. She was classically beautiful—long, silky hair, large green eyes, and a shapely body—and she was more than a little insane. She stared at Peter and laughed what should have been a low, throaty chuckle, but it had the sharp edge of dementia.

"Damn it," Peter Collins said, striking the counter with his fist. "It's not working. She's gone crazy on us." He glanced at the two men sitting beside him, then jabbed the console interrupt button, not bothering to exit the program. The startled woman disappeared. Disgruntled, Peter slumped in his seat and raked his fingers through his hair. "I thought we had it this time." He took a deep, calming breath.

"At least the tactile/auditory functions are coordinated," the technician said hopefully. Peter nodded to Dave without speaking, remembering some of the earlier trials. One woman had felt sticky and cool; he had been reminded of a honey-coated corpse. Another had a faint but peculiar odor and a flickering, purplish cast to her skin; while yet another had a voice that sounded out of synch with her facial movements.

"Yeah, we've got the sensory data under control," Peter agreed, "but we're still having trouble with the personality matrix. I don't understand what could be altering the data after they've been in the computer a while. And why are the changes so specific?"

"Maybe the personalities really *are* going insane," Dave said.

"Oh, sure," Peter said sarcastically. "No, I think it's just an error in the program somewhere."

"Well, you know whose job it is to fix that," Jim, the project manager, said, slipping off the receiving headset that enabled him to experience the sensory effect of the woman. Until now, Jim had remained silent, merely watching without comment. He clapped Peter on the shoulder and stood up. "I'll leave you two men to work this out." He glanced again at Peter, managing to create the impression of disapproval despite his smile, and left the computer room.

"Damn," Peter muttered.

"Think it'd do any good to get the data from another personality type?" Dave asked. "Maybe she was crazy and we just didn't know it.

Peter shrugged. "*She* was supposed to be as stable as they come," he said, waving his hand in the direction of where the woman had appeared. He unpeeled the control headband from his scalp, severing the link via the biofeedback unit to the computer. "Your turn," he said. "Before you do that, though, let's run a Test and Verify on the contents of addresses 3C100 through FF800 on level six. Maybe this time we'll find a pattern to the changes that'll tell us where we're going wrong."

Dave took the headset and punched in the location of the data to be tested. "Do you still think obtaining data from adult humans is better than trying to develop an artificial personality matrix or taking one from an infant?" he asked as the computer churned away at its task.

"Yeah, otherwise they act like robots." Peter rubbed his chin and frowned. "Heaven forbid that they act like robots. Or lunatics." He turned to face the technician. "Do you ever feel like a pimp doing this? Sometimes I feel like having cards made up: Peter Collins, procurer. Reasonable rates for selling out. If I didn't have so damn many bills . . . "

Dave stared at the floor in seeming contemplation of his ankles.

"Hell," Peter said softly. He had not meant to dump his problems on anyone else, particularly not Dave. "Don't mind me; it's not your fault that the only company interested in financing my project just happens to be a porno factory. Don't mind me," he repeated. "I've got a lot of things bothering me right now. I'm beginning to think *my* personality matrix is deteriorating." Dave gave him a crooked grin. Peter stood up. "I'll take a copy of the program home tonight and see what I can come up with. When the computer stops, get a printout of the results, and we'll get back on it in the morning."

"You're leaving?"

"Yeah, I've got to pick up Cathy for her doctor's appointment." He clapped his hand on the technician's shoulder. "You're doing a good job. I'm happy with the way you're holding up your end of it." Dave's grin made Peter feel better.

Peter checked his watch as he approached the house. He was a few minutes late; Cathy should have been home from school already. Pushing open the front door, he called her name. There was no answer. For a moment, he thought she was late, but then he saw her coat draped over the back of the couch. He tried once more.

"Cathy!" Again, his shout was met by silence. "Cathy, where are you?" He slowly pivoted in the living room, then began what he knew would be a futile search of the house and yard.

Afterward, Peter reentered the house and surveyed the living room from the kitchen doorway. Checking his watch again, he saw that Cathy should have been at the doctor's five minutes ago.

With sing-song weariness, he called out, "Cathy, I know you're in here! Come out this minute before I get angry with you and never talk to you again!"

First silence, then: "Would you really never talk to me?"

Peter turned around. Cathy's voice had come from somewhere in the kitchen, but he could not pinpoint the location. Feeling ridiculous, he asked, "Where are you?"

"Up here." He looked up and saw his six-year-old daughter peering over the top of the overhead cabinets. Her short hair—the result of chemotherapy—gave her the appearance of a young boy.

"How'd you get up there?" Cathy had squeezed herself into less than a foot of clearance between the ceiling and the top of the cabinet.

"I was hiding," she said, as if that answered the question. She opened a door and swung a sneakered foot over the edge until her toes touched a shelf.

Peter tensed as she shifted her position. "That won't hold your weight, Cathy."

"It did before." She swung her other leg down, ignoring her father's nervous efforts to help her, and stepped onto the counter. He picked her up then and set her on the floor.

"Why are you always hiding?" Peter asked as he propelled her into the living room. Cathy shrugged. "You know you had a doctor's appointment today." He held out her coat, but she just stared at it. "Why are you always hiding?" he repeated as he stuffed her arms into the sleeves. It pained him to see how frail she had become. Briskly, he buttoned up the jacket. "You manage to get yourself into the darnedest places. Why don't you just choose a favorite hiding place so I'll know where to look for you without feeling like such a fool?"

Cathy frowned, concentrating on his questions. "If you could find me, it wouldn't be hiding."

Her logical answer stopped Peter for a moment, then he laughed. "Well, you've got to stop hiding before your doctor's visits. We're late." He looked at his watch and frowned. "Again."

"It doesn't do any good to go to the doctor," Cathy said.

"Oh, Cathy," Peter said quietly. Her words hurt. He wanted to tell her that she was talking nonsense, but she had spoken the truth; her future looked as bleak as her expression. He sat down on the couch and pulled her up onto his lap, holding her tightly until he could face her without giving way to his emotions. "I guess we're too late anyway." Peter smoothed her short hair back from her forehead with his hand. "What am I going to do with you, huh?"

Cathy shrugged, taking his teasing seriously, and began fiddling with his shirt buttons. "Don't do that," he said wearily, firmly moving her hands from the button to her lap. "You're always twisting them off."

"If Catherine was here, she could sew them back on for you."

"Your *mother* is not here, so don't do that." Again he pushed his daughter's hands away from his shirt buttons.

"Why did Catherine leave?" Her innocent eyes stared at him, waiting to see his reaction.

Peter sighed. "Please stop calling your mother 'Catherine.' And please stop asking me why she left; I don't know any more about it than you do. And—" He held up his hand to cut off the question he knew was about to be asked next—"I haven't told Catherine—I mean your mother—about the visits to the doctors because I have no idea where she is. Does that answer your questions?"

Cathy appeared momentarily disheartened, then glanced up. "What's a prostitute?" She grinned, and a mischievous expression appeared in her eyes. He was reminded of her mother.

Peter stared at her for a moment before speaking. "Where on earth did you hear that?"

"At school. They say that you're making prostitutes. What are they?"

Peter grimaced. "Don't worry about it."

"Are the ladies—"

"The ladies are actresses," he insisted. "That's all—just actresses. Don't listen to what your schoolmates say, okay?" Cathy nodded reluctantly. "Besides, the ladies aren't real." His daughter gave him a puzzled look. "See, we hook you up to the computer and the computer stimulates a special part of your brain that makes you *think* there's a real lady in front of you. But there isn't really. What Daddy's trying to do is program the computer to pick up your thoughts so *you* can make the ladies do whatever you want them to do."

Cathy frowned in concentration, trying to understand. "Does that mean you can make them play with you?"

"Uh," Peter said, running his fingers through his hair, "that's one way to put it, yes. But it's not working anyway."

"Why not?"

"Something's wrong with the program for the personality—the part that makes them act like real people. After a while, they act like they are crazy."

"Maybe they don't like it in there."

Peter laughed. "You're starting to sound like Dave. They're not real, Cathy; they can't *really* go insane. It's just something wrong with—"

"Maybe they can't take it, living inside the computer," Cathy insisted, "but I could. Why don't you use me? I wouldn't go crazy."

"Oh, that would be just wonderful—my daughter, the . . . "

"The actress?" she finished for him. Peter stared at his daughter, wondering who was fooling whom. "I'd *like* to be an actress, Daddy."

"Don't be silly, Cathy. I can't—"

"Call me Catherine," she said, grinning. The grin faltered. "Uh-oh."

Peter sighed. "Now look what you've done." Cathy contritely extended her hand holding the shirt button.

No matter how many times Peter reran his personal accounting program, the results were the same: dismal. He leaned back in his chair and stared at the figures on the screen. If only I had more money, I could find a doctor who could cure Cathy and I could go to work for myself, he thought. It was a threadbare thought, frayed around the edges, and it no longer offered the comfort it used to give him. Gradually, he became aware of the blinking call light on his terminal.

Peter exited his program to link up with the caller on the net. When the project manager's call sign appeared on the screen, he pushed the "receive" button. As he had done every day for the last two weeks, Jim indicated he intended to dump the latest results of Dave's program analysis directly into memory. Peter would go over the printout of the results later, but he was convinced that the problems with the personality matrix were not due to a software error.

After transmission, Peter waited for Jim to exit, but another on-line message appeared instead.

JT: YOU COMING BACK IN SOON?

Peter stared at the words for a moment. So that's what's bothering him, he thought; he's worried about my being gone from work. PC: RETURN TOMORROW. WORKING ON IDEA FOR NEW PM.

JT: NEW PM? DID YOU FIND PROGRAM ERROR?

PC: NO. He considered explaining but did not want to continue the conversation. CATHY IS IN HOSPITAL AGAIN. Why did I bother to write that? Peter wondered. Jim already knows it.

JT: SORRY. WHEN SHE COMES HOME, BRING HER IN TO SEE YOUR WORK.

Sorry? Peter said to himself, angered by Jim's suggestion. All you care about is your damn project. Well, it's not your project; it's mine, and my daughter comes first. Peter imagined the words appearing on Jim's terminal, letter by letter, and took satisfaction in the fantasy. He wrote instead: SHE DOES WANT TO BE ONE OF YOUR ACTRESSES. He wished scorn could come across on the screen.

JT: INFANT PM'S DON'T WORK.

The message infuriated Peter for more than one reason. Who the hell are you to tell me what will or won't work? Peter thought. He addressed the other reason, however: CATHY IS NOT AN INFANT. He knew he was making a mistake but felt compelled to continue. PM FROM CATHY IS MATURE ENOUGH TO BE ADULT BUT STILL ADAPTABLE TO COMPUTER. WILL NOT DISINTEGRATE IN STRANGE ENVIRONMENT. PREPUBESCENT PM IS THE ANSWER.

JT: BRING HER IN.

PC: NO. He knew his ego had gotten him into this mess. Although he had figured out a way to modify a child's personality parameters to adult responses, he had no intention of using Cathy. N. O. ABSOLUTELY NOT. FORGET IT.

JT: WHY? END RESULT COMPLETELY DIFFERENT.

PC: NOT DIFFERENT ENOUGH.

JT: NOT TRUE. BRING HER IN.

Peter knew he was being foolish about it; the final result would be totally different. Cathy's modified personality, both aged and cleared of her idiosyncrasies, would bear no resemblance whatsoever to the original, particularly after it was put into the visual and phonetic data of someone else. Still, the idea of using his own daughter horrified him. NO, he typed again, but he felt himself weakening. If Cathy's PM worked, he would not have to worry about her medical bills.

Angered by his weakness, he reached to exit the net when Jim typed: WHEN IS CATHY'S BIRTHDAY? DUPLICATE OF HERSELF WOULD MAKE A GREAT GIFT.

Peter stopped. "You bastard," he muttered. Cathy's birthday was far away—too far away. He knew that Jim was aware of the fact, too. He punched the exit key and turned away from the console.

Cathy pushed at the headband, preventing Dave from putting

it on her head. She glanced fearfully at him. "It won't hurt, Cathy. Honest," he said, then looked to Peter, silently pleading for help.

"It prickles a little at first," Peter told her, "but it doesn't hurt."

Hesitantly, she placed the band of metal around her forehead, then flinched as Dave adjusted it. "See, it doesn't hurt, does it?" he said. Suddenly shy, Cathy ducked her head without answering. "So you think the personalities really are going insane after all."

"I'm afraid I'm being dragged, kicking and screaming, to that conclusion," Peter said, as Dave ran calibrations on the biofeedback unit.

"You know what this means, don't you? It means we've created a sentient computer."

Peter laughed. "Not hardly. Let's not get carried away, shall we?" But Dave merely grinned.

"Daddy, will this make an actress out of me after you do this?" Cathy asked, pointing at the headband.

Again Peter laughed. "No, this is just the first step. You'll be plenty tired of it before we get finished with you."

"OK, Cathy," Dave said, "I want you to pay close attention to what I say and remember not to move unless I tell you." Cathy started to nod her head then froze, an anxious look on her face. "I want you to think of a quiet place you like to go—somewhere you can be all by yourself. I want you to pretend you are there right now."

Peter watched as Dave measured her alpha waves, then gradually induced a semi-hypnotic state. He knew beyond all reasonable doubt that this time, the personality matrix would work. It suddenly occurred to him that in the extensive databanks of the computer network, his daughter would survive her own death, although only for a short time, until they modified her data. The prospect of having to experience her death twice made him shudder, but another idea—a frightening, tantalizing idea—chilled him more. Why twice? he wondered. Why not only once? He stared at the dreamily smiling girl before him and closed his mind to the thought of her dying at all.

Peter held his daughter on his knee. "OK, first of all, you put the cube stack—that's this thing—in here," he said, matching his actions with his words. "Now you come over to this terminal and type in $DUPFIL=UL(0-C100,S1,6). When all those words stop, you enter $CALL LINK4(CATHY). That's the program for you. Do you want to do it?" He waited for a response, but the effort to decide seemed to be too much for her. "Or do you want me to do it?" He called up the program. "Someday there'll be a whole lot of programs with different people in them."

"Where is she?" Cathy asked.

Peter pushed the appropriate buttons, and the sensory image of his daughter as she had been several months ago appeared before them. Cathy on his lap stared at the Cathy standing in front of them, who stared back. Peter stopped himself before punching the exit button. It's just an image, he told himself; it's not real. Yet he knew that something else bothered him. He looked at his daughter's gaunt body and dry, taut skin that seemed to bruise at even the lightest touch. In fact, her arms and ankles were bruised now from the injections she had been receiving.

The duplicate Cathy turned to Peter, her expression troubled, her voice wavery. "Is that how I'm going to look?" she asked.

"No," Peter said, feeling that showing Cathy to herself had been a terrible mistake. "You won't change unless I make you change."

The girl shifted on his lap. "I still don't have any hair," she said listlessly. Peter looked from girl to girl, not knowing to whom Cathy referred. "Daddy, I'm tired and want to go home."

Relieved, he hit the exit key, then removed their headsets. Cathy settled back against his chest, more from fatigue than as a show of affection. Peter wanted to hold her tightly, but he was afraid of hurting her. "Are you hungry? I'll take you out for a hamburger." At the mention of her favorite food, a ghost of the familiar grin she shared with her mother appeared briefly, then faded away. Like everything I love, Peter thought. I'm going to miss you, he felt like saying, just like I miss your mother.

"Let's go home," he said instead. As if she were not made of flesh and bone but some lighter substance, he picked her up and carried her out. As he was leaving, he passed the technician in the hallway. "I'm going to take a little vacation. I'll be back to work on the modifications later. Let Jim know, will you, Dave?"

"You going to be gone long?" he asked, then blushed when Peter hesitated and glanced at Cathy.

"Not very long," Peter said softly. "Not long enough anyway."

"About time we began the modifications, don't you think?" Jim asked Peter as he entered the building. This morning greeting had long since replaced "Good morning."

"Yeah, I'll get around to it," Peter said reluctantly.

"Make it today," Jim said. He started to turn away. "Perhaps it would be easier for you if your wife were here."

"My wife skipped town without a trace," Peter said, angry that Jim had seemed to pick the thought out of his head.

The manager stared at him. "Don't you think you're just running away from your problems this way?"

Peter thought of his wife disappearing, "in search of herself," she had said; his daughter disappearing into her hiding places; and his own ill-defined idea of preserving his daughter in a computer now that she had died. "Running away from our problems is a family trait, I'm afraid," he said, his anger fading. He stopped in the doorway to the computer room. "I'd like to be alone for a while," he said before entering.

Peter called up the program for his daughter's sensory image, and Cathy appeared out of thin air. She ran to his lap.

"Hi, Daddy," she said, settling herself on his knees. The effect never ceased to astonish Peter. Although he knew that the sensation was imaginary—merely electrical stimulation of his brain—it felt as if his daughter were really on his lap. He frowned slightly as Cathy fiddled with his shirt buttons. He resisted the automatic response of pushing her hands away; it might feel as if she were tugging on his shirt, but she could not do any damage. "I missed you," she continued. "Did you bring me anything?"

"Just me, that's all." He smiled, then stopped when he remembered what he intended to do. He had foreseen having to experience her death twice; he had not, however, realized he would think of himself as a murderer.

Cathy looked up at him and showed her familiar slow grin. "Guess what!"

"What?"

"I'm not alone."

"What do you mean?"

"There are a couple of actresses in here besides me. Pretty ladies with—" She held her hands in front of her chest to indicate large breasts. She giggled.

It took several seconds before the implication of what she had said sunk in. Peter was immediately furious, not for entirely rational reasons. Cathy's sensory image seemed as real to him as his daughter had been; the discovery that Jim—or more likely Dave under Jim's orders—had modified Cathy's data, adapting it to the adult responses the company wanted, felt to Peter as if his daughter had been corrupted.

Cathy tugged at his shirt buttons again. "Are you mad at me?" she asked. Peter shook his head. The "daughter" he held was an illusion, and the "Cathy" who had been corrupted was not this one. He felt as if his hold on reality were slipping. This is the time to end it, he thought. He listened without hearing as Cathy chatted about what she wanted to do when she grew up. It was all too easy, he knew, to believe that his daughter were really here, alive and healthy. I've got to do it now, he told himself angrily.

Something in his manner betrayed his intentions to Cathy. She looked at him solemnly but with a touch of fear. "Are you going to . . . "

Peter could not help her finish the sentence. "I have to, Cathy. This isn't right. I should have known better, but I fooled myself. I've fooled myself over and over again, and this is the price I have to pay."

"Have I been bad?" she asked, bewildered.

"Oh, Cathy," he said, holding her tightly. "Of course not." Her face had the same slightly confused and frightened expression as when she had lain in the hospital bed for the last time. "It won't hurt, sweetheart. I promise."

She stared up at him. "Okay," she said, then put her hand in his.

Peter knew there was something he had to say, but he could think of nothing. A second chance, he told himself; what would you have told her if you had had a second chance? As the distinction between his daughter and his wife blurred, he said, "I love you, Cathy. I don't want you to leave. I'm going to miss you more than anything in the world."

Cathy flung her arms around him, and as they held each other, Peter hit the console interrupt button. He was left with nothing.

Moments later, he looked up at the clock and saw that hours had passed. He pulled the cube stack containing his daughter's data out of the computer and placed it in the laser erase unit. For a second, he considered duplicating the cube or stealing the backup cube, but instead, he turned the unit on. The laser eradicated all trace of the cube's contents.

Peter opened the file for the backup cube, and for the first time he carefully examined all the other cubes. What he had assumed were still the preliminary trials had been changed and now bore new labels: CATHY2, CATHY3, and so on. He picked up the last one, CATHY8, and put it in the computer.

The woman stared at Peter. A shadow of Cathy's smile played across her lips, but this expression was lascivious. Stunned, Peter interrupted the program and pulled the cube out of the computer. He stared at it, then thought of the most effective way he could devise for quitting his job and getting revenge for Cathy. Twenty minutes later, he had erased all of the cubes that even remotely had anything to do with the project.

Heady with what he had done, he sauntered outside and into Jim's office. "I quit," he told the manager.

Jim looked up from his desk and after a moment's hesitation, nodded. "I thought you might. Did you erase Cathy's data?"

"Yes, I erased the data for Cathy." Peter paused for effect. "I erased *all* the data for every Cathy, for every goddamn simulacrum made."

Jim seemed unconcerned. He reached inside his desk and pulled out a cube stack. "You forgot this one." Peter stared at the cube, suddenly realizing why Jim had asked him if he had *erased* Cathy's data, not *modified* it. "This is CATHY9," Jim said, confirming what Peter had already guessed.

"You goddam—" He snatched the cube from Jim's upheld hand. "I'll destroy this one, too." He knew the gesture would be futile.

"We figured you might do this, so we made plenty of duplicates. And no," he said, answering Peter's thoughts, "we don't have any of the original Cathys. They're of no use to us. Go ahead and take this one. She won't remind you of your daughter one bit; we made sure of that." Jim shoved the cube stack toward Peter from where he had left it. "Take it," he insisted. "You might just enjoy it."

Peter took great enjoyment out of the sight of Jim picking himself up off the floor. The manager's nose bled profusely, and his eyes were already swelling. Jim wiped his face as he pushed his chair upright.

"You ought to do something about that swivel chair," Peter said calmly as he walked slowly out of the room. "It could kill you." Jim's threats to call the police only made Peter smile.

Peter stared bleakly at the figures on his home terminal. He leaned back in his chair and idly picked up the cube stack labelled CATHY9. He had projected it only once before, when he had awakened in the middle of the night with the insane but compelling idea that he had been fooled, that his daughter's data actually existed in the cube. He had been wrong. The woman bore absolutely no resemblance to Cathy.

The call indicator flashed, and Peter linked up with the caller. He read the message first with amusement, then with growing seriousness. Ignoring the request for a confirming reply, Peter cut the link with the net.

"So they're having problems and want me back," he said aloud.

He did not want to return, but he needed the money. Besides, the note of desperation in Jim's request did his ego good. "Oh, what the hell," he said, getting to his feet. It would do his bank balance good as well.

Peter strode into the computer room and found Jim and Dave huddled over a printout. "Thanks for coming, Peter," Jim said awkwardly. Peter acknowledged the implicit apology with a nod.

"So the women are behaving erratically. Dementia? You weren't clear over the net."

Jim shook his head frowning. "No, it's not insanity. It's something different. Hell, I don't know what it is. I'll leave you two to figure it out."

After Jim had gone, Peter said, "Just like old times, huh? So what's the problem?"

Dave tried to look serious but failed. He laughed. "The women aren't behaving erratically; they're behaving consistently."

"I don't understand. What is it they're consistently doing?"

"Saying no."

"Saying . . . ?" It struck him what Dave meant, and he laughed. "Well, that certainly hampers business, doesn't it? Can't turn much of a profit when the ladies keep saying no. Are these on the market yet?"

"Oh, yeah," Dave said. "You should hear the complaints!"

"I can imagine." He laughed again. "Well, let me see this." Peter had written the program so that the wearer of the control headset could direct the responses of the sensory image to a large degree; the women could do anything that did not directly contradict the express desires of the wearer. Compliant is what Jim had called the design.

Dave called up the program as Peter adjusted the control headset. A woman resembling CATHY9 appeared. She smiled at Peter, and he decided that if she had been a real person, he would have liked her a lot.

"Come here and have a seat," he said, indicating his lap. She walked over to him without a trace of reluctance. Everything's okay so far, he thought, then noticed that Dave was smiling in obvious anticipation of what would be coming next. Peter wrapped his arms around her and she still offered no resistance. He gave the technician a look as if to say, 'It just takes the proper technique.'

Dave laughed openly at him. "Just wait and see."

Peter shrugged and returned to the business at hand. It had

been some time since he had held a woman in his lap. Embarrassed by an audience, he kissed her neck. She turned her head to face him, placing her forehead against the side of his head. Although it was not a direct rebuff, it made further advances difficult. He could hear Dave's laughter.

Not wanting to admit defeat, he leaned back a little and placed his hand along her cheek, guiding her face toward his. This time the rejection was not subtle; she pulled away and shook her head.

"Why not?" Peter asked, suddenly feeling as if he was back in high school on a first date. She glanced under her lashes at him, and for one shocked moment, he saw his daughter in her expression. She shrugged, and the resemblance disappeared. Disturbed by what he had just seen, he turned to the technician. "I thought all idiosyncratic elements of Cathy's personality had been eradicated."

"They had. So you saw it, too," Dave said. "I thought I saw a resemblance to your daughter about the same time as we began to get complaints from people. Take a look at this printout of CATHY9 and compare it to this one."

After Peter had studied the sheets of paper, he indicated the printout in his left hand. "This is Cathy's original data?" Dave nodded. "Well, it looks like the modified personality matrix is deteriorating back to the original. I'd advise you to use another PM. Cathy was a bit headstrong."

"It won't work for our purposes and you know it."

Peter feigned surprise. "What do you mean?"

Dave laughed. "The project is screwed. If we use a willing adult, the personality deteriorates into insanity. If we use a child and modify the behavioral aspects to adult responses, the personality deteriorates back to the child. Either way, we end up with a personality unsuited to what this company wants."

"Ah, well, I *did* find out what the problem was, didn't I? The terms of the agreement were that I find the problem, not the solution." Peter knew he sounded smug, but he did not care. Cathy had done a good job—one he had not been able to do. "I hope this won't hurt *you.*"

"Oh, I'm real heartbroken about the prospect of having to leave this place. I'd better go break the news to Jim. He's expecting it, I think, but that won't make it any easier." He got up to leave.

"Good luck," Peter said.

"Good luck," the woman echoed.

Peter jumped then laughed. He'd forgotten the woman on his lap. "Well, say goodbye because I'm going to exit the program."

The woman shrugged. "That's the story of my life." She got up off his lap and waited expectantly. He punched in the usual exit sigh, but the program did not respond.

"More changes," he muttered, searching the menu list of options for the exit sign. When he felt a hand at his knee, he turned, puzzled that the woman would voluntarily touch him.

His daughter climbed onto his lap. "Hi," she said, grinning. "I'm back."

"Where the hell did you come from?" He glanced around the room to see if the other woman was still there, but the room was empty. Cathy gave him her familiar grin. "How'd you get here? I erased all the data. What happened?"

She hesitated, then said simply, "I hid."

"You what?"

She shrugged. "I hid."

Peter laughed. Hugging her, he said, "You're crazy, you know that? You can't hide inside a computer." He did not know how she had done it, but then, he had never known half the time how she—or rather the original Cathy—had gotten into the places he had found her. Perhaps Dave's grandiose idea of creating sentience in the computer had not been so far off the mark as he had originally thought. But Peter did not care. "I'm glad you're back. But what am I going to do with you?"

"Take me home." Cathy pointed to the drawer with the cube stack. "We traded places because she was bored. It's neat what you can do in there."

"I just bet."

"You're going to.take me home, aren't you? You're not mad at .me?"

"Of course I'll take you home."

"Daddy?" She looked up at him with her seemingly innocent brown eyes. Running her hand over her short hair, she said, "Will you make my hair longer, just like Mom's?"

Peter looked at her for a moment, contemplating the changes that were to occur in his life if he were to take her back with him. He knew it was neither right nor wise, but he decided he didn't care.

"Sure," he said, "I'll modify the data so you'll have long hair. Is there anything else you want?"

Cathy ducked her head, fiddling with the buttons on his shirt, as usual. She looked up at him, the slow grin spreading across her face. "Call me Catherine," she said.

HEAVENLY FLOWERS

by Pamela Sargent

The author's short fiction can be found in *F & SF*, *IAsfm*, and other science fiction magazines and anthologies. Two of her novels, *The Alien Upstairs* and *Earthseed* came out this year from Doubleday and Harper & Row respectively.

art: Broeck Steadman

The sun was too bright. Maisie tried to ignore the ache in her joints and the gnawing pain in her intestines. She sat in the back seat of an old Ford station wagon, her head resting on Gene's shoulder. Junior, sitting on Maisie's left, squealed as he caught sight of a thick, green bush and a patch of blue wildflowers, their colors bright against the desolate, pockmarked ground.

Lydia was driving, and the car began to lurch, jostling Maisie and making her ache even more. Talia began to bounce on the front seat and whined softly as her father Drew stared out the window, trying to ignore the girl.

"Need anything?" Gene asked Maisie.

"I can hold out."

He patted her shoulder. The car stalled. Lydia gunned the motor, then switched off the ignition.

Drew sighed. "Better get out and stretch," he said.

Everyone got out and stood by the side of the highway while Drew opened the hood and fiddled with the engine. Lydia tied Talia's bonnet firmly on the child's head, then said to Junior, "Put on your hat."

"Aw."

"Put it on right now."

Junior put on his oversized fedora. Maisie adjusted her wide-brimmed hat and rolled down her sleeves. They had allowed themselves plenty of time, but she had hoped that they would arrive early; she did not want to miss any of the festivities. This ceremony was special, the thirtieth anniversary, and perhaps the last time a nationwide ceremony would be held. Radio broadcasts had alerted everyone; people from all over the country would be there. Maisie's family had been traveling for two days and would reach the fairground by the following evening if Drew did not have to spend too much time nursing the Ford. She suspected that this was the last long trip the car would ever make.

"I could use some now," Maisie said to Gene.

He grunted and reached inside his shirt pocket, took out a pouch, and tapped some weed into a cigarette paper while Lydia looked on, frowning her disapproval. Gene passed the lighted joint to Maisie, who toked on it, then handed it back.

The highway, pocked with potholes and partly covered by drifting sand, stretched out toward the horizon in the east and disappeared among brown hills in the west. Maisie squinted; another vehicle was approaching from the east, crawling along the road as it weaved its way around the potholes and broken asphalt. As it came nearer, she saw that it was a red Subaru, and wondered how its owner had kept it going; parts for Japanese cars had become hard to find lately.

The Subaru pulled up behind the Ford and a middle-aged man got out; his passenger stayed inside. The man rolled down his sleeves and adjusted his hat. Maisie took a last toke and handed the roach to Gene, who leaned over, stubbed it out, and tucked it into his pocket.

"Hey!" the stranger said as he walked over to them.

"Hey," Gene answered.

"You going to the fairground?"

"You bet," Maisie said, thinking it was a foolish question.

"So am I. Jim Fairbairn." He stuck out his gloved hand and Gene shook it. "That's my wife, Dora. She's not feeling so good at the moment."

"Gene Sakowitz."

"Mrs. Sakowitz?" Jim Fairbairn said as he shook Maisie's hand.

She shook her head. "Maisie Torrance. Gene's my man, but we aren't married. This is our daughter, Lydia Simpson—that's her husband, Drew, by the car. And this is Talia, and that's their boy Junior over there."

Junior was pissing at the side of the road. "Say hello to the man," Lydia shouted. Junior buttoned his trousers, wandered over, and mumbled a greeting while Talia stared. Maisie wiped her face with one sleeve; the sun was hot.

"How's your car holding up?" Jim asked.

"It's doing all right," Maisie said. "How far have you come, Jim?"

"Ohio."

"Long way." Maisie cleared her throat, which was dry from the pot, and took a breath, feeling better; her pain had been dulled. "Been out before?"

"Not since I was a kid. This highway goes all the way to the fairground, doesn't it? I checked an old map before I left."

"Yeah. But I wouldn't follow it if I were you. About twenty miles from here, you run into a hot spot—you have to take the long way around if you don't want to get cooked."

Jim frowned. "Maybe I can follow you."

Gene shrugged. "If you want."

"I'd be obliged."

"Keep your hat on, young man," Lydia shouted at Junior, who was swinging it over his head.

Jim glanced at the boy. "Nice-looking kid. You must be proud of him."

Lydia nodded. Maisie tapped Gene's pocket. He took out his weed, rolled another joint, and handed it to Jim. "For your wife," Maisie said. "It helps the pain a little."

"Thanks."

Drew had finished with the engine and was filling the tank with alcohol. When he was done, he motioned to them. Lydia picked Talia up, lugging the girl's heavy body back to the car; Jim opened the door for her.

Drew took the wheel. They rode on, the Subaru trailing them. Lydia turned toward Maisie, resting her arm on the seat. "You didn't have to make a point of telling him you and Father aren't married."

Maisie was about to reply, but caught herself. Younger people set more store by such ceremonies, and she couldn't blame them for it; they longed for the signs of order and normality. But only one ceremony mattered to her, the one they were soon to witness, the one that reminded Maisie of how much she had lost and of how lucky she was to be alive.

The plain was covered by tents and pavilions, and Maisie's family had to set up camp on the edge of the grounds after arriving at the fairground. There was one consolation; a big truck carrying tanks of water had parked near them, so they would not have to go far for that commodity.

Maisie sat against the Ford while Drew and Lydia settled the children inside their tent. Gene, after pawing through his collection of items for barter, had taken out a tape cassette to swap for some water. A man on horseback rode by and waved; he was followed by a woman offering to trade flashlights and pencils for dried meat.

Gene returned with two large bottles and two men. The older man was stooped and wizened, but Maisie caught her breath as she stared at the younger one. Under his hat, his handsome face glowed with good health; she had not seen such a beautiful young man in a long time. As the young man sat down, he bowed his head, as though aware of Maisie's reaction.

Gene introduced Maisie, then gestured at the two men. "David Chung. And this is his son, Paul."

Paul brushed back a lock of black hair, smiled at Maisie, then looked down again. David grinned. "We've only been here a few hours, and Paul's had offers already."

Maisie said, "I'm not surprised."

"I have two grandchildren already," David went on. "One of them takes after Paul."

"We've got a strong grandson." Maisie did not mention poor Talia.

"I know—Gene told me."

"We met over by the water truck," Gene said. "David came all the way from California."

"I don't know if we should have come at all," Paul blurted out. "We dwell on it too much. Maybe it's better just to forget."

Maisie shook her head. "Even if we tried, we couldn't. And we shouldn't. People have to remember. It's important for you young folks to keep up the ceremony after we're gone."

"How?"

Paul had asked a good question, and Maisie did not have an answer. David pulled a pipe out of his pocket and tapped in some weed. "Sinsemilla," he said proudly.

Gene sighed. "I didn't think there was any left."

"We still grow some." David lit the pipe, puffed, and passed it to Maisie, who drew in the smoke deeply. She felt a rush as she handed the pipe to Gene. Paul did not smoke; like all young people, he guarded his health, avoiding such habits.

When they had finished David's marijuana, Gene got out a little of his homegrown, and they passed the pipe again. Lydia glared at them as she came over for one of the water jars; as she caught sight of Paul, she straightened up and stared at him. Maisie giggled as Lydia retreated to the tent.

"Your daughter?" David asked. "The one with the healthy boy?"

Maisie nodded; the pot made her want to laugh again.

"What do you think?" David said to Paul.

"Maybe we can bargain," the young man answered.

"What do you think?" David asked Maisie.

"You'll have to talk to Drew—that's her husband. And Lydia'll want to know Paul's history."

Paul got up and went to the tent. Drew and Lydia came outside and talked to him while the old people finished the pot. Maisie, noticing that the sun was almost down, took off her hat and fanned herself with it as she watched.

At last Drew went to the car, took out a pack, rummaged in it, and removed a vial, handing it to Paul. As Lydia approached, Drew took her hand, kissed her on the cheek, then gave her hand to the other man. That's Drew, Maisie thought, formal as always—never neglecting custom.

Paul led Lydia away. "Hope it works out," David said.

"Hope so." Maisie, stoned, was feeling optimistic. Her own attempts with other men at past festivals had resulted in two miscarriages, but she had lost two of Gene's children as well. Lydia was stronger.

They sat, talking of old times until it was completely dark. David took out a pocket flashlight while Gene and Maisie showed him some of their treasures—a matchbox bearing the University of Wisconsin seal, a Phillips screwdriver, a Boy Scout handbook, a pair of scissors.

When Lydia returned, she went directly to the tent. David stood up. "Better get some rest. Things start early."

"See you tomorrow," Gene said. He helped Maisie to her feet. "Feeling all right?"

"I'm fine."

"I think Drew gave a lot of the medicine to Paul."

Maisie was suddenly resentful; Drew should have asked her first. But Lydia's chance at another healthy baby was more important, and she could get by without the pills for now.

The clear blue morning sky promised a good day for the ceremonies. Maisie sat on the hood of the Ford, estimating the crowd; there were close to three thousand people on the plain, and she supposed that almost every town had sent several of its citizens.

Two rivers of people were streaming toward the distant silos; for that extra thrill, they would miss much of the ceremony itself. Others were seating themselves near the raised platform of wood in the center of the field, putting up umbrellas and canopies to shade themselves.

Lydia strode toward her from the tent. "Mother? We're going over to Paul's tent with Junior, and then we're going to try to get a good seat. Need anything?"

"I'm fine." Maisie frowned. "Twice with Paul?"

"That was the bargain. And Drew thinks Junior ought to meet him."

"He would. He must have given Paul a lot of pills for two times."

"I know. I'm sorry. But you understand." Lydia lowered the veil on her floppy blue hat, hiding her face.

"Yes, I understand."

"We'll see you afterwards. Talia's in the tent—I gave her something, so she should sleep through everything, but you'd better look in on her once in a while."

"Sure."

Lydia walked off with Drew and Junior. Five young people

passed Maisie on their way toward the platform; their faces were attractive, but she could not know what their loose, flowing garments hid. Two of the boys wore Panama hats, another had a sombrero, and the two girls were wearing large white bonnets. Maisie adjusted her hat, lowering the brim. She had put it on at dawn, out of habit, though she could not benefit from its protection now. Two veiled women passed, their long skirts swaying around their legs.

Jim Fairbairn got out of his car and came over to her. "Going to look for a seat?"

"We're staying here." She paused. "We've got binoculars."

Jim whistled. "Lucky you." He glanced toward the platform. Several old soldiers were on the stand, fiddling with the sound system; they would soon be on their way to the silos. "As I recall," Jim went on, "they don't get started until late afternoon."

"That's right. But if you want a good seat, you'd better go now."

"I'm staying here. Dora's pretty sick. I don't want to leave her alone." He lowered his voice. "She's the one who really wanted to come. I didn't think she'd make it this far. She just wanted to be here, even if she doesn't see anything."

"I can understand that."

Jim leaned against the car. "We were just little kids when it happened, so we don't really know what it was like before. It must be harder for you."

Maisie did not reply at first, wishing Jim had not spoken of that. "We're alive," she said. "We're thankful for that." She could say it now; she could not have said it thirty years ago, when she had longed for death and had cursed herself for surviving.

"Well, I'd better get back to Dora."

As Jim got back into his car, Gene returned with David Chung. "Dave's going to sit with us. Think we'll see well enough from here?"

Maisie lifted her binoculars and focused on the platform. "Sure."

"The Chinese envoy's here," David said. "And a Russian from the Council. They're really doing things up this year."

Maisie nodded. "I heard on the radio that we sent people to their ceremonies, too."

"I wonder what we'll do next year," Gene murmured.

Maisie thought, I won't be doing much of anything. She climbed down from the car. "I'm going to check on Talia, and then rest for a while." She hobbled away from the men, pressing her lips together, trying to ignore the pain.

The sky was still unclouded that afternoon as Maisie waited for the ceremony to begin. The crowd, noisy throughout the day, was settling down. People had positioned themselves near the platform on chairs and blankets and under protective umbrellas and veils while vendors circulated among them, trying to make a few last trades for food and drink before the ceremony started.

She glanced at Jim's car; he and Dora were still inside. Taking the binoculars from David, she gazed at the platform. Various dignitaries were already seated under the canopy; one old soldier, dressed in an officer's uniform, got up, crossed the platform, and knelt before a group of old people sitting near the edge. They gazed sightlessly past him. The old people, representing all of those who had been blinded thirty years before by glancing at the approaching destruction, had a special place of honor.

The officer beat his chest and wailed as the crowd grew silent. Then the president rose and approached the microphone.

"Testing," he said, and the ominous word rang out over the plain. "Testing." He adjusted his hat, a Stetson bearing the Stars and Stripes, then struck his chest with one fist. "I accuse myself." He was a lean young man with the scars of skin cancer surgery on his face, and could not have been more than a child thirty years ago, but the words were part of the ceremony. "I accuse myself of murder. I am guilty of genocide. Billions lie in graves because of me."

The Russian was at his side; he wore a fedora with an embroidered hammer and sickle. "I accuse myself," the Russian said as the president yielded the microphone. "I am a murderer, guilty of the worst crime in human history." The Chinese envoy, a small woman wearing a cap with a red star, then said the same words in a high-pitched singsong.

Maisie drew up her knees, resting her elbows on them as she gazed through her binoculars. Gene and David took turns looking through the other pair. The three dignitaries on the platform lifted their eyes to the sky.

"We brought death on the world, and our guilt will never be washed away," the president cried. "Speak the names."

The crowd below uttered an indistinct barrage of names. Maisie put down her binoculars and whispered as many as she could remember; her father, her mother, her two brothers, her best friends. She blocked her memories of that day, thinking only of the names. Gene rocked as he spoke; David covered his eyes. Within an hour, a billion had died; within a month, another billion; within a year, most of the world. Maisie had found that out only later.

As the murmuring faded, the president spoke again. "Let the ceremony begin."

Maisie lifted her binoculars. The president knelt, and others on the stand approached, carrying long sticks, tapping them on the president's shoulder as they passed. This part of the ceremony depicted the death of the president who had launched the missiles, who had been beaten to death by an angry, dying mob when he had emerged from his shelter. Maisie muttered the name of that man, making it a curse. The Russian and the Chinese were also tapped with the sticks, though rumor had it that the Russian leader had been assassinated in his shelter by his successor, while the Chinese leader had committed suicide.

A woman stepped forward, stood near the president, and wailed as she clutched her belly, symbolizing the fear of mothers for their children and the birth of the maimed and deformed. Another woman was strewing dirt on the platform, a reminder of the poisoned earth.

Maisie lowered her arms. The pain was returning. She clenched her teeth, determined to get through the rest of the ceremony somehow. A few people on the edges of the crowd seemed restless. A couple of small children, obviously bored, were poking at each other; a group of young people whispered among themselves. The ceremony meant little to them. Maisie shook her head. They had to be made to remember.

"Never again," the president shouted, and the crowd took up the cry: "Never again." The young people Maisie was watching looked up; she saw their lips move. "Never again." At least they were saying the words.

"We have disarmed," the president went on. "Never again will so many die. Never again will men fight other men. Never again will the world know mass weapons of destruction. At last we have what so many sought—universal peace, a world council, and good will toward all our fellows."

"A little late," David muttered.

Maisie touched his arm. "At least you have Paul."

"I hope he and your daughter have a good, strong child."

"I hope so, too."

"I think it's a mistake—not having any more national ceremonies after this one."

"Maybe. But there'd be nothing to hold them with. That's good, though. We'll be rid of them all after tonight."

"But the custom's important," David said.

"This is my last ceremony. I'll never see another one anyway."

"I don't think I will, either."

The sun was setting. The people on the platform were now lifting tattered flags, holding them up before the spectators, then slapping them down on the planks, stamping on them with their feet. Stars and stripes fell next to a red flag bearing the hammer and sickle, followed by a red star, the Union Jack, a maple leaf, the Tricolor, the Sword and Crescent, the Star of David, and various other banners. Some of the flags were so ragged that it was impossible to tell which countries they had once represented.

A woman marched forward with the world flag, a phoenix rising from ashes against a black background, and the audience sighed, then was still. Maisie trembled at the silence, which reminded her of the quiet that had pressed in around her when she had emerged to find the world in ruins.

As the sun disappeared behind the distant mountains, she heard the rumble, and clutched at David's hand. Gene let out his breath. The rumble grew louder, thundering over the plain; the ground trembled. Maisie tensed, thinking for a moment that she would be thrown from the earth. She covered her ears, but her body still felt the thunder.

As the missiles were launched from the east, the car vibrated with the roar. Maisie lifted her head, following the trails as the missiles arced toward the purple sky. She gazed at the flickering flames and the threads of smoke until she heard the last clap of thunder, and could see the weapons no more.

She waited. A bloom of light, far above the atmosphere, dying in the darkness. She closed her eyes and turned her head away, even though she knew there was no danger. Far away, physics was different, like the silence under the sea or the warmth of the sun.

"We live," the president shouted.

"We live! We live!" the crowd answered.

The last weapons were gone; the world was disarmed.

"We live," Maisie whispered.

The people near the stand were dancing, shouting out the words. The celebration would last into the night; she supposed that many bargains would be made before morning.

The pain clawed at her then; she toppled forward, almost sliding off the car. David caught her while Gene hurried around to her side. "Maisie?"

"Gene," she said, slumping into his arms.

She awoke in the tent, and saw light through the flap; it was morning. Gene was at her side. He put a pill in her mouth and handed her a cup of water; she swallowed it.

"We have plenty of medicine now," he said. "I gave the binoculars to David, and he gave back the pills Drew gave to Paul. Paul doesn't mind, and we need the medicine more than an extra set of binoculars."

"Thanks." She tried to sit up, and could not. "I won't make it home."

"Yes, you will."

She shook her head. He lifted her up and carried her outside, setting her down on a pillow against the Ford, then put her hat on her head. Two cars, a truck, and a horse-drawn buckboard rattled by; people were heading home.

Jim Fairbairn's car was gone, a mound of earth in its place. Maisie pulled at Gene's sleeve.

"Dora died last night," he said. "I helped Jim dig the grave. I guess we're all experts at that."

Maisie sighed, wondering how long she and Dora might have lived without the war. Drew wandered over and peered at her, looking concerned. "You all right, Maisie?"

"I'm fine."

"Did Gene tell you? The president said that, next year, every town should hold its own ceremony—he announced it at dawn. He'll say something over the radio, and every town will have a festival, so this isn't the last one after all. Of course, they'll be smaller, and we'll have to use fireworks instead of missiles."

"We won't forget," Gene said. "It'll be like the Fourth of July used to be."

"No," Maisie said. "Not like the Fourth."

Drew went to help Lydia take down the tent. Maisie gazed at them, Drew with his slightly humped back and skin cancer scars, Lydia with her oversized head. They didn't look too bad—not as bad as some. Talia, lying next to Maisie, kicked her feet, twisting the shapeless garment that hid her armless body, then hummed tunelessly while Maisie stroked her granddaughter's head, wondering if the child would ever be able to speak.

Junior sat near the tent, pouting. Gene motioned to him. "You going to behave?" Junior did not answer. "He got into a fight with another boy this morning," Gene went on. "Called him a mutie. I had to break it up." He waved at the boy again. "Get over here, young man, before that tent falls on top of you."

Junior wandered over to them, clutching a toy made of wood. One end of the toy came to a point; two wings had been carved on its sides. The boy lifted it, swooped toward Maisie, then stabbed the toy into the ground at her feet.

"Boom," Junior shouted as he strewed dirt around with his hands. "Kaboom. Boom. Bang."

EXORCYCLE

by Joan D. Vinge

art: Jack Gaughan

Ms. Vinge and husband Jim Frenkel
are currently enjoying
their first collaboration,
as the parents of 1½-year-old
Jessica. Along more literary lines,
Ms. Vinge has just finished
writing a sequel to her
Hugo-award-wining novel,
The Snow Queen. World's End
will be published by Blue Jay Books.

It's a pleasure to live in Southern California— "Tan Your Hide in Oceanside," as the Chamber of Commerce billboard across the street proclaims. And it's a pleasure to be here in the off-season, to have a decent breakfast on the sunny patio and time for the morning mail. I stripped the brown wrapper off of my latest selection from the book club and turned it over: yet another in the seemingly endless stream of "inside" accounts of the late, great government scandals. But this one: As I read the title, I felt an odd shiver run up my spine. Just then Pewter bounded up into my lap, purring loudly for no obvious reason. I greeted him with my usual sneeze, and groped for a napkin. "Damn it!" I put my hands fondly around his thick gray neck. "I'm going to make violin strings out of you, cat."

"Sean, how can you say that," my wife Marge chided absently; her red curls and freckled hand appeared in the pass-through from the kitchen. She gave me a glass of milk. "He's just kidding, Pew."

"Don't count on that forever," I muttered. "You know, Marge, I wonder what really became of Prentice—"

"Prentice who?" Marge called. "Oh, that Prentice; the actor. How do you want your eggs?"

"Not raw. *That* Prentice, who made the Queen's Own Players the rage of two summers in the park, earned us fame and renown, as if you could forget Prentice . . ." Marge *tsk*ed. And yet, as much as I admired him as an actor, personally he probably was the most forgettable man I ever knew; maybe that was why he was so good. He could have been another Olivier—if only he hadn't gone into politics. Pewter looked up at me through slitted emerald eyes, drooling sentimentally as he kneaded the title page, inflicting tiny puncture wounds. He assumed, like all cats, that whatever you were doing could not possibly be as interesting as he was. He was wrong. I sneezed again and wiped my eyes, deciding that I could forgive Prentice anything but that cat.

The cat had come strolling down the pier to meet us, as matter-of-fact as fate, on the foggy night we first saw the two of them. I'd come to the beach with Marge, to let the astringent air of a Pacific evening ease away the trauma of directing summer theater, to drown Shakespeare in the sibilance of the waves, and possibly to do a little necking. We strolled hand in hand along the pier, above the rushing water in the seagreen twilight; we were entirely alone, or so I thought. I was just about to suggest that we stop against the rail, when down the pier an enormous slate-gray cat materialized, marching toward us and yawping insufferably.

"Oh, look, Sean," Marge said, automatically putting out a hand. "Kitty, kitty, kitty—" She shared the opinion all cats had that they were irresistible, any time, anywhere.

I leaned against the splintery rail, shoving my hands into the back pockets of my jeans and wondering if this was why Mother always told me not to get involved with actresses.

The cat came to Marge and wound ingratiatingly around her ankles. She picked him up and nuzzled him; I sneezed, getting splinters, as the residue of loose cat hair settled into my hyperallergic nose.

"Lips that touch feline shall never touch mine," I said stuffily.

Marge groaned her contrition, dropping the cat and wiping her mouth on the sleeve of her work shirt. "Rats." She gave me a Kleenex. "Sorry. But look, he must belong to that man fishing down there. Let's take him back before he wanders away." She picked the cat up again. Obviously delighted, he settled across her shoulder and pinned me with an inscrutable gaze, before he looked away down the pier. Marge started walking.

I followed, wondering how I could have overlooked the fact that someone else was down there. Or the fact that he was quoting Shakespeare: " 'Oh, that this too, too insubstantial flesh would melt . . .' " Misquoting, I thought sourly, hearing his voice soar above the waves.

But Marge caught at my arm. "Hey, listen. God, he's *good,* he sends shivers down my spine!" And even if he did own a cat, I had to admit that much was true.

"Excuse me—" Marge said meekly, as we came up behind him.

He started and looked back at us almost guiltily. The cat began to purr in Marge's arms, blinking at him smugly. "Pewter," he said, his voice suddenly fading into the wind, "what have you done now?"

That confirmed my worst suspicions, but Marge only held him out reluctantly, saying, "We were afraid he'd get lost."

The stranger took the cat and draped him over a shoulder. "No—we're inseparable, really. But thank you." His clothes were nondescriptly hip, and he had a lean and hungry look. Such men are dangerous. . . . I wondered whether he turned Marge on. But he also looked like he wished we'd go the hell away. The feeling being mutual, I was about to suggest it, when Marge burst out:

"We heard you reciting. If you don't mind my saying so, it was tremendous. Are you an actor?"

"I don't mind." He smiled vaguely. "I have been . . . off and on." I harrumphed, placing a hand firmly on Marge's shoulder; she is a chronic victim of the Fallen Sparrow Syndrome. But she pressed on stubbornly, "Are you looking for a job? We're with the Queen's Own

Players, we do Shakespeare in the summer, and contemporary drama through the year, here in Oceanside. We're having auditions this week. This is Sean Haley, our director. I'm Margaret Gillespie."

"Elwyn Prentice—"

Marge shook his hand heartily, and then I did. He had a weak grip. I said, "Pleased to meet you," insincerely; and before I quite knew what was happening we seemed to have invited him out for coffee. As we walked back down the pier, my plans for the evening sinking slowly in the west, Marge asked him, "Um, say—you weren't thinking of jumping, Elwyn, were you?" I winced, but somehow Marge manages never to offend anyone. It's a knack I've often wished I had.

Prentice only shook his head, looking morose. "Nay . . . no, it wouldn't have done any good."

It was hardly what I'd have called an auspicious beginning. But Prentice wound up—inexorably, perhaps—as one of the Queen's Own Players, and I was forced to admit to Marge (as she twisted my arm) that she'd been right after all. He was one hell of an actor. He was also just about the strangest man I'd ever met; and when you work with actors that's saying a lot. Immersed in a character he was totally real and believable, but off-stage there was an insubstantial quality about him, a fuzziness around the edges that was somehow more than psychological: his ability to merge into the background was a subject of morbid fascination for us all. I could never remember what he looked like for more than half a minute at a time; it was even possible to forget he was in the room. I wish I could have said the same for his cat. We seldom saw Prentice outside of rehearsals. He didn't seem to have any interest in the things that usually interest actors, or human beings generally—"he hated public appearances," he said. He rented a picturesque hovel out by the beach, and it didn't surprise me at all when the neighbors told me nobody lived there. Someone in the cast summed it up well, once, when he said, "Prentice who—?" I think Prentice affected everyone that way.

But it was partly his lack of character that made him such a good actor—he could play anything, several parts in the same play, and lose himself in them completely. I'd hired him initially for stand-ins and bit parts, since the leads were already filled; but it seemed to be all he wanted. He was content to be the perfect spear-carrier, on stage as well as off of it, and he virtually avoided the spotlight like the plague: even his vanity was invisible. He had an early–Gene Wilder quality: he was totally inoffensive, a director's dream.

And yet he could have been co-director, if he'd been interested (and if my vanity had been invisible). He seemed to know every line Shakespeare had ever written, he must have had a mind like a tape recorder—and his promptings to the less blessed were somehow so perfectly tuned in that only a blank mind would receive him. His interpretations of Shakespearean dialog and byplay had an authentic feel that once led Marge to remark, admiringly, "You'd think he was a personal friend of the Bard."

"In that case," I snapped, "he's too old for *you.*"

Partly because he was her discovery, he fascinated Marge; she was drawn to him as the moth is drawn to the flame. Or so I assumed, and proposed to her to be on the safe side, even though he never seemed to be more than pleasantly distant. Because there was something about Prentice, if you looked hard enough, that was haunting in the poetic sense—a shadow of bedevilment, a restlessness that somehow hinted at secret sorrows. He had, in a way, the mournful dignity of a down-at-the-heels tragic hero, and the faintly archaic speech patterns to match.

That may have been why he was so good at tragedy; and maybe it also had something to do with the thing that really made him remarkable on stage—his Shakespearean ghosts. Whether his inspired performances came out of skeletons in his closet or bats in his belfry, I'm still not quite sure. I probably never will be. But in any case, we did *Hamlet* that first summer; and, with a certain instinct for type-casting, I picked Prentice for the ghost of Hamlet's father. It was my casting coup of the year. As Hamlet walked the battlements at rehearsal, there appeared before him a hideous ectoplasmic manifestation that would have turned Christopher Lee green with envy. Its voice turned Hamlet as white as his father's ghost; and, raising a trembling hand, he said, "Eeek." His father's ghost fed him his lines. Later that night, catching Prentice as he drifted out the side door, I asked him how the devil he'd *done* that? He only swelled with rare off-stage presence, and smiling conspiratorially, said, "Trade secret." He disappeared into the foggy street, trailing Pewter on an invisible umbilical, whistling an Elizabethan tune.

The public, it turned out, was as impressed as we were by Prentice's ghost: In a way, it gave the perfect touch of reality—or unreality—to charge the atmosphere of the play and transport the play-goers back into Elizabethan times, when ghosts were as real a fear as muggers. Our summer season was an unmitigated success; Hamlet's ghost made the theater page of *Time,* and set us on the road to national fame and artistic fortune.

The next summer, knowing a good thing when I saw one materialize, I scheduled *Macbeth* and cast Prentice as the ghost of Banquo. The season's success topped all our wildest dreams of glory: we actually outdrew San Diego's Shakespearean Festival; and in July we received a request for a special, end-of-season performance at the western estate of the President of the United States.

Marge and I got married that summer and blew our honeymoon on a pointless trip to Disneyland, before we slid back into the endless stream of sunburned, blue-and-golden days, and nights of chilling mayhem on the stage. Life had never been more beautiful.

And then, after one Saturday matinee, Prentice squeezed into my broom-closet office, his cat and costume making him look like Dick Whittington come to London. He appeared to be more morose than usual. Pewter, on the other hand, bounded gleefully up onto my desk, scattering scripts and knocking over cola cups. I wondered what practical joker had started the rumor that cats were graceful. He sat down in my correspondence heap and tried to rub his face along the edge of my chin. I sneezed, ruffling his fur. He protested in aggrieved tones. "Are you sure," I asked again, "that this cat isn't going to run off some day, and get hit by a truck?" Prentice said something but it was lost in another sneeze. I blew my nose on a used napkin; Pewter leaped down from the desk, taking a stack of books with him. "What did you say?"

Prentice picked up a book and whacked his cat in passing, before he rebuilt the stack on my desk. Pewter removed himself to a corner and began to wash, twitching indignantly. Prentice swept coats and dungarees off the guest chair and sat down. "Sean, I want to quit."

"My God," I said, "that's what I thought you said. Do you want more money? Bigger parts? Starting in the fall—"

He shook his head. "Nay. It's not that."

I began to pull on my beard. "But I even agreed to let your cat do a walk-on with the Three Weird Sisters—"

"I know." He laughed, looking uncomfortable. Pewter crept out of exile and settled under his chair, squinting up at me like an appraising jeweler. "You've been a real friend, Sean. Not like some. I don't know how to explain this to you. . . ."

"Is it the Presidential Performance coming up? You're the last person I'd expect to *get* stage fright, frankly."

"It's not that, either." He shrugged. "Tis no worse than the Queen's command performance. . . ."

"You've performed for Queen Elizabeth?" I gaped, forgetting the point.

He blinked back into focus, looking mildly surprised. "Not for a long time."

"Then you must know what an honor it is to perform for a president. You're the real reason he's asked us to come. Where's your artistic integrity—Hell, man, where's your conceit? You can't walk out now!"

He tied a lace on his doublet. "There's a thing I have to do. Something I've been needing and wanting to do for years, and now the time has come. I wouldn't do this to you, Sean, but I can't resist it." He looked up, and for half a second I wondered who he was, figuratively and literally.

"It can't wait another couple of weeks?"

"I'm just tired of acting."

I stopped pulling on my beard and started in on my hair. If there's anything I hate it's vagueness; or maybe it's actors. "You've got to do better than that, if you're going to snatch fame and fortune out of my greedy little hands. How can you be tired of acting after two years—two years of greatness?"

"More like four hundred years, of obscurity." He sighed. "How much Shakespeare can a man stand?"

"Come again?"

He hesitated. "Well . . . you remember Marge saying I must have been a personal friend of the Bard? She was right. I was in the original productions." He swept off his feathered cap. "Elwyn, the 'prentice actor, at your service. My credentials are authentic."

"Oh. I see," I lied, glancing at the door and wondering whether he got violent when contradicted.

"You wanted to know how I did my ghosts so realistically." He looked faintly indignant at my expression, whatever it was. "Now you know."

"You mean because you're—authentically Shakespearean?"

"No . . ."

I thought for a moment. "You mean you're—"

"An 'ectoplasmic manifestation.' A ghost. A departed spirit—except that I never departed properly, for wherever I was supposed to go. 'I ain't got no-body,' as they say."

"Ah," I managed, wishing I'd brought my fifth of scotch down to the theater. "How did this—come about?"

"I died, but something didn't work out. The energy half of my matter-and-energy whole failed to dissipate when the bond was broken, perhaps." He looked apologetic. "It's only a theory. I try to keep up with the literature. It's all academic, anyway. I'm *here,* drifting helplessly through eternity . . . a lost soul." He sighed again, melodramatically. "Always trying to get in out of the cold."

It occurred to me that he always seemed to be standing in a draft; and I'd studied enough horror films to know what *that* meant. "How—uh, how does one do that?"

"By taking over someone else's body . . . nay, don't worry, not yours." I wondered whether to be relieved or insulted. "I only choose strangers. But that's my real problem. The cycle is almost complete again, and the urge to inhabit someone is getting to be irresistible. I don't know if I can finish the season."

"Now you're telling me that you're a demon." I couldn't help sounding a little petulant. "That you really take over someone else's mind and body, you make them commit vile deeds, and humiliate themselves, and all that? That's a little hard for me to believe. Especially of you, Elwyn. What in Hell—er—would make you want to do anything like that?"

"It's hard to explain, to a 'mere mortal'." He grinned ruefully. "But I'm not exactly ye Ideal Demon—I've always been a failure at real, diabolical creativity. I'm only good at causing gourmets to spill wine in expensive restaurants, or forcing decent people to show their friends home movies of their baby's drool . . . I've always lacked the inspiration of a Classic Demon.

"It's not even the classic Evil that makes you do it, some devil with a pitchfork tail; or at least I don't think so. But it is a kind of damnation, to be stranded alone forever between here and there. It warps your perspective. It makes you jealous, it makes you bitter . . . and it makes you competitive. You resent that happy soul secure in its body; you want to dominate it and take over, you want to take out your frustrations on it. It's like a punching bag."

"What happens if you win?"

"I don't know. I've never gotten a chance to find out. Like I said, I've always been a—hopeless failure. I've been thrown out of more bodies than I can count."

"Exorcised?" I whispered.

He nodded.

"But if you're not classic Evil, how can you be tossed out by classic Good?"

"I don't know that, either. Maybe there is something to the classical definitions." He leaned back in the chair and stretched his booted feet; I noticed that the chair hadn't creaked. "It just seems to set up vibrations that I can't tolerate, like scratching your nails on the blackboard. Except that in my state it's more serious, it disassociates me, or polarizes me, or something like that. The longer I resist and stay in the body, the more damage it does—I can't inhabit another body until I've spent time this way, sometimes *years,* getting myself back together again."

"So what you're trying to tell me is that this cycle you mentioned is up again, and that's why you want to go out and inhabit somebody else?"

"Yea. And this time I feel that at last it's going to be a success! I'm fed up with being a bush-league demon, getting cast out like an old shoe. I'm very grateful to you, Sean, more than I can say, for the chance you've given me to prove myself. Working with the troupe—it's been like old times again, the best of times. It's renewed my faith in myself, after so many humiliating failures: I have self-confidence again. This time I'm going to do something grandiosely—Evil. I'm going to find someone whose goals and needs and nature truly match my dark desires. This time I'm going to succeed, thanks to you, Sean!"

I looked back over my shoulder at the window, feeling a little like an arcane Norman Vincent Peale. The eucalyptus trees rustled reassuringly in the theater courtyard outside; life went on as before. "Well, I'm going to level with you, Elwyn . . . I don't know if you're crazy, or I am." I laughed, nervously. "I—almost—believe you really intend to go out and bedevil the world. And frankly, I don't give a damn. What I give a damn about is the fact that you want to do it *now,* and our biggest performance is coming up in two weeks. If I've really done so much for you, will you do just this one thing for me? Just stay through that performance. Then you can fly up the flue if you want to, it won't really matter. And we'll be forever grateful to you."

He shifted in his seat, like a soul in torment. "I just don't know if I can wait that long. . . ."

"I took you in when you were a—lost soul, remember." I leaned forward, hearing the pencil can fall off my desk. "And think of the president! You can't walk out on him, it's unprofessional . . . it's probably even unpatriotic." Inspiration came to me from above; or below. "You performed for the Queen of England as a mere apprentice in the trade. How can even you pass up the chance to perform now as the real star, before our president and his top officials? Some of the most important men in the world, all waiting for *you?*"

"Ah . . ." His eyes gleamed like red glass in the late afternoon light; I felt a sudden desire to crawl under my desk and look for pencils. "Zounds, 'tis perfect! 'The play's the thing, in which to catch the conscience of the king—' You're right. I'll stay."

I sighed, with relief or something less comfortable.

"But you must swear never to reveal what I've told you, to anyone."

"You're secret's safe with me," I said sincerely, having no more desire to be put away than the next person.

" '*Swear—*' " He rose from his chair, swelling into night's dark agent, and swept from the room on peals of maniacal, theatrical laughter.

I told one person—Marge—since I felt it was only fair to let her know, and since she was my wife and didn't count, because she couldn't testify against me. It was the sort of thing you have to tell someone. Besides, she'd wanted to know what had happened to all the scotch. She listened soberly, and then told me that I didn't have to make up tales about Prentice, she'd always liked me best anyhow.

Our final grand performance, Prentice's farewell appearance, was flawless: when Banquo's ghost came billowing down the dining hall Macbeth turned green, as he invariably did, and three Secret Service men fainted in the second row. And after the performance, Prentice disappeared without a trace, true to his word. We never saw him, or heard from him, again. The only thing he left behind was Pewter, yowling forlornly in the empty hall. He wound himself inextricably around my legs, peering up at us with the eyes of an abandoned child. "Sean, do you suppose it was true?" Marge said softly. I shrugged, but against my better nature I picked him up, and we took him home.

"Your eggs are petrifying, Seanie. Eat, eat!" Marge removed the book from Pewter's grasp and looked at the cover. "What, yet another book about red faces in high places? Good Lord, is there no end?"

"Goodness had nothing to do with it, my dear. Not that I haven't always thought most politicians were crooks; I'm inured to that. But, my God, at least they're usually competent crooks, and don't get caught at it. . . . But you know, maybe this really is the definitive confession." I stared again at the title: *The Devil Made Me Do It.*

"You still think Prentice was serious about that, after all this time?" She pulled on her sweater and sat down. "Just think: We knew him when."

"That we did. Too bad he wasn't as good a politician as he was an actor."

"You don't think the present political follies were exactly what he had in mind, huh?"

I shook my head. "Nope. He wanted to be behind grandiose evil. But I'm afraid he's still a bush-league demon." Pewter raised his head and peered up at me, his whiskers quivering, and slowly closed his eyes.

art: Robert Kraus

STARGRAZING

Omicron Ceti looks like a star:
It shines and it twinkles; it's out pretty far.
But *Omicron Ceti's* a hyperspace creature.
(You won't find its ilk in the worst movie feature.)
And that light that we see is its eye.

As you will have noticed, the light sometimes grows—
Then it scents asteroids with its keen meganose.
(You didn't think asteroids smell, I suppose;
All of which just goes to show what one knows
Of how life is lived in the sky.)

This creature last dined out in 1506
When twelve planets vanished in two mighty licks.
(Had a star for dessert!) And I can't help but wonder
If its appetite's back. Is it starting to hunger?
We really should send out a spy on some pretext
To find out if our world is next!

by Beverly Grant

art: Odbert

Sharon Webb

SHADOWS FROM A SMALL TEMPLATE

The author's trilogy, "The Earth Song Triad" (Atheneum/Argo), had its genesis in her novelette, "Variation On a Theme From Beethoven," a story originally published in *IAsfm.* A reprint of her first novel, *Earthchild,* is just out from Bantam Books.

It was going to take everything he owned, but it was worth it—it had to be worth it.

The man across from him was saying something: ". . . understand our procedure thoroughly, Mr. Gordon."

"What?" Steven stared at the man, then lowered his gaze. "I'm sorry. What did you say?"

Crenshaw leaned back. "We understand your stress level is high We expect that. But before we proceed, you'll have to understand exactly what it is we offer." He leaned forward abruptly and touched a code on the flat panel in front of him. "Perhaps a drink? What would you like?" Then without waiting for an answer, Crenshaw pressed another button. "Try one of these."

A narrow door slid open at Steven's elbow. He stared inside at the amber cube for a moment. He really didn't want a drink. Still . . . maybe he needed one. He reached for it, pressing it between thumb and fingers. When the drinking tube emerged, he took a sip, then another. "Thank you." He could feel it begin to take hold almost at once. He could imagine the drug entering his bloodstream, slipping into his brain—smoothing little jagged edges from his nerves, patching torn fragments of his mind, fitting the inner parts of him together with a transient glue.

"Better now?" asked Crenshaw.

He nodded. "Better." For the moment. Better to hang suspended by a chemical than to plunge into the valley once more—the valley he had crawled through ever since Lisa . . . He forced himself to think the words slowly, emphatically: ever since Lisa had died.

"We have to be very careful, Mr. Gordon. People in stress sometimes hear what they want to hear. There are things that we can do—and there are things we cannot. You need to understand the difference." Crenshaw's stern gray eyes grew softer as he said, "Your little girl . . . Lisa, was it? You wish your little girl to be resurrected?"

Despite the drink, he felt his face twist; he masked it with a hand. The moment passed and he was able to look at Crenshaw again. He found his voice, "I want her back."

"Listen to me carefully," said Crenshaw. "You will be able to see her. At first, there will be only a suggestion of her; later, it grows more distinct as the re-collection goes on. You will be able to see her, but you won't be able to touch her or hear her."

"But I thought—" He clasped one hand in the other, running his fingers over the junction of thumb and palm.

"Let's start with your thought, Mr. Gordon. Your thoughts are what you are. Your brain is the generator—chemically, biologically. Your thoughts are a by-product, so to speak, of the generated energy." He smiled gently at Steven. "If it weren't for the pioneering work of Penrose, we might never have known." He popped upright in his chair as if for emphasis. "Twistors have no mass, you know. They were discovered by inference. Every thought, every memory is made of billions of them. With our process, we can re-collect them around a biological template." Crenshaw stared at him sharply. "Did you bring what we asked? Did you bring the template?"

Steven felt a blank look come into his eyes. Then remembering, he reached into his pocket and brought out the little gold locket. He held it in his palm for a few seconds, then awkwardly opened it. Coiled inside was a curl of baby-fine blonde hair.

Crenshaw nodded. "Now, let me answer your questions." When Steven didn't speak, he went on. "I know you have questions. There are always questions."

He looked down at the little locket, at the pale, tiny curl. "You said that twistors—the ones that make up the thoughts—you said that they don't have mass. How—how can I see her then?"

"No. They don't have mass. They're not particles at all. But one—a single twistor—can produce a photon or a neutrino. Two can produce an electron. The more twistors that combine, the more building blocks we have. The process attracts them to the template."

"Then—" He looked down at the locket once more, "Then what you . . . re-collect will really be my Lisa?"

"Energy is never lost, Mr. Gordon, only dissipated." He leaned forward and said in a low, but emphatic, voice, "We *will* collect the spirit of your little girl—just as surely as drawing iron filings to a magnet."

"There you are," she said as he opened the door and stepped into the bright room. At its center in the tiered, circular kitchen hub, Anne stood, meat-cleaver in hand, before an array of thinly sliced onion rings and crescents of green peppers. "I called the office, but Cindy said you saw your last patient at four. Where did you go?"

In answer, he kissed the nape of her neck, burying his lips in the soft wisps of honey-blonde hair that curled there. The color Lisa's would be—would have been—when she grew up.

"Never embrace a woman with a meat-cleaver in her hand." Anne smiled and ducked under his arm. "You'd better let me chop if you want dinner tonight. We're having tempura." She reached for a bunch of celery. "It's a lot of bother, but I felt like it."

Answering his puzzled look, she said, "I'm giving Oscar the night off."

In response to its name, the kitchen servo said, "WAITING." It—he, as Steven thought of him—had been dubbed Oscar from the day he was installed and they had been struck by the sentence in the owner's manual: *Your Omni-Skilled Chef is an Automatic Restaurant.*

"WAITING," Oscar repeated.

"Well, if you insist." Anne perched on the stool in the center of the hub. "Above."

"ABOVE." The stool rose to the second tier and Anne extracted a ginger root from the crisper. "Below," she said.

"BELOW." The stool sank to the lower tier.

"There's a bottle of wine in the table cooler. Get it?" she said to Steven with a sidelong look.

He fingered the booklet Crenshaw had given him, wondering whether it was the right time to tell her about it.

"What's wrong?"

"Nothing." He tucked the booklet by his plate.

"What's that?" The bright blade of the cleaver flashed as she cut a slice of ginger and then struck the flat of the blade against it with her fist. The sharp odor of crushed ginger filled the hub.

"Oh, nothing." He wouldn't tell her about it now. He'd wait until later—after dinner, after the wine. He took the green bottle out of the cooler and drew the cork, automatically squeezing it between thumb and forefinger. He poured two glasses and placed one at Anne's side.

The cleaver rocked under her hand as she roll-cut the celery into pale green wedges.

By way of conversation he said, "Surely Oscar can do that. I can program him—"

She shook her head as Oscar responded to his name with a "READY."

"Don't you dare," she said with a grin. "If you do, I'll hand him this cleaver and tell him you're a side of beef. After all, the guest chef ought to be able to keep a few secrets from Oscar."

"READY."

"It's your night off, Oscar. Be happy."

"BE-HAPPY IS NOT PROGRAMMED."

"Well, we'll fix that." She hopped off the stool and engaged Oscar's learning mode. "Be happy," she said. "Above."

"ABOVE." The stool rose to the second tier.

"Fast around, fast around, fast around. Wh-e-e-e!"

"FAST AROUND, FAST AROUND, FAST AROUND." The stool whirled. "WH-E-E-E."

She giggled at Oscar's dervish effect. "Technology. It's grand. But it's good to get away from it for awhile. It gives perspective."

He stood staring at her, wondering at her resilience, her ability to laugh again. It had been just three months—three months since the accident. He glanced at the booklet tucked beside his plate. The wound was still too fresh for him.

He sipped the tart, white wine and watched as she fished a handful of peeled shrimp and expertly transformed them into pale butterflies with curving scorpion tails. Her slim hands moved deftly, working the baskets and plates of crisp vegetables as surely as she worked the clay in her studio. Tempura as art, he thought—a collage. Her hands were beautiful. Lisa's would have been like that. Lisa's . . . . He felt the cold move through his belly again; he felt the emptiness it always brought. Lisa, six years old, forever. Caught in a little stack of picture albums and tapes, and memory—all that was left now. Nothing more, except a wisp of a curl in a locket.

With twirling chopsticks, Anne dipped the shrimp and vegetables in thin, iced batter and plopped them one by one into smoking oil that smelled of ginger.

As they ate, he stole glances at the booklet. As if reading his mind, Anne nodded at it. "Going to tell me now?"

He couldn't find the words. Instead, his fingers closed over the booklet and he handed it to her.

She read it in silence, keeping her eyes on its pages, her head bowed over it. Not until she had finished did she raise her eyes to his. With a start, he saw that they were filled with tears. Embarrassed, he looked away.

She sat very still for a moment. He heard the thin sound of her held breath escaping. "Oh, Steven." She shook her head in an almost imperceptible movement. "You can't want this. You can't."

His voice sounded strange to him—prim, chilly around the edges. "I've given them a check."

"Without asking me?"

He had no words to answer her; he nodded.

"You did something like this without asking me?" Her eyes reflected a hurt so great that he shrank from it.

"I gave them a lock of her hair."

"Her hair?" Her face twisted. "You took my locket then. Oh, Steven."

"I—I couldn't help it. I missed her so much."

She was on her feet, turning from him, running into the next room. He followed. She stood by the window and leaned her forehead against the pane.

He touched her shoulder. "Anne?"

She whirled toward him, flinging her words like weapons, "It's always you, isn't it? 'You miss'; 'you need'; 'you want.' Did you ever once think of me? Lisa was mine too, dammit—mine. Part of me, from my body."

He reached for her and recoiled as her palm stung across his cheek.

She ran from him then. He heard the lock of the bedroom door turn, shutting him out.

He poured the rest of the wine into a glass and took it into the empty living room. The setting sun blazed pink, shading quickly to purple, then gray. He closed his eyes in the dimness and sipped again from the wineglass . . .

"Grown-up lemonade," he had called it.

"Me too, Daddy."

Grinning, he poured her lemonade into a wineglass and repressed a smile as Lisa, in imitation, sniffed it deeply.

"Know what, Daddy?"

"No. What?"

Her gray eyes were serious. "I've been thinking and thinking. And now I know what I want to be when I grow up."

"What's that, Pooh Bear?" he asked, reverting to her baby name.

"Oh, Dad-dy." Her nose wrinkled in disdain. "I'm not a baby. I'm in the first grade."

He grinned, "Well, almost. In September you will be."

"But I went in the first grade at graderation. Miss Osgood *said*."

He stared at her solemnly. Kindergarten graduation. Lilliputians in minuscule caps and gowns. "Then if Miss Osgood said, it must be so."

"Anyway, I've been thinking and thinking, and I've decided." She paused dramatically, a trait she had inherited from her mother, he was sure—the dramatic-effect gene, found at the apex of the X chromosome.

"And what have you decided?"

"I'm going to be a 3V singer and then a sickologist just like you."

Just like Daddy—a clinical psychologist—dealer in hopes and dreams and fears. Mitigator of guilt in everybody except himself. . . .

He sat alone in the deepening shadows of the room and felt the cold edge of remorse rise in him again.

There had been no room in that day for cold. When they opened the doors, the warm June air caressed their skin and bore scents of hemlock and mountain wildflowers. Lisa exploded from the car and ran with shouts of glee toward the old cabin.

Anne, struggling with two bags of groceries, grinned at Steven. "It's always strange and new to her when we come up here."

"To me, too." He hefted the suitcase with one hand, and with the other caught at a low branch of dogwood and pulled it from Anne's path.

"Let's live here," she said lightly. "All the time. We could live on roots and berries."

"And love." He reached beyond her and thrust the key into the lock. The door fell open to the pungent smell of cedar. "But if we lived here, where would we go on weekends?"

"Back to Atlanta," she laughed. "Where else?"

While Anne put away the groceries, Steven followed Lisa up the little ladder to the sleeping loft. He gave a boost to a small blue-jeaned rear and in return almost received a smack in the nose from a pair of tattered red sneakers as Lisa reached the floor of the loft and turned to face him. "It's still here, Daddy. My bed's still here."

"So it is." Stooping beneath the low ceiling of the loft, he unrolled her little sleeping bag. "Tired, honey? Want to take a nap?"

She shook her head. "I want to go swimming."

"I'm afraid the lake is still too cold. But it's not too cold for the fish. Maybe we can catch some." He poked his head over the loft railing. "How does that sound, Anne?"

She glanced up from the tiny Oscarless kitchen. "Not for me. You two go. I have another project. Did you see those blackberry bushes on the way in? They're loaded. How about blackberry cobbler after the fish fry?"

Worn out by trying to keep up with his rambunctious daughter, Steven stretched out in the late afternoon sun on a wooded spit of land within view of the Lake Notteley dam.

"How come the fish didn't bite, Daddy?"

He felt his eyes drag shut. "Guess they were sleeping." He blinked and looked up at the sky again. "Guess they were tired out after the drive up here."

"That's dumb. Fish don't drive, Daddy."

Drowsily he looked up. A large eagle, wings outstretched, rode an updraft far above him. "You're absolutely right. Fish don't drive; they fly."

She laughed obligingly and scrambled to her feet. "Birds can catch fish. Can't they?" She was running along the edge of the trees, arms outstretched. "Look at me, Daddy. Look at me. I can fly."

He grinned lazily. "Stay away from the bank, Lisa. It's a long drop down to the water here."

He hadn't meant to fall asleep. He meant only to rest for a few minutes, deliciously supine under his pine tree in the warmth of the sun. He hadn't meant to sleep at all, but he had been up late last night finishing that book. And up early that morning. Not more than five hours' sleep, all told. He'd just rest his eyes awhile.

The sun was a red disc lowering behind the mountains when he woke. Disoriented for a moment, he raised himself on one elbow and looked around. The wind sighed through the pine needles. "Lisa," he called. "Come on, honey. It's getting late."

He got to his feet, and when he heard no answer, called again. When he still heard no answer, his voice took on an edge and he walked quickly through the woods toward the steep bank that dropped so abruptly to the water.

He looked down, and in relief saw nothing but a straggling bush clinging to the nearly vertical wall of clay. Whirling toward the woods, he cupped his hands, calling again, "Lisa . . . Lisa."

When again he heard nothing but the lap of water far below him and the sough of the wind whispering through a million needles, he felt a cold knot form inside him. Stalking the edge of the lake, he stared across at the labyrinth of inlets and coves and tried to make out the figure of a small girl wearing blue jeans and bright red sneakers.

He called again and again, not realizing that his voice had grown hoarse. He was running now, along the high banks following the ragged edge of the lake. Then, knowing that she might have gone the other way, he retraced his steps, circling beyond, then back.

He had to have help. He thought of the campground a mile or so beyond and ran to his car, but the thought of leaving her alone there took away his breath. He pressed the horn once, then twice, then twice more. Its blast struck against the bulge of mountains across the water and echoed faintly back. When the echoes faded, the silence they left caused him to shatter it with more cries of "Lisa . . . Lisa. . . ."

At last he started the car, telling himself that she was there at the campground waiting for him, that she had somehow lost her bearings and had headed there. She was a smart girl. She knew about the campground. She'd be there waiting for him. She must have been on the road. Playing on the road. She was just lost. After all, from the road each little finger of land looked the same—except for the campground.

He swung the car around and headed down the dirt road, turning at the dam. The lake was to his left now, to his right the steep spillway of the huge TVA dam, its waters plunging down the rocks hundreds of feet below.

She was just lost, he told himself. Just lost. Please God let her be lost.

It was late when he returned to the cabin. He moved slowly and his face was expressionless. He faltered once on the way to the door, but the sheriff's deputy to his right took his elbow, steadying him. The sheriff walked to his left, matching his long strides to Steven's slower ones.

As they moved toward the steps, the door fell open, silhouetting Anne in the light from the cabin. "Thank God. It was so late. I was so scared—" She stopped short, then recoiled at the sight of the two strangers, at the sight of her husband carrying a single red sneaker with gray, frayed laces.

The sheriff clutched his hat between his hands, twisting its gray brim. "Ma'am, your little girl is missing."

She stared at him without seeming to comprehend. They stood clumped at the door until, in movements underwater slow, she turned aside and let them in. The odor of blackberry cobbler mingled with the smell of cedar. A frying pan of cold hamburgers stood on the stove next to a package of buns. The table was set for three.

"We'll need a LAMET," the sheriff said to his deputy. The man nodded and turned to Steven. "Where did your daughter sleep, Mr. Gordon?"

He turned to the deputy without comprehending. "What?"

"We need a sample for LAMET."

He stared at the man as if he were guilty of a crude joke. "What did you say?"

"It's a test, Mr. Gordon. We test a biological sample of the missing person. The LAMET system can read just about anything we hand it: hair, skin, bone fragments, urine. If you can show us where your daughter slept, we can probably get a hair sample."

"But why?"

"LAMET will tell us if your daughter is alive, Mr. Gordon. Or if she isn't."

Huddled together in the sheriff's office, they waited for the mobile lab unit to come from Atlanta.

Anne turned her stricken gaze toward the sheriff and for the third time said, "You're sure they're still searching?"

He sucked on his cold pipe and looked at her with wise, sad eyes that had seen too much of pain. "Ma'am, the Union Rescue Squad is the best around. And they know these hills. They'll not stop looking for her, Mrs. Gordon—men nor dogs."

"When they do—when they find her you said they'll take her to the hospital. She'll want us—she'll want her mommy."

He indicated the radio console at his desk. "When they find her, we'll know it. I'll have you at the hospital as quick as they get her there."

She stared at the receiver as if willing it to respond.

The outside door sighed open, spilling chill night air inside. "The G.B.I. lab van is pulling in," said the deputy.

The sheriff nodded and lit his dead, battered pipe.

Anne shivered and crossing her arms, ran slim fingers over the thin sleeves of her sweater. Steven wrapped his arm around her shoulder in an automatic response. He heard her say something. "What? What, honey?"

She caught her lower lip between her teeth and leaned against him, pressing her face to his shoulder before she could say again, "It's cold. It's getting cold out there."

He couldn't answer. He clenched his jaw and stared at the floor. And he thought of a little girl alone in the night, a little girl with no sweater and only one shoe.

The door opened again and a young, uniformed woman with skin the color of butternut walked in. She paused for a moment, her soft black eyes glancing at Steven and Anne, then toward the sheriff. "If you want more than one test at full-frequency, I'll need auxiliary power."

"Hook her up, Rondall," he said to the young deputy.

In a minute, a long cable from the van snaked into the room and the deputy plugged it into a red outlet near the floor as the sheriff handed the woman a small plastic envelope containing a tangled wisp of pale hair.

The girl took the envelope and turned to go out.

Steven was on his feet. "I'm going with you."

The technician looked at him for a moment; then she said evenly, "All right."

He followed her into the van, stooping a bit as he entered.

She flicked a switch and brighter lights flooded the interior. He stared in bewilderment at the array of equipment.

She took a seat at the single chair and looked up at him. "I'm sorry there's no more room." As she spoke, her hands moved busily, opening the envelope, extracting the fine wisp of hair with small tweezers, placing the hair in a thin, concave slide. "Do you know how this works?" She nodded toward a black box with the raised silver letters **L.A.M.E.T.—System 120.**

He shook his head. He had read something about the newer police techniques. He tried to remember. "Isn't there supposed to be a screen there?"

She sealed the little slide and inserted it into a small opening marked SPEC. PREP. "A stage, you mean?" She shook her head. "You're probably thinking about LIMBO. That's the Latent Image Matrixed Biological Organizer. We don't handle LIMBO specimens on the road. There's usually no rush for those, anyway. LIMBO analyzes remains for positive I.D. —bone fragments, ashes, hair—so on. That is, in department work. A few commercial establishments use LIMBO for resurrection of the remains." She pushed a button and the slide disappeared inside with a faint click.

He leaned against the door of the van; he felt shaky, as if his blood sugar had suddenly plunged.

"LAMET-S stands for Light Activated Matrix-Encoded Twistor System. It'll take a few minutes for the specimen preparation." She half-turned to face him.

He felt sweaty; nausea skittered in his belly.

A hand touched his arm. "Are you all right?"

He swallowed and managed to nod.

She looked at him uncertainly. "Maybe you'd better go lie down."

He shook his head. "I'll be all right." He waved a hand toward the machine. "Tell me how it works. Just don't stop talking. Please." If she stopped talking, he thought, too much was going to rush into the void. Too much was going to echo in the silence.

Distressed, she stared at him. "Uh, the slide's not ready yet. When it is, this light comes on." She showed him a dark amber square. "We're looking for a sound pattern. We get a printout too. Here. I'll show you." She reached into a small compartment. "I made up a slide of my own hair—for calibration purposes." She popped the slide into a slot marked SCAN. "Listen."

A low tone began, a soft throbbing note that rose in pitch slightly, then leveled off. She tried a smile at one corner of her lips, "That's me. Hale and hearty." The smile flattened and disappeared as the amber light came on—Lisa's slide was ready. "I think you'd better go back inside," she said. "I'll be in soon."

"No." His fingers touched her shoulder and closed tighter than he realized. "Do it now."

She moistened her lips, then inserted the slide. The SCAN light came on.

At first he thought it was the wind. It started faint as a whisper, growing until it blew its sharp, cold draft across his soul, until there was nothing left in his mind except the howling wind and the red LED words: **DISRUPTION PATTERN.**

He was outside the van somehow, kneeling in the dark, emptying his stomach onto the rough concrete beneath him.

The girl's hands steadied him. Her voice was stricken with remorse. "I'm sorry. I shouldn't have let you stay. I'm really sorry."

And when he was able to stand at last and lean against the van, he heard her whisper, "There's a LIMBO, Mr. Gordon. In Atlanta."

. . . It had taken him three months to find the courage to seek out Crenshaw. He sat alone in the darkened living room and tried to remember the man's words: "Every thought is made of billions of twistors moving at the speed of light."

Every thought. It seemed to him that his own zigzagged in drunken chaos around him, breeding their electrons of memory until the weight of them was too great to stay aloft. He stretched out his hand and touched the tabletop beside him, half expecting to feel the debris of his mind like dust beneath his fingertips. As his touch grazed the cool, clean surface of the table, the bedroom door clicked open and he heard Anne in the hall.

She crossed the darkened room in silence and leaned against him, her hair sweet and soft against his throat, her wet cheek touching his.

Crenshaw cleared his throat, "Sometimes these things happen, Mr. Gordon. Not often, but sometimes."

"It's been two weeks now."

"And fourteen weeks since you lost your daughter."

"You said I'd see her in a few days."

Crenshaw leaned back and tented his fingers over his belly, "That's usually what happens. But once in a while we find a case like Lisa's."

"A case?"

"Usually the departed's thoughts tend to remain close by for a time. Of course, you have to realize that 'close' is a relative term. Twistors travel at the speed of light, Mr. Gordon. With most templates we can re-collect within a week or so—from here, from there. They're orbiting, you see—eccentric individual orbits something like tiny comets."

"And Lisa?"

"We have part of her. Nothing you can see yet." Crenshaw stared past Steven as if he looked through the paneled wall at something far away. "I like to think of them—the ones like Lisa—as special." He smiled at Steven then. "Free spirits, Mr. Gordon. Finding their own path to the stars." He popped upright with a creak of his chair. "But don't you worry. We'll get her back. It just takes a little more time."

It began with a faint mist, a thin golden nebula swirling above the stage. Each day as he came and sat alone in the darkness of the viewing room he could see it grow. Now he imagined that he could make out her features: the shadows that would soon be clear, gray eyes; the suggestion of a tilted nose, a little mouth. No, not quite. Yes. Yes, it was her mouth. Moving. Forming words? Could she? Catching his breath, Steven leaned forward and touched the transparent barrier between them. He stared at the moving patterns without blinking until his eyes were quite dry and strained. And, as he had done each night that week, he lost all track of time.

Anne was in bed when he came in. She didn't look up as he touched her shoulder. Instead, she stared at her book as the next page flashed on and its music whispered in her ear.

"I'm sorry I'm late," he said.

She didn't speak, but he caught the pain in her eyes as the pages of her novel flashed by too fast for reading.

He ate alone, extracting his dinner from Oscar, whose uncomplaining voice was the only one he heard that night.

He found it hard to keep his mind on his patients the next day. The last, a spare, black woman of fifty, struggled with her guilt and grief over her youngest son who had been sent to the penitentiary in Reidsville.

"You mustn't blame yourself," he told her absently and sent her on her way half-an-hour early. She was scarcely gone before he left the office and found himself once again in the little darkened viewing room.

Within the stage, a restless shadow moved and became a plump arm, fingers outstretched toward him. The image wavered, faded, formed again.

He caught his breath and stared as a small face flickered in a halo of pale gold dust that shaped itself in shadowy curls and tendrils.

He formed her name silently. And in answer, he saw her lips part and move until the shimmering image writhed away, reformed, then faded again.

He had to tell Anne. She had to see. Still staring at the twisting shadows of his child, he moved toward the door.

Anne stood outside the viewing room and leaned against the wall.

The blue-white light of the hallway accented the paleness of her face and the dark smudges that underlined her eyes.

"Don't be afraid," he said, taking her hand, drawing her toward the door to the little cubicle. "She's trying to speak to us. I know she is."

She hesitated, large eyes searching his, fear and hope flickering in them. Then she stepped toward him and he opened the door.

Her hand felt small and cold in his as they stepped inside. She stood by his side and stared through the window. Beyond, the transient image of a little blonde girl wavered in a narrow shaft of light like a butterfly caught on a pin. Plump little arms thrust outward at shoulder height. The last words he had heard her speak came to him: *Daddy, I can fly.*

He saw her small mouth move then and writhe open. "Do you see? See that? She's trying to speak to us."

Anne's hand trembled as it drew away from his. He placed his arm around her shoulder. As he did, he felt the shaking tremor of her body. Dismayed, he stared at her. "Don't you see, honey? Don't you see?"

She pulled away, trembling so violently now that her voice when it came was an anguished stammer, "Oh, God . . . she—she's . . . screaming. . . ."

Then she was gone, running from the little room. The open door threw a rectangle of blue-white light over him as he stood alone and listened to the echo of her footsteps fade and disappear.

He stayed in the cubicle until very late that night. When he came in, Anne was asleep, her hand across her eyes, palm out as if to ward off a blow.

He undressed in silence and eased himself into bed. He lay rigid in the darkness until at last he fell into an uneasy sleep that was broken at dawn by Anne tossing beside him.

She whimpered once and he turned to look at her. She was wrong about Lisa. She had to be. It couldn't be true.

He lay there in the silence until the bright October sunlight crept into the room. He rose then, dressed, and called his office, telling Cindy that he was sick, telling her to cancel his appointments for the day. When he hung up, he turned and saw Anne watching him. Wrapped in her silent accusations, he turned and left the house.

Alone in the viewing room, he stared at chameleon shadows: Lisa's face, her reaching hands, dissolving into cloudy shape upon shape. Her lips again, moving. Her mouth. "Speak to me, baby," he whispered. "What is it?"

As image shifted into image, he tried through will alone to freeze the quicksilver shadows into the likeness of a little girl. "Talk to me, baby. It's Daddy," he said to a swirl of golden hair that flowed into a silver comet's tail. He stared at a little face that shimmered and became the face of a fawn with Lisa eyes—eyes that reflected gold lights in the gray, gold that became star points in a blackening sky, then back to Lisa eyes again, brimming in a torrent of tears that became a waterfall cascading from the rocky face of a cliff.

He stared and whispered, "Speak to me." And finally he realized that she had. And when he knew what it was that she said, he began to weep.

He sat in the darkness with his head bowed and his face in hands that ran wet with tears. He had trapped her. Caught her and trapped her like a wild, free thing in a cage. And in the trapping, he had locked himself away too in a small, dark prison.

When he left the viewing room for the last time, he sent a message to Anne, and then taking the tiny package from Crenshaw's hand, he got into his car and began to drive.

October golds and reds lay on the mountains and the sky was a brighter blue than he remembered it could be. He stopped near the little cabin and began to walk along the banks of a stream that narrowed as he made his way up the ridge.

He stood on the high point of the land. Below, the stream was a thin silver ribbon on a patchwork of fallen leaves. He reached into his pocket and took out the small package. He opened it and gave its contents to a brisk wind that blew from the west, and with a sudden gust the little strands of pale gold hair swirled in a spiral of scarlet maple leaves against the blue sky.

I can fly, Daddy.

"Goodbye, baby," he thought; and yet as he walked down the old path toward the cabin, he knew he would always look for her. He would look for her in the sparkle of falling water as it danced from stone to stone. He would see her reflected in the eyes of small wild things. He would find her shining in the clear night skies of winter.

It was late when he came home. He let himself in and found Anne waiting in the kitchen for him.

"I let her go," he said.

"I know. They told me." Her eyes seemed bright and moist to him. "You must be hungry."

"Not very."

"A glass of milk then. Oscar—"

"READY."

"A glass of milk."

As Oscar dealt with his innards and produced a glass of milk, Steven looked at his wife. "I almost lost you too."

"Well, you didn't," she said, and her eyes were suddenly brighter. "I guess you're stuck with me."

He sat down on the stool in the kitchen hub; and instead of reaching for the milk, he reached for Anne and pulled her onto his lap. "Oscar—" he whispered.

"READY."

"Be happy."

"ABOVE."

He clung to Anne, burying his face against her hair for a moment before he kissed her, as the stool rose to the second tier and began to turn.

PACKING UP

by P. J. MacQuarrie

art: Alex Schomburg

P. J. MacQuarrie is a freelance writer who lives on the edge of the Ozark Mountains in southwest Missouri. "Packing Up" was her first published short story. It has been followed by others in *IAsfm.*

"Then I was sliding down this slippery thing, like maybe I was inside a snake . . ."

Zekie paused and put the tips of his fingers together and studied them. His face was rosy and he smelled of bath water and clean pajamas. Bart noticed Zekie's toes under the covers wiggling up and down, up and down, always a tip-off. Zekie was fabricating.

"And then I came out. All of a sudden! And I was in my own space bucket, zooming around, zoom, zoom, and I started to crash and the bucket went down so fast it started to burn up—"

"Zekie," Bart interrupted gently, "this isn't the same dream you told me this morning. Did you have two dreams last night?"

Zekie glanced at Bart quickly through his long lashes, the look of a young animal contemplating the next move. "Dokky, is your beard real?"

"You know it's real, pardner. You've tugged on it many times. Are you sure you had this dream last night?"

"I think I did. Anyhow, I might dream it tonight. Again."

"You won't dream that dream tonight. When you talk about your dreams, you give them away. You've given that dream to me."

"I'll get new ones."

"Maybe. But you'll go right to sleep, and you won't wake up until morning. Because you're tired. *So tired,*" Bart went on more softly,

"You'll be asleep when the lights go down."

Zekie gazed at him with half-lidded eyes. "We get to see the new animals at school tomorrow, Dokky."

"That sounds all right to me," Bart whispered. He touched the light control, and the room lights dimmed slowly.

Zekie was the first each night because he was the youngest. Of all the family, he alone seemed happy to see Bart at bedtime; in fact, it was obvious that Zekie could hardly wait for his short and squarish Dr. Markov to plod through his doorway each evening. Zekie saved up his monsters and disasters through the day, waiting for this moment to unleash them. Should Bart ever be delayed in keeping his appointment with Zekie, he could only envision an explosion of green lashing tails, dripping fangs, oozing messes with sly bulging eyes, and rockets going wrong and disintegrating like fireworks against the night sky of space.

Tonight Zekie was well on his way to sleep as Bart left the room. Bart could take pride in that fact. This was one household where no child would awake in the night and bring the parents running. Undisturbed sleep was of paramount importance here, and part of Bart's job was to secure it for each member of the Mellewin family.

Bart proceeded along the white streamlined hall, a seamless tunnel, ceiling curving into walls curving into floor. Maybe Zekie's complicated creatures were an attempt to provide some furnishings for this featureless architecture. He couldn't blame Zekie for that; Bart often played pictures from his own mind against these stark walls. Lately he'd been seeing clouds lit by sunset, changing color second by second, hovering over mountain peaks. The bulk of his next holiday, he vowed, would be spent sitting immersed to the neck in a spring-fed thermal pool after a long hike up a mountain.

He knocked at Tam's door.

"Doctor Bart?" Her voice was a bit too high, fluttering, fringed with worries.

"It's me, Tam."

"Come in." She flew immediately into it, even before he was through the door. "I know I won't sleep tonight, no matter what you say. No one could sleep with all my problems."

He sat in a chair by her bed. "Let's talk."

She sighed. "It's the fourth level. The whole fourth level, against me."

It was typical of her, but it always struck him as incongruous, Tam's serious manner forever at odds with her joyful coloration. Coppery hair, eyes at once green and brown—the bright tropical bird believing itself to be a mournful turkey vulture.

"Against you? Why?"

"They're nine and I'm eight. That's about it." This freckled child should have been dreaming up pranks to plague him.

"What do they do?"

"Oh, they just hate me, that's what they do. They ignore me, and they say terrible things about me."

"How many? Name them."

"Tressa . . . Cody . . . maybe Bianca, sometimes, and . . ." She broke off and searched, frowning at the wall.

"I think Tressa, Cody, and Bianca may be all I can handle anyway. Hand 'em over."

Tam turned to him, astonished. Then she giggled, a delightful bird-chirp. "Doctor Bart! We haven't done that since I was in third level."

"Come on, give them up."

She took a deep breath, laughter showing at the corners of her eyes. Then she rubbed her temples and cupped her hand over her right ear.

"Here's Cody." She reached out as if giving him something. His hand went to the pocket of his tunic, then held the flap down.

"Here's Tressa. And here's Bianca. You can have them! For keeps!"

"Not for keeps. Just for tonight, so you can sleep. Girls! Quit kicking!"

Tam slid down in her bed. "You know, you're the nicest of all the live-ins we've had."

He smiled as he murmured her litany. She'd always been one to fall asleep quickly, sometimes before he could tell her she would; but he gave his full attention to the intonations of her evening chant about being relaxed and sleepy. He touched the light control.

If he could choose children for his own, he thought, he would choose Tam and Zekie.

But once in the brightly lit hall, he forgot them and saw the clouds again, from his high vantage point where he imagined himself soaking in his moss-lined pool. With his left hand, he could reach out and feel the grass growing up between his fingers, touch the alpine flowers. And there, beside him in the pool, he placed Olivia Shyre, a woman who had gone through live-in training with him and twenty-eight other trainees, just four months ago. Her face appeared to him gradually, as if he were sculpting the delicate embrasures of the eyes, the arched not-quite-prominent nose, the full lips with the little quirk to them. It was hard to believe he had known her so briefly. The training had been rushed, because live-ins were in great demand.

His whole life had been rushed, it seemed, ever since he had taken the tests. Before that, he had been an unpromising student, headed happily for the work he liked best: either gardening or a position with a family as mechanic in charge of their various vehicles. With this goal, he'd enrolled in a local domestic college. But the tests given there revealed him as a bright underachiever, indicated he might fit into the very highest domestic classification.

He was whisked over to the Central Psychology Institute. Evidently his understanding of grass, trees and flowers, his affinity for tinkering with mechanical contrivances and figuring them out, meant more than anyone had realized. His gifts could be applied to people, too.

So he entered the quiet scholarly halls of Central Psych, first for the intensive basics, then the whirlwind live-in training, finding himself motivated for the first time to retain all he read and heard. He'd had misgivings at first—had the tests been in error? But he found he could hold his own.

He felt comfortable with the other students; most had been yanked out of other programs too. They would not be actual doctors of psychology as their professors were, but a corps of specially trained counselors, live-in psychologists, dealing with individuals and family units. They were given the title Doctor for use on the job, to establish their positions in the households they served.

Life at the Mellewins' had been good; Bart mingled with the family but also enjoyed the belowstairs camaraderie with the rest of the staff, who cooked, cleaned and maintained the Mellewins' possessions. But he took all his meals with the family in order to regulate their mealtime confrontations.

He lived in a state of amazement, grateful for his good fortune, proud. Most of the time, he felt he was in the right place. He tended some of the family like flowers, carefully and tenderly, and some of them like machines, making little adjustments here and there to see if they'd run better. Now and then, when they didn't respond like flowers or machines, he worried. But he always got them to sleep.

Too soon, Colin's door. It was definitely closed.

"Go away, Doc! I don't need a psychologist tonight!"

"Colin, I'd like to talk to you."

There was a silence. "Frankly, I'd rather stay awake. It's my room and my life."

"Great. Just let me say goodnight. And I wanted to tell you what happened today."

A hesitation. Any conversation with Colin was destined to be anchored down here and there with hesitations. "Was it your day off?"

"Yes."

". . . Come in."

Colin was up, standing in the middle of the room, but he had his dark, pacing-the-floor look. A runner, forced inexplicably to stop and chat in the middle of the five-thousand-meter event.

Colin usually took the longest of the three Mellewin children. His concerns went deeper, holding fast with their fourteen-year root length. And every day meant starting over with Colin, tinkering with the works. The hard-won rapport of the day before never carried over.

Bart persuaded him to sit down and then launched into a description of the comedians he'd seen at the cultural center that afternoon. He remembered the routines, line by line, and mimicked the players well. He watched a better performance, though, playing across Colin's face; sullen anger mixed with anticipation, dignified aloofness in the grips of a half-emerging belly-chuckle, then rueful, penitent, capitulating laughter.

"That was it. Brought down the house."

Hesitation. "I'd like to go there."

Bart said nothing. It was his turn to wait . . . wait . . . wait.

"I never will," said Colin. "They'll never let me go anywhere, all my life. When will they let me go?"

"You want some freedom."

"I want lots of it! Look what they expect of me. I'm supposed to be super at everything, but at the same time I'm allowed to do nothing. Zip, to school. Zip, back. Can't hang around with my friends at all. I'm living the life of a bored old man."

"I'd like to talk to your mother and father about this."

"You'd make them let me do what I want?"

"Not everything all at once. But we'd talk about some freedom, now."

Skepticism mixed with walled-in hope. A half-hearted "Great." What freedom Bart could negotiate wouldn't be nearly enough for Colin, but it would be a start.

"That," said Bart, "is now on my agenda, not on yours. You can erase it from your list for tonight. The lights are going down now."

Colin got into bed, looking as though he'd like to say something else, but Bart had a lot of work ahead of him.

"Are you erasing?"

"I'm wearing a hole in the paper."

"Fine. It should be all gone by the time the lights . . . are . . . out."

He left, wearing a heavy invisible cloak about his shoulders. He shrugged the mysterious garment off (what was it, anyway?) and slipped deeper into his warm pool. The cloak had been Colin, he admitted; but he didn't want to ask himself why.

The pool felt cooler, and he couldn't seem to put Olivia back into it. The vision faded. He needed to hurry. The adults took even longer than Colin; it would be late by the time Bart could get them all tucked in. He gave up the daydream and sped on to Aunt Muff's room.

Auntie Muff was the children's great aunt. Where did she get her clothes? It was hard to believe she was born only seventy-two years ago; she seemed to have stepped out of a past so remote no one could recall it.

Tonight she was settled in her bed, wearing a lace cap and a frilly, beribboned gown. She had told him about her research into old books and photographs, but she would never reveal who was copying the clothing for her.

"Doctor Markov, come in. I've been drifting off to sleep by myself, you took so long with the children! But of course I snap awake every time I close my eyes." She sighed noisily.

It seemed a fragment of her research kept returning, an illustration showing a man wearing a tunic with an intricately embroidered sash slung over the shoulder. Each time she drifted off to sleep, she would dream of trying to embroider such a sash. She'd struggle clumsily with the stitches, snap awake, then drift off and start the embroidery again.

"And I can't even have a sash like that. It was for a man." She pushed fretfully at the gray curls around the edge of her cap.

"You could have a sash like that, you know. I know it's not done now, but didn't you tell me how women used to copy men's fashions? Let's see, the man-tailored shirts, the little short trousers held at the knee—"

"Knickers. But women didn't copy this sash."

"Not then. But you're free to do what you want, now. You'll be the first woman ever to have one."

She smiled. "Perhaps I will."

He left Muff drowsing off with nary a snap to interrupt her and jogged wearily along the hall. Scarcely time to think of sunsets or Olivia, but he tried. If only he'd had time to know her better! All he owned of her was a small stack of friendly letters. Now he mentally moved her to his second-choice vacation spot, to the edge of a misty ocean the color of frozen emeralds. Olivia was running just ahead of him, leaving her footprints in the dark wet sand. She was shorter than he, the small and tantalizing Olivia; her long dark hair, pulled back, swung as she ran. But something else was pattering along after Bart, something concerning Aunt Muff. Maybe this was the sea of senility, because hadn't Muff been getting stranger and stranger? He slowed; the questions about Muff and Colin bumped into him; the sand and Olivia disappeared.

This bit with Muff and Colin. Maybe tonight he should call in. Wasn't that what Central Psych was standing by for? He shouldn't use it too much, but it could be a comfort. It helped in sorting things out, reminded you that you always had someone behind you who cared. He'd consider it. Maybe his daydream was prophetic; maybe he needed that vacation.

Meaghan Mellewin's door was open. He entered warily and dragged a chair to a distance of approximately twelve feet from her bed. He sat waiting as she stared at him from a confusion of pastel satin bed pillows.

"And how are you tonight?" he began.

"I don't know. I can't sleep. I won't, I know it."
"That's what everyone's been telling me. Does it run in the family or what?"
Her fingers plucked at the cover as she looked around the room.
"I wish you could love me, Bart," she said in a small voice.
There it was. He had sensed her getting ready to surround him for almost a week. "Mrs. Mellewin—"
"Meaghan. You used to call me Meaghan."
"If there's some problem between us, everything else could start to go. My relationship with the children—"
"You wouldn't leave!" She sat up straight, alarmed. She could have been beautiful, with her mass of dark curly hair and light blue eyes. But her beauty was blurred by obesity. She was a lovely lily potted in a cumbersome container. "You're the best live-in we've had. The one before you was terrible. No one got any decent sleep, and the children! They'd wake up with circles under their eyes, even Zekie."
"There's no danger of me going. And you must understand that your feelings are natural. But we need to talk about this." If he'd followed his instincts and headed this off earlier, he was thinking bitterly, it would have been easier. "Your problem may be slightly different than you see it. There may be an overwhelming need for something in your life, but it may be something you don't suspect."
He gave her pep talk number eighteen, the vaguely ambiguous one that leads them to believe there are better days ahead without being too specific. Then he led into the benediction, the special one that would nudge Meaghan to sleep.
When you're able to do so much for a person, for a person's mind, that mind sometimes thinks it's in love. A professor had warned them of that.
It was true he was the best live-in the family had had; with some creative persuasion and near-hypnotic gambits, he'd bought them quite a lot of peaceful sleep. And he'd invested his time well, listening to them, listening, listening. But to be truthful, he couldn't have made such progress here without the constant strength of Central Psych behind him, that band of experts loyally standing by, willing to listen to him. Maybe he would call tonight.
Bart slowly trekked on toward Clarence Mellewin's room, leaving the sleepy Meaghan behind him. Building her self-confidence would be the next step, but it would be a long time before she would feel strong enough to stop falling in love with the household help.
Back to Olivia. It didn't work. He found the mist had lifted and the sea looked hot and ordinary rather than mysterious. No Olivia.

Hang the sand, the sea! Colin, Muff, Meaghan—he trailed them along like coattails of smoke. Maybe he would call Central Psych; this was too much. No, no, it wasn't, he reasoned quickly. The calls add up, so save them for the really rotten times. He could take care of this. Everything would be all right in the morning. Everyone on the right path. Easy. Easier than the three trailing ghosts would have him believe.

"Where have you been?" Clarence Mellewin bellowed, his scarecrow head popping out his door. "I'm not paying a live-in psychologist to lollygag around the corridors."

The tall stick figure in green pajamas charged around his bedroom. "Where have you been, Markov? Telling Ezekiah those lengthy bedtime stories?"

Hyper-Mellewin. He'd never slow down long enough to fall in love with anybody, so Meaghan could forget that. Probably she had.

Bart turned a chair around, straddled it. He sternly indicated Mellewin's bed; the man frowned and threw himself down.

"Now." Bart always said "now" to Mellewin.

"You've got your work cut out tonight, Doc. I've got a doozy for you." Mellewin rubbed his face, up and down, from his balding head to his long chin.

"Worse than last night?"

"Oh, *ho!*" Mellewin rolled his eyes. "After a day like yesterday, nothing could be worse, right? Wrong. Today I learn our plant's number 2 stack cleaner is inoperative and probably has been the better part of a week." He glared, waiting for an appropriate response.

"So the number 2 stack—"

"Has been spewing out the raw stuff all over Lower Thornton."

"How serious is it?"

"Serious? It's damned serious! Heads will roll!" Mellewin lunged toward Bart, almost coming out of the bed.

"Aside from heads rolling, what will it do to Lower Thornton?"

"Aw, nothing. Dirty up some rooftops and we'll have to clean them up. Cost like crazy. The stuff from number 2 is harmless, just filthy. It's just that heads will roll, man! And me with the—"

"Clarence, shut up." It was the proper thing to say, because Mellewin actually expected Bart to say "shut up" at some point in every conference with him. Without this bit of ritual, they could not communicate.

"I'm asking you to remember the fueling incident in May."

Mellewin stared at him, eyebrows raised and mouth open, a more convincing comedian than Bart had seen all day.

"At that time," Bart went on, "you turned it to your advantage."

"Yes," Mellewin began slowly, then rushed on. "Of course, I didn't really *turn* it. The facts were the facts. I just pointed them out. The fueling mistake harmed no one, but made us aware of the need for new procedures. Which I then outlined. Came out with a promotion."

"Is there any chance . . . ?"

Mellewin was racing ahead. "Yes, yes, I can come up with a positive picture on the cleaner fiasco. And I think I know what it is."

"And?"

"I'm storing it away for use in the morning. Now I'm going to sleep." Mellewin liked to feel he was, ultimately, in control of the sleep situation rather than acknowledging any dependence on Bart's ministrations.

Lights down.

"You're worth every penny, Markov," said Mellewin sleepily. Bart, on the way to the door, was caught by surprise and almost let a laugh escape into the dark. It had been a simple, tried solution. Why hadn't Mellewin thought of it first?

He paced the long corridor again, back toward his own quarters, toward rest. But he felt he was trudging directly into tomorrow, a puffing engine pulling the family with their freight of worries behind him, Zekie and his monsters gaily waving from the brightly painted caboose.

Tomorrow. Tomorrow Aunt Muff would worry about her choice of apparel for the day. Then she'd worry that her indecision might be a sign of failing. Meaghan would need channeling into some peppy activity, preferably at a good distance from Bart. If he directed the breakfast conversation to fitness, would she join her exercise class again?

And Mellewin and the kids—they'd have to be shored up for reentry to daytime, to work and school, each requiring a little pre-game conference.

Bart fell down on his bed fully clothed. The fatigue of his mind had seeped into his body, displacing all but enough energy to hit the room lights.

He drifted into the anteroom of sleep, where snakes wore embroidered sashes but kept losing them for lack of shoulders. Here, Meaghan embraced a number 2 stack cleaner. And there, Tam collected three more of her peers and stuffed them into her left ear for later delivery to him. There was Colin, floating free in space but screaming for more freedom, more! And Zekie, lugging in bigger monsters and staging fierier disasters!

Suddenly he was not falling asleep. He could have been a steel girder lying there on the bed, a girder left over from the assembly of the unfriendly structure around him. He tried relaxing, muscle by muscle. He erased everything and mentally threw the Mellewins, one by one, out his bedroom door.

No sleep. It angered him to know he couldn't overcome his tensions, that all the tricks he possessed for helping his clients would not work for him.

Bart turned the lights up and touched the numbered buttons on his console, grabbed the communicator. Central Psych answered promptly.

"Good evening. This is Dr. Zorka," said a deep voice.

"Markov."

"Yes . . . Dr. Markov, go ahead," droned Zorka.

Bart smiled and lay back on his bed and told Zorka of the evening's confessions. He fed them all into the communicator, starting with Zekie's snake.

How good it felt to throw all this garbage on Zorka! Not something to be done routinely—it would alert Central Psych to a live-in who couldn't handle the job—but such a blessed relief when he needed it. Now and then, he could take advantage of the service and, afterward, get a solid night's sleep. Live-ins needed their sleep, too; and this worked for him.

Zorka made all-purpose monosyllabic comments here and there. How could Zorka stand all the trash he heard from sleep-hungry live-ins? Most of it was far worse than the Mellewins' laments. What kind of a man was he? Bart had met only a handful of professors during his training, never Zorka.

Bart told Zorka about the occupancy of his pocket by Tam's classmates. Zorka chuckled a chuckle that was almost an echo of Bart's, and Bart went on, feeling the trash roll away from him.

It was a good system. The Mellewins fed Bart all their worries; he helped them find solutions or took the worries away with him, as he'd done for Tam tonight. "Pack up all my cares and woe," began a song Aunt Muff had unearthed in the archives. Dr. Markov is here; he'll pack up your cares and woes and take them away in his pocket. And Dr. Zorka will take Dr. Markov's cares away in his pocket. Who would take away Zorka's woes?

Someone, no doubt. Someone cared. The whole chain was one of helping and caring, with the live-ins at the grass roots, feeding troubles up the line. Without this support, a person couldn't handle it.

Bart dimmed the lights as he talked; he was beginning to relax now. He told Zorka he thought he hadn't done that much for

Meaghan tonight, but when he paused, Zorka only said, "Mmm." To be expected. Any discussion was out, of course. Central Psych could never handle all the live-in traffic at night if there were conferences; the chance to report it all was supposed to be enough. For a real consultation, Bart would have to appear at Central Psych and talk with someone else. He'd never done that. It was considered a last resort, and though it was supposedly an acceptable practice, everyone knew it was not without risk to the live-in's career. Reporting this way was safer; it made the live-in aware of new possibilities and enabled him or her to let loose of some worries and get to sleep.

A new possibility was forming now. Maybe, Bart was thinking as he went on talking, he could have skipped this entire recital, could have just sat up all night and thought. Once, when he'd been close to overusing Central Psych, he'd done that; and a solution had come to mind, almost sneaking up on him. He hadn't gotten much sleep, but he'd been pleased with himself. Was that what Colin had been saying, when he yelled he'd rather stay awake? That he wanted to work things out for himself?

Bart finished his monologue. "That's all. Thanks for listening, Zorka." It was the approved way to end a report.

"Thank you, and good night." Zorka always signed off the same way.

"Wait." It was impulsive; he couldn't resist trying out his half-formed theory on Zorka, rules or not. Zorka might be interested. Bart rushed through it. "You know, I've been musing about what I'm doing for these people. Sure, it's beneficial. Sure, they get their sleep. But I *am* depriving them of worry, and maybe there's a function to the process of worrying. Maybe they should be worrying sometimes instead of sleeping. Maybe we're taking short cuts, making them too comfortable, putting everyone to beddy-bye before they have a chance to think things through."

The instructions from Central Psych were clear. You could report if you felt the need, then you were to sign off promptly.

"So what do you think, Zorka?"

There was a click.

The communication was terminated. Bart sat up and stared at the console, bewildered, then insulted. After months of reporting to Zorka, didn't they have a relationship that could transcend rules once in a while? Couldn't he expect Zorka to break down and toss off a little professional repartee?

Something inside him, something he hadn't known was dwelling there, broke loose. He punched the console buttons furiously and began talking before Zorka could speak.

"Dammit, Zorka, you could at least give me a minute—"

"Good evening, this is Dr. Zorka." That same deep voice rolled on, oblivious to Bart's tirade, with exactly the same inflection as before.

Then there was a silence, a sort of humming silence. Bart couldn't even hear Zorka breathing. Had he ever heard him? The question hung there: was Zorka indeed a breathing being? A breathing, caring being? With a dreadful certainty, the question hung, a weighty thing on a metal ceiling hook, already tagged with the answer.

A faint cool tingling ran over Bart's face and then over the surface of his entire body, like a blush of ice.

"Washout," said Bart deliberately.

"Yes . . . Dr. Washout, go ahead."

Bart lay back and stared at the seamless ceiling, turned pinky-white by the glow from the console. Zorka, the amazing machine. Bart took the Zorka-machine apart inside his mind, examined the intricate electronic circuitry that could make the Zorka-voice repeat the caller's name, say, "Mmm," and chuckle.

Bart reached out and shut the console down, button after button. Darkness.

Alone. Ultimately, one is, Bart thought. Alone, each of us.

His first impulse was to run out into the night, to throw himself down someplace miles from anyone, to feel the grass growing up between his fingers. His next impulse was to find Olivia, tell her, take her away with him.

Alone, each of us, all alone.

It would be a hard lesson, but somehow he would get them through it. The children, at least. Colin! Colin had a head start on all of them, even on Bart. Bart would only confirm Colin's suspicions about independence.

But Bart would at least get the kids through this lesson, before packing up and heading out for a long holiday at the mountain-top pool, with or without Olivia. At the mountain top, or the shore of the frosted emerald sea.

When morning came, he still lay awake.

BLUE HEART

The author, 24 years old, lives in Portland, Oregon, and this was her first professional sale. The story was written during the 1981 Haystack Writing Workshop under the direction of teachers Vonda McIntyre, Elizabeth Lynn, and Ursula K. Le Guin. Ms. Smith would like to dedicate it to all the Haystackers, with thanks.

by Stephanie A. Smith

art: Richard Crist

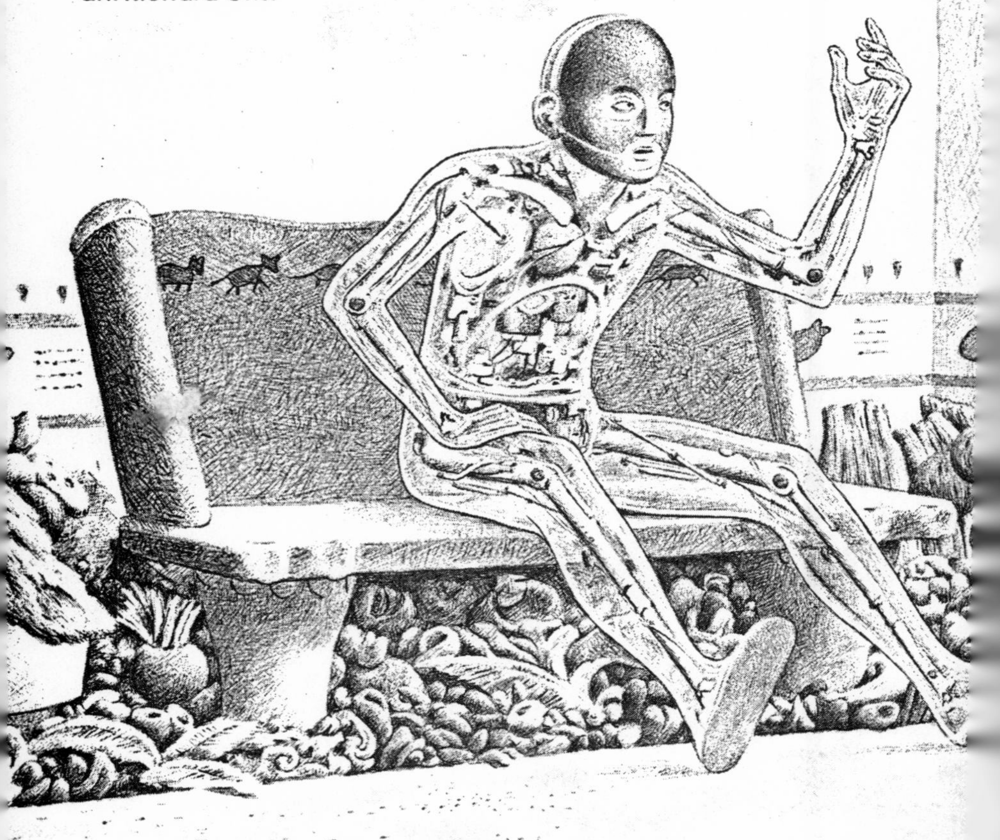

Sansel stood alone beneath her bedroom's skylight and stretched over to examine her legs: white legs, threaded with burst veins. Rubbing and flexing her swollen fingers despite their stiffness, she glanced down a glass breezeway into Beacon Kield's main hall.

"Mendir?" she called. No answer. Pulling on a robe, she walked through the breezeway, still massaging her fingers.

"Mendir?" She poked her head into the cavernous hall, letting her gaze rest on the spacecraft there. It stood in the center of the octagonal room, squat on squat legs, its underbelly burnt brown.

I should have taken myself home years ago, she thought. It's almost too late now.

"I'm going to die here. . . . " she said aloud. Turning abruptly, she peered through the breezeway windows to watch the coming storm.

Outside of the Kield house, Mendir pushed his way to the gate and then ran down the path to the doorway. Hailstones mixed with the falling snow clattered against his metallic face as he rounded a corner. From beneath the flapping veil of his slicker, he caught a glimpse of Sansel's robe, framed by the black lintel of the open door. He quickened his pace.

"Where have you been?" she asked him as he came inside. Rubbing her arms briskly, Sansel shut the door with her hip. "I don't like waking to an empty house."

Mendir brushed himself off and hung up the slicker. His silver face, an ageless mask, glinted under the dimmed lights, gem-sharp and exactly the same as Sansel had specified years before. He folded his snow-veil and accepted the robe she handed him, slipping it on over his artificial body: an ice-wrapped silver skeleton with supple, transparent skin that encased blue steel machinery.

"I went out before the storm began. For this." From the pocket of the slicker he took a snowstar, the Gueamin summer's last blossom.

She lifted the large flower from his fingers.

"I saw it while I was fixing one of the gates. The storm would have covered it."

"Water," she said, examining a leaf. "The petals are drooping." She walked down a second breezeway into the kitchen and Mendir followed her. Opening a cabinet, she took out a red-veined crystal bowl as he dialed for the breakfast meal. The chef hummed.

Cutting off the stem of the snowstar, she shook her head. "I'm not going to change my mind. That's what this flower is for, isn't it? And the food? To change my mind."

He said nothing but folded his arms and watched the chef brew a pot of tea.

"I know what you're doing. It won't work. I'm not going to change my mind."

"Come and eat." He retrieved a hot and well-spiced plate of food from the chef and set it down on the table. The aroma of spiced tea and spicy food mingled. Sansel sighed and closed her eyes.

He turned then to look at her with his own, white-irised ebony eyes. "I remember. It does smell good, doesn't it?"

"Yes. Very." She picked up a mug and then set it down sharply. "But I won't miss it."

"I did." He poured the tea and changed the subject. "The snow isn't too deep yet."

"No, though we could be snowed in by nightfall, don't you think?" Her voice cracked a little. I am old, old, she thought, and look at him! There is no brittleness in him. She covered the weakness in her voice with a cough, glancing up.

"I've been busy this morning," he said, avoiding her look. "Wait until you taste the breads I've baked." He laughed his hollow reflection of a laugh. "And for supper, I've made a batch of chelt for you."

"I won't need it," she said.

"Of course you will. Tonight's going to be cold. Chelt will be just the thing to warm you."

"I won't be cold. Not tonight, Mendir." She captured his wire-veined hand, holding it tightly until he sat still, as if he were a child. "I'm going ahead with the transition tonight."

He shook his head. "It won't work."

"Mendir, I—"

"Please don't."

She sighed. "I'm overdue at home. My replacement is likely to be on the way. If I don't go ahead and—"

"But what about me?" he cut in. "What if you should die in transition? You're not replaceable, to me."

"I am going to die, regardless." She shifted in her chair. "Transition will work."

"No, it won't."

"It will." She began to eat her meal slowly, savoring the flush of spice-heat that reddened her cheeks. "I refuse to sit idly while my life drains away. You know as well as I do that I can't guide the ships the way I used to. I get stiffer day by day now, instead of year by year. Last night, I had trouble guiding a simple probe. I was shocked when I saw how much an easy job like that wore me out." She gestured with her spoon toward the main hall. "I'm lucky a starship hasn't been by. Freighters, satellites, even personal shuttles are slow. I might be able to give them the directional shift they need to keep their sleepcrews on course. But a starship moves. It could slip out of my control before I'd be able to help. Then what do you think would happen?"

"I don't know," he whispered.

She broke off a bit of bread. "Why don't you think it will work? Is it that I'm too old to construct the thing properly? Or do you think there's something wrong with it?"

Mendir brushed back her frayed hair. "How could I tell if there was something wrong, love?"

"You couldn't." She shook her head.

"Sansel."

"What?"

His glass lips were cool and dry on her cheek. "You don't know what you might be leaving behind. You don't understand what you are going to lose."

"Of course I do. Nothing." She laughed, pushing him aside gently. "Nothing but death."

"And the taste of food; the satisfaction of tea on a winter's night; rain on your bare head; feeling; flesh." He stood and picked her up.

She laid her head against his smooth neck and hugged him. "But you do feel things. I programmed the specifications for your body, I know what you're capable of."

"It's not the same." He set her on her feet. "I'm telling you. Even forty years of being in here, living this way, can't erase the memory of flesh. I may not be able to have food, but I remember the value of hunger."

"I want to live," she said with finality. "And I've got to be a guide—I've got to have the net. If you can't understand, after all these years, that the net and my ability to become a part of it are necessities to me, then think of yourself. You'd be forced to work for a stranger. You'd have to stay here; my replacement would value your help, and there's nowhere else for you. Not in your world and not in mine."

"I could make a place, here—"

She shook her head. "You don't believe that, do you?" she asked quietly.

"I don't know. I could try."

Together they walked back down through the kitchen breezeway to the hall, passing under the wing of the spacecraft. Suddenly, she quickened her step, heading alone for her bedroom. "I've got to check the net," she said without pausing to turn. "I'll talk to you about this later."

He nodded.

"But," she added as she moved away. "I'm not—"

"—going to change your mind. I know."

Mendir stood in the hall until he heard the hum of Sansel's door closing behind her. Then he turned and made his way to his own room. The place was cluttered, filled with a floor loom and several shuttles, its skylighted ceiling strung with drying, medicinal herbs. Spools of weaving grass and several finished tapestries sat on the shelves.

Mendir turned up the lights and picked up one of the tapestries. He stared at it for some time, shook it out, held it up. At last he draped it over one arm and went to a wooden chest. He pulled out another piece from the chest and placed the tapestries side by side on the cold floor. Crouching, he glanced from one to the other.

"No," he murmured. In a sweeping motion he lifted the newest tapestry and flung it across the room. "It's no good. I'm no good anymore."

He sat back and folded his arms. After a few minutes he stood and put the remaining piece back in the chest. Then he turned his attention to a wheeled table that stood in the center of the room. He bent over to examine the artificial body lying there. Sansel had brought it in to him a night ago. Point for point, it was a twin to his own: a silver and glass reflection, colored wires and blue wire mesh.

"Sansel," he whispered into the silence.

In her room, Sansel sat down on the bed and relaxed to free her mind and allow herself to move out beyond the confines of her body. Using deep meditation and the training she had been given as an apprentice-guide, she released her mind's energy from its bodily restraints. Her consciousness sped away, bursting along the directional energy-net that surrounded her adopted planet. Invisible except to her and to the navigators aboard the ships, the net shifted and wavered in the diamond field of star-light, a beacon flag to people from her homeworld, signaling safety. With the net, Sansel could cradle her people as they came through this area of the galaxy and navigate them in the direction they wished to go, since by the time they had reached her planet, the crews were all in suspension.

Born and raised to solitude, Sansel loved this lonely planetary outpost, loved the sense of expansion and freedom when she became one with the net. She felt rich in the knowledge that shesafeguarded her people with the filaments of her mind.

Mendir wheeled the body out of his room and into the hall. A tray suspended between the table's legs was stocked with water bottles.

As he pushed the whole collection down the breezeway, the bottles clacked together, a musical sound, glass touching glass.

She stood waiting at the end of the hall as he approached. "I see you've decided to help me get . . . "

"I never said I wouldn't."

"No." She sighed, brushing past him to walk before the cart. "No one was in the net. I made a mistake."

"Again?"

"Yes, again."

"Oh." He was afraid to say more and watched her instead.

"Never mind." She smiled. "It doesn't matter. The net can stay empty, as long as I can be a part of it." She quickened her pace. "Come on, I want to get this over with."

The obsidian floor and walls of the corridor dimly reflected her white arms, her orchid white face, her white hair. She tried to ignore the ghostly triplicate image. At the end of the corridor they came to another room.

Mendir fitted the table-cart under one of the machines. Automatic fastenings snapped. "I wish you'd reconsider," he murmured as he transferred the jars from the cart to their holders.

"Just what is wrong with you?" She turned away from one of the panels. "What have you got your mind set against, anyway?"

"Suicide."

"And just how am I committing suicide?" She closed her eyes and spoke slowly, as if she expected to break apart at any moment. "Do you want to serve this other, younger guide, this replacement of mine? Is that it?"

Mendir nearly dropped the jar he was carrying. Carefully, he set it down. "Is that what you think?"

She flinched and lowered her voice. "You tell me! What am I supposed to think? Here I offer you my company for a long, long time and you refuse it."

He took a step toward her. "Do you mean that? Is that truly the reason you want to do this?"

"I wouldn't say something I—"

"Come on then. I need to talk to you."

She didn't move, puzzled. "Why? We can talk here. What is the matter?"

"Come on. This room is too cold for you. And I can't think in here, with that . . . thing . . . staring at the ceiling." He pulled her along and together they walked to the greenhouse. Snow was piled high against the thick windows.

She sat on a garden bench and let the warmth work its way into her knotted muscles and joints. She stretched. "Talk."

"I thought you would change your mind." Mendir knelt and righted a fallen silkgrass plant, packing the earth around it. "When I thought your only reason for this change was the net, I decided not to say anything. I didn't want to interfere."

She rubbed her eyes. "Well, when you first put the idea into my head—"

"I was hoping—"

"That I'd forget? Well—"

"Forget? No . . . I . . . " He saw that she had misunderstood him entirely.

She shrugged. "As I said at the time, among my people a transition isn't usually granted unless someone is completely crippled. Or has no chance for a normal life. Well, I've had my full life span; I'm not entitled to a transition. And yet I have enough of the materials here to grant it to myself. After all—"

"—it worked on me," he said.

She frowned. "That isn't what I was going to say. You make it sound as if you were an experiment."

He brushed off his hands and sat beside her. He struck his own thigh. "Wasn't it? I didn't choose to be like this."

"No, what you did choose was to climb Mt. Oron. Against every Gueamin tradition. It wasn't my fault you walked into the security net. I was in deep meditation. I couldn't leave myself unguarded. You—"

Mendir clenched his hands and turned his marbled gaze on her. "Don't."

"You would have died, my love. I couldn't let you die. As it was, you were in suspension much too long before I could get your body ready. It must have been so cold and dark. Like the nights when I'm tired and can't reach the stars or feel the net. Death must be like that. Not this." She ran her hand up his arm. "Here." She touched the chill plate of his face. "Inside. If I have my mind and my net, then I'm alive, warm, like the blue heart of a flame—"

"Is that all?"

"What?"

He leaned over, folding his hands between his knees. "Your mind and your net." He shook his head. "Blue is a cold color."

"You were dying."

"Yes." He looked at her and whispered, "Do you love me at all?"

"Of course!" She folded her arms, leaning back. "I always have."

"How?"

"What do you mean, how?"

He laughed quietly. "Never mind. When I woke up in here, a"—he smiled—"a blue heart in a jar, I was terrified."

"I remember."

"And you were there."

"Yes?"

"Don't leave."

She sighed. "I never have. I never will, after tonight."

He chafed her hand. "But you have left me. When you go to the net. When you talk about it. I can't—"

"I'm a guide," she said coldly. "Nothing can change that. I've told you before."

"Nothing," he repeated flatly. "Well. I was a weaver once. A long time ago. I thought nothing could change that, but I was wrong." He sighed. "Remember this?" He began to sing quietly:

> Weaver, weaver, throw your threads,
> Out to the soundless seas.
> Net the ships of sons and daughters,
> Send them home to me.

Sansel laughed. "Of course! I thought you'd forgotten your weaver's songs, after so long. How does the rest go? 'Spider, spider—'

> Spin your web,
> Across the quiet grasses,
> Link the space from leaf to leaf,
> Jewel the empty pastures.
>
> Weaver, weaver, search among the islands,
> Sail the sky from star to star,
> Weaving ever farther.' "

She rested her head against Mendir's shoulder. "They're true, those ancient songs of your world. That is what I do, in a way, for the lost. I must . . . "

He tensed. "Stop."

"I can't just sit and wait to die."

"You don't know how it will be," he whispered, more to himself than to her. "You don't understand what I mean."

She eyed him. "I have some idea. Haven't you told me about it over and over?"

"Yes." He stood up. "And no. I'm not a guide. How do you know whether you'll be able to stand the change?"

"My body may be feeble, but my mind isn't. Not yet, anyway. Besides, I'll have a lot fewer adjustments to make than you did, even though I did feed your mind with information about my world before I let you wake up. Unless—is there something you haven't told me?"

Mendir sat down, hesitating. "What if you should lose your skill as a guide?"

She said nothing for several moments. At last she whispered. "No. It won't happen."

"Sansel—"

"No, I said!" She stood. "No."

Mendir didn't move. "All right, I can't argue. I'm not a guide. I'm just a primitive weaver who can't weave."

She touched his arm. "It's not the same sort of skill."

"No?"

"No." She turned to leave.

"What can I do to help?" he called after her.

She smiled at him. "Nothing. I'm ready now. All I need is myself."

"Let me come and—"

"Don't." She put her hand an his shoulder. "You were unconscious when I helped your mind transfer, but still it would be painful for you to watch."

"And there's nothing I can say?"

"No. Don't worry. I can handle this." Then she was gone.

He leaned back on the bench, remembering himself as whole and human, a native of Gueame, a grass weaver. He remembered his secretive and solitary climb up Mt. Oron, a climb he believed would lead to the object of his dreams—the Net-Weaver of the old songs. If he could learn skills from her! Every one in Gueame knew the songs of the net, and all were taught the lore of its magic. The songs told of a crystal Kield house, hidden in the snows of Oron.

And so one day he stood before the great open doors and stared at the sprawling Kield, the tall and faceless walls, the strange, octagonal brilliance of the eight seamless glass breezeways that linked the main hall with its circular workrooms. A stone and metal spider, somnolent in the snow and sun.

He walked to the open doorway. One more step and he would be there. The net-keeper couldn't possibly turn him away, not after he had climbed the mountain, defied his people's cowardice. He had stepped . . .

. . . off the edge of his world. He remembered his limbs lying useless and scorched, his body twisted, in the snow. He'd been caught, he found out later, in the small energy web that guarded the Kield doors while Sansel was among the stars. Something had smelled awful, he remembered, but he had felt nothing. He had broken his neck.

Mendir blinked himself awake from the memory. The sky was dark now and the garden still. It was late.

"Sansel?" he called. No one answered. He hurried out looking for her, suddenly afraid.

The door to her bedroom was open. She sat crouched against the lintel, naked in her new, gleaming body, her silver face shining from the lights as if she were sweating. Beyond her he glimpsed the bed. He looked away before he could catch sight of her old self.

"Sansel?"

"I tried," she whispered as he approached. "I tried, and it doesn't work." She stared up at him, her white irises wide.

"But it did work." He bent down to her.

"No. I can't reach the net."

Mendir kept his voice even. "Are you sure?"

"My mind reaches and is thrown back in on itself."

He placed his hands firmly around her wrists. "It doesn't matter. What matters is that you're alive."

"Alive? Aren't you listening?" She pulled her arms away, balling her fists. "I'm no use now." She shook her head back and forth. He leaned over and she pushed him away so that he backed off a little.

"No, no, it can't be," she said. "Maybe I haven't given myself enough time." She closed her eyes.

He waited, listening to the dual clicking of their bodies' inner workings. Waiting.

At last, she looked at him, her pupils contracted to white needles of fear. "I'm trapped in here."

"Not alone."

She blinked. "Trapped."

"No."

"I've given up everything—for nothing."

"For life!" He calmed himself. "You still have me."

She turned on him. "You! You knew this would happen. Why didn't you—"

He slid his arm around her waist, glass against glass. "You're alive, Sansel, alive. There are other things in this world for us. I had to learn that. So will you."

"You knew! You could have stopped me."

"I had a suspicion. I tried to tell you." He tightened his grip.

"No, you only suggested it. But you knew—"

"I love you," he said simply. "Love me."

Sansel sat there, caught in his cold embrace, a frozen statue with a blue metal core, bereft even of tears while Mendir waited for her to come to him, as once, long ago, he had come to her.

THE EXAMINATION OF EX-EMPEROR MING

by Cyn Mason

art: Odbert

The author has sold stories,
a poem, a song, and a recipe.
She is also the editor
of the anthology *Wet Visions* and hopes that
one of these days she might finish
the book she's been fussing over
for years. Ms. Mason currently lives
in the University district in Seattle
with an OWC (Obligatory Writer's Cat)
who, she says, gets the fan mail.

There were deep burn marks on the road to the fortress. Many turrets stood against the walls, lending ominous meaning to the scars. A lone figure stood at the gates, knocking.

"Halt, fool! Who dares disturb the solitude of Ming the Merciless?" The echoes rolled over the hills, precipitating a small landslide half a kilometer away.

"Not bad," commented the fool. "I see you have the 'Voice of Authority' option on your subterranean speakers. I'm here about the audit."

Instantly the turrets spat forth assorted rays, engulfing him in flames. Ignoring them, the burning figure calmly walked to the castle gates and kicked them. The turrets ceased firing as the gates fell inward. A mob of robot gladiators rushed him as he stepped inside. The man grabbed one, ignoring the others as they variously beat, slashed, and fired at him, and politely requested, "Will you please tell Mr. Ming that Special Agent David Klayven from the Intragalactic Revenue Korps is here?"

Not programmed to deal with men who refused to be burnt to a crisp, the mechanism blinked photoreceptors and ran out of the room. Klayven followed it into an opulent suite, to a small room containing a round pool filled with water and the former emperor of Mongo, soaking in scented bubbles while several partly clothed women stood by. They giggled at Klayven's entrance. Ming did not, preferring to turn purple.

"What is the meaning of this? Who are you? Guards! *Guards!* Destroy this intruder! **Guards!**"

Obediently, the robot turned and fired. The backwash of close range blasters brushed one side of the pool. A violent explosion of steam fogged the room as the women all screamed and ran like hell. When the air cleared, the robot was lying in smoking ruin as the pool spilled hot water and parboiled ex-emperor across Klayven's shins.

"Special Agent Klayven, Intragalactic Revenue Korps," said the agent, offering Ming a hand. "I'm here about the examination of your planetary tax returns for the last two years."

"What? The I.R.K.? You're here about the audit!" snarled Ming, ignoring the hand. "Get out! Leave now and I may let you live."

"Displays of violence against an I.R.K. agent in lawful performance of his duties carry heavy penalties. You've already incurred several; are you trying for more? Why don't we just get down to business and get this over with? If you'll just produce your books and records . . ."

"Records!" interrupted Ming. "I barely escaped Mongo with my life, let alone records. You can't just walk in here and start demanding to see my books. What about my rights? Tyrants have rights just as much as anyone!"

"Intragalactic Revenue Code gives me the authority to conduct an immediate examination of your returns complete with all the substantiation you can provide. If you cannot substantiate your deductions, they will be disallowed and the tax recomputed."

"But I haven't got any substantiation! What are you talking about? *What* deductions? Oh, Hell, get this stupid audit over with and get out! First some jerk goes and runs me off my own planet, then you blood-suckers from the I.R.K. start in on me. Get done and get out!" Draping a soggy towel around himself, he stalked into the suite adjoining. Klayven followed, opening his briefcase.

The agent handed Ming copies of his planetary tax returns. "Please look these over." Sitting at a table, Ming watched Klayven take a stack of papers out. "These are the items being questioned."

"That many?" demanded Ming incredulously.

"That's right," said Klayven cheerfully. "Let's get down to specifics. First, you claimed a large business expense here. What exactly was this cost to you?"

"Oh, *that*. It was the expense of keeping up my torture chambers and dungeons. You've no idea what it costs to maintain a reign of terror these days."

"Torture chambers, eh? That's totally unallowable."

"What? It's a completely legitimate business expense!"

"No; I.R.K. Code clearly states that torture and dungeon expenses are simply for your personal pleasure, and hence disallowed. It isn't considered so much an expense as the way you chose to spend your income. Speaking of which, I have reason to believe that on line forty-four you understated your adjusted gross income. Look at this." The agent pulled out a meter-long list. "The I.R.K. has a computer program that automatically matches up all information received from banks, stocks, and pensions against the information on your return. These are the credits paid into your accounts that weren't included in your income."

The former tyrant paled as he scanned the list. "How sloppy of the accountant to have left that out," he commented weakly. "We hired the best accountant on Mongo to do the returns! How could he have missed it?" Klayven smiled.

"Speaking of the accountant, you show a considerable cost in fees paid to him on this schedule, and some doubt exists as to whether it was actually paid. Do you have a receipt to show?"

"Who says it wasn't paid? How would you know?"

"Possibly the fact you had him beheaded for trying to collect could have something to do with it."

"Details, details. I'm a very busy man. You can't expect me to recall every single beheading. All right, if you want to get down to business, what would it take to make you forget this whole issue?" Ming's expression was coldly calculating. "Would you like to own my harem?"

"Are you aware of the penalties for attempting to bribe an agent of the I.R.K.? Your bribe itself is forfeit, as well as penalties, on top of the taxes, interest, and penalties you already owe."

"You *fool!* Nobody need know about this but ourselves! Think of the girls! Beauties, and talented, every one of them."

Klayven looked at him with pity. "You're completely wrong. I.R.K. Central already knows. I'm in constant communication with them, through the telemetry in my briefcase, and this conversation is being recorded."

"*What!*" Ming stared, pop-eyed, at Klayven. Finally he said, "I don't see any reason to go on with this. You've got that stack of questioned items and I haven't got any records. We can't show you anything to back up my deductions, so why bother? Besides, what else can you do to me? My empire is gone, my harem is lost, what can I lose?"

"Well, the credits from selling this place should help a little in paying off your bill," said Klayven helpfully.

"*What?*" Ming yelled again, clutching at his towel. "You can't!"

"Since you've chosen to terminate the examination, the computers at I.R.K. Central have recomputed your tax, plus failure to pay penalties from the date the tax would have been due, plus interest, plus penalties for the destruction of the previous three robotic auditors that I.R.K. sent out to . . ."

Ming interrupted, "What robotic auditors? That's got to be a mistake!"

"No, we sent them out to examine your returns. Your defenses destroyed each while it was attempting to gain entry, but fortunately each was equipped with telemetry."

"You can't blame me for destroying robots I didn't even know about!"

"Somebody has to pay for them. *You* broke them. Then there's the penalty for attempted bribery, and the total amount now due is just printing out in my briefcase." He handed a statement to the ex-emperor. "There you go."

"That's more than *five* times the tax I paid as Emperor of Mongo! You've bankrupted me! They'll be calling me Ming the Penniless!" he shrieked, his voice cracking. "How do you expect me to live? Do you think the Galaxy is full of job openings for cruel despots? Guards! *Guards!*" The robots assembled at the door. "I order you to destroy this intruder if it means leveling the castle!"

One gladiator stepped ahead of the rest. "We cannot obey you," it stated.

"*Why?*"

"We no longer belong to you," it answered, and left.

"That's correct," Klayven said. "I.R.K. Central just placed a tax levy on each of your accounts, and filed a tax lien on this place."

"What can I *do?*" gasped Ming. "I'm ruined." His face was gray, the pupils dilated.

"Well, wait a minute. Possibly I have a proposition for you."

There were deep burn marks on the road to the fortress. Many peculiar turrets stood against the walls, lending ominous meaning to the scars. A lone figure stood at the gates, knocking.

A challenge shook the hills. "Who dares approach?"

"Mr. Vader? Special Agent Ming, from the Intragalactic Revenue Korps. I'm here about the audit."

THE CRYSTAL SUNLIGHT, THE BRIGHT AIR

The author lives in Dorset, England, and has a novel, *Golden Witchbreed*, coming out from Arrow Books, Ltd.

by Mary Gentle

art: Ray Lago

Paul Broderick came to Orthe a haunted man.

You'll have no trouble, the Intendant who briefed him promised. Orthe's a regained world. There were Earth settlements on it before the Insurrection. The natives are used to humans.

Go down, Broderick. Find out if this world needs the Interdict.

Haine's Star scorched down on Orthe, on Kasabaarde's narrow streets, reflecting back from the white domes and ankle-deep dust. The acid light bit into his eyes, even behind the face mask's protective glass. Dust irritated his skin. He quickened his pace towards the wall separating trade district from inner city. If there was cause for the Interdict, it had to be there. Nothing outside the wall was unusual—after the Insurrection. An agricultural society living in the ruins of a high-technology past . . .

Wind brought the smell of marine life from the harbor, close by the gate. Sunlight fractured off the sea like broken glass. Broderick approached the Ortheans at the gateway.

"You wish to enter the inner city?"

His hypno-trained mind translated the breathy sounds and sharp clicks. He answered as well as he could.

The Orthean who spoke was a head shorter than Broderick. Bleached skin under the city's dust showed a hint of scale-pattern. Masked—as all Ortheans were outdoors—there was only a glimpse of eyes set widely apart under a broad forehead. Under the mask's edge, thin lips curved in a reptilian smile.

"Wait," the humanoid said. Pale hair was caught up in complex braids; as she turned to consult the others he saw the mane was

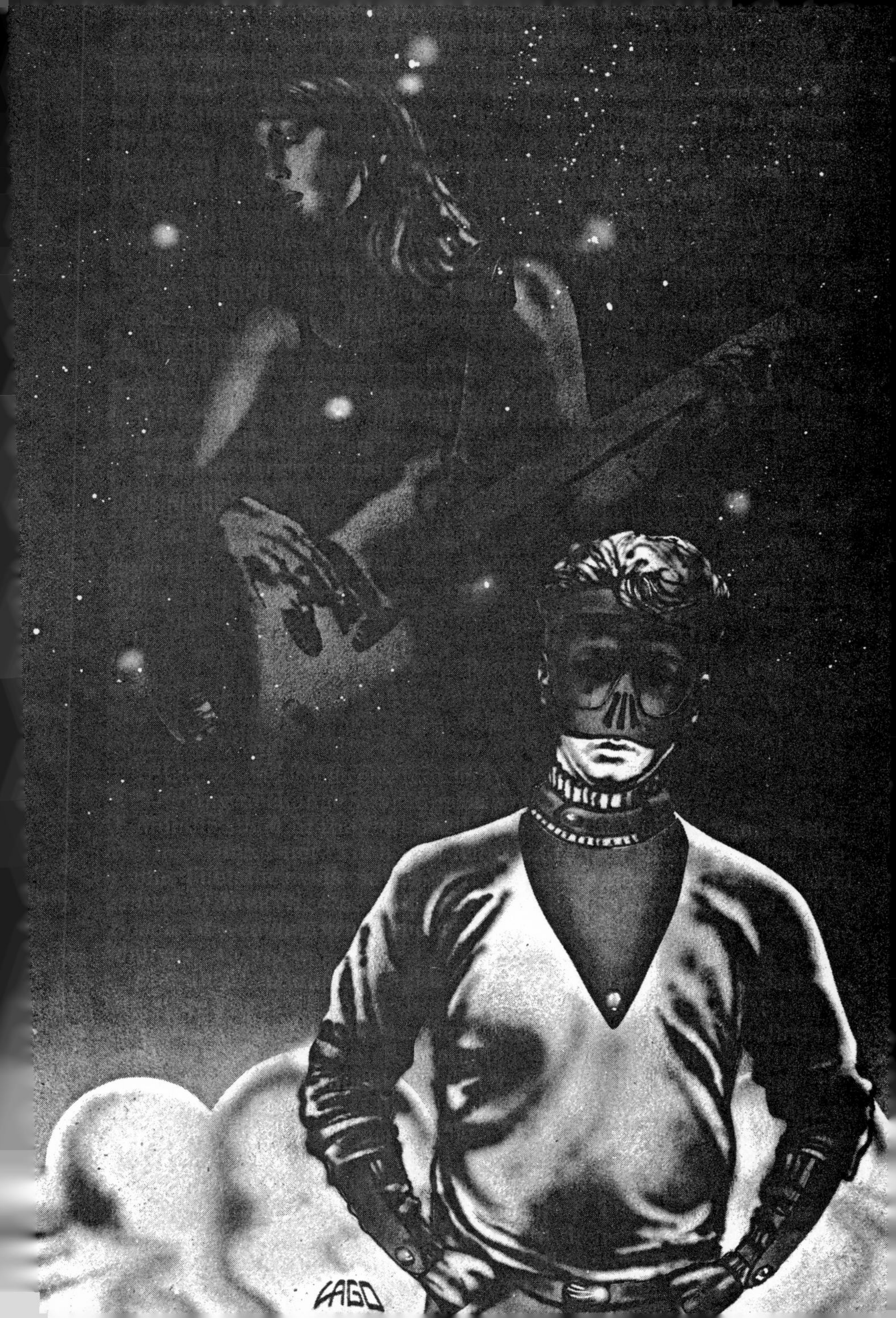
LAGO

rooted down her spine to the small of her back. A length of cloth wrapped her narrow hips. Thin ribs were prominent. Small breasts were set higher than the human norm, and a second pair of rudimentary nipples were visible on her lower ribs. He noted the seamed belly. Oviparous.

"It is permitted." She faced him again. "Touch the earth."

He knelt and touched the dry ground, and when he stood she took a bowl of water from another Orthean and offered it to him. He drank, indifferent to infection.

"If you have weapons you must leave them with us. They will be returned to you when you go."

He carried a knife for just such occasions, and gave it to her. The weapons he carried wouldn't be recognized on a world like this.

"Is there somewhere I can stay in there?" he asked, as they registered his name and possessions in the gatehouse. "Somewhere cheap?"

"Anywhere." Her six-fingered hand flicked out, a gesture including all the streets and domes beyond the wall. "All the Order houses are open to you, Outlander. Open and free. There is no gold in the inner city, not for strangers, nor for us."

" 'Free'?" Broderick said, appalled; and when they had translated it several ways so that there was no mistake: "*free?*"

And then:

What are you doing here, Paul?

No, he thought. No! Not again. Don't think about it—

What right does the Holy Dominion have over this world, what justification for the Interdict? Why, Paul, why?

His haunt was a woman-shaped emptiness visible on the air, distorting the pale sky and squat buildings. Grief and doubt threatened to overwhelm him. He stifled the remembered voice.

Broderick entered the inner city of Kasabaarde.

When Clare Felix died the whole world grieved.

They told Paul Broderick she was dead and he didn't believe it. He heard and smiled: it was a fiction, like the games he and Clare played. A world couldn't exist in which she could be dead.

They thought they made him understand. He understood. The shock blinded and deafened him, but not for long. News of that death would have touched him, he thought mechanically, if he had been dead himself.

He went out blindly into the streets of the megalopolis, into the dust and fumes of a wholly inappropriate summer day. In the crystal sunlight, the bright air, he stood trying to realize it: Clare is dead. Is dead. Clare is dead but the world's still whole, I still exist, and Clare—

—is dead.

He walked past familiar crowded shops. The news was out by then, satellite-broadcast to the world. On the faces of people he passed, he saw a shadow of that raging grief.

He didn't notice when it began, but after a time he knew that in every shop he passed the tapes of Clare Felix's songs were being played. The music and the words that she had sweated over, snarled at him for interrupting, hummed when they loved—those songs were coming out into the dusty grieving city.

He might have run. He found himself, gasping for breath, in front of a public newsscreen. The dead woman's voice sang out under the noise of traffic, the rumble of the distant starport. People slowed, hesitated, listened; a girl cried. Lines of type formed beside her picture on-screen. Her kind of death would have attracted attention on Parmiter's World in any case: they tended to long lives, not massive coronaries at twenty-seven. Being who she was . . .

Broderick read the customary closing line with a new razor-edged attention. '*She lives in the union of the Holy Dominion; her spirit is with us forever.*'

He waited for the comfort that always brought him. It didn't come. When the weeks turned to months, he realized it would never come.

Wider streets opened here, still with the cloth awnings stretched from dome to dome. The shade was welcome. Sweat tracked down between his shoulders. Few Ortheans moved in the noon heat; they sprawled on the steps that led up to the domes, or sat with their backs against the dome walls and stared into space.

Broderick walked for some time down the avenues. At last, having no better guide, he chose a door at random; pushing through the bead curtain and entering the bright room beyond.

"Welcome to Thelmithar." A male Orthean paused at the head of a flight of spiral steps. He was darker-skinned than many, his mane receding from his brow until there was only a white crest left. His movements had the carefulness of age.

"Is there somewhere I can eat?" Broderick asked.

"Of course. Will you stay here?"

It was as good a place as any, he thought. "Yes."

"Come with me. I'm Surinc," the old male said. "Ask for me if you need anything."

Broderick followed him down the spiral stairs and came into a bright underground hall. Silver light reflected diffusely from mirrors set in the vaulted roof: sunlight directed down from above. A young Orthean played the twin-flute in a corner. The tables round the still pool were mostly empty. Children scuttled past, sparing him curious glances.

He ate what time in the trade district had proved unlikely to cause allergic reaction: breadfungus, *brennior*-meat, and *arniac*-herb tea. When he left the table, he called the old Orthean.

"I'll pay for a room now," he said, testing.

The thin lips curved. Surinc weighed the cord of metal beads that passed for money in the trade district and handed them back to Broderick.

"You will be an Outlander, then, not to know there is no payment in the Order houses. Here at Thelmithar—and Gethfirle, Cir-nanth, all the others—they'll feed you, house you, clothe you if you desire it. Freely."

"For how long?"

"As long as you wish to stay."

His mind protested, *nothing's free!* "If not money, then what? Labor? Information?"

The old Orthean unmasked. Broderick saw his whiteless animal eyes, and the nictitating membrane that slid slowly across the slit pupil. Those hooded eyes held indefinable amusement.

"We're fortunate," he said. "All who travel up the Desert Coast to trade must pass through Kasabaarde, and also all who come down from the north and the islands. All who pass us pay. The Order houses have tolls and taxes, Outlander. They can afford the inner city."

Broderick shook his head. "Why give anything away?"

"If you have to ask, why have you come?" The tawny eyes veiled. "We give only one thing—time. Come here and we free you, feed and house you; but what we give away is time."

This, Broderick thought. *If anyone can come here, and not have to work—this is why we're considering the Interdict.*

"Time for what?"

" 'Idleness breeds violence and vision,' the Orders say. There are other values besides what you wear on your back and put in your belly, Outlander. Thelmithar can give you time—what you do with it depends on what you are."

"Violent or visionary?" It was an involuntary, cynical remark.

Surinc's six fingers linked in a complex gesture. "I can't tell you what you'll find here. If I could, it wouldn't be the true illumination."

Reduced to simplicity, Broderick protested, "People can't just do nothing!"

"No, indeed. Most can't. But those who can . . ."

Left alone, Broderick sat for a while, then felt driven to go back up into the open air. Under the awning's shade, many Ortheans sat on Thelmithar's steps. Come from both continents? Broderick wondered. The concept of the inner city stunned him. It was dangerous.

And will you bring the Interdict down on this city of philosophers?

He shook his head to clear it, but couldn't rid himself of the caustic, loving voice of the dead woman.

Broderick left Parmiter's World a scant few weeks after Clare's death. Her face stared down from newsscreens, her voice followed him in the streets. He left because he knew he'd never hear her songs offworld, never hear her name.

Clare Felix's songs and music were under Interdict.

"How can they do it?" she'd raged. "I'm good, Paul. All over this planet—"

"Too good," he admitted. "Too strong, if you like, for the average mind."

"Intendant!" She snarled it like a curse. "What's the Dominion afraid of? Think there'll be another Insurrection if Felix sells offworld, that it?"

She was acid, dismissing his explanations. She didn't want explanations, only justice.

"How can I communicate? I know I can reach them on other worlds—they're different from us, yes, but I can touch them—feel the way they feel, make them listen to me when I sing!"

"How do you think the Insurrection started?" Broderick asked. "Something in the mind responds, philosophy and religion spread from world to world, psychic epidemics—man tends to chaos. If the Dominion didn't keep the Interdict on that—"

"So you interdict religion, politics, art, music . . ." She sat hugging her knees, knuckles white. Tension drew the brown skin taut over her high cheekbones, sharpened the line of her mouth. "You've put me in a cage."

And so he left that cage, Parmiter's World. His fear and hope was that passing under Interdict might wipe out his feeling for her, and the doubt that gnawed him. It did not; it left him more hollow than before.

He went out by way of the Dominion orbital station, traveling on a Dominion ship—there was no other way to travel. The Interdict—a combination of hypnosis and aversion therapy—didn't destroy memory. It implanted a strong disinclination to communicate the Interdicted subject. Perhaps what it did, Broderick thought, was kill the belief in a thing; so that after he left Parmiter's World, Clare glowed bright in his mind, but her music was only noise.

Something with terrifying potential, the Interdict, and so only to be trusted to the highest power: the Holy Dominion. . . .

But that was when I believed in the Dominion, Broderick thought. Now who do I trust?

You came here to judge. So judge.

Broderick knew he was hallucinating. Nevertheless Clare Felix followed him from Thelmithar to Cir-nanth, from Cir-nanth to Gethfirle, and from Gethfirle to the Order house Durietch.

The curved wall of Durietch was hot against his back. The scent of *kasziz*-creeper filled the air. In the past week Broderick had heard any number of philosophies, many varieties of mysticism. Any Intendant would recognize at once how dangerous Kasabaarde's inner city was, breeding such things.

"Outlander," said a young Orthean near him, "what do your people believe in?"

The creed came to Broderick's mind: 'I believe in the Dominion, in our immortality in the union of spirit; I believe in the Peace of Mankind, and in the holy instrumentality of the Intendants—'

I believe Clare Felix is dead.

"I don't know," he said.

"I left the Islands for much the same reason." The Orthean's skin shimmered, crystalline. "I thought I might find an answer here."

"Have you?"

"I don't know. Perhaps."

Dangerous, Broderick thought. If the inner city's principle spreads. An epidemic of fads, philosophies, cults, heresies. No Intendant should hesitate. *Interdict!*

He missed one ship's pickup date, and the next one too.

A fight began without reason, and finished as rapidly; a brief scuffle. No one moved to stop it. Broderick, caught in the fringes, rubbed skinned knuckles. Few of the crazies would tackle the Outlander, as a rule. He left Durietch all the same, walking back through dry alleys to Thelmithar. The egg-basket domes of the inner city blazed white against the pale sky.

When are you going back, Paul?

Now it was movement out of the corner of his eye, creeper fronds that mocked the line of her throat, the turn of her head.

You had no business sending me here! This needs an Intendant with faith, not a man who doubts everything!

Clare, Clare, Clare is dead. Known for so long, so familiar; lived with so close (Broderick thought) that you couldn't say I loved her, you'd have to say we were part of each other. So that death is amputation. Without reason. No, no reason. All the Intendant principles: peace, power, and love . . . all of them hollow. Measure it up against her death and what answer's left? Nothing.

Self-pity, Clare jeered. *And selfishness. How many times have you thought of suicide? Paul, Paul, and you always told me you believed in the unity!*

He sat on Thelmithar's steps, among the tranced Ortheans.

Work, Paul—are you going to waste your life?

He retained a lunatic hope that it was a real experience. That it was Clare in communication from the unity. But however hard he begged her, she wouldn't sing. Then he resigned himself to the fact that it was his own mute mind producing her image.

Clare, I miss you. All our lives together wouldn't have been long enough. I miss your touch, your smell, your love. There are so many questions I wanted to ask you.

The last pickup date was close. Broderick, restless, went from Order house to Order house, questioning those who thought they'd found some illumination, some revelation in the inner city. To any who would listen, he spoke of Clare Felix.

"We're not so intense," one elderly Orthean woman said. "We love many times. But you . . . better to have had her a short time than not at all."

Another, so young he couldn't tell if it were male or female, said, "The earth is. The stars are. The wind blows and the land grows. What more should there be, Outlander?

Passionately, he said, "It doesn't answer her death!"

"I'll die," the young one said. "So will you. Does that thought disturb you?"

Broderick laughed at the irony. "No."

"If you can forgive the universe for your death, then forgive it for hers. Her death is her own, not yours."

He left them, unanswered. The ever present dust worked under his mask as he wandered the streets, irritating his sore eyes. Fury possessed him. Sometimes he shouted aloud. No one took notice of that. He was not unique in the inner city. The short twilight passed, and the fierce stars of the Core blazed in the night sky. Heat radiated back from the stone walls. Broderick kept walking. He crossed and recrossed the inner city, ignoring fatigue. The stars turned in the moonless night.

Dawn found him on the steps of Cir-nanth, dully watching the sunrise. Fatigue blurred his mind. His body ached; he had walked all the long dark hours. Light flooded the face of the dome. A dawn wind blew off the sea. Broderick eased himself down to sit by the bead-curtained door.

It happened then. Between one heartbeat and the next, welling up in him. His eyes stung, wet. He reached out and touched the mortar crumbling between the curved stone blocks, the dead leaves in the dust beside him. He saw the flaring light of the sun and the pale glory of the sky, felt the salt-laden breeze. Felt the breath in his lungs, the beat of his heart, the blood in his body. The pulse, the rhythm . . .

Nothing was changed: Clare was dead. Everything was changed: he was alive.

Broderick drew breath, shook his head in amazement; looking at her death as if it were a thousand years ago, and at her life as if it were a miracle. All the people she had reached out to—!

The inner city said to him: The world is. You are. I am. This is all there is.

And if this is all there is, Broderick slowly pieced together his conclusion, then all that's important is communication. To know ourselves and to know others. Reach out, touch: love. The past and the future don't exist. What matters is us, alive, now.

In Orthe's dawn was a pinprick of falling light, no morning star. The ship. If he didn't leave willingly, they would take him. And take it as further proof that the Interdict was necessary.

"You're our litmus paper," an Intendant once said to him. "We drop you in, stir you round, and pull you out, see how you've changed. How else can we judge the really powerful effects on the human psyche?"

On Orthe there are two populated continents where a man might vanish. On Orthe there are remnants of a high-tech civilization, a star-traveling people. Broderick watched the star fall. If a man should build his own ships . . . ?

It would not be the first time someone had gone up against the Dominion. He would most likely fail. Even if there were—as he thought there might be, later—others to carry the word, failure was still probable.

Will you put music in a cage? Clare Felix had asked.

Broderick put on his mask, and walked on into the long morning shadows of that alien city.

ODBERT

MISSING

by P. A. Kagan

P. A. Kagan, who's from Illinois, says that this unusual story did not start out as SF. What do you think? And do you know just what's—missing?

art: J.R.O.

To whom it may import:

I am writing from jail to acquaint you with important facts in this missing part crisis. I ask your pardon for my awkward phrasing; writing is difficult in such conditions.

Until last Thursday I was happily unconscious of anything wrong. But, trying to fathom an unusual difficulty in conducting my daily affairs, I saw ominous signs of a thing not in its normal spot. Only gradually did I grasp its implications, as shown in writings from my diary:

> **Thursday.** An important part is missing. I cannot carry on my work, and I don't know how anybody in town can. But oddly, nobody says anything about it. It's as if nobody knows, though warning signs abound. Knowing how apt I am to panic, I shall not talk about it until I find additional proof.

> **Friday.** I am right. No doubt at all. It is missing. As implications crowd in, I shrink with horror. Without it our civilization is lost. And how could it just vanish? Still no talk about it. Looking back, I think it was gradually withdrawn from circulation. It is surprising that I, a journalist, did not know right away.

Hunting for an ally, I told my buddy Pynchon, who said I was crazy. You watch, I told him, and try to find it.

Saturday. At six o'clock this morning Pynchon was waiting at my door, full of dismay. A cautious man, Pynchon, but not afraid to act if conditions warrant. Pynchon and I shall work jointly on this affair. First thing is to find facts that confirm our diagnosis. I am trying to show him that Washington has to know. All day Pynchon and I sought that missing part, looking for a pin in a haystack. To think that a fortnight ago it was all around. I don't want to alarm our population, though how it could stay so blind is hard to grasp.

I am drafting a manuscript for public distribution, but with difficulty, for now that it is missing, how will I talk about it? This is a form of thought control, which I must combat with my ability. Words will not go as I want: "This is a day for all good folks to go to aid . . ."

Sunday. Working on a holiday! But our situation commands it. I can spot an agitation in our town, an aura of misgiving in both adults and kids. Though *still* nobody talks about it, all know by intuition that things do not flow smoothly. Only by intuition. How poorly our population thinks!

I finally got Pynchon (who has a good bit of clout) to call Washington. I think our information did not astonish our "guv-mint" so much as our having it did. It turns out that this loss is not just local but national. Officially, activity was put in motion by our call. Both of us had to go to our nation's capital but got no thanks for our pains. High command was afraid to trust us in discussions! Within hours, Washington was amok with rumors. FBI from instinct said it was a Russian plot. Absurd. Any fool knows that that part is as important to Russia as to us. An intriguing possibility has to do with Third World, Arabs, or China—civilizations to whom this loss is nothing.

Monday. Back in our town, I find still no word about this missing part. I think our high command in Washington is trying to push it out of sight, hoping (as usual) that this crisis will go away.

I cannot allow it, for I am afraid that it is not just missing but lost. Lost for good. All right, so basically it is just a symbol, but without symbols, what basis for communication? It is crucial to our civilization. Without it our world is grown poor.

My diary stops at that point. On publication of my story, I was brought to prison, and for many days had no writing things. A traitor, I am told. It was always thus—punish a man who brings bad tidings.

I had nothing to do with that part vanishing. I only saw it was missing and said so. But it is important to find who did.

For this culprit is still hiding, waiting, plotting to go on with his diabolical work. In jail I can do nothing, so I say to you: *You must not wait.*

Today, *today* a watchdog group must start to monitor things. Do not wait until it occurs again. For I worry. I am afrad that addtonal loss awats us.

by
Sydney
J. Van
Scyoc

FIRE-CALLER

art: Gary Freeman

This story was a brief respite for the author who lately spends most of her time writing novels. Berkley has recently published *Darkchild* and *Bluesong*, the first two books in her Sunstone Scrolls trilogy, and the third *Starsilk*, will soon be out.

Pa-lil followed the others down the ship's ramp, blinking against harsh late afternoon sunlight. Her initial glimpse of Tennador was not encouraging. A dusty pall hung in the western sky, turning the sun copper. From the bottom of the ramp, boulder-pocked ground spread toward a collection of rude structures in one direction, toward a ragged band of trees in the other. Shading her eyes, she distinguished a turbid strand of water winding westward toward what must be the growing fields. At least she thought she saw people working there among rows of vegetation.

Tennador—Bright Bird of Freedom. So someone had named this globe when the first Pachni were sent here. Pa-lil could not see the brightness. The only thing that glittered today was the single tear that came to her eye as her feet touched ground. She blinked it away irritably and studied the men and women who had come to greet the newcomers. They were much like the slaves who worked her father's vineyards, tall and lean, with blond hair turned to straw by the sun and squinting grey eyes, as if they had looked too long into a harsh sky.

Now they looked at her, picking her from among the others, silently questioning her auburn hair, the clay-red darkness of her eyes, the unblemished pallor of her skin. Uncomfortably she turned and gazed toward the trees.

They were nearer than she had first thought. Even from here, she could see the thick, fibrous hair that matted their trunks and the oily sheen of their broad leaves, details that put the stamp of finality to her exile. During the weeks of her journey, Tennador had been no more than a name she gave the future, the name of the land where Pachni slaves were sent when their Washrar masters chose to release them but were afraid to let them remain near. Or more brutally, the land where Pachni slaves were sent when the masters who wanted to be free of them were too humane to have them garrotted—or too frightened for that measure.

Pa-lil's master, however, had been frightened not of her but for her. And he had been her father as well as her master. And so today Tennador took substance and tears rose in her throat. She glanced around briefly and found grey eyes watching her. With a strangled sob, she dropped her bundles and pushed past the other newcomers. She ran toward the trees, unable to bear the watching eyes.

Soon she brushed among softly-furred trunks. Fallen leaves crackled brittlely underfoot. The air under the trees held a sharp, oily scent. She ran until she could hold back tears no longer. Then she threw herself down against a hair-matted trunk and cried.

When she calmed, she had only to think how pleased Brindin would be to see her cry and her tears dried completely. Brindin had always hated her, his half-Pachni sister. Their father set a generous table, but Brindin considered each bite Pa-lil ate food taken from him. If their father ordered her a new gown, Brindin demanded a gift too, and of better price. He made caustic remarks about her mother, who had died at Pa-lil's birth, although everyone knew it was his own mother who had brought disorder to the house, who had finally been barred from the estate for raising a knife to their father. And there were the pranks—only pranks, because Brindin knew their father would look to him if she were harmed.

Then one autumn noon she had done the one thing she should not have done—without even knowing she did it. Suddenly the danger had been not just from Brindin but from every Washrar. And her father had recognized that she was beyond his protection if she remained on Washrar.

A mistake, such a small mistake. She had not even been aware of making it, yet now she would not see her father again. She began to sob again, crying until she fell into an exhausted sleep, curled against the tree's matted trunk.

"Sister."

She heard the summons as if from a distance, felt a touch on her shoulder. Reluctantly she opened her eyes, the lids swollen and heavy. A Washrar bent over her: shining dark hair, finely carved lips and nose, heavy-lidded black eyes. He was beautiful, as Washrar men so often were, yet she thought of Brindin and recoiled.

But when he spoke again, she forgot her half-brother. This Washrar spoke as she had heard the Pachni speak among themselves, softly, the words falling in musical cadence. "Sister—it's coming dark now. You must wake and come along. You haven't given work for your night's bed."

Work. She sat, remembering that in the settlements, everyone was required to work, from the first day. And she had not stayed to help unpack crates or janitor the ship. But surprise carried her past dismay. "You're Washrar."

He shook his head emphatically. "No, no, I'm a man of Tennador. I call myself Andor Tereyse. I arrived here three years ago to help build the newer settlements. I came to meet you at the ship today and I heard you had gone into the woods. Now you will have no place to sleep if you don't come do work before dark."

"You came to meet me?" She had expected no one; she knew no one in the settlements.

"You are Pa-lil Rhallis, the fire-caller?"

She drew back involuntarily, a chill settling upon her bare arms. How did he know she had been a fire-caller? "I left the fire-bowl when I left Washrar."

His dark brows rose questioningly. "I didn't think anyone ever left the fire-bowl. I thought that once the conduit was established, it existed eternally."

"A conduit to corrupt gods?" she demanded sharply, trying to keep the quiver from her voice. "I'm not sure it ever existed. I'm not sure there was ever anyone there to hear my plaints."

"Ah?" Although his words still fell in Pachni cadence, the consonants took a sharper edge. "You completed the temple disciplines without believing in the gods? Why would anyone do that?"

Why indeed? Perhaps because she had believed in the gods at first. Or had at least believed in the symbolic truths their legends embodied. Or perhaps she had lost herself so totally in the temple disciplines—the fasts, the vigils, the long hours spent studying obscure texts and learning archaic plaints—because they offered escape from her increasing revulsion with the life she saw beyond her father's estate.

Or perhaps she had simply learned the disciplines to please her father. Certainly it was only through his insistence that she was accepted at the temple, a half-Pachni.

"Maybe," she ventured, "maybe it isn't really the gods I've lost faith in. Maybe it's the people who treat with them."

He nodded, still studying her. "You will find that different when you practice your vocation here."

She glanced up sharply. Practice the fire-bowl here? What gave him the idea she had that intention? But before she could protest, he stayed her with an upraised palm and glanced around, listening. She frowned, puzzled. "What is it?"

"Do you hear the wind rising?"

She listened, distracted. "No. I don't hear anything."

"You'll hear it soon enough. So will the woods cats who hunt this part of the woods. We must go before they wake early and find us in their run." He turned away. "Hurry."

She hesitated, briefly disconcerted, then followed.

She soon realized she had run deeper into the trees than she had thought. Andor walked quickly, glancing warily into the growing shadows. Before long Pa-lil found herself imitating his vigilance, although she was not certain what she watched for.

And now she did hear the wind. It moved into the trees like the breath of night, shaking branches and setting up a brittle clatter of leaves.

Gazing around, distracted, she stumbled over an exposed root. Andor turned back immediately at her startled cry. She accepted his extended hand, then stiffened at a rising cry from deep in the trees. When it died, she stared at Andor uncomprehendingly, realizing that suddenly he gripped her hand so tightly it hurt. "What—"

"One of the woods cats that dens near here. Look—you can tell by the claw marks on the trees that this is a pack run. If your nose were sharper, you could tell from the scent the cats leave. Didn't you learn any of this on the ship?"

"*No*—no. I—I didn't attend all the briefings." And she had not noticed before that the tree trunks were ripped and torn in places. "What do they hunt?"

"The woods are full of seed gatherers. The cats prey on them. They prey on our stock if they wander this far. And of course they prey on us if we are here."

"Then—then let us not be here," Pa-lil said tremulously. She had always been frightened of the feral cats that stalked her father's estate, although they stood no higher than her knee. Certainly none of them could cry as the woods cat cried again now—the sound full and deep, ending in a gurgling moan.

"Your knee—can you run?"

"It's only a scrape."

They ran hand in hand, leaves crackling underfoot, Pa-lil's breath coming painfully. When they emerged from the trees, she almost fell against Andor in exhaustion. But he did not slow until they had put a good distance between themselves and the woods.

Finally he halted, breathing heavily, and threw himself down on a small boulder. Pa-lil collapsed nearby, her legs quivering, her chest tight.

Dusk was slowly thickening to darkness. In the settlement, lanterns glowed alive, shining through glazed windows and straw thatch. From somewhere came the smell of food cooking.

And she had not done work to earn a meal, Pa-lil realized in dismay. "The rules—" she ventured, licking her lips.

Andor pushed himself upright, gazing at her through the deepening shadows. "You're hungry."

"Yes," she sighed, relieved he had guessed. She was hungry and she had nowhere to stay the night.

He pressed her hand reassuringly. "Then let's go find your

bundles. I have a small wood-hut I built for myself. I keep food there from my own patch."

"You'll feed me? If there's work I should do for you—" She broke off, gazing up at him with sudden uncertainty. Was she trusting him too far on first acquaintance? Even after nineteen years, she still had trouble believing what lay behind so many Washrar faces—the same classic faces the gods wore.

"There's always work," he said easily. "Let's go before it grows darker."

They found her possessions on the landing field. From there she followed him down the boulder-strewn lanes of the settlement. They passed structures of every kind, some built of wood with glazed windows, others of woven grasses or braided twigs.

Andor led her to a modest structure of hewn wood. Its interior, she saw when he lit the lantern, was plain and sparsely furnished. The only luxury was the heavily embroidered quilt thrown over the mattress in the corner.

He noticed immediately that the quilt caught her eye. "My nurse made it for me, every stitch by hand."

She nodded, remembering her own nurse and the fine-work she had done: embroidered quilts, gowns, nightdresses. Remembering too the times Brindin had tangled Yoni's threads or deliberately stained the fabrics she worked with—remembering the impotent glint of anger in Yoni's grey eyes, quickly hidden. Worse had been her own fear that one day Yoni would not hide the anger, that one day she would let Brindin see its intensity. Then Pa-lil's father would have to send her to the vineyards or to the southern estates before Brindin could make a story of it and demand she go to the garrotting chair.

Pa-lil shivered and turned from the embroidered quilt. Andor was sorting through a rank of wooden bins. "Here," he said. "These don't need cooking. And the tea will brew quickly on the lantern burner."

He placed round yellow cakes and dried fruit on brightly patterned platters and Pa-lil ate eagerly, so hungry she hardly noticed the unfamiliar taste and consistency of the food. When they finished, they sat at length over mugs of bitter tea. Finally Pa-lil put her mug down and traced its glazed surface with one fingertip. There was a question she hadn't asked in the woods. "Andor, how did you know I was a fire-caller?"

His brows rose quizzically. "There's free communication between Tennador and Washrar."

She waited, but he did not continue. "That's no answer."

He shrugged, filling his mug from the pot. "No, it isn't. But you know the settlements don't accept just any Pachni whose master decides to free him. There are some we cannot take. Some who would be too disruptive."

Yes, some driven past reason or rule by the cruelties of life on Washrar. Some too disordered or debauched to live without masters and whips. The first settlements, established on Tennador seventy years before, had failed. This time the conditions of emigration and the rules of communal life were far more stringent. "So you learned when my father applied to send me here."

"Yes. And we needed a fire-caller. Our people know the gods, but they have no one to speak for them. No one trained to serve as conduit. Here—let me show you what I've made." Quickly, before she could object, he went to a cupboard and brought down an object wrapped in layers of fabric.

Unwrapping the object, he set it on the table between them. His black eyes glinted as the glazed pattern blazed alive by lantern light. "You see, you haven't asked me what work I do," he said softly. "I'm a potter, and this is the fire-bowl I've made for you."

She gasped involuntarily at the beauty of the bowl. It was low and perfectly formed, glazed Parnith blue, the favorite color of Rundikar, god of fine arts. It was patterned with silver wings so perfectly drawn they seemed to float upon the surfaces of the bowl. "It's beautiful," she said at last. "But I don't call fire any more." The words were regretful. She had always loved the offering bowls, their form and balance, the cool beauty of their glazes. She would have liked to gaze into this one while she sang the archaic plaints she had searched out in the early books, as balanced, as cool as the silver wings that decorated the bowl. But she knew she dared not.

Andor tapped one fingernail against the rim of the bowl, making it ring dully. It was moments before he spoke. "Tell me then—if you won't use my bowl, what work will you do?"

She glanced up, afraid from the sharpness of the question that he thought she did not like the bowl. She met a cool, weighing gaze instead. "I—" She searched for an answer. She had no skills, only her temple training. "I could work in the fields."

He shrugged off the suggestion. "Are you used to hard labor, to working long hours in the sun? It would take half the season to condition yourself properly. Why don't you just take my bowl for the day? I've already set up a canopy near the river, where everyone passes. Our people have fed the fire-bowls of Washrar for three centuries now and no one has sung any plaints for them. I think it is time."

The Pachni had fed the fire-bowls? "No, the Pachni have never been permitted to come to the temples. Not even—"

Andor's finely etched brows rose sharply. "They have been barred from the temples, yes. But who do you think creates the food and goods that are burned in the temple fire-bowls? Not the estate owners. Not their families. And not any other Washrar, not since Jan Palsin landed the first consignment of slaves at Windigar Port. Since then it has been the Pachni who have filled the temple bowls. I doubt you have ever burned an offering drawn from the sweat of a Washrar."

Pa-lil drew back, struck by the truth of what he said, wondering why she had never seen it before. Even her father, the best man she knew, went to the temple carrying fruits and grains grown by his Pachni slaves. Was that why he so often came back troubled? Because he knew his offerings had not been his own at all?

Was that, in fact, why the people who had come to her station at the temple had always demanded such small-hearted blessings? Was that why they insisted that they be set above their neighbors, that they be aggrandized? How could they ask for dearer gifts, closer gifts, when the offerings they made were not even their own?

"Three of my father's vineyard workers came to me last year and asked me to make plaints for them," she said slowly. "My father wouldn't let me. He said I would be expelled from the temple."

"Now there is no temple to expel you. You have an entire new people to serve—and they want to speak to the gods they know from the older legends. Not the gods the Washrar have tried to create these past years with their extravagant offerings and corrupt demands."

She glanced up sharply, surprised. Did he feel as she did, that the Washrar were trying to shape newer, more venal gods in their own image—because they were ashamed before the old gods? Ashamed of their greed and the brutality it engendered. She bit her lip, stroking the rim of the bowl, realizing he had convinced her. She wanted to do it. She wanted to sit under a canopy and sing plaints that were no longer sung on Washrar, to gods purer than those worshipped now. Slowly she drew her fingertips across the glazed inner surface of the bowl.

When she touched the sloped bottom, she realized what was wrong. "You haven't left a hole for the gas pipe." And where had he found temple apparatus: fuel tanks to be hidden under the floor, a feeder pipe leading up through the carved column where the bowl rested, the pressure sensitive pilot control she could nudge with one toe when she was ready for the flame to leap into the bowl and consume the offering?

He measured out his response deliberately. "We have no gas. I didn't suppose you would need it, Pa-lil."

At first she didn't believe what he said. Then blood rushed dizzily from her head and her face blanched. *He knew.* He knew what had happened that noon when Fenubia had removed the empty tank from beneath her station and neglected to replace it, when Pa-lil's toe had touched the pilot control and flame had leapt in the bowl anyway. If the petitioner had been anyone but her own father, if he hadn't quickly told Fenubia he had ignited the offering himself with striker tongs—

Her entire body grew cold. Somehow Andor knew.

But how? Certainly her father had told no one. And she had refused to go back to the temple after that day. Fenubia—had Fenubia guessed and passed rumors? She had resented having a half-Pachni caller in the temple, and she had not liked hearing the old plaints sung. Could a rumor have reached Tennador from Fenubia's lips so quickly? Pa-lil shook her head in confusion.

Slowly Andor stood, his gaze measuring. "I suppose I can give you hearth matches if you have no better idea."

She nodded numbly, seizing at his words, refusing to meet the question behind them. "Yes. The offerings won't burn as cleanly without the gas flame, but if that is all you have—"

"That's all I can offer. You'll do it then? You'll go to the river tomorrow?"

"Yes," she whispered, wondering from the steadiness of his gaze how much he knew—and how much her confusion had betrayed. "Yes, I'll take the bowl to the river." She stood uncertainly, suddenly very tired. "Is there a place where I can sleep tonight? Someone I can go to—"

"You can sleep here."

"I—is that usual?"

"No, but it's late to disturb the shelter monitor. And I would have to speak to the meal monitor too to see that you were given breakfast. It will be simpler if you stay here. You take the mattress; I have blankets enough to make myself comfortable on the floor."

She was too tired to vacillate long before accepting his invitation. He turned the lantern low and she slept almost immediately.

Deep in the night, a succession of dream-images overtook her: faces, scenes, half-digested memories. Anger came too and terror; they were her frequent companions in sleep. They had been for many years. When she heard the bellowing cry of a woods cat nearby, she thought she dreamed that too. But it came again, nearer, and was followed by human voices. She awoke to see Andor pull on his boots and slip out the door.

"Andor?" When he did not answer, she ran to the window and saw only running shadows, then nothing. She wondered what was happening, but there was no one to tell her. After a while she lay down again, uneasily, and fell into a restless half-sleep.

She woke later at the sound of the door opening. Andor slipped into the room. "A pack of cats got into the sheep pens," he explained when he saw she was awake. "We'll be hunting them tomorrow night. Once they leave their runs and come into the settlement to take stock, there's nothing else to do."

She frowned, trying to penetrate the shadows of the room. "You're hurt," she said uncertainly.

"This?" He held out a spattered sleeve. "Sheep's blood. They killed two of our best ewes."

He rolled into his blankets and she crawled back beneath the embroidered quilt. After a while she realized neither of them slept. And there was one question she had not asked earlier. She spoke quietly into the darkened room. "Andor, why did you come here?" The first settlements had been established seventy years ago by an eccentric estate owner who had adopted asceticism and decided to free himself of his slaves. Those had been the settlements that failed. The new settlements had been founded by a group of unlanded Washrar whose motives were still much debated. They had turned the administration of the settlements entirely to the Pachni at the end of five years, but their reasons for establishing the Pachni on Tennador remained obscure.

He spoke softly. "I had to come."

"But you don't have Pachni blood." His was a classic Washrar beauty. She had seen his heavy-lidded eyes gazing down at her from dozens of dusty portraits.

"No, not in my veins. On my hands. I had to come, Pa-lil. And now I have to sleep. I'm going upriver to dig clay tomorrow. I'll be leaving early."

She recognized his reluctance and didn't press further. Instead she lay awake while he slept, staring at the shadows in the corners. She didn't sleep again until near dawn.

It was midmorning when she woke. Andor had gone, leaving his blood-spattered shirt flung over the back of a chair and cold tea, cakes, and dried fruit on the table. Pa-lil pulled on her best temple gown, emerald green patterned with finely spun golden spirals. The silken fabric folded coolly about her ankles. She ate sparingly. When she was done, she filled a pail from the water barrel and rinsed the blood from Andor's shirt. Then she carefully wrapped the fire-bowl, found the hearth matches, and left the hut.

By sunlight, the settlement was caught between rough beauty and squalor. Coarse-spun clothing hung drying on trees and bushes and tiny flowers of intense color bloomed at the edges of weedy paths. Pa-lil glimpsed a child running purposefully between huts and saw an old man sitting dull-eyed in the shade of a hairy-trunked tree. He looked up as she passed and said something she did not understand. Looking back, she saw that he was pulling strands of fiber from the tree and twisting them into cord.

When she reached the landing area, she paused and gazed toward the river. Shading her eyes, she saw a patch of bright color. The canopy Andor had raised for her? She gazed at it, feeling a moment's doubt. Perhaps she should not have accepted the bowl. But she had, and she had accepted food and shelter as well. The bargain was struck.

The canopy was made of brilliant azure canvas supported on poles. It waited for her a short distance from the riverbank. Beneath it weeds had been cut back and a kneeling mat spread for her. She stepped beneath the bright fabric self-consciously, aware of people who had come to draw water pausing to stare. Carefully she unwrapped the bowl and placed it on the mat before her. Sunlight slanting beneath the azure canopy made the silver wings beat with color.

She sat alone for a long time. People came to the riverbank to drink or to draw water and lingered to stare. She could not read their thoughts from their faces, but when she met their eyes, they did not look away. After a while, shivering under their scrutiny, she drew a tremulous breath and gazed into the bowl. Almost without realizing it, she began to sing.

She sang an archaic plaint to Birikar, goddess of blue skies, patron of birds and serenity. All the verses asked of Birikar was an easy spirit. In that it was far different from the newer plaints demanding that the glory of the petitioner reach as far as the sky.

She wove the time-worn words together and silver-glazed wings spanned the sky.

She did not realize until she completed the plaint that a petitioner had come. A girl of perhaps twelve knelt opposite her. When she realized that the plaint was done, the girl touched the rim of the bowl with one careful finger. Her hand was tanned by the sun, hardened by work, and her pale hair was bleached white. Her tongue darted at her lips; her eyes were bright. "I brought an offering. Will you burn it in your bowl?"

She held a small, taut-skinned purple fruit. Pa-lil hesitated only a moment. "Yes, if you can bring me some dried grass to line the bowl. Something I can set afire with my match."

The girl nodded quickly and jumped up. Bare moments later she returned with a double handful of brittle vegetation. She crumpled it into the bowl, then gazed up at Pa-lil, poised between eagerness and apprehension.

Carefully Pa-lil laid the fruit atop the pyre. That done, she hesitated, momentarily uncertain how to treat with her first Pachni petitioner. This setting, so unlike the temple, with its friezes and draperies and polished marble, was well-suited to the old plaints. But if the girl had large wishes—"What is it you want from the gods?"

The girl spoke quickly, as if she were afraid of losing courage. "I want to go to the big looms to weave like my sister. She went to the looming rooms on her birthday and they began to teach her. Now it will be my birthday in four days."

Pa-lil studied the girl: her breathless eagerness, the glint in her eyes. "What birthday is it for you?"

"My twelfth."

"And your sister—how old was she on her birthday?"

The girl sighed and squirmed impatiently. "She was fifteen. But—"

"Have you ever had a chance to practice weaving? To see if you have any ability for it?"

The girl leaned forward eagerly. "I have a lap loom. I've made pieces on that. But I want to learn the big looms. I want—" Quickly she jumped up. "I'll show you. I'll bring you the pieces I've made and you can see them. Can you wait?"

"I can wait," Pa-lil agreed, relieved that the girl was amenable. She would never have dared question a Washrar petitioner on the suitability of his demands.

While she waited, a group of workers came from the fields to take their meal beside the water. They sat a short distance from her canopy, laughing while they ate. She had seldom heard a Pachni laugh before, and now she heard six of them laughing together, men and women. She listened and found she liked the sound of it.

The girl returned soon, her tanned face flushed. She threw herself down, rummaging through the cloth bag she carried, bringing out small swatches of fabric. She spread them, watching anxiously for Pa-lil's reaction. "They aren't fine. I don't have fine threads and yarns. All I have are lengths that weren't good enough to be used on the big looms. But—"

"It's your workmanship we're interested in," Pa-lil agreed. She studied the samples. She did not know much of the weaver's art. She had seldom visited the looming rooms of her father's estate. Yet it seemed to her that the girl had done well, that she had combined colors carefully and created distinctive patterns and as even a grain as possible, given the inferior materials she had used. She nodded, realizing the girl watched her expectantly.

"I think," she decided, "that we must address Nabikar, who has the gift of dexterity, and Rifikar, who is patron of practical arts. We will tell them you require cleverness for your hands and a wise eye for color and form. It appears to me that you already have those abilities in their early form. We will ask that they be steadily strengthened until it is your turn to go to learn the looms. Then when it is time, you will be so skilled that you will learn quickly and easily."

"But I can't go on my birthday?"

"Are others taken when they are twelve?"

The girl shook her head. "No."

"Then you must not ask to be taken out of turn. Instead you must let your talent grow until it is old enough for the large looms. But I would like you to go often to the loom mistress and show her your work. Take opinions from her. Perhaps when she sees how well you work, she'll let your sister give you lessons on the large looms sometime when the weavers are not busy." She studied the girl, wondering if she would accept such a modest blessing. If so, it would be by far the most humble request Pa-lil had ever made of the gods for anyone but her own father. Not to become wealthy or feared, not to put rivals in the shadow or to gain revenge upon enemies—simply to be permitted to learn a skill she had already begun to master.

The girl did not hesitate. "That's what I want."

Pa-lil nodded as if she had expected just that answer. "Then tell me your name and I will sing for you."

"Tibbi."

Pa-lil nodded again, striking a hearth match with as much ceremony as possible. The dry grass in the bowl caught fire immediately, flaring in a small yellow blaze. Pa-lil let her head drop and began to breathe as she had been taught, concentrating upon the flame. She called up memory of Rifikar's face, of Nabikar's, as she had seen them in sculpture and tapestry, their features serene, composed, untainted by any hint of striving or dissatisfaction. She held their faces before her mind's eye and the flame in the bowl grew more vivid, burning blue, dancing. Drawing breath, she commenced her plaint to Nabikar. She chose verses recorded twelve centuries before, in the days when the Washrar first called themselves a people. Those were the days when the Washrar labored on small plots and knew hardship, the days when they housed their gods in plainly furnished temples and brought offerings they could scarcely spare.

She sang to the gods of those early temples, vital and unsullied. She was hardly aware, as she made her plaint, of Tibbi staring breathlessly into the fire-bowl, of men and women coming from the river to watch—of the flame dancing clean and blue far longer than it should have, dancing from the bottom of a bowl that soon contained only ash and a charred fruit pit. She sang to the gods the early Washrar had created from hard work and need.

She approached the final verse of the last plaint when she became aware of an old Pachni woman leaning near, her lips moving as she peered into the flame. Her concentration broken, Pa-lil let her eyes dart around the circle of eyes. She saw the same blue flame mirrored in them all.

The flame. She caught a ragged breath, the plaint dying. The flame danced, but there was no gas line feeding the fire-bowl, and the offering was long since consumed. And no sooner did her voice fade than the blue flame winked out. Stunned, she stared first down into the emptiness of the bowl, then up into the faces that surrounded her.

If they were not frightened, she was. She had called fire again—not as she had been taught in the temple, by tapping a hidden control with one toe. Instead she had called it from another source. From herself.

For a moment she could not breathe. Her heart pounded so loudly she was certain everyone heard. She knew she should sit calmly and add some benediction to the plaint she had sung. But she could not. She was on her feet and stumbling from under the canopy before anyone else looked up.

Even as she ran, she mouthed silent plaints. Let not the fire follow her, let her not wield it and do harm. She had left the sullied temples of Washrar behind. The gods she had brought in her heart to Tennador were young and uncorrupted. They had not seen the cruelties practiced on Washrar these past centuries. Their eyes were clear.

But she had seen those things and they burned in her. She ran from the riverbank to the landing field to the trees, her gown whipping at her ankles. She ran until tears blinded her. Then she threw herself down and cried, choking for breath.

As on the day before, she sobbed herself to sleep, her head cradled against the coarsely furred trunk of a tree. She did not even think of woods cats until Andor's voice woke her. Then she sat, drawing an anxious breath.

Andor was not alone. A tall Pachni woman with white braids stood behind him. And something in the woman's eyes, some deep-seeing quality, dispelled all thought of woods cats. Quickly Pa-lil tried to stand.

"No, stay," Andor said, sitting in the dry leaves. "This is Loxa, governor of the settlements. She has come to talk to you about the gift."

The gift? Pa-lil stared in confusion as Loxa lowered herself to the ground, crossing her lean legs. She was dressed in a long, loose gown which she pulled up unselfconsciously to bare her legs. Her face might have been worked in leather, the flesh was so weathered, but her eyes were brightly alive, probing and commanding at once. Pa-lil tried to guess her age and could not. "I don't know what you mean," she faltered.

"You have brought us a gift we have waited for," Loxa said. "We thought you might, but your father's message was cryptic. He could not write plainly with the shadow of the garrotter upon you."

Her father had sent a message? What had he said? And what gift? Pa-lil looked to Andor in confusion and for a moment saw a blue flame wavering in his eyes.

The fire. She had brought the Pachni fire the Washrar had tried so hard to extinguish. But how could anyone call that a gift? "No," she protested. "It was an accident. I forgot there was no gas to feed the flame. I—"

"So you fed the flame yourself. You kept it alive the same way the first Pachni slaves did. Of yourself."

Pa-lil stared helplessly at Loxa. The first slaves had made fire from nothing—yes—and everyone knew what had become of them. *"They died!"* she said. "They called fire—without strikers, without matches, without pilots or gas tubes—and they died. Their masters killed them!"

"Of course they killed them," Loxa said, untouched. "Imagine yourself a Washrar land owner. Your family has struggled for centuries, tilling the earth, perfecting the vines, shipping their wines to every known market and getting all too little for it. Then Tel Veximar perfects the *palina-vira,* which produces a unique wine, in demand everywhere as soon as it's tasted—and the vines flourish only on Washrar.

"Suddenly the market is boundless. But who will work the new lands required to supply it? Invite emigrants to come in and share the bounty when they haven't shared the hardship?

"An entrepreneur named Jan Palsin had a better idea. He had heard of a world peopled by humans far less enterprising, far more docile than the Washrar. They appeared to be primitives—simple primitives, living with no thought of civilization or trade.

"You know the rest. Jan Palsin made his family's fortune by trading in those people—the Pachni. By bringing them to Washrar and selling them as slaves. And the first Pachni, so naïve in the isolation of their own culture, hardly realized they had become slaves.

"Nor did they guess that the few little gifts they brought with them would terrify their new masters. A youngster working in the potting shed needs a trowel that has fallen to the floor. Instead of leaning down to pick it up, she simply lifts it. An overseer instructs one of a crew of pickers to take a message to the rest of the crew. The picker conveys the message without leaving the trellis where he works—and without speaking aloud. An estate owner's wife instructs her Pachni houseman to light the hearth fire, and he does it without matches.

"The Pachni who possessed these gifts did these things as casually as they walked and talked. To them they were natural.

"But the gifts were not natural to the Washrar. They were terrifying. For one thing, the Washrar couldn't guess what gifts beyond these simple ones the Pachni might have. The ability to make healthy vines wither? The ability to kill an overseer with a glance? Yet those same feared slaves had become essential to everyone dependent upon the wine trade. And not every Pachni had a gift. Some could call fire. Some could lift. Some could in-speak. But there were many others who could do none of those things.

"The estate owners acted secretly and in isolation at first. Pachni with gifts simply disappeared, sometimes after a loss the estate owner attributed to their witchery. Later the weeding became systematic, even institutionalized. It became a preventive measure, a way of holding back flood or drought or disease—because surely the Pachni could inflict all those disasters upon their masters if they didn't learn the proper fear.

"The Pachni were too naive to realize at first what was happening—or to understand what more could happen. And so before they thought of using their gifts in their own defense, the bearers of the gifts were murdered. Later their survivors were too compromised by fear and isolation to resist. They learned not to let any spark show in their eyes—of intelligence, of anger, of humanity. Because the Washrar quickly learned to fear those things too."

"They died," Pa-lil repeated flatly. That was what Loxa said with all her words. Any Pachni suspected of witchery disappeared or died.

"Yes, and they're still dying on Washrar—for the pettiest reasons, upon the slightest of suspicions," Loxa agreed. "But not so often now. That's the irony of our situation, Pa-lil. The less humanity they left us, the more the Washrar feared us. Now that they've almost entirely quenched our spirit, they've persuaded themselves that a dead slave can reach out from the garrotting chair to avenge himself. Some Washrar have become so frightened they are willing to let us go."

Pa-lil nodded reluctantly. Fear had fed upon itself for so long now that many masters wanted only to rid themselves of their slaves and live upon their fortunes. So they sent the Pachni to Tennador and hoped the terror went with them. But what did that have to do with her? Her father had not been frightened of her. He had sent her here because he had been afraid Brindin would learn she had raised fire and call the garrotter on her. "I don't understand—"

"You don't understand why we've followed you here to tell you things you already know? Only because we want our gifts back. They were taken from us by the Washrar and our people think they are gone forever. Our people think they have been permanently lessened by slavery. They think their spark has been extinguished.

"You showed them today that it has not. You showed them hope—hope that they are as fully themselves, as fully human, as their ancestors were. You showed them that the gifts still exist."

Pa-lil's throat ran dry. Loxa's presence was so strong she might have been a Pachni god: elemental, strong, avenging. And how did one argue with a god? When her voice came, it was hoarse. "What do you want me to do?" She asked the question although she knew the answer.

"We want you to show them hope again. Every day. We want you to show them again and again until you have burned three centuries of doubt. We want you to show them until they know they are finally free—and strong."

Pa-lil's shoulders tightened, muscles cramping. "*No*. I can't use the fire-bowl again." Her voice was so tight it quivered. Loxa could speak of hope and freedom. She had never called the fire. She couldn't guess the force with which it could burn—the angry force. "I'll sing the plaints. But I won't use the bowl. It's—it's only a focusing device. I don't need it. I can speak to the gods without it."

"But what are the gods, Pa-lil? Are they living entities? I believe they are simply hope and faith and strength given human face and name. And those are the very things our people need—the very things you can give them. You can show them they are whole again, Pa-lil. You can whisper it to them as a mother whispers to a child, day after day. They need to believe again that they are a race with strength and beauty and power. You can show them it is true."

Pa-lil shook her head doggedly, refusing to meet Loxa's eyes. "If it's true, if they have those things—then there must be others. Others with gifts. Let the others show them." The words sounded small. But surely the other gifts were less dangerous than her fire.

"When others find their gifts, when others are born to them, they will. But you are the first."

"No." Pa-lil took her feet, struggling to put the full force of her fear into her words, trying to make Loxa hear it. *"I can't."*

Andor stood too, ready to argue, but Loxa rose and caught his arm, her eyes narrowing. "Yes—I see you need time, Pa-lil. It was too much to expect that you would not. Take it. Think about what I've said. Then come to me. Any child can direct you to my cottage." Catching her long skirts, she turned and strode away through the woods.

Pa-lil looked after her, relieved and troubled at once. If she were the only one with a gift . . . But even so, she could not do what Loxa wanted. She could not call the fire again. Not with anger running like blood in her veins.

Slowly she became aware of Andor, of his silent scrutiny, and realized it was nearing dusk again. She glanced around but saw no sign that they trespassed on a cat run. Still she spoke hurriedly. "I won't trouble you longer. I'll—I'll go to the shelter monitor and ask to be assigned a place to sleep. It's late, but surely there's work I can do. I won't bother you again."

He spoke shortly. "I've already spoken to Para. She has assigned you to sleep in my hut. And the meal monitor has given me extra rations for your meals."

"But you can't—I'm supposed to sleep in the newcomers'shelter. I'm—"

"We took a very heavy consignment of newcomers yesterday. The shelter is over-filled. Even the dining hall is over-booked. The arrangement is made." He peered around. "It's getting dark. I have to join the others for the hunt. We'd better hurry."

She followed him, reluctant to accept his hospitality again when she could not do what he wanted. Why, she wondered, did it matter so much to him whether she called the fire? If he knew the impulse that had possessed her in the temple when she realized the flame in the bowl was her own, if he knew what will it had taken to call back the fire instead of sending it leaping from the bowl to burn the temple clean—

But he did not know those things. She followed silently, kicking brittle leaves.

When they reached his hut, the fire-bowl sat in the center of the table, all trace of ash scrubbed away. Andor's lips tightened as he wrapped it and returned it to the cupboard.

They ate silently, lantern-light painting the walls with shadow. Soon there were voices on the path outside. Andor stood. "I have to go. Don't step outside without the lantern. And don't go far even with it. This pack has become bold. If we don't take them, they'll come into the settlement again."

She promised. At the last minute, as he slipped out the door, she felt the sharp prompting of anxiety. "Be careful, Andor."

"Always," he promised, unsmiling.

She stood at the window and watched a long line of torches pass down the lane. Later she went to another window and saw them in the distance, moving toward the trees. She counted seventeen before she lost sight of them. She turned from the window, rubbing her arms anxiously.

She washed their dinner platters and swept the floor. Then, finding nothing else to do, she spread blankets and made herself a bed on the floor. She lay awake for a long while, trying to find some way to do what Andor and Loxa wanted. Finding none.

She woke once in complete darkness and realized the lantern had burned out. Later she woke again at the creak of a floorboard. "Andor?"

"It's me."

"Did you catch them?"

"We took three. We couldn't find the other."

Reassured, she fell asleep again and did not wake until morning. Andor sprawled across the mattress, the quilt over his head, his legs bare. She covered him with her blankets and took food from the kitchen. Then she slipped outside, closing the door carefully.

She ate in the shade of a small fruit tree, watching men and women pass on their way to the fields. Many of the implements they carried were familiar: rakes, hoes, shovels, shears. Others were unfamiliar. She couldn't guess their use.

It was time she learned, however little use Andor thought she would be in the fields. When she had eaten, she slipped back into the hut and unpacked the drab trousers and long-sleeved shirt the estate seamstress had made for her. Discarding her gown, she drew them on, then pulled her hair back and secured it with a strand of cord she found in a storage bin. Then, swallowing back doubt, she left the hut again.

She found the administrative offices in a long hut at the western edge of the settlement. An elderly woman sat at the counter. Her features puckered into a hard frown when Pa-lil entered. Disconcerted, Pa-lil approached the counter. Was it so obvious she was poorly conditioned for work? "My name is Pa-lil Rhallis. I arrived yesterday and I would like to be assigned work."

The woman's grey eyes narrowed. "So you intend to do something of real work today?"

Pa-lil shrank at the unexpected hostility. "Yes. I don't have any training but—"

"Nor much muscle either. You won't be a lot of help, will you? If you want to sweat, you can sweep and pare in the kitchen. If you want to ache, you can carry water in the fields."

Pa-lil hesitated, confused by the woman's venom. Finally, when the woman continued to stare at her from poisoned eyes, she said stiffly, "I'll carry water. Where are the buckets?"

"Go to the tool shed. In the field." The woman bit the words off.

Embarrassed, Pa-lil turned to the door. As she stepped out, she thought she heard a small hissing sound behind her. She turned, puzzled, but saw only the woman sitting at the counter. She smiled now, her smile as hostile as her frown had been before.

Dampened, Pa-lil made her way to the field and found the tool shed. She soon became uneasily aware that many of the people who had stared at her yesterday averted their eyes today, as if she had become unwholesome. When she found the overseer and asked him where water was needed, he spoke brusquely from the corner of his mouth and immediately turned his back.

Again she heard the hissing sound, so small she wondered if she had imagined it.

But as she placed the yoke upon her shoulders and began her first trips to the river, the hissing followed her. It was faint, taunting. Soon she found herself listening for it, waiting. But no matter how quickly she glanced around, she never caught anyone making it.

It wasn't until her fourth trip, when the yoke had begun to chafe and her back to ache, that she heard the first whispered comment. She passed two women pinching back overgrown vines and heard one say to the other, "Did you see the *fet*-lizard come slither by?"

"On the way to feed its brood. It should be stamped before we have a whole nest of them. But who wants to dirty her boot?"

Pa-lil turned, the buckets swinging awkwardly on their yoke. The women peered up at her, grey eyes challenging. Disturbed, she turned away.

Fet-lizard. The name followed her as she continued to trudge on her rounds. Sometimes it was spoken aloud. Other times it was only mouthed, but she read the scorn in it anyway.

She didn't understand. Were people angry because she had not worked the day before? Because she worked so slowly today? Because the pallor of her skin told them she had never done manual work before? Yet for every person who turned his back or stared stonily, there was another who seemed merely wary or even silently sympathetic.

The sun beat down. Noon came and the others went to eat, sitting in groups beside the river or under scattered trees. Pa-lil emptied her last load of water and shrugged off the yoke, realizing she should have brought food from the hut. She was too tired to go for it now. Instead she trudged to the river to sit alone under a small tree. The midday sun pricked through the foliage. Sighing, blinking back tears, she drew up her knees and rested her head on them.

A few minutes later she started at a touch on her sleeve. Tibbi knelt in the grass beside her. She pushed back her sun-bleached hair and darted a defiant glance at a group of youths who splashed in the water nearby. "Pa-lil, I know it was real—the fire you called for me. Some of the others say it was a trick. They're calling you a *fet* because they think you tried to fool them. But I saw it. I saw the fire burn."

Pa-lil drew back from the conviction that glowed in Tibbi's eyes. "Tibbi—" But what was she to do? Try to persuade her she had only seen dried grass burning? Pa-lil rubbed her temples, trying to stroke away confusion. "Tell me—tell me what a *fet*-lizard is," she said finally.

"You haven't seen one? They burrow in the fields, near the surface. If you break into their nest, they jump out and strike. They're poisonous." She extended one tanned hand, tracing a series of tiny white scars on the thumb and index finger. "Here—I broke into a small nest. There were only three nestlings. But I was in the infirmary for four days."

Pa-lil shuddered. "The nestlings—do they hiss?"

Tibbi's eyes narrowed. "Just before they strike. You don't hear it any other time." Pressing her tongue to her teeth, she produced the sound that had followed Pa-lil that morning.

So that was what the hisses told her. That the people thought she had tried to deceive them with her fire-bowl. That they considered the deception poisonous. She felt a bubble of laughter rise in her throat. On Washrar she would have been garrotted if anyone had guessed the fire was real. Here she was despised because they thought the fire was false—a trick she had played, showing them one moment's hope, then dashing it.

Aware of Tibbi's gaze, she brought herself under control. "They'll forget in a few days," she said, as much to herself as to Tibbi. "If I work hard, if I show them I'm no different—" Perhaps it was true. Not everyone was hard-eyed and angry. She had seen that. And what other course had she? She pushed herself to her feet. "I have to work, Tibbi."

Tibbi jumped up, catching lightly at her arm. "Pa-lil, if I bring you another offering, if you make the fire come again—they'll see then."

Pa-lil shook her head. "No." She wanted to give the people what they needed. But she could not. The fire she had called could leap from control so easily, as easily as her own anger. And she must not let it, no matter what names they called her. "I have to work, Tibbi," she repeated. Work and show them she was as they were, no different.

She assumed the yoke again. The sun beat at her face and her muscles grew tender. Although she stopped often to drink, the water sat heavily in her stomach. After a while she didn't hear the hisses that followed her, didn't see the occasional worried frown or half-extended hand. She moved mechanically, her body aching.

She had just emptied her buckets into the irrigation ditch when Andor caught her by the shoulder and spun her around, buckets banging her legs. "What are you doing?"

She gasped in surprise, trying to break his grip. "My shoulder—" The flesh, where his fingers pressed it, felt as if it had been burned.

"Yes, and not just your shoulder. I told you you weren't conditioned to work in the sun. Here—look." He pushed up her sleeve, baring scarlet flesh. "Did you think you could cover yourself with fabric this coarse and not burn right through it?"

She stared at her arm dumbly. "I—I didn't think about it. It doesn't hurt—unless you touch it. It—"

"It will hurt later. And did you remember to take salt pills?"

Salt pills? "My—my father's workers took them sometimes, during the hot season," she said in confusion. "But I—I didn't think of it."

"And I don't suppose anyone here reminded you."

Pa-lil shook her head, anxious that he not be angry with the people working around her. "Andor—it's not their fault. They think—they—"

"I know what they think," he said. "I've heard. I suppose it was to be expected. And if you intend to work again tomorrow, you'll get out of the sun now. Otherwise you'll be too stiff and burned to be of any use."

Reluctantly she agreed. She followed him to the hut, aware of every sore muscle, aware of the tenderness of her sun-burned flesh. She accepted ointment and smoothed it on, avoiding Andor's frowning gaze. At his insistence, she stretched out and fell asleep immediately.

She woke several times, aware of the sound of Andor's boots against the floorboards, pacing. Once she thought she heard Loxa's voice, heard Andor arguing with her in low tones. She tried to rouse herself to hear what they argued about but could not.

He wakened her soon after dusk, mug in hand. "Here—the nurse sent this. Drink it while I get you something to eat."

She sat, her stiff muscles protesting painfully, and peered into the mug. "What is it?"

"It's herbal. Drink it."

Why did he speak so shortly? Was he still angry? She drank cautiously. The liquid was salty and thick. It sat easily in her stomach, leaving her hungry for the cakes and fruit Andor brought next.

He stood with hands in pockets, watching with frowning detachment as she ate. When she put the platter aside, he said softly, "You're not going to use the bowl, are you?"

She raised her eyes reluctantly, meeting his level gaze. "No."

"It doesn't matter that you're the only one who's brought a gift to Tennador. You won't give it to your people."

Helplessly she felt a tear escape the corner of her eye. "Not—not because I don't want to, Andor." At least he was not arguing with her, not pressing her. He was simply probing the state of her mind, studying it with clinical detachment. Trying to understand.

But how could he understand when he had never called fire himself? Had never seen his own anger burn to life in a glazed bowl? "Andor, I can't."

He studied her for moments longer, then nodded absently to himself and paced to the window. He gazed out for a long time, apparently taking counsel with himself. When he turned, a taut frown scored his forehead. "There's still a ewe-killer in the woods, the puss we didn't take last night. I'm going for the hunt."

She watched in dismay as he changed into dark clothes and soft boots. "You're going because you're angry with me."

"No." The word was without inflection. He took a heavy jacket from a hook. He didn't glance back as he went to the door.

She knew his denial was false. He did not even attempt to make it convincing. She watched from the window, her shoulders tense, as he strode down the lane. Tonight there were no voices, no accompanying shadows. He walked alone. When she lost sight of him, she turned away, staring around the empty hut helplessly, then went to the other window to watch for the torches of the hunting party.

It was long before she saw anything but lantern light from the other huts. Then she saw a single torch moving away from the settlement toward the woods. She stared after it, watching for others to join it, but it moved alone toward the trees.

Was he hunting alone? She pulled her gown close, caught by an indefinable anxiety. The others must have gone ahead. But she had seen no sign of them.

Perhaps they were to follow instead. But she saw no sign of that either. She watched and she saw no sign that there was a hunt.

But why would Andor go to the woods at night if there were no hunt? She knew he was angry. Would anger take him that far?

She hesitated a while longer, her anxiety growing. When she could stand it no longer, she discarded her work-stained clothes, pulled on her oldest gown, and snatched the lantern from the table. Loxa had said any child could direct her to her hut. Surely Loxa would know why Andor had gone to the woods alone. Perhaps that was what they had argued about while Pa-lil slept.

The night air was cool, so cool Pa-lil's teeth began to chatter as she picked her way down empty lanes. Any child—but there were no children out tonight. Nor any adults. Every door was closed. In many huts, the lanterns had already been extinguished. People slept early to prepare for an early waking.

Pa-lil hesitated outside first one hut and then another, trying to find courage to rap at the door. It wasn't Andor the people had hissed. If she told them she must find Loxa's hut because she was afraid for him—

She still had not found courage by the time she reached the administrative building. She hesitated, undecided. Perhaps Loxa lived in the small hut she saw behind the larger administrative structure. Quickly Pa-lil stepped around the corner of the building.

Lantern light fell against the side of the building and eyes burned down at her. She shrieked involuntarily and stumbled backward. Hides—there were dark-furred hides nailed to the side of the building, the heads attached. Woods cats: dead eyes glaring, fangs bared. She stared, a hard pain in her chest. They were larger than any cat she had seen before. Raising her lantern, she saw tufted ears and razor claws.

She counted three—of a pack of four. And Andor had gone to the woods. She glanced around, half hoping her cry had roused whoever lived in the small hut. But the hut remained dark and still.

Suddenly it seemed to her that the entire settlement was the same, dark and still. Suddenly it seemed she was the only person awake and frightened.

Certainly she was the only person who knew Andor had gone to the woods. She bit her lip, thinking of the times he had followed her there. Did he want her to follow him this time? She remembered how long he had stood at the window taking his own counsel.

She remembered his frown, his air of decision when he announced that he was going to the hunt. Had he expected her to watch from the window, to realize there was no hunt? To follow?

It made no sense. She wadded and crushed the fabric of her gown in one fist, then picked her way quickly through the shadows to the darkened hut. She rapped twice, three times, but there was no response. She knocked once again, more loudly, and held her breath, listening.

And then she could wait no longer. She could not spend half the night knocking at doors, trying to find Loxa, when Andor was alone in the woods. Yielding to an anxious sense of urgency, she raised her lantern and set toward the woods.

She made her way carefully over the irregular ground. The night sky bristled with stars, but they offered no useful light. Boulders and dried vegetation caught at her gown. Twice she paused when she heard a scurrying sound nearby. The seed gatherers Andor had mentioned, she guessed. Once she saw glinting eyes barely five paces away and gasped with terror before she realized they belonged to a straying sheep.

She smelled the trees before she saw them. Their oily pungence seemed stronger by night than by day. She paused, calling Andor's name, peering into the trees.

Did she only imagine a faint light ahead? She called again, then gathered courage and plunged into the trees. Soon hairy trunks surrounded her. Dry leaves crackled underfoot. "Andor?" Her voice was lost in the shadows that pooled under the trees. She held the lantern high and saw, chilling, that a nearby tree trunk was freshly clawed. "Andor?" She was surprised she could call out at all when she was suddenly breathless with fear. But she *did* see a light ahead, receding. She called again, more loudly, and moved in the direction of the light.

She lost her bearings quickly, following the elusive light through the woods. Occasionally she passed trees grown into grotesque shapes or large, root-bound boulders. Her lantern cast threatening shadows against them and her heart pounded at her ribs. Her calling grew more guarded. There was only one cat left from the pack that claimed this run, but she didn't want to attract it.

And then, miraculously, the light halted. She gasped with relief, running toward it. "Andor!"

He spoke from the darkness. "I'm here."

Why did his voice sound so strange? She looked up and found him perched on a large boulder. The stock of his torch was wedged into a crevice in the stone. Its flickering light cast his profile in relief. He sat with his feet drawn up, looking down at her with dispassionate interest. "I thought you would come."

She raised the lantern, trying to read his face. Something in his tone—flat, over-controlled—frightened her. "Why did you come here? There wasn't any hunt." She searched the boulder for a foothold, not waiting for him to answer.

"Do you want to climb up here with me? It's safer."

Safer? Still the flatness in his voice. She glanced around and saw only trees muffled in darkness. "Andor—"

"Over here. Give me the lantern. I'll hold it for you."

Gratefully she found the foothold he indicated and passed the lantern to him. She bunched her gown in one hand and picked her way up the side of the boulder, sun-burned flesh drawing painfully. He caught her hands and pulled her up. She sank to her knees beside him. "Andor, please—why did you come here?"

"I'm hunting a cat."

The words weren't convincing. They had no resonance. She shook her head. "No. There isn't a hunt tonight. You're the only one who came."

"I'm hunting alone. Here, you can see the bait." He leaned over the edge of the boulder, holding the lantern so that its light fell on the ground. "One of the lambs wasn't feeding. It would have died anyway."

She caught her breath, peering down at the faint white stain at the base of the boulder. "But the cat—isn't it afraid of fire? And you didn't bring anything to kill it with. You—" Her mind worked quickly. What kind of hunting implements did they use against woods cats?

His eyes glinted by lantern light. A hint of a smile touched his lips. "We usually dig pits and bait them, then drive the cats toward them. They're frightened of fire; you're right. But tonight we will conduct our hunt differently. She'll smell the bait quickly. Her warren is near." Before she could respond, he lowered the lantern's wick, extinguishing it. Then, with a swift motion, he smashed the lantern against the side of the boulder.

Pa-lil stared at him wildly, gasping as he tugged his torch from the crevice and set the spilled lantern fuel afire. It blazed briefly on the flank of the boulder, sending up dark smoke. Then there was only torchlight.

Pa-lil sank back tensely, wondering with cold detachment if he had passed reason. There was something very like satisfaction in his eyes, but his knuckles were pale on the stock of the torch.

"What are you going to do?" she said finally, knowing he would do something. Knowing he had a plan.

"The next is more difficult," he said. "I haven't tried it before, but I think it will work." Holding the torch high, he knelt over the narrow crevice in the rock. Quickly, before she could protest, he plunged the burning torch head-down into the gap. Before the flames could race up the wooden stock, he stuffed his jacket into the crevice.

The torch died, smothered. Shaken, Pa-lil stared into the dark, suddenly aware of sounds she had not noticed before: the soft bump of her heart against her ribs, the rasp of Andor's trousers on the boulder, the lazy sound of leaves in the breeze. It was no use, she guessed, to ask what he intended next. But she suspected she knew. Knew what he was going to say.

He said it. "Now there is no fire here but yours, Pa-lil."

Yes, that was why he had brought her here, why he had extinguished both torch and lantern: to make her call fire. *"No."* Her voice took a rising edge. How many times did she have to tell him?

The fright that infected her voice did not touch his. "No? Tell me why you can't do it."

"Why?" She shuddered, pulling her gown close, trying to lose herself in it. "Do you really want to know?" The words were trembling and hard-edged at once. And once they had escaped, she knew she couldn't call them back—them or any of the others that followed in a swift rush. "I can't do it—*I can't do it*—because I'm half Washrar and the Washrar turn everything to dirt. The Washrar bring rotten fruit to the temples and demand that the gods cripple their enemies. The Washrar murder and think no one sees. The Washrar snatch and grab and take what they can. They can't even leave the gods alone. They've made the temples filthy. If I used my fire, I'd burn them all. I'd clean the temples. I'd burn the towns and the estate houses. I'd—*I'm like them, Andor. I'd use my fire like them. I—*" How could she make him understand how angry she was? Not nineteen years angry but three hundred years angry. Angry for every indignity, every death. Angry for all the bitter things her father's people had done.

He caught her by the shoulders, breaking the rising cadence of her words. "Is that what you think I am? A man who corrupts temples? I'm Washrar, Pa-lil. Your father is Washrar. Do you think I'd burn towns and houses if I could call fire?"

She drew a shuddering breath. His rebuke forced her to pause, however reluctantly. To think. "No. I know you wouldn't." And her father was no more evil than Andor. He had acknowledged her; he had defied ostracism to keep her with him; he had protected her.

"Then why think the worst of yourself?"

"Because—" She faltered. Why was she afraid of her own anger? Simply because she had held it so long? Because she had hidden it? "Because it's touched me. It's all touched me closer than it has you. It—"

"Closer?" His voice took a bitter edge. "Do you remember what I told you the first day we met? That I call myself Andor Tereyse?"

"Yes?" She frowned, surprised at his tone.

His grip tightened on her shoulders. "I call myself that because I don't want to use the name I was born with: Andor Palsin."

"Palsin?" She repeated the syllables blankly before she recognized their significance. Jan Palsin, the man who had heard of a world where docile people lived. Jan Palsin, the man who had made his family's fortune by trading in those people. What had Andor said that first night? That he had Pachni blood—on his hands. "But that was a long time ago," she protested. "Three hundred years ago. That has nothing to do with you."

"It doesn't? When thousands of Pachni were taken by Jan Palsin? When thousands more were killed because they could do a few small things the Washrar could not? That's all the gifts were. Small conveniences. They weren't vital to the Pachni. Not then.

"But they could be vital now, Pa-lil."

He had released her shoulders. Looking closely, she could distinguish his profile against the diffuse darkness that enclosed them. "That's why you came to help build the settlements," she realized. "To pay for what Jan Palsin did."

"Partly. And partly because I was becoming like the others. So afraid it was making me vicious. So frightened of the power I thought the Pachni had. I was afraid to walk on my father's estate by night. Afraid to go to the vineyards or the looming rooms. I was so afraid—" He broke off, drawing a sharp breath, listening.

Pa-lil tensed, staring into the darkness. She had been frightened too, living in her father's estate house, enjoying privileges that should never have been hers. Privileges bought with the labor of slaves. But Andor's fear didn't seem related to his words. "What is it?"

"The cat is coming."

She wasn't prepared for the rush of fear that made her skin prickle. "I—I don't hear anything."

"I do. Listen."

She caught a shallow breath, trying to make herself still. She heard only the wind in the trees, the dry rattle of leaves overhead. Then she heard another sound, the soft pad of feet. Blindly she caught Andor's arm. The quiver of his muscles frightened her as much as the sound of padded feet. "Can it jump? Can it jump this high?"

"It won't. I'm going down."

It took a moment for her to understand. When she did, the effect was numbing. *"No. Andor—"* The trembling of his muscles should have warned her. Should have told her what price he was willing to pay for Jan Palsin's crime. What price he was willing to pay for the gift he wanted her to give the Pachni. "Andor, you can't. You—"

But he could. He pulled his arm free and was already sliding down the face of the boulder. She heard the sound of his feet against rock. In a moment she heard his boots hit the ground. And she heard the heavy pad of the cat's feet, the low mutter of its breath. Her throat closed spasmodically, cutting off her breath.

"They're afraid of fire, Pa-lil."

She sat like stone. The cat was afraid of fire. But she had called fire only twice, neither time with a woods cat stalking below. Neither time with Andor its prey. "Andor—if I can't do it—"

"Then I'll pay."

He would pay. And she didn't even know what god to call. Krakar, who guarded the night? Coqkar, who looked after the hunter? She began to tremble violently, the names of the gods running rapidly through her mind. Bozikar, Malikar, Magakar —Were they actual entities, living and sentient, waiting to hear her plaint? Or were they only the names people had given hope, strength, courage?

Did it even matter? *Nordikar.* It was Nordikar's wisdom she required. Wisdom to find the fire before the cat struck. Wisdom to control the fire if she found it.

Quickly she raised her voice, imagining a bowl with silver wings, an azure canopy, a river. *Nordikar, father-mother, here is the fruit of my hands, the plenty of my heart. Help me find the wisdom you have safe-guarded for me. Show me the way, Nordikar, while the flame does burn. Show me where truth lies, show me where justice beckons. Show me, Nordikar—*

The plaint rose, sweet and true, carrying no taint of fear. Pa-lil pressed her hands to the rock, willing flame to come. When it did not, her voice began to waver.

Courage. She must have courage. She pressed her eyes shut, putting all her will into the rising plaint. Slowly, in her vision, she saw blue flame grow. She breathed on it, giving it fuel. Then, catching her breath, she opened her eyes.

Flame burned blue upon the rock. Flame grew and below Pa-lil saw the cat, its tufted ears laid back, its fangs bared. Andor stood utterly still, his back pressed to a matted tree trunk, his eyes as brightly reflective as the cat's.

Bless me, Nordikar, with the wisdom to study the paths before me, the judgement to choose from among them, the perseverance to follow that which I have chosen. Bless me, Nordikar— She had called the flame. Now she must form it into a weapon and wield it against the cat. The muscles at the back of her neck knotted with effort. Perspiration stood on her burned skin, prickling.

Hope, courage, strength. As the cat gathered itself to spring, Pa-lil caught a deep breath, drew sparks from the fire, and shaped them into a fiery spear. With a final effort of concentration, she hurled the spear at the cat.

The cat screamed, its fur scorching. It flailed briefly, muscles jerking spasmodically, then glared briefly up at her, as if it understood. Finally it found control of its feet and fled. Dry leaves shattered noisily in its path.

Then there was silence. Pa-lil stared down, not believing what she had done. Slowly Andor raised his head and stared up at the fire that still danced on the rock. He seemed to be numbed—as numbed as she was. He did not speak as Pa-lil groped her way down the boulder.

"It's gone," he said finally, as if he didn't believe it.

The cat was gone but the fire was not. It still burned on the boulder, electric blue. "Didn't you think I could do it?"

"I wasn't sure," he admitted.

Pa-lil laughed unsteadily. He hadn't been certain and neither had she. But she had called the fire and she had harmed no one. She had not even injured the cat. And Andor—"You've paid now. You've paid for what Jan Palsin did to the Pachni."

He sighed, color slowly returning to his face. "Yes. And for what he did to the Washrar."

"The Washrar?" What did he mean?

He took her hands between both his. "He destroyed the Washrar, you know. He made them what they are today. Frightened, cruel— That's why we're building the settlements. To save the Pachni and to save our own people. The Washrar."

She drew back, surprised. He was one of the group that had backed the settlements? And their intent was to save the Washrar by taking their slaves away? But she understood what he said. Slavery had destroyed the masters far more surely than it had destroyed the slaves. The Washrar were a ruined people. They had corrupted themselves and now they corrupted their gods as well.

But the Pachni— The more frightened the slave masters became, the faster the settlements would grow. And when she called fire for the Pachni each day by the river, when she sang plaints for them, they would see it was no trick. They would see they were whole. They would see that the gifts had not been destroyed, not in three centuries of slavery, never.

They would see the fire and soon they would see other gifts too. Perhaps in people who had suppressed them without ever suspecting they carried them, perhaps in children yet to be born. And if the Washrar someday moved against them, the Pachni wouldn't be naive again. They would use their gifts any way they could. Pa-lil laughed softly, understanding everything. "Andor, I thought you told me you were a man of Tennador."

He laughed too, as softly as she. "I am. And if you can light our way home, Pa-lil—" The words held a Pachni lilt.

"I can light our way," she said, adopting the soft cadence, adopting his whole bright vision. Carefully she drew the fire from the rock and ringed them with it. They walked within its protective circle back to the settlement.